War of Three Waters

Under the storm clouds of a dark lord, the armies of three realms clash, turning once verdant lands into barren battlefields littered with the dead. The Man of Three Waters is no longer alone. At his side stands the Woman of Three Waters. Given new life by the powers of each realm, they share the same magic, the same strength, the same fate. Heroes in a world that desperately needs them. Guardians of a way of life that stands to be destroyed. Legends who will surpass any who have come before . . .

The stunning conclusion to the brilliant epic fantasy of wonder and terror, magic and heroism, and good versus evil . . .

A Breach in the Watershed
Book One of The Watershed Trilogy

"Douglas Niles and I worked on *Dragonlance* together. This book captures all the adventure and romance of *Dragonlance*."
—MARGARET WEIS

"In *A Breach in the Watershed*, the landscapes are sweeping and complete, and the various races are believable . . . new and exciting. The detailed pantheon of gods gives the readers a deeper and richer understanding and appreciation of the motivations of the characters. Any reader will come away from this book fully satisfied."
—R. A. SALVATORE, *New York Times* bestselling author of *Siege of Darkness*

Darkenheight
Book Two of The Watershed Trilogy

"Like Book One, this is filled with action, courage and fantastical beings—the stuff of riveting fantasy." —*Kirkus Reviews*

"Douglas Niles . . . writes so well that his characters come to life after only a few lines . . . This middle book . . . keeps the trilogy moving." —*Starlog*

Ace Books by Douglas Niles

THE WATERSHED TRILOGY

A BREACH IN THE WATERSHED
DARKENHEIGHT
WAR OF THREE WATERS

WAR
OF
THREE WATERS

DOUGLAS NILES

ACE BOOKS, NEW YORK

This Ace Book contains the complete text of the original trade paperback edition. It has been completely reset in a typeface designed for easy reading, and was printed from new film.

WAR OF THREE WATERS

An Ace Book / published by arrangement with the author

PRINTING HISTORY
Ace trade paperback edition / August 1997
Ace mass-market edition / June 1998

The Penguin Putnam Inc. World Wide Web site address is
http://www.penguinputnam.com

Check out the Ace Science Fiction / Fantasy newsletter, and much more, at Club PPI.

ISBN: 0-441-00532-2

ACE®
Ace Books are published by
The Berkley Publishing Group, a member of Penguin Putnam Inc., 200 Madison Avenue, New York, NY 10016.
ACE and the "A" design are trademarks belonging to Charter Communications, Inc.

PRINTED IN THE UNITED STATES OF AMERICA

10 9 8 7 6 5 4 3 2 1

To Troy Denning,
and the secret trout lakes of Gold Dust

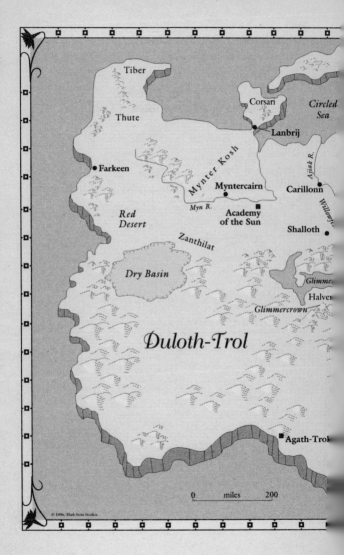

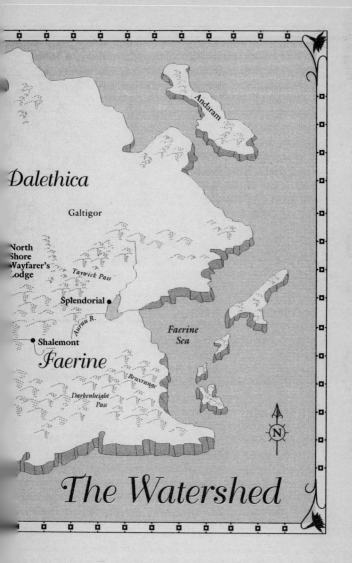

Dalethica

Galtigor

Andaram

North
Shore
Wayfarer's
Lodge

Taywick Pass

Splendorial

Aurun R.

Faerine
Sea

Shalemont

Faerine

Bruxrange

Darkenheight
Pass

N

The Watershed

PROLOGUE

A task is not completed until the tools have been
cleaned and sharpened . . . and with clean, sharp
tools, who can resist starting on the next job?
—Diggerspeak Proverb

*When my fingers failed in their last, frantic grasp at the lip
of the precipice, my death became certain, three or four
heartbeats away at the most. Still, some desperate instinct
for preservation caused me to twist, spiraling like a bird
without wings as I plunged past the rock face. Frantically
I bent my spine, tucking to avoid the dizzying approach of
jagged outcrops. I tumbled, my last thought a memory of
Rudy's face as he saw me fall, my final sensation the stinging force of the wind.*

In retrospect, of course, my maneuvers were laughably
futile. The cliff was so high, my speed so great, that I was
certainly killed after the first, or at the latest, the second
impact against the protruding crags. Later, Rudy would tell
me—reluctantly—that I bounced at least a half dozen times
over the rough, sloping terrain at the foot of the Tor of
Taywick. Mercifully, I knew nothing of the pulverizing of

my bones, the smashing of my body, before I came to rest amid the springs at the base of that thousand-foot pillar.

The fact of my foot settling in one of those pools, a natural well of pure Aura, suspended some spark of my being for the time immediately following death. Much as Rudy had been smashed down the face of the Glimmer-crown by an avalanche of Aurasnow, my later resurrection could be attributed to the enchanted water of Faerine.

It was hard for my beloved—the hardest thing he had ever done, he told me later—to take the Sword of Dark-blood in his hand, to raise the hateful weapon over my corpse, and to drive the ink-black tip through my unbeating heart. Rudy's only hope was to re-create the circumstances that had, nearly a year earlier, altered his own lifeless body—as, within a cocoon of Aura and through the thrust of that same dark blade, he became the Man of Three Waters.

He had reason to hope that these three elements—the fall from a great height, the immersion in Aura, and finally the stab of that venomous sword—might have the same effect upon me. I can only imagine his anguish as he beheld my broken corpse. Once he admitted to me that, after piercing me with the blade, he cast it away and wept. And he remained by my side, unprotected from mountain weather, subsisting only on Aura, for a fortnight of waiting.

But before my outer awareness returned, I would languish for a timeless period in a wasteland between life and death—and here the experiences of our transformations differed. Rudy emerged from his tomb of ice with no knowledge of what had transpired around and within him, as if he had spent a period of deep and dreamless sleep. For me, the time was not oblivion—rather, it was an interval of wandering, a period of constant search through a landscape of impenetrable fog. Only rarely did a feature or a being materialize in that murk, but as it arose, each encounter locked another piece of my destiny into place.

I met ancient Pheathersqyll, both as the vibrant teacher he had been, and as the wasted hulk I saw after the fatal kiss of Lord Minion Nicodareus. Pheathers talked to me, but the words that emerged from that shriveled corpse were spoken in a strange tongue. I cried and I pleaded, but he would not make himself understood.

Rudy, too, appeared before me in this timeless vault. Often he was the lanky, shyly grinning young man who had captured my heart. Occasionally I saw him as a mighty avenger, a being beyond such concerns as love, loyalty, and affection. There were times, too, when I beheld him as an image of basest evil, a being who made my skin crawl and sent me shrieking in terrified flight through the formless void.

Always thrumming in the background of this vaporous nothingness was a deep, steady cadence, a meter that I gradually recognized as a heartbeat. It was not the pulse of any living creature—the pounding was too infrequent, too sonorous and grave to be formed by mortal muscle. Instead, this was the measured pace of something vast and eternal, a being not terribly distant, yet not a thing of our world.

A shred of tale from my early education gradually took form, a scrap of verse here, a lyric there, coming to me as I wandered. At first I was not aware of the memory's significance—why would I recall an epic poem, a version of a story I had first heard from my childhood tutor? Perhaps I viewed it as a pastoral anchor to times that had definition and meaning, when, even in the midst of countless questions, I knew that I was a human girl, with hopes and desires and fears and aspirations. And those were days when Pheathersqyll was always there, with an answer for every question—and a question for every answer.

My tutor had drawn me onto his knee for this story when I was perhaps nine or ten years old. No doubt the old sage recognized the potential for terror in his words. And, too, he was fond of using proximity to emphasize the importance of the story he was about to impart. In any event, I sat so close to him that I remember the cinnamon he used to spice his tea as a pleasant fragrance on his breath. The earnestness of his eyes, as clear and blue as the ice of a deep glacial cave, impaled me, settling the fidgeting tendencies of a restless girl.

"The Heart of Darkblood," he told me, and even through his measured articulation I knew that the notion frightened him. "It is said that a great valve of mortal flesh exists in the depths of Agath-Trol, grim fortress of the Sleepstealer."

"But isn't Agath-Trol a mountain of black rock?" I asked, logically. "How can it have a heart of flesh?"

"To understand, you must first think of the Great Betrayal," my tutor explained.

Vividly I recalled my lessons about Dassadec's most perfidious act, when the Sleepstealer tricked his siblings, Baracan, God of Man, and Aurianth, Mistress of Magic. All three immortals had pledged to depart the world after forging the Compact of the Watershed. Yet when the time came, Dassadec seized the bedrock of the land and remained behind, lord of the wasteland called Duloth-Trol.

But Pheathers, as always, pressed me to ask questions. He noted that, in order to work this treachery, the Lord of Darkblood needed an anchor, a thing to which he might fasten his will, insuring that he would not be drawn into the vastness of the godly planes. For the first time I wondered how he had done so, and gave voice to the question.

"No one knows," my teacher intoned, vexingly. He continued then, as I had known he would. "There is but legend, the oldest of which is recorded by the Sylvan Bard, well before the time of the Sleepstealer War." Pheathers looked at me, inviting amplification before he continued.

"The Sylvan Bard is Wysteerin Hallowayn," I explained dutifully. "And he scribed the *Tally of Lives* almost a thousand years ago."

"Very good. Of course, the bard wrote other things too, some more ancient . . . and others quite a bit more recent. One of the oldest of his epics is *The Heart of Darkblood*."

"I've never heard of that one," I admitted.

"It is not generally a story for children. It is a tale of two heroic mortals captured by minions in the time before the Great Betrayal. They were taken to the depths of the Sleepstealer's blackstone lair—a human warrior of strapping muscle and great courage, and a sylvan sorceress of abiding magic and purity of soul. Both were chained to the walls within a deep and lightless chamber.

"It pleased the Nameless One to imprison a mighty snow lion, as well. He mocked his prisoners by having them showered with precious stones, their dungeon paved in diamonds and rubies and emeralds. And unknown to the Sleepstealer or his minions, a tiny beetle also crept into that dank lair—at least, so the Sylvan Bard tells the tale."

I nodded with all the sagacity of a ten-year-old who is certain she has learned all of life's greatest lessons, but has not yet become aloof to wonder.

"Into this cell Dassadec released a mighty Elder Brutox, one of the greatest of his minions. Driven to a frenzy by the beings of two waters, the minion killed them all, streaking the chamber with the blood of Faerine and Dalethica, draping the shredded pelt and flesh of the snow lion over a bed of precious gems.

"Then it was that Dassadec killed his brutox, and mingled the blood of his own realm with that of the other two. The combined essence of the three he fashioned into a great, pulsing muscle—a heart that he immersed in the blackness of pure Darkblood, in the very well from which the water of poison and blight first arose. With this heart as his anchor, Dassadec was able to thwart the will of the immortal compact, and when his sister and brother departed to their ethereal homes the Sleepstealer remained behind.

"But only later did Dassadec learn that there was another effect to his dark sorcery. The tiny beetle was touched by that magic, as were the very stones of the floor. Enchanted transformations occurred, the gemstones fusing with the flesh of three waters to become a living, sentient creature standing upon two legs. The beetle, too, absorbed potent magic, becoming a being of great size and power. And both the stony walker and the monstrous, crawling bug-creature were born to a sense of duty that the Nameless One could only despise.

"Thus were the Guardians, in orders High and Deep, formed as a result of the Great Betrayal. Dassadec was enraged—he seized the Deep Guardian and managed to entomb the creature in the bedrock within his mighty fortress. But the High Guardian escaped to the Watershed, and there it bore the larvae of its cousin as well. The eggs of the lone beetle would become those Deep Guardians that still, today, dwell beneath the divides."

"And where did all the rest of the High Guardians come from?" I asked.

"Diamonds!" Pheathersqyll declared with a laugh. "And rubies and emeralds, too. Gems that were clustered to the skin of their ancestor when it emerged from Agath-Trol. These stones were scattered across the mountains, and each grew into a protector of the heights."

My teacher could not avoid one final conclusion to the lesson. "And, too, in this tale we see the balance so characteristic of stories by the Sylvan Bard: Out of an act of treachery and evil comes a force for stability and law."

And through these long wanderings in the realm between life and death I reached my own solid conclusion: It was this piece of mortal flesh, the Heart of Darkblood, that I discerned in the near distance. The measured cadence was a sinister background to all my seeking, growing ever louder, threatening to crush me with each thunderous pulsation. In the timeless nothingness of death, I dreaded that pounding beat, cringing in long anticipation of every new, doomful knell.

Yet, gradually, a softer rhythm interceded. This was not a sound that drowned out, or even competed with, the rhythm of the great, black heart. Instead, it was like a background accompaniment, barely audible, yet more vital than the infernal bass beat of the Sleepstealer. I comprehended that this second, underlying sound, was the restored pulsing of my own heart.

When I finally awakened, it was with a feeling of numb

separation. I was unable to share Rudy's tears or his joy—and his own happiness was rapidly muted by my detachment. It was the epic of the Sylvan Bard, *Heart of Darkblood*, that finally focused my thoughts—the rote recitation of a childhood lesson was safer than a consideration of more recent dangers.

My Iceman raised an Auracloud and we returned to Spendorial. I told him of the deep and steady cadence that had thrummed in my head, and my words disturbed him—though in my own mind they might have been a tale as distant as the sylvan ballad. Only when the skyship lowered us into the middle of a cheering throng did my emotions awaken . . . and then I was very much afraid.

I wanted to proclaim my unworthiness, to rail against the expectations that glowed with such fervor in a thousand desperate faces. Instead I recoiled, realizing that destiny had imprisoned me more firmly than ever before—and wondering at the bitter irony that once again laid my future before me in a series of hard-set stones.

Rudy took my hand, and when I looked at his face I saw the same sense of reluctance and dismay reflected in his eyes. His gaze met mine and I saw a naked plea there, a need that only I could meet.

In that glimpse of his own frailty, I began to understand myself—my dreams and darkest nightmares, my weaknesses and strengths.

And finally, with that conviction, I was ready to embrace my challenge, and to vanquish my fear.

From: *Recollections*, by Lady Raine of the Three Waters

ONE

Tides of Darkblood and Death

When an enemy's hopes have been shattered
and his courage jellied into fear, strike the killing
blow without hesitation, and without mercy.
—TOME OF VILE COMPULSIONS

— 1 —

Bristyn Duftrall's silk slippers scuffed against the flagstone
floor, eerily loud in the empty halls of Castle Shalloth.
Thousands of memories assailed her—of gay parties and
elegant banquets, of the tutors and servants who had devoted their lives to helping her grow up in comfort and
ease. She passed the great throne room where her father,
the duke, had ruled his people with the wisdom and benef-
icence that had been the hallmarks of his great life.

That life had been cut short by the vagaries of a weak
heart, an ironic failing in a man who had symbolized physical strength and undying love to his young daughter. Still,
with the passing of the duke, Duchess Bristyn had assumed
the mantle of his rule, the Duchy of Shalloth, and the long-

cherished legacy of strength and independence that was a stamp of the realm.

Yet now, she would never sit on his throne.

That knowledge made her melancholy, brought a wistful sense of longing for days of peace and security—days before the war. Bristyn's steps carried her outside the keep, to the foot of a tall, slender tower. As she climbed the stairway that spiraled up the outer wall of the shaft, she looked toward the expanse of darkness that blackened the lands and skies to the west. The minions of the Sleep-stealer were close now, only a few days' march away, and it was time for her to leave.

Yet she had one more task remaining, a thing that conscience and pride demanded she attempt—even as she knew that her efforts were doomed to fail.

She found Gandor Wade where she had known she would, standing alone atop the castle's highest tower. The old veteran's eyes were fixed unblinkingly on the smoke clouds marking the enemy host, but when the duchess climbed to the parapet beside him he turned away from the vista, an expression of gentle concern belying the fierce warrior Bristyn knew him to be. In fact, Gandor's leathery face and handlebar mustache reminded her more of a genial grandfather than a capable man-at-arms.

"Your Grace," he said, bowing low. "You should be gone from here. The main road back to Carillonn will soon be threatened by the enemy."

"I know, Gandor. But I must plead with you to reconsider. Come with us, bring your men to the marbled city. There, at least, we have a chance of making a stand."

Her gaze avoided the bleak vista of the enemy's advance, the columns of black smoke marking swaths of forest destroyed, or sacked villages, towns, and farmsteads. Gandor, who had no doubt memorized the location of each hateful plume, held his own eyes of slate-gray upon Bristyn's face.

The captain of the castle garrison was a veteran warrior of dramatic height and impressive girth, with hair of silver-

salted chestnut falling past his shoulders. Straps of leather
crossed his chest, supporting the massive broadsword at his
right hip. Despite his bearlike size, however, Gandor
stalked with supple grace around the perimeter of the lofty
platform as he collected his thoughts.

"Your Grace knows my men serve here of their own
will—I neither command them to flee, nor compel them to
stay. Yet we are warriors of Shalloth, my lady, descended
of the same. Surely you understand why we cannot turn our
backs on our ancestral homes, our liege's castle."

"In truth, I *don't* understand. Lives are important, but
this is a place, this castle, a *thing*. And I know that if you
survive to fight again, you may even reclaim Shalloth some
day!" Bristyn's tone grew sharp. "And surely you know
that it's hard for *me* to abandon the realm of my fathers?"

"Lady, you *must* depart," declared the captain. "My
men and I can make a difference in the tide of this campaign—and though Shalloth may fall, the Lord Minion
shall know he's had a battle. The corpses of his dead will
scatter the landscape to the horizon!"

The captain halted, emotion thickening his voice.

"For all these hours, perhaps days, that we hold, you
and King Takian can be gathering the rest of humankind,
uniting Dalethica under your combined banners!"

"But Shalloth's time is almost gone, now—and what's
left isn't worth your lives!"

"Who knows? We might even gain time for the Prince
of Andaran to reach Carillonn—think of that, the High
King's heir arriving in time to rally the defense! If the pennant of the White Drackan flies once again from the King's
Tower, all the men of Dalethica will take heart—there's no
enemy they'll fear!"

The veteran of Shalloth continued, enthused by his own
visions. "Your husband's army of Galtigor is prepared to
stand at the River Ariak. Myntarians, Coastmen, Oxnars—
they're all marching to his trumpets. And you know as well
as I: Holding that river is the last hope of Dalethica. If we

can earn you more time to prepare that barrier, then our lives are well spent."

Gandor's mustache bristled sternly. "They will cross the field, and our arrows will kill them. Those that survive may batter down the gate, and we shall meet them with the steel of our swords."

Fixing his soldier's eye upon the duchess, Gandor glared down from the lofty vantage of his bulky frame. At once Bristyn felt like a little girl again, being scolded by her father's most loyal retainer for letting loose the hounds of the kennel, or wandering too close to an unbroken stallion.

She brushed the emotion aside—*she* was mistress of this castle, and Gandor was bound to obey her commands. For a moment Bristyn considered ordering the captain and his men to abandon the castle, knowing that he would obey.

But she would not do that—it was hard enough for her, who had a husband and a realm beyond Shalloth, to make that decision. She could not compel men who had nowhere else to call home, whose own lives as well as the lives of their forefathers had been devoted to the defense of that home, to turn their backs during its darkest hour.

"The last of the wagons are off," Gandor declared gently, raising his somber face to the northern horizon. A wide roadway extended from the castle gates, rolling over grassy meadows for several miles until it vanished into lofty pines. It was a good, dry route that ran all the way to Carillonn, and nearly all of the duchy's citizens had plodded up that road in the days since Bristyn had ordered the evacuation.

"Has there been word from the Willowfen?" asked the duchess, her eyes sweeping to the low, flat wilderness that extended from the near horizon all the way to the great river winding its unseen path fifty miles to the east.

"Nay, my lady. It is as if the men of the swampland, my kinsmen though they be, have vanished into the heart of their wilds. My messengers have been unable to make contact—and, in fact, two of them have failed to return."

"The swampmen have always been stubborn," Bristyn said with a sigh. She turned to her captain with a tight smile. "Even those who come out of the wilderness to join the ranks of men."

Gandor chuckled, but his laugh had a grim edge acknowledging the truth of her statement.

"And what of the other refugees, those who have fled toward Halverica? Is there word on their passage?"

"The minion army has yet to probe around the city to the south," explained the captain. "My outriders report that the road is unthreatened all the way to the North Shore Wayfarer's Lodge. And once there, as you know, the refugees will reach safety beyond the Ariak and the Glimmersee."

"If there's safety to be found anywhere," Bristyn whispered, half to herself. She vividly recalled the splendid travelers' inn on the shores of the pristine, mountain-flanked lake. The North Shore Wayfarer's Lodge was a place of hallowed beauty, revered history, and gentle serenity. Now she shuddered at the thought that the sprawling complex of sleeping wings, great rooms, barns and stables lay in the path of irresistible onslaught.

"Sergeant Major Katlan will command your escort, my lady. We have appointed five good men to ride with you— though I will not hesitate to send more, should you desire."

"Five, and Katlan will be more than sufficient. No doubt we'll reach the outposts of Carillonn's knights within a few days' ride."

"Aye, Your Grace. And the treasury wagons, they should already be secure in the marbled city." When Gandor spoke of Carillonn, Bristyn suddenly sensed the veteran captain's melancholy—and she fully understood the depth of the sacrifice he and his men had chosen.

"Last word is that the minions remain far from the bridges over the Ariak," explained the duchess, trying one more time. "Takian will keep the gates open until the last. If you should change your mind, if the situation here becomes too dire—promise me that you'll try to reach us there!"

"Lady Duchess, you have my pledge—but only if our

efforts here can do nothing further to delay the enemy advance. Otherwise, as you know, we stand here till the end.''

Moved, Bristyn reached up and hugged the burly officer. Her gesture brought a blush of embarrassment creeping upward from the tangle of his whiskers, but Gandor awkwardly returned the embrace, patting her slender back with a brawny paw. ''Ride quick, now, understand?'' he said gruffly, guiding her to the landing.

''Good luck, Gandor. May Baracan smile upon you,'' Bristyn said as she stood atop the tower steps. Looking over the vista of hills and lakes, the tangled wilderness of the Willowfen beyond, she thought fleetingly of the countless occasions when she had enjoyed this once-splendid view. Acutely aware that this was the last time she would look upon it, she suddenly found it very difficult to leave.

''Rather than smiling upon me, perhaps the God of Man might send rain,'' the captain replied with a grim chuckle—and a nod at the skies, clear except for the plumes of black smoke.

''A worthy prayer,'' Bristyn replied, knowing that on those rare instances when the skies opened up, the armies of the Sleepstealer ceased their advance and sought whatever shelter they could find, or create. It was a curious fact, Bristyn reflected: Subject neither to fatigue nor hunger, the minions had proven vulnerable only to something that was integral to human life.

Yet as the monstrous horde advanced, spreading a barren wasteland in its wake, rain clouds had literally been parched from the skies. Great fires blackened huge forests and sweeping grasslands, while the powerful, elephantine bovars labored on the fringes of the mountains, damming every stream as it spilled from the heights. Countless creeks, rivers, and lakes had been reduced to pathetic, muddy trenches. The resulting drought had extended beyond the swath of the Sleepstealer's conquest, so that even the eastern half of Dalethica had succumbed to dry weather and hot, unseasonal breezes.

Bristyn walked slowly down the spiraling stairs. She

blinked back tears as she remembered carefree childhood days sliding down the curving banister or, in the far distant past, climbing with her tiny fingers gripping her mother's hand, seeking the lofty vantage from which they could watch for the duke's return from some mission or adventure.

Though her mother had been gone for most of Bristyn's life, claimed in the failed birth of her second child, her daughter still drew a vivid mental picture—an image that was far more personal than the oil painting that hung on the wall of the great banquet hall. As her steps carried her into that vast chamber, she looked up at the life-sized portrait that had been rendered shortly after her own birth.

The high windows admitted rays of afternoon sun in slanting beams, casting most of the large hall in an eerie, silent pattern of shadows. One of those shafts of light struck the framed canvas directly, bringing to the image an uncanny sense of life. The Duchess Gracialyn Duftrall in the painting was a tall woman, serene and elegant in a blue gown—the same color favored by her daughter—and pearls. Golden hair, dazzling bright in the sunlight, coiled regally atop her head, elegantly braided to support a sparkling tiara of sapphire and silver. Her eyes of piercing blue seemed to look past the viewer, as if focused on some distant height.

Yet the woman of Bristyn's memory was a person of delightful laughter and boisterous high spirits, as ready to spin her young daughter through the air as she was to sit and sing a gentle ballad. Duchess Gracialyn had always been busy, but a great part of that busyness had been devoted to her only daughter. When she had died, shortly before Bris's eighth birthday, she had left a void in the young girl's heart that had never been completely filled.

Of course Takian, ultimately, had come close to doing so. At the thought of her husband, the duchess shook herself from reminiscences and walked quickly through the cool, shadowy hall. He was desperately worried about her, she knew. Indeed, barely more than a fortnight earlier he had forbidden her to make this trip to her ancestral home.

Bristyn felt no triumph in the recollection of her determined stance in the first impassioned argument of their marriage. She had traveled to Shalloth, of course, but at the same time she knew that her husband's fear stemmed from threats that were all too real. Unlike Carillonn, Shalloth had no significant river barrier between itself and the minion armies. The castle and duchy's fate in the face of that relentless advance was inevitable, and all that could be done was to see that people were evacuated as smoothly as possible.

In the end, Bristyn had made Takian see that she, like the king himself, bore a tie to her realm that was more than symbolic. Only her presence had convinced the populace of the urgency of the situation. She had worked to insure cooperation, to get the displaced people started along one of the two decent roads—north, to Carillonn, and southeast, toward the North Shore Wayfarer's Lodge. At the same time she had hoped to persuade Gandor Wade and the loyal men-at-arms who wore the blue and brass of Shalloth that they, too, should flee the city. In this last, of course, she had been unsuccessful.

Shaking off her regrets, Bristyn entered her dressing room, stripping off her dress and slippers in favor of leather breeches and riding boots. She girded on a sharp shortsword and even toyed with the thought of concealing a long-bladed knife in her boot. After a moment she decided that the weapon wouldn't be very useful—and besides, it would chafe.

Finally the young Duchess of Shalloth stepped through the great doors of the keep, deciding to walk one last time through the gardens on her way to the gatehouse. Following the aisle of smooth paving stones, she passed through the verdant arch of a well-trimmed hedge. Within lay a maze of pathways that she had long since memorized. Now she drifted aimlessly, past a reflecting pool where goldfish scooted beneath smooth lilypads and plump frogs croaked from the shallows, comically alarmed by her passing.

"I caught your grandfather when he was a tadpole," she teased wistfully, meeting the baleful eye of a monstrous spotted bullfrog. "I bet you're glad I let him go."

Abruptly the memories surged, too strong to resist, and she knelt beside the placid water, weeping softly. The frogs, as if sensing her distress, fell silent as she drew slow, ragged breaths. Finally, angrily, she wiped her eyes with the heel of her palm and rose, standing proudly beside the water.

Her reflection glared sternly back at her. Bristyn saw a tall woman, more well-rounded than her mother, with cascading golden hair, barely contained by a silver clasp. She held her chin firm and high, and allowed but a single, parting sigh as she turned toward the gap in the hedge, her horse, and the waiting guards of her escort.

— 2 —

Rudy and Raine, dressed in the plain white cotton gowns of Auramasters, walked side by side down the long, crystalline archway to the Scrying Pool. Casting a glance from the corner of his eye, the lanky Iceman saw that his partner's jaw was firm, her gaze locked straight ahead. He took her hand and squeezed it, stopping to face her.

"We don't have to do this, yet. If you want some more time . . ."

"Time for what?" Raine shook her head, sending a cascade of dark hair tumbling past her shoulders. Her eyes were focused tightly on Rudy's. "We both know that there *is* no time! It's been weeks since you've seen the pool—"

"Yes . . . but *I* can look now, can learn how Carillonn and Neshara fare, and wherever else we need to see. You don't have to. . . ."

"I *will*." Her tone would allow no argument, and when the Iceman nodded she continued more softly. "Are you afraid for me?"

He was silent for a moment. "Us. I'm afraid for us both.

You see, the pool showed me things before . . . I saw you falling from Taywick, *knew* you were destined to die at the foot of a tall cliff. And I've seen hints about *my* destiny as well. I think I'm afraid that you'll see the same thing."

"We both know that my fate is locked into yours," Raine said bluntly.

"I know . . . that's why I'm afraid."

"So am I." Raine drew a deep breath, standing straight and turning to face the ivy-draped archway leading to the Scrying Pool. She kept Rudy's hand in hers, starting forward with a firm step. "I'm ready."

Now it was Rudy who hurried to keep up. He fought against his own reluctance, knowing that he had to be there, to guide her as the Auramaster Larrial Solluel had guided him.

It had been Rudy's decision to bestow upon her the power of Three Waters. No other hope had existed—without his actions, she would have remained irrevocably dead. His own destiny would have become a bleak and solitary affair, a question for himself alone, when he knew that he needed Raine for the answer. Yet in saving her, he had changed her in a way that no one else in the history of the Watershed could hope to understand. At the same time he had cemented a link forged in the prophecies of Raine's birth under Three Stars Rising and his own transformation within the ice of Aura.

They passed through the arch into a large circular chamber domed with multihued crystal. The moist air of the surrounding garden, smelling of loam and bloom, was a physical embrace, familiar yet still mysterious to the Iceman. His heart pulsed to vivid memories of wonder . . . and fear.

Palms, willows, and ferns grew in thick profusion around the fringe of the round chamber. The center was occupied by the large, still pond. Lilies clustered in the narrowed ends of the mirrorlike oval, while a bank of white boulders bordered the roundel in the center of the pool.

A slender, golden-haired figure glided from a fern-draped

path, bowing as he faced the two humans. The sylve was nearly as tall as the Iceman, and his posture and bearing were possessed of a serene dignity that sometimes seemed to lift him above the ranks of other mortals.

"Ah, Mussrick," Rudy said as he recognized the Royal Scion of Spendorial.

"Welcome to the soul of my people's palace."

Though Mussrick Daringer was the closest thing to a monarch in all Faerine, he was dressed in a white robe identical to those worn by the two humans. The tips of his narrow ears emerged from his hair in a way that reminded Rudy of the scion's brother, Quenidon, who had fallen on a battlefield within view of the crystal city's walls.

The royal sylve opened the discussion bluntly. "I was a student of Larrial Solluel for more than a century. My own Testing lasted eight days—an unusual length of time for a sylve, even if not for the Man of Three Waters," he noted with a tight smile. "In the pool I have watched the legions of the Sleepstealer march across Faerine. I saw the victories won by yourself and by the field army—and I held my breath as the two of you floated to Taywick Pass, and battled the Lord Minion."

The sylve paused for a long time, but Rudy knew that he was simply arranging his thoughts. Time moved slowly for Faerines, and sylves in particular were far more deliberate than the human norm. Finally the scion turned to Raine, drawing a deep breath and taking both of her hands in his for a moment.

"After you fell, I couldn't see you in the pool—either of you," Mussrick admitted. The sylve released Raine and turned to the Iceman. He seemed shaken, as if he wanted to reach out and touch Rudy also, to make sure that he was really there.

"Then, when word came this morning . . . that you had returned to the city, I could only hope that you would come here."

"There's no other place to go—at least, for now," the Iceman replied.

"It is a place to start, in any event. Soon, I imagine, we will have a choice of many destinations."

Rudy waited, again knowing the sylve would continue—though this time the pause was very long.

"You know that the pool has gifts, wisdom to bestow that goes beyond a mere view of the events transpiring around the Watershed?"

"Larrial Solluel taught me. For a very few Auramasters, the waters can give a hint of future developments, destinies."

"Yes." Mussrick Daringer proceeded carefully. "I admit that I have seen at least one of the paths that your own lives might follow from here . . . and I want you to be aware that there are other hopes, real chances of defeating the Sleepstealer's scourge that do not entail the two of you. . . ."

"We all have our parts to play," Rudy replied. The sylve's words only confirmed the expectations he had about Raine's look into the Scrying Pool.

"Indeed." The Royal Scion drew a deep breath. "To that end, I have announced a council, a Gathering of Faerine. It has been my hope all along that you would return. Even more, that you could offer us guidance, leadership . . . hope."

"I think that we'll have something to say," Rudy said. "If you'll grant us leave beside the pool, we'll seek you as soon as Raine's testing is completed."

"Good luck to you . . . to you both. I will await word in my study."

Serene again, the sylvan leader bowed gracefully, and departed the Scrying Chamber. Rudy followed the slender figure with his eyes, then turned to see that Raine had walked to the very edge of the pool. Bare feet perched on a smooth boulder, she studied the Aura with an expression of skepticism.

Rudy stepped forward, taking a nearby boulder. The waters of the Scrying Pool were still, almost unnaturally so. Pulling his eyes away, the Iceman resisted the temptation to stare, to use his own power to set the pulse of Aura into motion. He would study the pool at length, but not until Raine had tested.

"It's beautiful," she whispered in awe. "I was here— but I never saw it before!"

"Watch the rhythm. Feel your heart beating . . . let the colors come in time with your pulse." Speaking slowly, Rudy wasn't even certain that Raine could hear him.

He remembered his first exposure to the pool, to the circles of bright color that cycled through the hues of the rainbow, growing in the center of the magical liquid and expanding to the edge in an ever slower pattern. When the hues had reached a measured cadence, one per six heartbeats, the magic of the pool was awakened. It was then that Rudy had seen revelations stark and frightening, portents ominous and hopeful.

He wondered whether Raine would see the same.

For a long time she stood rapt, staring into the circle of Aura. Rudy didn't have to feel the emanations from the pool—the expression on Raine's face was enough to show him that she was fully immersed in the spell of scrying magic.

Abruptly she staggered, one of her feet slipping from the rock. She moaned softly and Rudy was there in an eye blink, catching her as she lurched awkwardly toward the shore. Gently cradling her trembling body, the Iceman lowered her to the mossy ground. He hugged her until her shaking ceased.

Finally she lifted her head and opened her eyes—and those eyes were clear, cold and determined. With a return of her lithe grace she sat up and drew a firm breath.

"We have to do it, don't we?" she said softly. "The two of us . . ."

"What did you see?" Rudy's heart raced, and he guessed at—and dreaded—the answer.

Raine bit her lip, but was already climbing to her feet as she replied.

"It was our destiny—and it *is* locked upon us, despite

what Mussrick Daringer said. I saw enough of that pool to know that I'm not an Auramaster—that's your province, Iceman. But I know what must be done.''

"And you *heard* it, didn't you?"

She nodded. "It was almost taunting us . . . but we have to go there . . . you saw it already, even before the Tor of Taywick."

"Yes—but I didn't understand until you told me that story of the Great Betrayal, how the Sleepstealer was able to stay behind. But I see it clearly now," the Iceman agreed somberly. "We have to kill the Heart of Darkblood."

— 3 —

Anjell Appenfell reminded herself that it was really quite impossible for a day spent in Faerine to be a boring day. And it was a good thing, too—because if it *wasn't* impossible, then she would have to admit that life in the Palace of Time, for today at least, was uncommonly dull.

"How can a person be bored," she chided herself, "when there's magical fountains to watch in the gardens, and singing swans on the lagoon? And all those flowers that change colors through the day, and smell so sweet when the sun comes out?"

Indeed, the wonders of Faerine were beyond magnificent. Furthermore, she knew that she was lucky enough to have seen things undreamed of by any other human girl. And in no place were those enchanted surroundings quite so splendid as they were here, in the sylvan capital of Spendorial. Even the buildings, which were formed of crushed crystal in a variety of lovely pastel shades, were unlike anything to be seen elsewhere in the Watershed. And the people— sylves and twissels, diggers and gigants—were all so nice to Anjell and her mother that they had made them both feel right at home in this graceful, serene palace.

Still, a tiny part of Anjell admitted that it would be nice if something different happened today. It had been more than a week since Raine and Uncle Rudy had returned, and *that* had been terribly exciting, of course—especially the part where Rudy told everyone that now Raine, like him, was a magical person. "Woman of Three Waters," he had called her, which only made sense.

Following that tumultuous arrival, however, the pair had spent their time at the sacred heart of the sylvan palace, the Scrying Pool. And whatever they were doing inside, it wasn't much good to Anjell. As to the rest of it, the minion army that was camped across the lake stayed right where it was. Anjell had gotten a good look at that teeming horde, once, when she had gone with Danri to the bluffs beside the Aurun. They had hiked through the woods to visit the drackan Neambrey—*that* had been an interesting day—but Anjell couldn't shake the memories of vast destruction from her mind. She had been overcome by tears at the sight of the lands that had once been verdant hills and lake-dotted valleys. Now the whole Suderwild was a rolling expanse of blackness, all the trees cut and burned, the once-pristine waters filled with mud, soot, and ashes.

Since then, Anjell had spent her time in the city, visiting with her friend Darret, snooping around, wishing for something interesting to happen. Today she had decided to prowl the halls of the palace, stopping to learn about the exotic spices the cooks used in the kitchens, then moving on to watch young sylvan scholars study under a strict Auramaster. The pupils listened raptly to a discussion about the slender wands used to weave the steam of magic into clouds. Each of the young Faerines hoped to gain mastery in the use of Aura, and Anjell hoped that they all succeeded. She remembered her friend Quenidon Daringer, who had failed as an Aura-wielder and gone on to become a warrior leader of Faerine. It was that choice that had finally gotten him killed, Anjell understood, and if there was one thing that was *really* bad about this war, it was that so many nice people had to get killed.

Angrily the girl stomped her foot, wishing there was something she could do to punish the minions. In her petulance, she almost bumped into a sylvan attendant scurrying around a corner of the palace hallway.

"Oh—I'm sorry, Cillwyth," she apologized. "I guess I wasn't paying attention."

"Nary mind, little human," replied the slight, nervous courtier, who was dressed in a dazzling jacket and knickers of shimmering gold. "It was my undue celerity that brought on our impetuous collision."

"Oh?" Any cause for haste, Anjell knew, had the potential to be interesting. "What are you hurrying for?"

"I bear an announcement from the Royal Scion Mussrick Daringer himself!" declared Cillwyth excitedly.

The courtier was only about a century old, which was young by sylvan standards, and in his youthful zeal the sylve had found a soulmate in Anjell. Now he looked back and forth, determining that they were alone in the hallway, before he bent down to whisper.

"There's going to be a big council, as soon as your uncle is finished with the Scrying Pool. All the notables of Faerine are being summoned."

"What's it for?"

"I don't know the details, but it has to do with figuring out how to win the war!"

"Well, I should hope so!" Anjell exclaimed, pleased. "After all, *somebody* has to do something about all those minions across the lake!"

"That's exactly the idea!" Cillwyth cleared his throat as they heard footsteps. Trying to look inconspicuous, the pair strolled casually together as a troop of Royal House Sylvan Archers, resplendent in golden helmets with white plumes, marched briskly past.

"I don't think it's much of a secret anyway," the courtier noted with a shrug of his shoulders. "There's two dozen messengers already sent out with invitations. And I'd better be off—I'm to go to the waterfront, to let Captain Kestrel know."

"That's good!" Anjell agreed excitedly. She knew that

the bold captain and his stout galyon, the *Black Condor*, could play an important role in any plans.

As Cillwyth hurried away, the day seemed suddenly brighter and more hopeful to Anjell. This was good news—news that deserved to be shared. She decided to tell Darret, knowing that she'd find him by the lakeshore. It wasn't that the boy was always at the waterfront, but lately Anjell had been getting these feelings—like when she thought of someone, she could picture where they were, even what they were doing sometimes. It was kind of fun—and useful, too, as she now knew where to find her friend.

She made her way from the palace, passing between a pair of golden-helmed guards at the outer doors, then skipping eagerly through the wooded parkland that surrounded the crystal edifice. She stopped only to take a deep drink of Aura from one of the drinking fountains that were to be found throughout Spendorial. As she slurped from the narrow spume, she heard a familiar voice behind her.

"How can you drink that stuff all de time?"

"I've told you before." Anjell sniffed, turning to regard Darret as she wiped her mouth. "*I* think it's good—even if you and the other humans don't," she declared emphatically.

Squinting skeptically, the boy shook his head with a wagging of his many tightly bound braids.

"Hey! She knows good stuff when she sees it!" an indignant voice piped up.

The boy and girl whirled to see a third youth saunter into view, advancing to lean with casual ease against the marble base of the fountain. His hair was white-blond, and tattered garments—though they showed hints of very fine blue and gold silk—cloaked his rotund frame. The most arresting features of the newcomer were his eyes, which glittered in silvery brightness, as if they were flaked with the precious metal itself.

"Who are you?" Anjell gasped, startled and flustered by the stranger's appearance, and the knowledge that he had been listening to their playful bickering.

"Call me Haylor," said the fellow, skirting the fountain to regard them from the other side. He sat down for a moment, then bounced to his feet, fidgeting from one to the other. "And you're the two young humans, I know."

"Well, of course," the girl replied, a touch petulantly. "*Anybody* would know that."

Bending over the spout, Haylor took a deep drink and then stood straight, smiling and smacking his lips. Anjell noticed that he was shorter than Darret, though unusually stocky for a sylve. And he appeared to be just that—the pointed tips of his ears showed through his flowing hair, and despite his chubbiness the long sylvan features were still visible in his face. Though of course the girl had never seen sylves, or *anyone*, with eyes like that before.

"How come yer out here?" Darret asked, his chin jutting stubbornly. "I thought all you sylvan kids got to stay alla time wit' yer teachers."

"Not alla time," said the youth, perfectly mimicking Darret's speech. "I came to get a drink." His eyes narrowed and he cast a glance to right and left before whispering conspiratorially, "You know, this Aura here isn't bad—if it's all you can get."

"Well, sure," Anjell stated boldly, though she knew no such thing. "But where is it any better?"

"From the Scrying Pool, in the palace. I usually have that."

"I've never seen you in there before—and *I'm* a *guest* in the Palace of Time!" the girl declared importantly. She regretted her tone when Haylor merely shrugged and skipped away.

"I have friends there, friends everywhere!" he declared in a musical voice.

"Wait—where do you live?" asked Anjell.

"Spendorial, of course!" declared the youthful sylve, and then he was gone, vanished between the bushes of the surrounding hedge.

"Well, I knew *that*," she retorted peevishly, turning to Darret. "I meant, where in Spendorial does he live?"

"And I think he didn't want to tell you," the boy said with a chuckle, clearly amused at the sight of someone, anyone, getting the best of Anjell in a verbal sparring match.

She had far too much dignity to go looking through the hedge for Haylor, but Anjell found herself remembering those silver-tinted eyes. They had been lingering, pensive, serious—in short, not like a child's at all.

Thoughtful herself, she took another long drink of Aura, relishing the deeply satisfying way in which the water of magic quenched her thirst. "Here—you should try it," she urged.

Darret—who had lost this argument many times before— shrugged and slurped briefly at the stream, then shook his head in exaggerated disgust, once more sending the flopping tentacles of his long, tightly woven locks dancing around his thin shoulders. "I still like regular water," he declared. "But you can have Aura whenever you want, far as I'm concerned."

Though he was a head taller than Anjell, and growing fast, Darret rarely tried to argue with the girl—much, anyway—or to boss her around, and these were traits that she truly appreciated.

"Anyway, I've got news!" Swiftly she told Darret about the council.

The lad nodded in grim-faced enthusiasm for the idea. "'Bout time we did sometin' about dem scumdogs," he declared, spitting in the direction of the minion encampment.

The two continued toward the water in silent, mutual agreement on a destination. As they neared the shore, a gentle breeze wafted the smooth sounds of a lute to their ears, and they veered into the grove of lush pines where the sound originated. Anjell pictured the three people they would find before they came around a thickly limbed tree to see the bard, Awnro Lyrifell, and an audience of Dara Appenfell and Captain Kestrel of the *Black Condor*. Her mother, seated on a bench, had been working on the book she was writing, a tale of the human voyagers to Faerine, but Anjell saw that now Dara had set her writing materials aside in order to listen to the ballad.

"Hi, Mama," Anjell whispered, respectful of the song as she settled down beside her mother.

Kestrel paced rather tensely behind their bench, his face locked in a stone-faced expression. She had seen that a lot, lately—when her mother paid attention to Awnro, Kestrel looked unhappy, and when Dara was busy with the sea captain it was the minstrel who usually presented a mournful visage.

Now Awnro was animated, in a serious sort of way. He strummed a tune with many verses, a ballad about a young human woman who loved a prince in the time before the Sleepstealer War. The maiden was granted the gift of magic by a twissel who had flown across the Watershed from Faerine, and tried to use spells to capture the heart of the prince. She succeeded, but her magic frightened the people of his kingdom so much that, in the end, she was banished to Faerine—which wasn't such a bad fate, except for the fact that the prince had to stay behind. Anjell blinked back a tear as the last, minor chords faded away on the soft breeze.

"Splendid!" Dara cried, clapping her hands.

"Ah, but the music only pales in comparison to a fair lady's praise," declared the bard with a deep bow—and plenty of false modesty, Anjell knew.

Only Captain Kestrel seemed unmoved by the ballad. "Nice song," he said gruffly. "Now, I've got to get back to the ship." He cleared his throat awkwardly, and Anjell knew that he wanted to talk to her mother, alone. She could take a hint, but not until she'd spilled her news.

"There's a message coming for you!" she blurted at Kestrel.

The seaman chuckled, running callused fingers through his bristling gray beard. "Is there now, lass? Would ye know what it's going to be telling me?"

"Of course!" Eagerly she told them all about the council, pleased that the three adults seemed to welcome the news as much she did. "I'm going to tell Danri!" she added.

"Isn't he still up at the bluffs, with the drackan?" asked Dara.

"I think he came back this morning," Anjell replied. "He's at the Stone Goblet, now."

"How can you know?" demanded Darret skeptically. "You been in de palace all morning!"

"Well, I didn't know you kept such careful track of me," the girl sniffed. "But . . . I just *know*, that's all."

Dara looked at her daughter strangely, but gave her permission to go into Spendorial and look for the digger. Darret tagged along, and in a few minutes they had raced from the palace grounds. Sprinting frantically, then halting to gasp for breath, the two youngsters made their way along Spendorial's winding streets. They weaved through lush clumps of foliage, passed crystal buildings in the shapes of domes and towers, skirted the verdant swaths of fragrant gardens that were favored by so many sylves.

Anjell found the inn by memory—the Stone Goblet was a large establishment made of fieldstone in contrast to the Aurastone crystal of most sylvan buildings. Flanked by flower-draped outdoor patios, the Goblet shambled around an arcing street corner and commanded a splendid view of the Auraloch. Because of its shaded, smoky interior, it was a favorite haunt of diggers in Spendorial, and Anjell and the other humans had joined Danri here for several sumptuous feasts.

Darting through the crowd, easily ducking digger barmaids who hoisted three or four massive goblets in each fist, Anjell found Danri at his usual corner table. Kerri, seated beside him, saw the children first and waved them over.

"Hi Danri, Kerri," panted Anjell, struggling to draw a breath. "Did you hear the news?"

"About the meeting? No, I didn't," replied the stocky

digger with a twinkle in his eye. His rust-brown beard crin-
kled into a friendly grin.

"Oh, you heard!" retorted the girl, frowning. She
quickly brightened. "Isn't it a good idea?"

"Aye-uh, my lass, that it is," grunted Danri, his tone
strangely distant. "It's a job that well needs gettin' over
with."

Kerri nodded sadly, and Anjell shared her melancholy—
why did there have to be *more* war? Of course Anjell knew
why, but she also knew that Kerri and Danri were going to
get married and build a marvelous inn together, but not
until after the minions had been defeated. The girl sighed,
suddenly heavy-hearted as she saw the tiredness on the digger's face.

But then Danri's eyes, hooded by brows of bristling
brown, rose to regard the smudge-streaked sky across the
lake, and the digger glowered so fiercely that Anjell shivered, feeling as if it had suddenly grown very cold.

TWO

Neshara Pass

A battle is not always won by the general who
commands the most swords.
—SCROLL OF BARACAN
VOLUME III, GODSTOME

— 1 —

Roggett Becken leaned against an outcrop of granite, noting
that the surface had been worn smooth by countless other
Icemen propping themselves up, as was he, during a long
stint on the watch. This cradle of stone surrounded a
smooth, sheltered patch of ground, and was a natural vantage on the crest of Dermaathof Ridge, allowing a view
into the valley for miles in both directions. The Iceman's
heavy crossbow, and a quiver of steel bolts, were lashed to
his back, while the ice axe that he employed so effectively
in battle was in his hands, serving as a support now as he
leaned on the shaft while looking over the scene.

It could only be wished, the big man reflected pensively,
that the view was one worth enjoying. Instead, the once-
verdant vale of Dermaat was a wasteland of splintered for-

est, poisoned ground, and polluted, toxic stream. Even now
Roggett could see hundreds of minions, black spots moving
across the breadth of the trampled, lifeless landscape. Most
of these were kroaks, he knew, observing another great file
of the burly, blunt-skulled warriors. The column inched
down the valley toward the Glimmersee, adding strength to
the legion of monstrous invaders already mustered in the
lower valley. The Iceman couldn't take pleasure from the
fact that these reinforcements went to a different front, for
if the defenders failed either on the ridge or in the valley,
the defense of all Halverica would quickly become unten-
able.

And even when the monsters weren't attacking, there
was that damnable stream of darkness, foul poison making
a blight of a formerly wondrous creek. He had heard that
even the great Glimmersee itself, the lake so vast that one
couldn't see the far shore when standing at the water's
edge, was suffering from the Sleepstealer's pollution. Fish
were dying, and men who returned from trips down the
valley said that the 'see's pristine clarity was fading to a
dull murk.

Sparks, bright flares of light in the afternoon shadows,
trailed from a hulking creature at the rear of the minion
column. Roggett recognized the brutox as he considered an
ironic thought: A year ago, he wouldn't have believed such
creatures existed. Yet now they and their kin occupied half
of Dalethica, if the bad news from the lowlands was to be
believed.

A lot had changed in that year, the Iceman reflected
grimly, since the minions had emerged from the base of
the Glimmercrown. His friend Rudy Appenfell had been
the first to feel the threat, even fleeing the village when it
seemed that the monsters were there to seek him. The legion of darkness had attacked through a tunnel bored beneath the Watershed—a route pushed through the bedrock
of the world from Duloth-Trol into Dalethica. Dermaat had
fallen in the first onslaught, and it had become the task of

the bold warriors of mountainous Halverica to see that the situation didn't deteriorate anymore.

Now the men of Roggett's homeland, reinforced by a company of Galtigor infantry sent by King Takian, stood in uneasy stasis. The humans held this lofty ridge and the secure line down the valley, but had been unable to drive the minions back into their sunless hole. Not that they hadn't tried—within a fortnight of the incursion five hundred men had charged into Dermaat, determined to destroy the hated invaders. Barely half of the men had escaped, and the emboldened minions had moved after the retreating humans, seizing a stretch of the valley that was several miles long.

Roggett's eyes strayed back to the mountainside, rising from the crest of this rugged, forested ridge, to where the Glimmercrown rose like a challenge to the clouds, a gleaming white spire of glacier-draped mountain. Faerimont and Trolhorn flanked the mighty summit, the trio of mountaintops forming the massif known as the Crown of the World.

Movement attracted the Iceman's attention closer by as, around a shoulder of the ridge, a man came trotting along one of the well-worn foot trails. Even before he drew near to Roggett, the fellow slipped his waterskin from his shoulder.

The big Iceman did likewise, and when the runner came to a halt before him they extended their hands and splashed water over them before shaking. Ever since a party of shape-shifting stalkers had slipped through the lines, disguised as Icemen, the humans had resorted to this tactic as a preliminary to greeting—no minion could stand the touch of pure water against his skin, and the quick ceremony had been adopted as a way for strangers to assure each other of their mutual humanity.

"I'm Bekker Staylton. I've been stationed up near the mine," said the fellow, a sunburned mountaineer Roggett didn't recognize. There was nothing unusual in this, since the lines around the breach had drawn men from all the free cantons of Halverica.

"Aye—some men from my own village, Neshara, are there as well," Roggett acknowledged.

"Surely—Young Karlsted stands the nightwatch at my side."

The big Iceman was surprised by the news—Young Karlsted was a pimply-faced boy, in Roggett's recollection. Another fact about war: Boys became men far too quickly.

"I know the lad," was all he said.

"There's news," Bekker continued briskly, having recovered his breath. "A big column of minions comin' through the mine. There was a thousand or more before I left, and still comin' out the hole."

"Moving fast?" asked Roggett, feeling a knot form in his belly. The number of minions in the Dermaat wasteland had remained fairly constant for a long time. Now, it had apparently doubled, or worse, in a very short time.

"They were in as much of a hurry as any minions I've seen. Came with about a hundred brutox in the lead, it looked like. I wouldn't be surprised if they come into sight before too long, up the valley here."

Roggett squinted into the ruins of Dermaat Village, shading his eyes with a burly hand held to his brow. He saw a few minions plodding along the barren track of the main road, but as yet there was no sign of the enemy reinforcements.

If the minions attacked, the gap on the ridge just below Roggett's vantage would certainly be a major focal point of the fighting. To the north and south, the ridge crest rose in precipitous bluffs on the side facing Dermaat. Though a thin file of Halverican pickets guarded these heights, the humans knew that their enemy couldn't make a major push there—the kroaks and brutox would only be able to scale the height at a few crossings, and this one—Neshara Pass— was the closest to the breach in the Watershed.

"There they are," Bekker declared, pointing.

Roggett didn't need the assistance. The great file of minions looked like a thick black snake from this distance. Whether he imagined it or not, the Iceman thought that he could sense a thrumming through the soles of his boots, the plodding of monstrous feet that were still many miles away. Moving steadily, a column four or five minions wide, the file extended as far as Roggett could see, and continued steadily down the road.

Halvericans moved onto the narrow ledge of the vantage, and Roggett saw more of them take up positions in the gap of the pass or on the surrounding shoulders of Dermaathof Ridge. A block of men armed with long pikes would hold the key position straddling the roadway. Now those warriors lolled in the shade of the woods that flanked the saddle, with several lookouts posted right at the lip of the descending slope.

"Looks like you'll be ready," acknowledged the messenger. "I'd best be getting back to my own post."

"Thanks for the advance notice," Roggett replied sincerely. "I'll send word down the ridge."

He watched as Bekker Staylton jogged along the high trail, starting back toward his own position much farther up the mountainside. There a few mountaineers held a region of steep foothills, blocking yet another route into Neshara from a sudden minion advance.

Just before Roggett turned away, a faint shadow flickered across the ground and he shouted instinctively.

"Terrion!"

In another instant he saw the creature, the shifting camouflage of its skin a blue that nearly matched the sky. The flying minion tucked long wings and dove, narrow beak extended like an arrow, marking the path of that deadly descent.

At the shout of alarm Bekker Staylton hit the ground like the veteran he was, scrambling toward the shelter of a nearby pine.

Roggett thought first of his crossbow, then dismissed the notion—there was no time! Instead, gripping the smooth haft of his oversized ice axe, he sprinted along the trail, chasing the flying monster as it banked to follow Bekker. Against the high white face of the Glimmercrown, the

winged minion stood out in stark contrast for a second; then
its silvery-blue coat shimmered into the reflection of gray-
patched, icy glacier.

Bekker tumbled to the side at the last instant before that
stiff beak stabbed forward. The terrion squawked as it
struck the hard ground, then shrieked in fury and pain as
Roggett's axe bit into its scaly back. A leathery wing
slashed out, knocking the Iceman in the side of the head.
Dazed, he swung the weapon again, feeling the pick bite
into flesh at the base of the powerful membrane.

The monster hissed, then bit with a stabbing thrust of its
beak. Roggett, his fist protected by a heavy gauntlet, bashed
the strike aside and drove the pick of the ice axe down,
hard, against the monster's skull. Without another sound
the terrion collapsed, black streams of blood spilling freely
as the reptilian body faded to a pasty shade of gray.

Bekker rose to his feet, dusting the leaves and dirt from
his shirt. "Thanks, friend," he said, meeting Roggett's eyes
with the gratitude of a fellow warrior.

"I've seen too many good men fall that way," the Iceman replied grimly. "I'm glad that you weren't one of
them."

"It's not a good way to die," admitted the messenger,
with a brief, uneasy bark of laughter.

After a careful scrutiny of the sky, during which neither
man saw any of the telltale ripples that sometimes gave
away the location of a terrion, Bekker turned back to the
trail. Below, the minion column had begun to disperse,
kroaks in combat companies marching toward the base of
the ridge. Along the roadway below, a dozen brutox started
upward, marching shoulder to shoulder.

"That's the trouble with these times," Roggett murmured quietly. "There's altogether too many ways to die."

— 2 —

Danri's short, bowed legs plodded steadily up the steep
trail, each step carrying him higher on the rising ground of

the bluff. Kerri followed with the same tireless gait, barely drawing a deep breath as they neared the top.

"I should have had *you* training the field army," groaned the digger as he collapsed onto a mossy stump, puffing heavily.

"Oh, bosh. It's just that you insisted on bringing that heavy pack!" Kerri teased, taking a seat beside her betrothed. She clasped one of Danri's hands in both of her own, squeezing hard enough to let him know that he was never getting away from her again.

"It's like the old digger proverb," Danri said with a chuckle. " 'When you go to visit a drackan, make sure to take plenty of fresh meat.' "

"There's no such saying!"

"You're right. Guess I've been listening to Verdagon too much." He mocked the big drackan's pompous speech. "Heed me well, for it is written this, and it is written that!"

"Well, your saying kind of makes sense, though," Kerri admitted as the digger hefted the backpack, slowly rising to his feet. "It can't hurt to make a good impression."

"I wish that they'd just listen to Neambrey!" Danri groused, starting along the trail that followed the clifftop above the Aurun gorge.

"Surely you'll be able to talk them into coming down to the city, now that the Royal Scion has announced this council!" said the diggermaid encouragingly.

"You're right, babe."

In truth, Danri wished that he could feel as confident as he sounded. But the drackans were nothing if not aloof. The intervention of the mighty serpents had been decisive in stopping the minion advance short of Spendorial, yet that intervention had almost not occurred. Only the insight of young Neambrey had at last propelled the elder wyrms into the fight.

"Hi Danri! Hi Kerri!" The drackan's cheerful voice called out from a rocky overlook just ahead. In another instant Neambrey came into sight on the lip of the precipice, uncoiling sinuously around the trunk of an ancient pine. He spread his wings and pounced, gliding between the widely spaced trees to land in the meadow before the two diggers.

"What's in the bag?" blurted the drackan, forked tongue flickering from his narrow snout. "Is it food?"

"A little treat, if you'll let us share some of Faerine's bounty . . ."

"Ah, it is the digger who gave the treasured artifact to a human," sniffed a deep voice, as another serpent snaked into view around the shoulder of the rocky knob.

Verdagon was much bigger than Neambrey, and his scales were an emerald hue in contrast to the youngster's silver-gray. He came forward with measured dignity, stalking down the slope rather than gliding the short distance down to the two visitors.

"A human who used it to slay a Lord Minion," the digger retorted, his full beard bristling. "I daresay it didn't go to waste."

"Hmmph." Milky eyelids closed part way over Verdagon's slitted yellow eyes. Danri took some pleasure in the fact that the big serpent, uncharacteristically, seemed unable to come up with a pointed reply.

"We've brought a gift . . . and an invitation," Kerri said smoothly. "You should tell them, Danri."

"What is it?" squawked Neambrey. "Which first, the gift or the invitation?" The young drackan hopped from side to side on his taloned forepaws, his head, on its snakelike neck, bobbing eagerly between Danri and Kerri.

"The gift is here," said the digger, shrugging off his pack. He opened the flap and drew out a pair of leather-wrapped haunches. "Aurasheep," he said, presenting a morsel to each drackan. "I heard that was your favorite," he added, as Verdagon, in spite of himself, reached forward to snatch up the haunch.

"Yes . . . well, quite tender . . . indeed, rather nice . . ." the elder murmured around mouthfuls of fresh meat. Neambrey, too, squatted on the ground and began to gnaw at his own haunch. The two diggers took seats on a fallen tree trunk, and shared some cheese and Aurawine while they waited, quietly, for the drackans to finish their repast.

Danri drew a deep breath, relishing the fragrant breeze that, today, coursed eastward from the high mountains. The dry air, touched with a hint of pine, reminded him of Shalemont, his home. How long had it been since he'd last seen the slate roofs, stone cottages, and puffing smelters of that digger town?

Kerri had told him that he'd been gone for more than five years, and of course he believed her. Yet so consuming was the Digging Madness that had claimed him for so much of that interval, it still seemed no more than an eye blink of time in his own memory.

His thoughts turned to the diggermaid who sat so close beside him. Once again his hand had found its way into the clasp of her fingers—amazingly, he hadn't even noticed the touch. Chuckling wryly, he reflected that before his time with the Madness any such display of affection would have seemed embarrassingly inappropriate. Now, it only seemed natural.

Kerri's eyes met his, and her round-cheeked face broke into a shy smile, as if she sensed his thoughts. He grinned in return, warmed by the responding pressure of her fingers around his hand.

"See that speckled granite?" she asked softly, looking past him to the boulders atop the drackans' knolls.

"Aye-uh."

"What about stone like that for the bar? I mean, on a wood frame, of course."

"Hmmm." Danri thought about it. "A stone bar would be unique, all right—and fitting, I'm thinkin'. Still, I don't know about granite."

"What, then?"

"I remember some of the bluffs around Carillonn," he said. "White marble stone, as bright as clean linen. In fact, the diggers used it to make the arches and bridges all around that city."

"I'd like to see it someday," Kerri mused wistfully. "You make it sound like a real wonder."

"It is! And *that's* the stone that would make ours a bar worth talking about. Let's go there, after the war I mean. We can figure out a way to bring a slab of marble back for our inn—and I'll carve it into the bar!"

"It's a deal," the diggermaid said, before biting her lip and looking away.

Danri knew the reason for her bittersweet consent—it was hard for him, hard for everyone, to imagine a time when the war might be over, when life in Faerine and Dalethica could have some chance of returning to normal.

"Remember, I promised," he said seriously. "We'll have our inn, Kerri. You keep looking for the perfect place. When you find it, I'll start building."

"Oh, Danri." Kerri sniffled slightly, but the tightening of her grip only strengthened the digger's resolve.

"I say . . . that really was delicious," murmured Verdagon, running his forked tongue over the juices that trickled from his crocodilian jaws.

"Great!" Neambrey agreed, splintering the joint of his haunch to suck, noisily, on the juicy marrow.

"Perhaps there was another reason, beyond our feeding and comfort, that brings you to the forest?" Verdagon suggested with the serene patience of his kind.

"Yes, there is." Danri decided to get right to the point. "The Royal Scion of Spendorial has called for a council, a gathering of the leaders among all the Faerines, in order to make a plan for the war. Gulatch of the gigants will be there, and Garic Hoorkin of the twissels and Wattli Sartor. I myself will represent the diggers, and of course the scion will speak for the sylves."

"I see," murmured the sinuous emerald-colored serpent.

"The scion thinks, and I agree, that it's important to have the drackans represented in the council. Your intervention, after all, had a lot to do with the saving of Spendorial. The goddess only knows how important you and your kinsmen can be to all our ventures."

"That's a great idea, the council, I mean!" Neambrey blurted, looking to his elder for confirmation.

"An idea for the Lesser Faerines, perhaps," Verdagon concurred half-heartedly. "But we drackans are pledged to remain aloof from such concerns."

Danri had expected this initial response, but he still had to bite back a hot-tempered reply. "I know that the brown drackans have gone back to the Bruxrange," he said patiently. "And that all the greens but the two of you have returned to their lairs. But if you would attend, you would hear what our plans are—you could even make suggestions of your own. Then, if it meets with your approval, you could inform the other greens. I don't need to tell you that your assistance will greatly improve our chances of defeating the invasion."

"It would seem that the invasion was already defeated," Verdagon noted, raising his head to peer between the tops of the trees, looking over the wasted landscape across the river.

"The minion army was *stopped* at the river," Danri retorted, more sharply than he meant to. "But they're still over there—surely you can see that!"

"But they show no signs of attacking."

"Only because we—specifically, the Man of Three Waters and his Auracloud—destroyed their reserve of Darkblood. As soon as a train of bovars comes over Darkenheight Pass with replenishment, they'll return to the attack. And who's to say we can stop them again?"

Kerri laid a restraining hand on Danri's forearm as the digger bristled. He took a deep breath, knowing that a show of anger would only serve to solidify the elder drackan's stubborn refusal.

"It would be a bad idea for us to meet, to mix, with your people," Verdagon asserted. "For it is written: 'When the mighty mingle with the low, they are no longer the mighty.' "

"What does that—?"

Danri started to splutter an indignant response, but Kerri interceded smoothly.

"It's also written: 'When the parts of a thing come together, they can form a whole that is greater than their sum.' "

"Where is that written?" demanded the big serpent, scowling suspiciously.

"Since when does it matter *where* something's written?" Danri retorted. "Isn't it the *truth* that counts?"

"It was scribed by the sylvan bard, Wysteerin Hallowayn," explained Kerri. "A passage from *The Tally of Lives*. But Danri's right—it's a fact that should be evident to all of us. You drackans are an important part of Faerine. Surely you see that you should join forces with the rest of us!"

"*I* see," Neambrey replied enthusiastically. He turned to regard the much larger wyrm. "They're right, Verdagon. We've got to go and see what can be done!"

"It's another sign of the ruin of our world," muttered the elder, shaking his head obstinately. He glowered at Neambrey. "Still, I've seen that stubborn streak in you before—it's your brown half acting up, no doubt."

Danri bit his tongue to keep from remarking on stubbornness as he had observed that trait in green drackans. He sensed that they were close to victory.

"I suppose that I shan't be able to stop you if you insist on going," continued Verdagon with a resonant sniff of disdain. "For it is written: 'Let the youngster hear of wisdom, that he will know what he lacks.' "

"Then we'll go—or, at least, *I* can go?" Neambrey chirped eagerly.

"It is certain that I shall not be attending, so if there is to be a drackan presence at this council . . . yes, I would assume that it will be you."

"That's wonderful!" crowed the young silver-gray drackan. "I'll be there!" he promised. "When is the council?"

"The scion hoped it would be some time tomorrow,"

Danri told him, "though it partly depends upon the Man of Three Waters. He's still consulting the Scrying Pool."

"I'll come down to the city in the morning!" declared Neambrey. "That way, I'll be there whenever you need me."

"Great," Danri agreed. He turned to regard Verdagon, who had already swiveled his mighty wedge-shaped head away and was now probing under a massive rotting log, snuffling noisily.

"And Verdagon, my friend—I thank you," replied the sturdy Faerine quietly and sincerely, before turning with his diggermaid to start back on the woodland trail to Spendorial.

— 3 —

"I'm ready." Raine took a deep breath. She was dressed in her own clothes again, green silk breeches and a cotton blouse that rendered her, in Rudy's eyes, more dazzling than any noblewoman. Her hair glowed with a sheen like burnished metal, as she passed through the doorway with a barely contained sense of energy, reminding Rudy of a cat on the hunt, poised and alert, seeking the first sign of her prey.

The Iceman came behind, ready to return to a world of people and sunlight. For days he had observed the Watershed, in his own studies of the Scrying Pool. He had seen Takian patrolling the still-untested defenses of Carillonn. Though Rudy had been unable to find Bristyn, he was not particularly concerned—the pool was limited to viewing places open to the sky, and he knew that most of Bristyn's duties would be keeping her inside. Halverica was heartbreaking to see—Rudy wept at the devastation of Dermaat, and ached as he observed the loss of Neshara's pastoral existence. His mountain village was an armed camp, training ground for new recruits and hospital for men suffering from wounds or illness.

And he dared to probe to the south, into the realm of the
Sleepstealer. He saw little of detail, only barren landscapes
of plain and hill and chasm. Yet always farther on, still
mocking him with that resonant pulsation, there was the
Heart of Darkblood . . . calling them.

Raine's hand slipped through his arm as the pair walked
down the verdant, vine-draped aisle connecting the Scrying
Pool's dressing chamber with the heart of Spendorial's palace. She was strong, and he allowed her will and determination to pull him along, knowing that he would have
desperate need of her strength before their task was
through.

They found the Royal Scion in his chart room. Mussrick
Daringer was bent over a huge, low table, studying a vast,
dark canvas. Rudy knew without looking that it was a map
of the stars. When the humans entered, the Royal Scion
stood tall and greeted them from across his table, expectancy and hope lighting his eyes.

"Send out the call," Rudy declared without preamble.
"It is time for your gathering."

"May the gods smile upon us all," murmured Mussrick
Daringer.

— 4 —

The roadway crossed the face of the ridge some distance
below the defenders, then turned to curve through the
nearby pass. Roggett watched the minions on that rutted
track march upward from ruined Dermaat, monstrous troops
crowded shoulder to shoulder as they trotted steadily up the
Dermaathof.

Two hundred kroaks made the first rush at the ridgetop,
scrambling onto the rocky ground uphill of the road, grunting and barking, brandishing swords of black iron. Roggett
raised his crossbow and aimed carefully for the leading
minion, releasing the trigger to the satisfying *chunk* of the
powerful spring. The steel shaft flew faster than he could

follow, puncturing the big kroak and sending it cartwheeling down the slope.

"Stand firm!" cried the Iceman to his comrades, swinging the crossbow downward to recrank the spring. "And watch your front!" he added, as several young men nervously looked toward another band of minions advancing along the road toward the saddle of Neshara Pass.

Once more Roggett raised his weapon and released a killing shot. Then he slung the crossbow to his back in favor of the sharp ice axe, watching the snorting nostrils, the beady, glaring eyes of the nearest kroaks as the minions scrambled up the last portion of the slope.

The men of his village met the monstrous horde at the crest of the Dermaathof, slashing with swords and picks and axes. Perched on strong positions above the attackers, the humans made every blow count. In seconds, two dozen minions tumbled down the slope or lay motionless, spilling black blood across the rocks, while the survivors swiftly turned and fled back toward the road. Only the smell remained, that pervasive, familiar stench that was like a mixture of ammonia and carrion.

"That was just a test," Roggett said grimly, hefting the bloodstained ice axe. "They wanted to see how strongly we're holding the crest."

Around him, a dozen men of Neshara nodded grimly, while on the roadway below, a company of brutox advanced with heavy, plodding footsteps. Unlike the kroaks, the bigger minions didn't depart the track onto the brushy hillside. Instead, they trudged in a grim block along the course of the dirt road. Sparks crackled and hissed among the hulking, round-shouldered brutox, and as those in the lead turned their faces upward, the Iceman could see the tusks jutting from the monsters' lower jaws.

"Stand ready there," Roggett shouted to the pikemen who straddled the road where it crossed through the saddle of Neshara Pass. He knew that the men of that company, emplaced with bristling spears pointed outward, couldn't see the brutox yet because the attackers were still concealed by the shoulder of the ridge. "They'll be trying your neighborhood next!"

"Thanks for the warning!" shouted the grizzled captain of the pikemen, Kristoff Yarden. His company looked like nothing so much as a giant pincushion to the watchers on the heights above, as it waited for the first attack with a bristling array of steel spear tips facing down the road.

Kroaks, massed like a stain of ink on the ground, choked the route behind the brutox. Many of the lesser minions left the track to start back up the ridge, a wave of thousands trampling the ground bloodied by the initial probe.

The men of Neshara waited around Roggett, weapons ready. Those armed with crossbows shot volleys of deadly bolts into the tide, and each steel-shafted arrow punched through minion bodies. Still, the overall effect was lost among the rising wave of darkness, kroaks growling upward over the rocks. A sound like a distant rockslide rumbled from the monstrous throats, the mixture of panting breath, guttural threats, and sharp, aggressive barks. Occasionally a dark sword would clang against a rock, adding a background of staccato *dings* to the dull, rolling sound.

Roggett picked out a big kroak, watching as the monster advanced ahead of its fellows. Bloodshot eyes glittered, staring upward from the bestial face as the minion raised a curved sword. Using its free hand to aid in climbing the steep slope, the kroak kicked heavy boots into the ground with each step, securing purchase. Those hateful eyes met the Iceman's, and the creature's hunger for battle was a tangible longing in that wicked glare.

The big Iceman stood at the brink of a boulder, both feet planted firmly. The kroaks climbed closer, their growling shouts rapidly swelling into a roar—a sound that made Roggett imagine he was caught within that landslide he had earlier pictured. Abruptly cries rose from the pass, shrieks of minion pain mingled with hoarse challenges and grunts of exertion from the Halverican pikemen.

A quick glance showed Roggett that the brutox had met the first pikes. Some of the minions fell, sparking, howling in agony as they thrashed in the road, but others bored in to the attack, bashing the long spear shafts out of the way or snapping them with bites, or twists of powerful hands.

Then the kroaks were just below. Roggett sprang backward, avoiding the low sword swipe of the leading minion. Before the monster could swing again the Iceman struck, driving the pick of the ice axe through the heavy, knobbed skull. The kroak fell, slain instantly, but immediately three more of the minions crawled over the body, straining to reach Roggett with their swords.

Kicking away one of the blades, the Iceman struck to the right and left, sending two minions tumbling back down the ridge as the third cringed back, frightened of the deadly pick. The smell of the monsters thickened, nearly gagging Roggett as he spotted a slender, reptilian minion trying to slink between two rocks on all fours. The Iceman spun and hacked through the stalker's spine with a sharp, downward chop, then swung back to slash at the kroaks trying to scramble onto the ridge crest.

Clattering noises—the sounds of a *real* rockslide—rumbled from the right, where the defenders released boulders that had been piled atop the slope. Huge rocks tumbled through the wave of kroaks, crushing dozens, sending many more slipping back down the steep slope of the ridge.

"For Neshara—and all the Free Cantons!" shouted Roggett, splitting the skull of another kroak. On both sides the men of his village surged, slashing and stabbing furiously, showering the hated foe with a deadly barrage of blows.

"Remember Dermaat!" cried Tarn Blaysmith, who had lived in the neighboring village. His entire family had been lost in the first days of the breach.

Howling madly, Tarn led a contingent of axemen down from the ridge, and Roggett urged his own men to follow. Swinging recklessly as they skidded into the reeling minions, the men of Halverica swept forward. Some kroaks tried to stand, and these died quickly, hacked by the keen weapons of furious humans. Most of the minions tumbled back, rolling and scrambling down the ridge in the face of the sudden charge.

As the panicked enemy troops swept down toward the road, Roggett saw that the pikemen in the pass had held as well. The brutox, in danger of encirclement by the charging Icemen, backed away from the close confines of the ridge-top gap. In seconds they, too, were tumbling down the slope, taking the fastest and most direct route toward the base of the ridge.

"Hold up!" Roggett's shout was barely audible over the din, but several of his men took up the command and soon the line of warriors came to a halt. Tarn was the last to stop, and for several moments he stood alone, far down the slope of the ridge, shrieking his hatred at the retreating monsters.

Below, the retreating minions merged with a second line, presenting a wall of dark steel. Lacking the numbers to break that defense, the humans retreated slowly to the crest of the ridge. Messengers reported along the line, and from them Roggett learned that six men of Neshara had been slain in the brief skirmish, while three or four times that many had sustained nasty wounds. The pikemen, on his left flank, had fared similarly.

Looking at the hundreds of dead minions across the slopes, the Iceman knew that the bloody exchange had been a sound repulse for the enemy. Yet as he saw the teeming kroaks and their sparking masters gather on the valley floor below, he knew, too, that the monsters would be back . . . and soon.

THREE

Trails of the Willowfen

In ancient eras men of evil were drawn to the
Sleepstealer's banner like vultures to carrion,
compelled by the irresistible allure of Darkblood.
—TOME OF VILE COMPULSIONS

— 1 —

Bristyn knew Sergeant Major Katlan as a quietly competent
veteran, though a trifle too deferential for her taste. He
bowed low, then cupped his hands to offer the duchess an
assist into the saddle, but she shook his efforts away and
swung easily onto the back of her dappled mare.

The five swordsmen of the escort were already mounted,
their steeds stomping impatiently in the arched gatehouse.
Three of the men started through the open gates of Castle
Shalloth while Katlan pulled himself onto his chestnut gelding. Riding beside the duchess, the sergeant major set a
position two dozen paces behind the leaders, while the last
two men rode an equal distance to the rear.

Bristyn looked at the clean-shaven warrior, who appeared
remarkably young despite long service to the late Duke of

Shalloth and, in the last year, his daughter. Now she tried
to imagine the burden of guilt carried by Katlan and his
companions as they departed the ancestral fortress for the
last time.

Some three hundred elite warriors of the Shalloth Guards
remained in the castle, and the duchess knew that Katlan
and every one of the men of her escort detail would have
willingly—even preferably—stayed behind with them. Yet
these riders obeyed with stone-faced dignity, following
Bristyn's lead as she halted at the crest of the first ridge for
a final look at the vista of pastoral farmland and the lofty,
crenelated castle. Her eyes blurred before she at last looked
away, once again allowing the grim-faced Katlan to set the
pace as the riders passed into the first stretch of forest.

"We'll try to get some miles behind us today," the
young swordsman suggested. "That way—if we hold a
good pace—we might make it to Carillonn in four or five
days."

"Hard riding suits me," Bristyn said, suppressing a
smile as she remembered herself, barely a year before, in-
sisting on a sidesaddle and a pace that allowed for plenty
of rest stops.

Her good humor was short-lived, as the cantering riders
soon came upon the first group of refugees. A score of
villagers crowded the road, some men herding a ragged
collection of sheep, goats, and a few cows, while cloaked
women trailed behind, trying to serve as shepherds for a
dozen or so young children. Many of the little ones whim-
pered with fatigue, or limped numbly along the rutted track.

"'Ere now, keep it up for another hour—then we'll
rest," counseled an old crone, her voice soothing as she
stroked the head of a red-haired girl while the riders drew
up behind her.

"We'll help for a bit," Bristyn said immediately. She
and the guardsmen hoisted a couple of youngsters onto each
of the horses. The noble party clopped along at a walk,
accompanying the ragged, weary refugees until nightfall.
Only when the displaced farmfolk found a place to make

a camp did the children dismount, and the duchess urge her
men to make haste into the darkness.

Though the riders passed several inns, these were
crowded with people in flight. The duchess was heartened
to see that the available shelter had, for the most part, been
given over to the children and infirm. Many more people
slept in sprawling, impromptu encampments centered
around the infrequent crossroads.

Her own party eventually camped in the shelter of a
dense grove of pines, well-removed from other travelers.
Making do with a small fire, they ate cold trail-fare and
slept on the ground. The following day they started out
early, but soon found the road clogged with a slow-moving
exodus. Here the woodland pressed so close that the riders
couldn't pass without pushing the people on foot right into
the thickets.

"I know some paths fringing the Willowfen," Katlan
said as, by midmorning, the group had only advanced a
few miles. "One of the tracks leads off to the right up
ahead. It winds around a bit, but I don't think there'll be
many people down there. On the horses, we can make
pretty good time."

"Let's take it," Bristyn agreed. She knew of the Willowfen by reputation, and as Gandor Wade's home province. It was an extensive wetland that followed much of
the east bank of the River Ariak, forming a dense and tangled border for Shalloth. The folk who lived there were
rugged woodsmen and fishers, famed for implacable suspicion of outsiders—and keen knowledge of their swampy
domain.

Katlan's track proved much narrower than the road, with
moss-draped limbs often reaching eerie fingers down as far
as the riders' shoulders. Sunlight seemed incapable of penetrating the dense foliage, and the small party moved
through a region of perpetual shadow. However, the woodland routes were barren of other travelers, and once again
they proceeded at a canter. As before, three men rode in

the van, with Katlan beside the duchess, and two more bringing up the rear.

Bristyn found herself thinking about Takian as the day waned into afternoon. She imagined his anxiety, and determined to do everything she could to reach him as soon as possible. Propelled by her fresh resolve, she gave her mare a kick, urging the wiry animal into a faster gait. Her guards, sensing the change, picked up their own pace.

Abruptly the three men in the lead were slammed backward to the ground, swept from their saddles by a single, uniform attack. Groaning, the fallen horsemen twitched weakly as their steeds galloped down the shadowy trail.

Reining in by instinct, the duchess drew her sharp shortsword. Hearing a moan of pain behind her, she whirled to see the two guards at the rear tumbling from their saddles, three or four arrows jutting from the back of each.

To the front again she saw the rope stretched across the trail, grimacing at the old trick that had struck down three good men. Before she and Katlan could race forward, cloaked figures rushed from the woods, hacking viciously at the felled riders, then raising bloodstained blades to confront the sergeant major and the duchess.

Bristyn was about to put the spurs to her horse when she saw more men moving through the brush beside her. She pulled back on the reins, recognizing the futility of flight. At least a dozen bandits held cocked crossbows, the missiles aimed unerringly at the Duchess of Shalloth.

— 2 —

The lone being stirred in the depths of a vast, lightless chamber. A long and muscular arm, shiny with Darkblood, reached for a handhold, pulling a muscular body upward. Huge wings, taut and leathery membranes peaked like a bat's, flexed stiffly, then unfurled to their full, massive spread. The hulking form rose, first to its knees, then to its padded, taloned feet.

Nicodareus lifted his beastlike muzzle toward the unseen ceiling, probing the darkened corners of the chamber with his senses. Memories of punishment burned fresh in the Lord Minion's mind, and he flinched unconsciously as something stirred at the base of the far wall.

It was only a stalker, he saw with relief—and chagrin, for the snake-faced minion had seen his discomfort, and sneered slightly as it approached. *You will die for that,* the Eye of Dassadec pledged silently.

"What is it?" Nicodareus demanded, as the supple messenger bent more than double at its waist. The scaly tail lashed back and forth as the reptilian creature extended its forked tongue to lick the floor before the Lord Minion's feet.

"Our master bids you go to the Well of Darkblood. There he will speak to you."

Nicodareus nodded. "Stalker," he declared curtly.

"Aye, lord?" Again came that measure of insolence, in the sly, hooded drooping of the minion's filmy eyelids.

"Do not dare to show disrespect to the face of a Lord Minion—even in disgrace, I am your master."

The stalker's eyes opened fully, but it never got the chance to reply. Nicodareus' fist lashed out with the speed of a striking cobra, seizing the stalker around the throat. Tendons knotted like wire beneath the smooth black skin as he squeezed, slowly and deliberately crushing the life from the offensive creature.

Eyes glowing like infernal fires, fangs gleaming in a fierce grin, the Lord Minion tossed the corpse aside and pounded his mighty fists against his breast. Fully alive, monstrously powerful, the Eye of Dassadec stalked through the halls of Agath-Trol, moving deeper through the dark-walled passages hewn from the living bedrock of the Watershed. His steps carried him ever lower, down flights of slick black steps, along corridors that ran beside deep gutters, channels that carried steady currents of inky Darkblood.

The Well lay in the deepest part of Dassadec's fortress.

As Nicodareus descended the last, broad flight of steps he leaned forward and spread his wings, gliding to the base of the decline. Here he came to rest beside a pool of perfect darkness, a gathering place for troughs of Darkblood that flowed into this chamber from seven different places.

Look, my Eye . . . observe the labors of my favored son.

The command from the Sleepstealer entered the Lord Minion's mind like a hammer blow, staggering him with its humiliating reminder. Once it had been Nicodareus who earned the highest praise of his master, who had been the favored of Dassadec's Lord Minions. That reign had ended with the coming of the Man of Three Waters. Hatred flared anew as the Eye of Dassadec remembered a hundred insults delivered by the insolent Iceman, and imagined a thousand tortures inflicted by himself in return.

Yet now the humbled Lord Minion mutely extended his Sight across Duloth-Trol, over the lofty ridge of the Watershed, following the swath of destruction that led to Reaper's army. Probing through a vast, trampled encampment, the Eye of Dassadec at last found his serpentine counterpart, curled regally atop a knoll in the midst of his numberless horde.

The Talon of Dassadec was a mighty wyrm, slickly black in color, huge enough to shelter a dozen massive bovars under each wing. Slowly, with maddening impertinence, the mighty head lifted, a raised eye cocked above the crocodile snout, attentively turned toward the Sleepstealer's voice.

"It is I, Master . . . I await your command."

Your armies have been reinforced, your strength restored after the losses at Lanbrij.

"Aye, Master. We have fully recovered from the disaster brought on by Nicodareus' mistakes. Wagons full of Darkblood are on the way, and soon my legions will be fully replenished."

The Eye of Dassadec could only rage silently at his rival's base assertion. Any vocal outburst would be likely to draw his master's displeasure.

I command you to resume the attack as soon as you have replenished your bloodtrains. Destroy Shalloth and Carillonn, and send your armies into Halverica and Galtigor. Do not cease until all Dalethica is a wasteland.

"It is my pleasure, my honor, to obey," pledged the monstrous serpent, curling his lip in a display of long fangs. "Know that the attack will commence with all possible speed."

That is well, my favored son. But move with caution—I have dispatched the Dreadcloud *to support you. Wait until it arrives before you strike.*

The *Dreadcloud*! Nicodareus quivered with impotent rage. The potent skyship should be his, by right! Already Phalthak, the Fang of Dassadec, had failed to achieve victory, had allowed the mighty vessel to wither away. Now the power of Dassadec had restored the great vessel, only to dispatch it to Reaper! Yet, again, Nicodareus could only wait until he felt his master's attention turn toward himself.

"What of I, Master?" he dared to inquire then. "How may I strike at the enemy?"

Remain here, beside the Heart of Darkblood. Because of your unspeakable failure, my very center is vulnerable to attack. It shall be your task to protect me, and to slay any intruder.

"But how . . . ?" Nicodareus was at first mystified. No creature of Dalethica or Faerine could survive the poison environment of Duloth-Trol—how could the Heart, which pulsed steadily in the base of this fortress, be vulnerable?

Fool! The force of the word drove Nicodareus to his knees. *The Man of Three Waters—he who still lives because of your failure. He is the threat—and he must be stopped.*

Of course—the man who was more than human. Could it be that the admixture of water, Darkblood, and Aura would render the Iceman proof against the toxic surroundings?

"Allow me to fly, Master—to seek him across the Watershed. I shall slay him before he draws close to Agath-Trol!"

You dare to ask this—when you have failed, so many times before?

Nicodareus had no answer.

Your work is here. It is my will that the Heart be protected within a labyrinth. You, Nicodareus, shall create this maze.

"Master—" The Lord Minion, having struggled to his feet, spoke without thinking. "Surely bovar and brutox could work that labor more quickly than I!"

Nay. It is you who have created this threat—it shall be you who proofs against it! With hand and claw and fang you will dig at the rock of my fortress! Now, my worthless son—begin!

Abjectly Nicodareus hurled himself to the floor. He trembled at the thought of his master's rage and, frantically, began to tear at the rock, pulling away great chunks of the stone, swiftly burying himself in a growing cave.

— 3 —

Takian guided Hawkrunner through the crowded streets, hurrying as much as possible without forcing the big stallion to crush some unfortunate pedestrian's toes. Of course, as King of Galtigor and acting regent of Carillonn, he could have had an escort clear a path for him, but in these times of tension that seemed a criminal waste of soldierly manpower.

Too, though Takian was a king, Carillonn was not a city of his own realm. Perhaps that knowledge made him reluctant to rely overly much on the trappings of royalty. Of course, for now he was the only monarch the marbled city had, but this fact did nothing to encourage his aspirations. He looked forward to the time when the heir to the High Kingship would arrive in his capital and assume the mantle of command. Until then, Takian of Galtigor would do what he could to see that the City of One Hundred Bridges remained free of minion occupation.

And that would be no easy task.

Accompanied by his loyal sergeant, Randart, Takian had spent the morning touring the island, the high hills each crowned by majestic structures of white marble, crests and towers linked by the myriad alabaster arches and lofty spans of the fabled bridges. He had been circling the East-hill for most of the afternoon, and now he descended to ride over a much lower bridge, a marble slab crossing the Whitestream, the brook that bisected the city and its crowded island.

He entered the Royal District, the portion of the city dominated by the grand edifice of Castle Carillonn. Even from down here, on a street of crowded, dilapidated shacks, Takian could look up and see the white walls of the fortress encircling the hilltop, the highest elevation of the entire city. To the right, surmounting a lower crest, rose the needle of the King's Tower. The spire was connected to the castle by the highest bridge in the whole city, the Kingsbridge, which spanned the distance over a series of five high, slender arches.

Takian's progress took him around the high-walled castle and onto the wide avenue connecting the fortified gatehouse with the widest of the city's river bridges. Six impressive spans crossed the channels of the Ariak, three to the west of the island and three linking the city to the east bank. This boulevard, the Roseway, passed through the city gate and onto the Rosebridge, which was the centermost, and widest, of the western crossings.

Satisfied that his duty to the city was done, Takian set out across the bridge, bent on a more personal task. Randart's gelding cantered beside Hawkrunner as the two men reached the far shore and turned left at the crossroads, taking the highway toward Shalloth. A number of people were moving up this road, all of them apparently seeking to escape across the bridges to the island city.

"Ho, there, farmer," called Takian, spotting one strap-

ping, hard-eyed man. The fellow carried a stout staff and
marched at the head of a gaggle of children, while one of
the sons led an ox cart carrying a very pregnant woman.
At the summons, the man stopped and regarded the rider
skeptically.

Looking at the horseman with the straw-colored hair and
beard, the piercing eyes and the sturdy leather cloak, the
farmer would have little idea that he was being addressed
by a king. That suited Takian—he preferred that men related to him by the force of his own presence, not the title
that had come to him since his father's untimely death.

"What is it?" asked the refugee, as Hawkrunner pawed
the ground beside him.

"Do you come from Shalloth?"

"Aye—the pasturelands south of that city. Abandoned
my farmstead, I did."

"A wise precaution, I'm told. Did you have word of your
duchess?" Takian held his breath, waiting for the answer.
Although Bristyn had sent letters by courier, he had yet to
speak with someone who had seen her in person.

"'Twas upon her command that I departed," declared
the farmer. He glared at Takian and the burly Randart, flexing his brawny hands around the stout staff. "Think you
that any mere swordsman could have driven me from my
land?"

"No," replied the king in perfect honesty. "Nor could
the minions, I'm certain—save for your need to see to the
safety of your family. And know this, my good man: You
have done the right thing."

The fellow looked skeptical. "We would have given
them a fight, my boys and I." Three youths, beardless but
sturdy and as tall as their father, pressed forward to support
this claim.

"You'll have your chance to fight, I promise. But of the
duchess—had she started back to Carillonn when you departed?"

"Nay. She rode with a light escort, heading to the eastern
farms. That was six or eight days ago, now. But tell me,

horseman—what concern do ye have for the Duchess of Shalloth?''

''She's my wife,'' Takian replied simply.

The farmer's eyes widened. ''You'd be King Takian, then. My pardon, Your Majesty, for not knowin' ye.'' He bowed, and his three sons did likewise. Behind them, smaller children gaped upward in awe.

''Where's your crown?'' one bold youngster piped up, pushing between the legs of his older siblings.

''I left it in the castle on the hill, for safekeeping,'' replied the monarch with a chuckle.

''Word has it that the road from Shalloth is crowded back to the north for miles, still,'' said the farmer. ''Her Grace was insistent—she commanded folks to flee to Carillonn, though we could see the castle still standing in Shalloth!''

''Castles are not enough to hold the minions at bay,'' Takian replied. ''Our best hope is water, and Carillonn has the shelter of its river. But when you and your young men have crossed to the east bank, you'll find companies forming in the name of the duchess. I urge you to join—and with the help of Baracan, you'll be part of the army that reclaims your homeland and sends this dark horde reeling back to Duloth-Trol.''

''Good words, sire.'' The farmer bowed again as Takian thanked him and rode on.

They reached a low elevation on the road, and Takian saw the farmer's words borne out: A file of refugees darkened the highway for the several miles that were visible, spilling steadily from the swath of forest covering so much of the distance between Shalloth and Carillonn.

A detachment of city guardsmen stood to the side, allowing the column to pass freely toward Carillonn. The captain of the company recognized the king and stepped to Hawkrunner's side, bowing.

''There's more rumors, Your Majesty, about the High Prince—the king's heir.''

''Indeed. What are they saying now?''

"They're sayin' he's coming with a whole army, that he'll throw these minions clear back across the Watershed," declared the man-at-arms in tones of disgust. "As if another thousand men could make a difference."

"We'll take all the help we can get," counseled the monarch. "But I'd settle for the heir himself. Carillonn is too important to fall—and the city needs its own king to give it the strength to stand."

"Well, he couldn't get here too soon for me, either," the captain declared dispiritedly.

"There's possibly more help on the way. I've sent a courier with a personal letter to Duke Beymont of Corsari, telling him of our situation. He told me after the Lanbrij battle that he expected to raise a legion of ten thousand men. It's my hope that he'll be able to dispatch a good sized force to help us. They'll come up the river from the north, so the minions won't block them from the city."

"Good hope, sire. Not that I'd mind if we have to beat the bastards ourselves!"

"Let's allow the fighting to develop as it may," Takian said. "And until then, just try to keep these people moving."

"Aye, sire. Women and children to the camps on the east bank; men, to find a company and join up. And then we'll just have to hope."

"And pray," Takian said, half to himself.

His eyes rose to the dark storm clouds massed in the southwestern sky. He thought of his beloved Bristyn beneath that oppressive shadow.

Hurry home, my queen . . . hurry back to me.

These words he mouthed silently, raising a prayer to Baracan and Aurianth, hoping that the God of Man and the Mistress of Magic would shed their blessings on Bristyn Duftrall. Yet when he looked again at the dark shadow, he felt a penetrating chill, and despite pulling his leather cloak firmly about his shoulders as he turned and started along the road, he shivered all the way back to the castle.

— 4 —

With her hands bound to the saddle before her, Bristyn could only duck her head in a vain effort to keep the low branches from lashing her face. Her mount was led by one of her captors, a man who tugged roughly on the reins, urging the steed into a lurching, awkward trot. Helplessly the duchess was pulled along, an unwilling member of the file trailing through the tangled woods.

Once the bandit holding her horse turned to regard his prisoner with a pair of dark, frighteningly intense eyes. Bristyn had met his gaze with, she hoped, a glare of arrant disdain—but her fear lurked just below the surface. Silently the duchess prayed to Baracan that none of the dark men would scrutinize her too carefully and penetrate her haughty façade.

The silent, brooding intensity of the man closest to her was not the only unique feature of this cutthroat band. In the aftermath of the ambush, they had bound their two captives and started into the thickets of the fen with little talking. Furthermore, Bristyn had been unable to identify any of the men as a leader. Rather, the hundred or so bandits seemed to move as a pack, as if guided by some kind of mass instinct.

At first she had demanded to know who they were, why they had attacked her—but her questions were met with belligerent silence. Finally she had ceased to speak, fearing that her words might goad the strangers into violence.

Having stolen a few glances over her shoulder, the duchess knew that Sergeant Major Katlan was similarly bound astride his horse, forced to follow along just behind her. Their course took them down a series of narrow tracks, muddy routes through the tangled wilderness of the Willowfen. The air of the swampland was a dank, smelly blanket against Bristyn's skin, a wet cloak on her shoulders.

She winced, biting back an exclamation of pain as a thorny branch lashed her face. The hooked barbs left a

stinging welt, but she would not give her captors the satisfaction of voicing her discomfort.

They had traveled many miles since the ambush, and
Bristyn had learned that a surprisingly extensive maze of
trails crossed the Willowfen. Often these were shadowed
by mossy, overhanging trees, a leafy ceiling so dense that
most of the time she couldn't locate the sun. She had no
way to guess what direction she'd been taken, except that
they seemed to be working their way deeper into the tangled wilds.

Her horse's hooves sloshed wetly in muddy ground as
the file plodded around the fringe of a shallow, reed-fringed
lake. The sun set behind her, so Bristyn now knew that her
captives were leading her generally eastward. Then, once
again, the verdant dome closed overhead, and she ducked
away from vines and creepers, felt the lash of thorns against
her garments and skin.

Darkness came suddenly as the shadows cast by the trees
thickened, closing in from all directions. A few torches
sprang to life along the line of ragged bandits, spots of light
leading into the distance before Bristyn, vanishing behind
the frequent bends and turns. Now the duchess was forced
to lay herself along the horse's neck, lest she be strangled
by the unseen tendrils that swung across the path.

Men growled and barked, their accents unintelligible,
their tones hoarse and guttural. Raising her head, Bristyn
saw that the torches had spread out from the single file of
the march. The company had entered a large clearing, and
she felt a giddy, irrational sense of relief at the sight of a
thousand stars sparkling overhead.

The man leading her horse grunted violently as he came
to a halt, then tugged at the bonds securing Bristyn's wrists
to the saddle. Releasing the tie-down while keeping her
limbs bound together, the fellow pulled her unceremoniously onto the ground, then roughly supported her as she
staggered and almost fell.

"Here," he said curtly, pushing her toward the center of
the clearing. Most of the torchbearers had already gathered,

and the wash of flaring, yellow light cast alternating bright-ness and shadow across a dark shape looming upward from the ground. Flames crackled greedily as some of the torches were tossed onto a pile of timber. Dried pine boughs flared with the suddenness of lightning, and Bristyn gasped as she got a clear look at the hulking form in the center of the clearing.

It was a statue, crudely carved from the white marble quarried near the Ariak. Despite the lack of skilled craft-manship, the duchess recognized the image. Twin, upward-jutting tusks distorted the blunt jaw of a monster squatting on fat legs with broad torso and bestial head upraised. The rounded shoulders, the low, sloping brow were clearly in-tended to represent a specific creature—a beast that had recently become terribly familiar to humanity.

"Brutox," she whispered, trying to quell her horror as Katlan was prodded to her side. He flashed her a wink that was meant to be encouraging, until one of the swampmen cuffed him roughly across the face.

"Look," Katlan murmured, inclining his head slightly toward the side of the statue, where a group of men had gathered in the shadows away from the bonfire.

Even in the dim light, Bristyn could see that they were lining up there, forming a queue across the field. Those at the head of the line leaned over, and for a moment the duchess thought that they were kissing the base of the mar-ble statue.

Only when she heard them slurping, and noted that many of the bandits wiped their lips as they rose, did she under-stand: They were drinking from some sort of fountain or spring that rose from the ground at the statue's base. A cry of beastly exultation ululated through the clearing, followed by another as each bandit, after drinking, raised his head and uttered a deep, primordial scream.

The shadows cast by the rising fire flickered grotesquely, an effect that the men of the swamp did nothing to mute. Within a minute or two, dozens of men were shouting and dancing around the great fire, like marionettes with mad-

men operating the strings. The frenzy built, and for the first
time the duchess felt an acute stab of fear. She thought of
Takian, using the strength of her love to sustain her
hopes—she *would* return to him. Around her, the churning
mob seemed more like animals than men. Many bandits
dropped to all fours, howling and yelping with bestial ferocity. Even through her growing fear, Bristyn perceived
that the bizarre postures, the contorted leaps and gyrations
of her captors, were preternatural.

More of the brutes pushed from behind, forcing the duchess and Katlan closer to the great statue. Now she could
see the faces of those who drank, saw streaks of black ooze
running down cheeks and chins as heads rose from the
spring. A growing urgency seemed to possess the cutthroat
band, more and more of them pushing toward the fountain.
The organized queue collapsed, every man striving to push
his fellows aside, to be the next to sip the dark, sinister
liquid.

Abruptly Katlan was prodded toward the spring. The
duchess tried to reach for him, but restrained by her bonds,
she could only watch helplessly as he was pushed roughly
to the ground and dragged, struggling, toward the base of
the statue.

As Katlan disappeared into the mob, Bristyn saw another
man who had just drunk from the well drop to all fours and
lope like a wolf across the clearing. He veered toward her
and she recoiled from a glimpse of his gaping mouth, where
the dull canine teeth had grown into wicked, inch-long
fangs.

In that instant she realized the truth, an understanding as
horrible as any she had ever known. Though she had refused to recognize the black liquid, had been determined
not to allow her mind to accept its presence here, there
could be no more denial. Despite her terror, she pushed
forward, the surprise of her advance enough to break the
grips of the bandits who had held her arms.

"No!" she cried, plunging into the mob, seizing Katlan

by the arm and pulling him away from the men who were
dragging him off.

A hairy fist snaked out of the crowd, bashing the duchess
in the face and knocking her to the ground as the sinister
crew gathered around her in a growling mass. Bristyn felt
their anger as a physical force, a thick, putrid, clinging miasma. She climbed to her knees, pushing toward the sergeant major, but hands with a viselike grip dragged her
back, despite her kicks and frantic twists.

Katlan struggled desperately as his captors suddenly
grew silent, and then, with grimly shared purpose, lifted
him from the ground and carried him to a flat rock before
the statue. They tossed him onto the crude altar as if he
were a sack of meal, six or seven of them pinning his arms,
legs, feet, and head.

The man of Shalloth made no sound, but Bristyn saw
the veins stand out in his forehead and neck, sensed the
power of his sinew as he strained against the mass of
weight holding him down.

Dark metal flashed against Katlan's throat, and Bristyn
gasped at the sound of liquid splashing across the stone.
The doomed man's back arched and she saw the gaping
wound in his neck—and finally the sergeant major relaxed,
limp in the release of death.

Then her world closed in with a suffocating blanket of
terror, as the men who had killed her guardsman clustered,
panting and growling, around the stone. Lapping like dogs,
they slurped and licked the fresh, human blood.

FOUR

A Gathering of Faerine

Songs of harmony and hope must occasionally
give way to deeds of valor and violence, else the
songs may never again be sung.
—TALLY OF LIVES
BY WYSTEERIN HALLOWAYN,
THE SYLVAN BARD

— 1 —

The Faerines gathered on the vast lawns surrounding the
Palace of Time. A circular platform, girded by lush gar-
lands of flowers and carpeted in white linen, stood in the
center of the largest clearing, well removed from the copses
of trees that grew in so many parts of Spendorial's com-
mons. By early morning the grassy swath was thronged
with sylves, diggers, and sartors standing shoulder to shoulder, while gigants loomed above them, and at least a hundred twissels buzzed and hovered in the air.

A murmur of conversation, high-pitched enough to carry
a festive lilt, rose from the crowd. The sound rippled with
excitement—"Oh, look" "Here they come"—as Rudy
and Raine strolled from the palace doors.

The crowd parted to form a wide aisle leading straight

to the festooned stage. Smiling at a bashful sartor faun,
nodding to the respectful stares of stern-faced diggers, the
Iceman couldn't help but feel a surge of optimism.

"Their hopes are alive again," Raine whispered, tightening her grip on Rudy's hand as she looked across the sea
of expectant faces.

The Man and Woman of Three Waters ascended the
steps to the platform, where several stools had been arranged in a circle. Danri was already there, and the gigant
Gulatch glowered from beneath bristling brows in his version of a warm welcome. The two humans found a pair of
seats between the digger and the hulking chieftain.

Moments later a horned creature with leathery brown
skin hopped up the steps in an awkward-looking gait—
though Rudy knew that Wattli Sartor was a quick, nimble
warrior. His cloven hooves seemed like precarious perches,
but, like all of his high-spirited kind, the wiry, muscular
sartor was actually a graceful, well-balanced creature. As
he took his seat he nodded, tipping the goatlike horns of
his forehead in a display of aloof dignity.

Awnro Lyrifell was the next to climb to the stage, having
been nominated by Dara and Kestrel to represent humankind at the Gathering. The minstrel's feathered hat and elegant cape stood out even among the colorful robes of the
sylves as he waved cheerily to the assembled Faerines and
sauntered to a stool. There he sat, humming a pleasant ditty,
his lute strapped across his shoulder for now. The sea captain and Anjell's mother were just below the platform, at
the front of the crowd, and the bard gave Kestrel a wink,
then blew Dara a kiss when the sailor scowled and looked
away.

Neambrey came into view, flying from the gorge of the
Aurun, gliding low along the lakeshore. Wings spread wide,
the young drackan settled to the lawn of the palace in a
clearing that hastily appeared amid the scattering crowd.
The Faerines quickly formed a lane and cheered as the sinuous serpent trotted toward the circular stage. Pouncing up
the steps, Neambrey flashed a shy, sharp-toothed grin at

Danri, then coiled in the large space that had been reserved for him.

Rudy saw Anjell in the front of the audience and returned her enthusiastic wave. Darret was with her, and a young sylvan boy. The latter regarded the Iceman with a curious, almost sparkling gaze that Rudy found vaguely disturbing. When he looked back a moment later, the diminutive Faerine had disappeared.

Finally the white plume of the Royal Scion's headdress floated into view, drifting like a cloud above the throng. Mussrick Daringer, golden cape shimmering like a curtain of sunlight, advanced toward the stage with serene, reassuring grace and patience. He didn't walk so much as he glided, his pace slow by human standards but utterly fascinating to the spellbound Faerines.

A tall sylve of lean and sinewy build followed the regal figure of the scion. The fellow was dressed in simple garb of brown leather, and his face was bronzed and weathered—more so than any other sylve's Rudy had seen. Yet the golden hair, clasped in a braid dangling nearly to his waist, and the beautiful, slender face, clearly marked him as one of Faerine's elder race. The two sylves completed the gathering on the stage.

The Royal Scion began with little formality, welcoming all who had come to listen and to speak. He introduced the participants in the council, and Rudy learned that the lean newcomer was Wistan Aeroel, a chieftain of a clan of woodland sylves.

Mussrick paused, his green eyes flashing like emeralds as they swept over the rapt audience. After a moment he turned, regarding each of those gathered on the platform with a measured stare.

"All of us must be strong and steadfast. We all have roles to play, and it is to this council that I turn—that we may determine what those roles will be."

"It's time to attack!" Wattli barked, hopping to his hooves and waving a gnarled fist over his head. "We see the enemy, blighting the far shore of our lake. Let us go and slay him there!''

The suggestion was greeted with a rumble of assent from the throng, and a few voices echoed: "Attack!"

"Perhaps I might interject a thought?" Awnro Lyrifell ventured with the polite cock of an eyebrow. The bard had spoken softly, but his words clearly reached the crowd and immediately silenced the muttering.

"I am reminded of the late Quenidon Daringer, who so heroically saw his army out of the mountains, to the safety of your splendid city." The human's tone was cautionary. "He understood that our lives are precious, while the enemy will spend his warriors with callous lack of concern."

"We cannot wait here for the next onslaught!" argued Gulatch, shaking his head so firmly that his long beard swung wildly through the air.

"No," Danri agreed, his tone pleasant. "But I see what the minstrel means. We must attack, but we could do better, perhaps, than to strike directly at our enemy's army."

"Where, then?" growled Wattli. "Would you have us attack the trees of the forest, or the bedrock of the mountains?"

"Of course not." Danri took no visible offense at the sartor's gruff tone. "Those are things of no use to the minions. But determining what they need, where they are vulnerable, is not a terribly difficult challenge."

"Say, then!" snapped Wattli. "We waste time with riddles and word games."

"Perhaps," Mussrick Daringer suggested, "we should review the threats, insofar as my investigations in the Scrying Pool have been able to ascertain them."

An air of expectancy settled over the grounds, and Rudy waited for one of those long Faerine pauses to pass. Many heartbeats later the scion again began to speak.

"A great army of minions is encamped in the Suderwild, a direct menace to Spendorial and all Faerine. However, in the recent battle that force lost its commander, as well as its reserve of Darkblood. As a consequence it has remained in place, but made no attempt to attack."

Garic Hoorkin cleared his throat, flying excitedly up from the crowd. Wings buzzing, he hovered at the edge of the stage. The scion recognized him with a patient bow.

"We've spied over there, some of us—that is, when we're invisible," the twissel explained. "The minions aren't doing anything—most of 'em aren't even moving!"

"They're dead?" growled Wattli Sartor.

"Nay." Mussrick Daringer again took the reins of the discussion. "I have seen in the pool what our courageous cousin describes. The minions slumber, torpid, waiting for that which sustains them—Darkblood."

Pausing, the scion allowed the thoughts of his listeners to focus. "Of course, I cannot use the pool to see into Duloth-Trol, but it is possible that another train of blood-wagons is already approaching Darkenheight Pass to bring sustenance to this army."

"I have seen these wagons, and they do approach the pass." Rudy spoke quietly, the low sound of his voice nevertheless carrying across the crowded field. "They have long to travel within Duloth-Trol, but will come across the mountains before the end of the year—unless they are stopped." All knew that it was his Auracloud that had rained destruction on the previous bloodtrain, and they waited to hear what he would add. But the Man of Three Waters merely nodded, allowing the Royal Scion to continue.

"So we have at best, a temporary respite . . . until yon legion is restored, and once again bangs against our door."

"Attack the bastards!" roared Wattli. "Kill them while they sleep, or torpate, or whatever they're doing over there!" There was a roar of assent, more than a few diggers and gigants echoing the sartor aggression.

"We—well, some of us tried that," Garic said hesitantly. "As soon as we got close, the minions woke up and chased us away. They seemed as fierce as ever—I think they come out of their torpor if they get attacked."

"And despite our recent victory," the Royal Scion noted, "the number of minions across the river greatly exceeds the count of our own troops."

"So instead we should strike at their bloodtrain again—literally, their lifeblood," Rudy suggested.

"But will they again gather the wagons into a convenient target?" Awnro wondered. "And how else do we strike those wagons, without destroying the army first?"

"The Darkblood has to get down here, where the minions can use it," Danri pointed out. "And that can only happen along one route."

"The route through Darkenheight Pass," Gulatch said, his bushy brows lowering into a formidable glower. "But how can we strike at the pass and not at the troops, when the enemy army stands astride the road into the mountains?"

"I have a suggestion." With a bow, the woodland sylve had risen to his feet. As Wistan Aeroel scanned the crowd and the council, Rudy saw that his face was in fact quite weathered, much darker than the typical sylve of Spendorial. Yet he stood with the supple grace and serene bearing of his city-dwelling cousins.

"I believe that we might be able to forge a new route," the sylve began. "A way to reach Darkenheight that would go around the gathered minions, and still allow us to bring a force against the pass."

"But how?" asked the scowling gigant.

"There is a suggestion I have discussed with Captain Kestrel of the *Black Condor*," the woodland sylve offered with a genial smile. "Many of you have noticed his ship scouring the shores of the lake over the last fortnight. He has been scouting the various inlets, and last night he confirmed a suspicion of mine."

"And?" growled Wattli impatiently.

"The fishers of my tribe have known for a long time of a deep channel extending far up the Rainbow River, a fjord that penetrates into the heart of the Bruxrange. The galyon and a fleet of sylvan longboats can follow this passage for many miles, landing an attack force in the very heart of the mountain range. There is a pass—admittedly steep and rugged almost beyond belief—that connects the water passage with the Darkenheight Road. Traveling from the lake by ship or boat, an attack force could bypass the minion army, striking upward and closing on the Watershed before the enemy can react.''

''And we could claim the pass, and hold it,'' Danri speculated. ''There'd be no way—no way at all—for any more Darkblood to reach the Suderwild!''

''But what if the minions down here get wind of the plan?'' Awnro pointed out. ''Could they not move back to the mountains and disrupt your attack? Perhaps even trap the field army?''

''Not if there's a show of an attack down here,'' the digger countered quickly. ''Something to hold their attention, so to speak!''

''We'll do it!'' Wattli Sartor cried. ''The sartors will see these minions don't have a moment's peace—until we hear that the pass has been closed down for good!''

''This plan is sound,'' the Royal Scion declared. ''A strong diversion, and a chance to utterly choke the enemy's supply line.''

''And without Darkblood the army will wither, and die,'' added Wattli with a deep chuckle. ''A good plan—I endorse it!''

''And I!'' shouted Gulatch, standing and raising his clenched fists. ''The gigants will lead the attack against the pass!''

''Will we encounter problems with the Guardians at Darkenheight?'' asked Mussrick Daringer.

''Don't see why,'' Danri countered. ''In a sense, we'll be trying to do their work for 'em—stoppin' the minions from coming over. I was thinking, we diggers should build a wall across the place after we throw the cruds out. There'll be no more wagons passing over Darkenheight!''

Mussrick cleared his throat. ''I hereby announce the reforming of the Faerine Field Army, with the assigned task of closing Darkenheight Pass. Danri of Shalemont shall be general in command.''

The announcement was greeted with shouts of approval, and the Iceman was pleased to see that sylves, gigants, and even sartors all joined in the vociferous support.

"This is a good start," Mussrick Daringer affirmed, after the wave of rippling cheers had begun to settle. "But there are more dangers confronting us. For example, do we dare turn our backs on Dalethica? Know you all that if human-kind should fail to hold the realm of water, Faerine can be doomed as easily through Taywick Pass as through Darkenheight.''

"Perhaps I could speak about the dangers facing my own realm," Awnro Lyrifell said. "Dalethica is menaced in two places. A breach in the Watershed exists beneath the Crown of the World itself, a place where Darkblood seeps under the divide and pollutes Halverica.

"On a grander scale, the legions of the Lord Minion Reaper have occupied half of the realm of man, drawing almost to the line of the River Ariak. They advance against courageous resistance, bringing destruction and death in their vanguard.''

Rudy spoke up. "I've observed this attack, through the pool. The horde advances in three mighty armies, one concentrating on Shalloth, the other two coming together against Carillonn. The number of minions is countless.''

"And we are too few to send an army to aid in man-kind's defense," Garic Hoorkin, the twissel, stated, with an apologetic look at Rudy and Awnro.

"Remember the twin threats," interjected Mussrick Daringer. "One is the numberless horde, which we cannot counter with a legion of our own. But the other is Dark-blood through the Watershed—and what might be the best counter to this?''

"The best counter to Darkblood is Aura," Danri said quickly, then blinked, as if his audacious words had surprised even himself.

"Ridiculous!" Wattli snapped, then scratched his head

in delayed confusion. "That is, we know that there is no Aura in Dalethica."

"Why don't we take some there?" Neambrey asked, raising his head in question.

Wattli snorted, but Danri looked thoughtful. "Not a bad notion," the digger acknowledged. "If we could figure out a way . . ."

"How about another breach in the Watershed, only this one bringing Aura?" Awnro Lyrifell suggested.

"Can such a thing be dug?" Rudy asked Danri, immediately intrigued by the idea.

"Perhaps . . . if we could find the right spot . . . I'm thinking maybe a canal, with a tunnel or two if need be. Yes, you know, it *might* be possible!" Danri agreed. "A real hope—Darkenheight closed, and then the water of magic flowing into Dalethica!"

"But where?" asked Mussrick Daringer.

"Halverica." Rudy spoke from his heart, certain that the idea made rational sense as well. "More specifically, into the Wilderhof. We know that the Watershed is already a little porous there—that's where Danri came through after his Madness. And it would put the Aura very near Dermaat, where the Darkblood comes under the Glimmercrown."

"It could work," the digger concurred, nodding his head. "Of course, we'd have to find the right location—a *big* spring, steady flow and all."

"I know the place! That is, I might have an idea." Kerri of Shalemont spoke up from the front of the crowd around the platform. She faced Danri, explaining earnestly, "When you were gone, with the Madness I mean, I used to go up into the mountains above Shalemont—the heights near the Watershed. I guess it sounds kind of silly, but I'd walk around imagining you were somewhere down below, even that you might feel me thinking about you."

Danri's eyes misted and he gruffly cleared his throat as he waited for her to continue.

"Anyway, one time I hiked into this hidden valley, a place where there were no trails. I found a big spring of

Aura right below the ridge of the Watershed. The thing is, the mountains weren't that high there! I had the feeling that if I went a little farther I could hike right out of Faerine. . . ."

"And into the Wilderhof," Rudy completed. "And there wasn't a high ridge?"

"I didn't go any farther. But I knew I'd damned near reached the end of Faerine, and I didn't see one," Kerri explained.

"The idea has real potential," Mussrick Daringer noted. "But I have a fear that, in this case, the Guardians may well act to intervene."

"You're right—but there's something we might be able to do about that," Danri said. He turned to the Iceman. "I need to talk to you about it—sometime later," he added breezily. "And if this idea works, we should be able to ward a path through the divide without getting trouble from the Guardians."

"So the prospects of the canal, and even the location, have promise," Awnro Lyrifell summed up, before raising a hand in question to Danri. "But can even a digger be in two places at once?"

"That's true," Danri said. "And I'm afraid the mission to Darkenheight has to take precedence."

"Of course. But why not let me, and perhaps Kerri as well, go through Shalemont and up to the Watershed to have a look?" Awnro suggested. "I have some experience with surveyor's tools—I'm certain that we could at the very least establish a plausible route. Then the Field Army can follow, after leaving a garrison at Darkenheight."

"The *Condor* can bring you back from the mountains, though I fear I can't sail her up the gorge of the Aurun," Kestrel called up to Danri.

"That's fine. Get us back to Spendorial after we close the pass, and we'll march to Shalemont, and all the way up to the Watershed," Danri pledged grimly.

"These are encouraging plans—they offer hope of halting the enemy on many fronts." The Royal Scion spoke slowly, and Rudy sensed that there was great meaning in the things Mussrick was *not* saying. "But these tactics are primarily defensive in nature. That is, they only strike at the enemy where he has claimed our realms. Is there any possibility of defeating the Sleepstealer decisively?"

"Yes, there is." The Man of Three Waters spoke quietly, drawing all eyes to himself and Raine. A hush fell across the Gathering, and he drew a deep breath before laying out the plan that he and his beloved had formulated.

"Raine and I intend to embark for Duloth-Trol, riding an Auracloud over the Watershed," the Iceman said, ignoring the gasps, the expressions of horror and shock that rippled through the throng. "We will take the artifact Lordsmiter, and enter the Sleepstealer's fortress at Agath-Trol."

"But . . ." Danri's objection died unspoken, perhaps quelled by the determination in the Man of Three Waters' eyes.

"We seek the Heart of Darkblood, the Nameless One's anchor to our world. When we find it, we will drive the artifact through his mortal flesh—and banish Dassadec, finally, into the realms of the gods."

— 2 —

Water. Everywhere he looked, the terrified brutox beheld an expanse of lake and stream, or soaked, verdant landscape. The vast swaths of forest greenery were an affront to his eyes. The vitality that was obvious in the fields and pastures of the farmlands caused him to squint and look away.

And the worst thing was, Direfang could do nothing about it.

The brutox, desperate for a taste of nourishing Darkblood, clung to a shrinking wisp of tarcloud, drifting through the skies of Dalethica. This remnant was all that remained of the mighty *Dreadcloud*, the skyship Direfang had commanded on its epic voyage from Duloth-Trol.

It had been the Lord Minion Phalthak who had set the mighty vessel on course for destruction. The only bright spot in Direfang's bleak existence was a memory of pure, ecstatic violence: Phalthak, the Fang of Dassadec, pierced by the sword Lordsmiter, plunging to his doom at Taywick Pass. It was only fitting that the Lord Minion's reckless hatred had gotten him killed. Still, it seemed tragic that the disaster had left the brutox alone and adrift in the sky.

Since that day, dozens of sunrises ago, Direfang could only drift with the winds, watching as the remainder of his ship slowly disintegrated in the disastrously pure air of Dalethica. Though he floated generally westward, he had not yet reached the broad river that divided the realm of man. The brutox felt certain that his cloud would be gone long before he arrived above the regions held by the armies of Lord Minion Reaper—the only place he would be likely to find Darkblood, short of a miraculous return to Duloth-Trol.

But then a swirling waft of breeze caressed his nostrils, bringing an acrid stench that promised hope. Direfang looked down, observing a vast region of swampland fringed by a deep, mighty river. Many of the trees were withered and barren, while others drooped beneath the weight of brown, leaden leaves. Though there was life in this place, it was like a wasteland, wracked by . . . and then he knew:

Somewhere within that marsh Direfang would find a source of the Sleepstealer's nectar.

— 3 —

Rudy stood beside the palace fountain, carefully sweeping the long, supple wands through the air as he wove the spell of Auramagic. Above, filling the sky over his head and over most of the palace grounds, a huge cloud drifted on the tether of steam that rose from the Iceman's brazier. More of the enchanted liquid spumed from the fountain onto the coals, and a steady plume of white vapor billowed upward, expanding the size of the great skyship.

For a long time he had been weaving his spell, and for a longer time still he continued. The Auracloud expanded steadily, thickening, growing longer, swelling like a force of nature. Vast and pure white, it floated placidly, steadily nourished by the rising vapor.

Finally the casting was completed. Rudy exhaled slowly, lowering his wands, shaking the tension of the long concentration from his limbs. He turned toward Raine, who had stood beside him for the last few hours, and was surprised to see that a small crowd had gathered around her.

"Nice ship," Danri declared gruffly, leaning back to appraise the massive Auracloud with a critical eye. "D'you think she'll last you all the way to Agath-Trol?"

"I hope so," the Iceman admitted simply.

"At least, if any weapon on the Watershed is capable of destroying the Sleepstealer's heart, it's Lordsmiter," the digger added. "Actually, I was a little worried about that—but both Mussrick and Awnro think you've got a good chance. Something about a poem, by this bard fellow."

"The Sylvan Bard," chuckled Rudy. "Yes, Raine knows that poem, too—one of Wysteerin Hallowayn's first epics. She recited it to me when we were flying back to Spendorial, from the Tor. And in it the bard has a verse about the Heart being well-guarded, for it would be vulnerable to an artifact of the gods."

"Aye-uh. 'Course, he didn't tell me the whole poem, but that's what Mussrick was sayin', too. And speaking of bards—"

"All our wishes go with you," Awnro Lyrifell offered, strolling up to Rudy and Raine.

"Thank you—but I know that we all have our challenges," replied Rudy, clasping the bard's hand. "Have you figured out how you're going to deal with the Guardians when you try and survey that canal?"

"As a matter of fact, I'm glad you asked. And the answer is yes—Danri's had an idea, actually."

"Remember when we first bumped into each other?" the digger explained to Rudy. "I was being chased by a Deep Guardian. But when it touched you—"

"My blood, really," the Iceman noted.

"Right—and you make a good point. It stopped attacking me, turned around and left us alone, even though I had tunneled through the Watershed."

"I remember."

"And then when we were caught by the gigants it was the Guardians who came and set you free."

"They freed all of us," noted the Iceman.

"Aye-uh, but only because *you* said so. You have some pretty real power over them."

"But how is that going to help Awnro and Kerri?"

"Well, what if we could extend that power to the whole canal route?" Awnro declared. "Ward it with the Blood of Three Waters?"

Rudy laughed, a trifle uneasily. "How much blood would that take, are you thinking?"

"No—no!" declared the bard in mock horror. "Just a little prick in the finger, and a few drops into a small cask— of Aura, naturally. That should be enough to get it up to the Watershed, and I'll just add more Aura until I have enough to mark a whole route!" So saying, he held out a flask he'd brought with him.

"If you think so . . ." Skeptically, the Iceman allowed the digger to stab the tip of his finger with the needle-sharp pick of the reverse side of his hammer. Rudy squeezed a small trickle of blood into the flask and watched as Awnro tapped a cork into it.

"Good luck," Kerri said, stepping forward beside her digger. She clasped Rudy's hand in both of hers, and he felt her sincerity in the pressure of her fingers. Nearby he saw Garic Hoorkin, the twissel, buzzing beside the hulking form of Gulatch. Wattli Sartor spoke softly with Wistan Aeroel, the woodland sylve who, as always, had his bow and quivers lashed to his back. Dozens of feathered shafts jutted from the leather sheath.

A shadow flickered beside the Auracloud, a serpentine form winging downward. Neambrey spiraled through leisurely circles, gliding gradually lower. Finally he came to rest within the circle of pines, a powerful downswipe of his wings gusting air into Rudy's face.

"Where've you been?" demanded Danri crossly.

"Up in the mountains, where you told me to go," Neambrey replied cheerily. "That fjord goes a long way, and it looked deep enough for the ship to sail the whole way."

"There's good news to start with," Raine remarked.

"Yup. And there's a place you can get off the ship, and then you'll have to climb pretty steep hills, but Garic and I can show you how to get to the pass!"

"That *is* a start," the digger allowed, turning back to Rudy. "May Aurianth grant that your voyage goes as well."

"You're going to a pretty scary place," the young drackan observed, his filmy eyelids drooping pensively. "I hope that you'll be careful."

"We will," Rudy assured him, then turned to Anjell, who stood with Dara and Awnro Lyrifell nearby. "And you be careful, too. It's a long walk back to Halverica."

"Oh, I'll keep an eye on everybody. And Kerri will too," his niece promised. "We'll be all right. I . . . well, I just hope Neshara's okay. I never thought I'd get homesick, but I think I'd like to see it again."

Rudy's throat tightened. "So would I, Little One . . . so would I."

He couldn't help wondering: Would he and Raine ever see them, ever see *any* of their fellow humans, again? Or would the tale of their lives end in the bleak wasteland of Duloth-Trol?

— 4 —

"I wish we could go somewhere exciting!" Anjell groused, her homesickness entirely forgotten. She and Dara were collecting their few belongings in their palace quarters, since Awnro had announced that they would start for Shalemont before midday. Her mother was distressingly cheerful as she packed her papers and quills, as if she were looking forward to having something new to write about.

"Do you have a waterproof cloak?" Dara asked, just the sort of boring and practical question that Anjell would expect.

"Over here," she grumbled, still sulking as she crossed into her dressing closet. She lifted the cloak, and spotted a bulging waterskin hanging from the hook—just that morning Haylor had given her a sack of Aura that he said came from the Scrying Pool. Impetuously, she pulled the cork and took a long drink.

She threw her cloak into the backpack she would be wearing, her emotions rising within her like a dark cloud, threatening rain. She knew that Darret and Kestrel were about to set sail, bearing Danri and the Field Army on the way to Darkenheight. She sensed that her mother was saddened by Kestrel's departure, but that Awnro Lyrifell was rather pleased. The bard was *very* pleased that Dara and Anjell would accompany him to the Watershed, and back to Halverica.

As her thoughts turned to Rudy, Anjell had a sharp, almost painful realization of her uncle's current sense of unease. She was sure he would have felt better if only she'd had the chance to make him laugh once or twice before he started his journey.

Abruptly the girl's thoughts focused on Rudy and Raine with a shocking, terrifying clarity. She felt a stabbing burst of pain between her eyes. The jolt of fear knocked her over backwards, and when Dara rushed to gather her into a mother's embrace, Anjell could only sob about a nightmare of awful, impermeable blackness.

Within that darkness a single image appeared: a person sitting next to her bed . . . a very strange person. He whispered one phrase over and over:

"It isn't time to go yet."

FIVE

Darkfen

Water and air are splendid conduits for
befoulment, for a dose of toxin introduced at
one source can quickly and thoroughly infest a
township, realm, or world.
—TOME OF VILE COMPULSIONS

— 1 —

The file of refugees coming along the Shalloth road had
dwindled to a trickle. Takian straddled Hawkrunner, pacing
the stallion beside the beaten, rutted thoroughfare where it
emerged from a vast stretch of forested land. Behind the
king, the highest towers of Castle Carillonn jutted above
the trees that skirted the steep banks of the River Ariak.

For now, this hill was as far as Takian dared to go. From
here he could see the crossroads before the Rosebridge, and
the darkened swath of the Willowfen far south along the
river bank. The clouds of the minion advance had grown
more imposing, looming as two distinct columns—one
closing in from the west, and the other from the south.

The city of white marble, on its hilly island in the center
of the flowage, had begun to seem a prison to the young

monarch, so much so that today he had been unable to
remain there. Together with Randart, he had galloped
southward along the road, only halting when the sunless
forest closed overhead.

To go farther would be too risky. Though every one of
Takian's instincts cried out for him to ride, to hunt until he
found Bristyn, he could not abandon Carillonn now. So he
had returned here, where he could look to the south, where
his hopes lay, and off to the west where he saw only fear.

Involuntarily his eyes turned toward the darkness in the
sky. How much of the oppressive mass was smoke and
cloud, and how much was the lightless soul of the Sleepstealer? Takian had ceased to wonder. It was enough that
the pollution swept across the world steadily and inexorably. From the growing presence of the murk, which extended from the southern horizon all the way across the
sky, the king knew that only a few days remained before
Carillonn was fully cut off from the western side of the
river.

And his greatest fear was that Bristyn wouldn't be back
by then.

A group of refugees caught Takian's eye, two dozen people traveling together, a trio of husky young men in the
fore. Two carried heavy sticks, while the third had a large,
double-bitted axe slung over his shoulder. At the sight of
the riders, the woodsman lifted the haft of his weapon in
both hands, eyeing Takian and Randart warily as they approached.

There was nothing even vaguely threatening about most
of the party. Several older men shuffled along, trailed by a
motley group of youths. Women of all ages came next,
while another trio of sturdy fellows brought up the rear.

But it wasn't the people that attracted Takian's attention.
In the midst of the women, bearing four small infants
strapped to its back, plodded a tired-looking horse, a steed
with the powerful size and sleek musculature of a warhorse.
When Takian looked closer he saw that the bridle bore a
brass bit and a strap of blue leather. He remembered, with

foreboding, that these were the colors of Bristyn's escort.

"Good farmers," Takian said quietly, but in a tone that could not be ignored. "You are close to safety—in a few miles you will cross the bridges to Carillonn."

"Not soon enough," growled the axe-bearer, pausing at the shoulder of the road while the others trod past.

"Have you come all the way from Shalloth?" inquired the king.

"Aye—just south of the castle."

"Tell me, if you will—what word of the duchess?"

The man squinted, as if noticing for the first time Takian's golden hair and beard, the regal sweep of his cloak. Perhaps he even recognized the Golden Lion emblazoned on the king's chest.

"You would be King Takian?"

At the monarch's nod, the fellow dropped quickly to one knee. "Forgive me, Your Majesty. Had I known it was—"

"Rise," interrupted Takian. "If I wished to be feted, I would travel with my crown. But you can help me, perhaps, with information."

Now the man appeared stricken, and when he turned to look back along the Shalloth road Takian felt a stab of sudden, violent fear. "What? What do you know of my wife?"

"I grieve to tell you this, sire—but we had reliable word she was slain by swampmen, ambushed as she and her company passed through the Willowfen!"

— 2 —

Bristyn shrank within an enveloping cocoon of horror. Her hands remained bound at the wrists as she stood, momentarily forgotten, watching the obscene feasting of the swampmen. Katlan's body was soon drained of blood, but even that wasn't enough—ultimately, the captors tore at the sergeant major's pallid flesh, rending with fingers grown

into curling claws, tearing with teeth that had become
sharper, wickedly animalistic under the influence of the
dark, seeping liquid.

The nectar of Darkblood.

The duchess couldn't conceive an explanation for the
presence of the Sleepstealer's vitriol, here in a region of
Dalethica that had yet to feel the tread of invading minions.
Yet she was fully certain that she was right in her identi-
fication of the vile effluent emerging from the ground.

Trying to ignore the horror and revulsion that threatened
to paralyze her, Bristyn sought some explanation. Fully expecting that she, herself, would be the next to fall victim
to the greedy ravenings of these men, she nevertheless tried
to grasp what was happening.

First, she corrected a fundamental aspect of her thinking.
Though the men of the Willowfen still walked upright, con-
versed in guttural sounds that were undeniably speech, still
bore the features of mankind on the surface, they were no
longer human. Instead, the Darkblood had worked some
kind of monstrous corruption on the swampmen.

She looked at the wretched creatures as they fed like a
pack of jackals, and she knew that humanity was something
they had already left far behind. The taste of Darkblood
should have killed them, yet it hadn't done so. Growls rose
in a bestial chorus from the seething, snapping curs, and
she shuddered with revulsion as she saw one shaggy brute
whirl and bite another who had apparently edged too close.

Moving slowly and carefully, the duchess sidled away
from the frenzied group. The dank, mossy limbs of the
marsh had seemed bleak and oppressive when she'd been
dragged along the narrow trails. Now, that same vegetation
seemed to offer the only hope of shelter against the nightmare unfolding before her. Gingerly she took another step
backward, and another. The growling, snarling darkmen ignored her, intent on their grotesque feeding. She sensed
celebration in the grisly ritual, an act that completely, irrevocably, drove them from the ranks of humankind into
the legions of the Sleepstealer's beasts.

Still easing away, the duchess backed through the trampled ground of the clearing, grateful for the shadows that grew thicker as she got farther away from the fire. Then, with shocking abruptness, she felt cruel claws bite into her arm, smelled the carrionlike stench of a swampman who had waited, unnoticed, behind her.

"Stop here," snarled the brute in a breathy, barely articulate growl. "Ain't goin' away . . . no."

Poised to flee like a startled doe, Bristyn was shocked by the raw, animal power in the bandit's grip. His fingers were a clamp of steel and she felt a trickle of wetness running over her elbow, knew that the press of his sharp nails had punctured her skin.

Her mind worked frantically, rejecting any consideration of failure, knowing that she had to stay alive.

"No—I'm not going away," she said, surprised that her voice could emerge so calmly from her trembling body. "Just seeking a place to rest, to sleep."

"Rest?" The fellow growled over the word, as if it was a strange concept. She cast a sidelong glance, seeing a darkly shadowed brow creased in concentration over the bright spots of gleaming eyes. Abruptly, the darkman threw her to the ground.

When he knelt beside her, an evil leer on his caricature of a face, she remembered in despair her decision not to carry a knife in her boot. His hand traced the outline of her leg. The rough paw moved across her belly, onto her breast, and she almost gagged in revulsion. But then the groping fingers moved past, around her shoulders, pushing and prodding mercilessly.

He's searching, she realized through her fear. Looking for a weapon, or perhaps valuables—but she allowed herself to hope that this was the extent of his desire. Indeed, when the clawlike hand closed around the purse belted to the small of her back, the fellow gurgled a bark of triumph and roughly pulled the coin sack away.

Crowing in delight, he tore open the purse and leapt to his feet. Golden coins shimmered in the firelight as the

circlets of metal tumbled to the ground. Shrieking mania-
cally, he gathered them up, tossing them into the air to
shower down on the gathered pack of his fellows.

"She brings us gold!" he croaked, throwing back his
head and laughing madly. "She would buy her life!"

Snarling wetly, another of the bandits came over, dropping to all fours and sniffing at the duchess's body. Bristyn
forced herself to remain still, biting back the bile that began
to surge in her throat. Abruptly, the newcomer turned her
onto her belly and she tossed her head, straining to pull her
hands from beneath her, to lift her face above the choking
mud.

Then bonds encircled her ankles. She gasped as they
were pulled tight, then bit her lip in determined silence as
she was dragged roughly across the ground by two growling, muttering darkmen. At the base of a sturdy tree she
was turned again, pulled into a sitting position while coarse
ropes were draped around her torso, then drawn tight.

Rough bark scraped her back, and several brittle
branches prodded her with thorny spears, but still she
forced herself to remain silent. After checking that her
bonds were secure, the two swampmen, without a backward
glance, started across the clearing to join their comrades
around the base of the ghastly statue.

Breathing deeply, Bristyn tried to calm herself. She was
grateful to be alone, even if she couldn't move—just
having the two bandits walk away from her gave her some
slim cause for hope.

That brief flare of optimism quickly faded as she began
to struggle with her bonds. Each twist seemed to drive the
ropes deeper into her flesh. Her arms were pinned to her
sides, and her legs—jutting straight out from the trunk of
the tree—were bound so tightly together that she could
barely twitch. After nearly an hour of futile straining, she
gave up trying to free her hands. Her wrists were chafed
and bleeding, but all her struggles had only seemed to draw
the bonds tighter. Likewise, she had no luck in her desperate efforts to loosen the lines that lashed her to the tree.

Finally, exhausted, she leaned her head back against the rough bark. For a brief moment her eyes grew wet, tears of hopelessness gathering, ready to flow. Angrily she forced away the self-pity, turning her attention toward the hateful creatures gathered in this swampy clearing.

The celebration accompanying the slaughter of Katlan had gradually waned. Bristyn knew with grim certainty that there was nothing left of the sergeant major with which the swampmen could indulge their barbaric appetite. Still, they had not turned to her. Instead, the bandits had gathered in growling, crouching groups. Only when she strained to listen did the duchess realize that the snarling had, for the most part, given way to gruff snores.

"At least they sleep," she whispered to herself, grateful for even this tiny semblance of humanity. The minions of Dassadec, after all, had no need for slumber. One of her worst fears, a thing she had not dared to articulate in her own mind, had been the awful thought that these former humans had been corrupted into actual minions.

Even so, the evidence of their transformation was of dire import for all mankind. Reluctantly, her eyes turned to the hulking statue, illuminated in pale orange from the hellishly glowing pile of embers remaining from the massive fire. The living brutox she had once seen had been distant creatures, whip-cracking commanders of the minion horde observed from the walltops of Lanbrij. Even as they plodded far below, their dull features had glowered with uncaring cruelty. Whoever had carved this statue had also seen a brutox, for the likeness was unmistakable.

But why had the sculptor chosen the image of this minion for his labors? Bristyn studied the facial features, the sloping brow and prominent, tusked jaw. Perhaps it was the heat that the marble had absorbed from the fire, but the duchess shuddered under a sudden impression that the stony form was a living, breathing menace.

She wondered, too, about the murky spring at the statue's base. When had the toxic liquid first started to flow here? And where did it come from? Bristyn remembered Rudy's description of the breach in the Watershed, a tunnel carved by minions through the Crown of the World. That mountainous route had allowed the Sleepstealer's poison to seep into Halverica, down a mountain creek and into the Glimmersee.

The Willowfen lay along the River Ariak, the main flowage to emerge from that vast lake. Could some Darkblood have seeped into the ground, somehow following the course of the great river, then emerging here in the lowlands without being absorbed by the mundane waters of Dalethica?

She could think of no other explanation. But with this suspicion came another dire fear: If it happened here, was it also happening somewhere else? In how many places was the venom of Duloth-Trol seeping into the realm of man? And how in the Watershed could mankind have any hope of resisting the dark tide?

Her feeble hopes faded further with the deepening hours of night. For a brief time she gave way to despair, hanging her head and allowing the tears to fall. Yet soon she cast off the mantle of hopelessness, vowing that as long as she lived she would continue to believe in the eventual triumph of humankind.

At some timeless point in the darkness she fell asleep, slumping awkwardly against the abrasive bark, shifting position frequently within the restriction of her bonds. Finally she awakened, and immediately probed the clearing with her eyes, seeking signs of movement. The hour was well past midnight, she felt certain, but there was as yet no sign of even the first glimmerings of dawn. Still, she noticed that the camp was astir. Shadows passed before the fading embers of the fire, and in moments the entire band was roused and moving.

Bristyn vaguely discerned approaching figures, and immediately she was fully, tautly awake, watching the shadowy forms materialize in the darkness. Now she recognized the same two men that had dragged her to the tree and tied her here so thoroughly. Rat and Weasel, she thought scornfully, noting the pointed nose of one and the upraised, animal ears of the other. Her limbs ached with cramps and scrapes, and her throat was parched by a deeper thirst than any she had ever known. Somehow, the pain was easier to bear as she imagined using the insulting names against her captors.

She managed to lift her head and regard the pair with a haughty, scornful gaze. Weasel knelt beside her legs and began sawing through the bonds with a keen knife. She half-expected the blade to slice her skin, but the swampman worked swiftly and surely, cutting away the ropes without tearing her leather breeches.

The one she thought of as Rat grabbed her wrists, which were still bound together, and lifted her roughly to her feet. As soon as he released her arm, the legs that had been bound so tightly collapsed. Bristyn cursed beneath her breath as she fell against Rat's vile, stinking form. He jerked her upward and pushed her roughly away from the tree—and this time she sprawled headlong on the ground.

By the time the brute reached for her hands again, she had begun to get some feeling back in her legs. Kicking, she drove him back, then wriggled around and pulled herself to her feet. Only when she was upright, supported by legs growing firmer with each heartbeat, did she raise her face and glare into her captor's eyes.

"What do you want?" she demanded, speaking with all the royal arrogance that she could muster.

If the fellow was annoyed by her tone, he gave no sign. Instead, he took her wrists and tugged her along, toward the tangled pathways of the Willowfen.

"Come," he said, without explanation. "It's time for us to climb."

— 3 —

The Talon of Dassadec was the mightiest of the Sleep-stealer's Lord Minions. Always so in size and power, Reaper had now, finally, achieved the position of his master's most trusted lieutenant. Knowing that Phalthak was dead and Nicodareus disgraced, the great serpent allowed himself the glimmer of a smile, fangs rippling into view along the crocodilian length of long, powerful jaws.

In truth, the mighty wyrm felt that he had earned a greatness that was, for all intents and purposes, equal to his master's status. Of course, it would be some time before Reaper would dare to verbalize this dawning awareness, but it was a pleasant thing to contemplate. The knowledge of his superiority gratified the Lord Minion as he coiled about a craggy knob of bluff and watched the endless columns of his minions marching eastward, converging on the center of Dalethica. The Lord Minion's black, serpentine body lay like a plume of dark smoke across the lofty vantage, a scaly image of perfect darkness on the grimy, befouled rocks. The Talon of Dassadec knew that he was visible to the numberless warriors of his host for miles across the wasted plains.

This lofty bluff provided a perfect overall view, which Reaper had recognized immediately as he had soared eastward, basking in the continental scope of destruction. From this promontory the Lord Minion could observe the glorious extent of destruction—a desolate expanse of blackened ground sprawling to the far western horizon, perhaps a hundred miles away. Of course, much of the distance was obscured by smoke—but those black plumes were themselves marks of Reaper's triumph.

The lines of minions were great, crawling snakes, writhing across the ruined ground. Tirelessly marching, kroaks and brutox advanced without rest, pausing only for an hour or two each day for the sips of Darkblood that sustained them in this once-hostile environment. Stalkers, light and speedy, scuttled in the vanguard of the invasion, attacking farms and villages, now finding most of these human dwellings abandoned. The stalkers rushed on, leaving the wooden structures to be torched by the slower moving legions.

Yet there was a glimmer of bad news as well, for when

Reaper looked westward he saw no sign of the bloodtrains, the great, stone-wheeled wagons that carried the Sleep-stealer's nectar. Without Darkblood to sustain the tireless legions, the army's advance must inevitably grind to a frus-trating, if temporary, halt. It had been reported that a freak rainstorm had left the tracks a sea of mud, slowing the great wagons across the entire front. Unfortunately, the infuriated Talon of Dassadec had eaten the messenger before he had learned just *how* late those supplies would be.

Ironically, Reaper reflected with a glower of displeasure, it was the effluent of Duloth-Trol that placed the greatest limitations on the army's movement. Darkblood was trans-ported in great, iron vats, each mounted on a wagon hauled by a team of stolid, elephantine bovars. Hundreds of these precious containers had lumbered steadily in the wake of Reaper's army, trailing out of Dassadec's realm.

Yet as the tentacles of the vast horde had dispersed, the wagons of Darkblood had been hard pressed to keep up. Northward into Tiber, watching the new strait at Corsari and proceeding strongly against Shalloth, the spearheads of the minion advance had been limited only by lack of sus-tenance. Soon Reaper would hurl his main force against Carillonn, centerpiece of Dalethica—but even that on-slaught would have to be delayed until sufficient supplies of Darkblood had been gathered.

On the positive side, nearly half of Dalethica had already fallen to the invaders. A waterless wasteland now covered this side of the continent, nothing but parched ground and blackened, burned timber stretching from here to the coast.

To date, only one assault had failed, when the humans had destroyed the landbridge of Corsari, making that realm into an island—and thus, immune to the minion troops. Still, even that shadow had a bright spark within, for Das-sadec regarded the destruction of the isthmus to be the fault of Nicodareus, not Reaper. After all, it had been the Eye of Dassadec who had been present for that offensive, and though the troops he commanded had been dispatched from Reaper's army, it had been Nicodareus who succumbed to

the Man of Three Waters' trap, who had been immersed in
Aura and, in the resulting explosion, destroyed the solid
link of rock that provided such a perfect invasion route into
Corsari.

At the thought of his fellow Lord Minion, who was no
doubt still suffering unspeakable punishment and humilia-
tion at his master's hands, Reaper chortled grimly. He knew
the glory that would be his, and his alone, when the war
was concluded in victory. Nicodareus would never dare to
challenge him again. Instead, he would be reduced to a
mere puppet, an errand-boy whose keen, far-reaching Sight
would prove useful to Dassadec and Reaper, but nothing
more.

Keening shrieks pierced the air and the Talon of Dassadec raised his massive head. He saw a dozen terrions
winging in serene circles around his perch. Two of the
winged flyers dove, sweeping past the single, narrow trail
that gave access to this lofty summit. Reaper saw three
brutox there, the minions laboring upward on the steep
path, growling and sparking and pulling themselves along
with the aid of their long, muscular arms.

Good, reflected the Talon of Dassedec. *Let them work
hard to reach me.*

When the Lord Minion turned his eyes to the east, he
saw only opportunity. The towers of Castle Shalloth were
visible, barely, along the horizon. His stalker scouts had
reported to him that the fortress had been abandoned by
the craven humans, all except for a handful of warriors who
still manned the lofty battlements, awaiting a battle they
could never win. Reaper was glad for their presence—there
would be little triumph in the capture of an undefended
outpost. Here, at least, he and his armies would have the
pleasure of killing to leaven the relentless advance.

The Talon of Dassedec knew that north of Shalloth, invisible across a vast expanse of forest and plain, lay the
real prize. The white marble city of Carrillon was the key
to the entire campaign. Reaper had flown high, had seen
those gleaming towers and the "One Hundred Bridges" of

the fabled city, and now his crocodile lips curled into a true smile as he pictured the destruction of that ageless center. Once Carillonn was destroyed and the River Ariak dammed, his army would pour across central Dalethica and Galtigor and all the other realms of humankind would be doomed to inevitable destruction.

"Lord Reaper . . . we have come in response to your summons."

The panting voice attracted the wyrm's attention to the three brutox who had at last crawled, gasping and exhausted, onto the upper slopes of their master's peak.

"I see you, Firetusk—and Kroaksmasher, and Burner, as well," he murmured, greeting these mighty captains. Each of the brutox threw himself flat upon the rocks, averting his lowly eyes from the glorious sight of his master, until Reaper commanded them all to rise.

"You will take your foremost column, Burner, and turn to the north. I want you at the outskirts of Carillon within seven days."

"Aye, lord! My kroaks will march through the night, and gather like a scourge about the city of marble."

"You, Kroaksmasher, are to bring your own legions in support, coming against the city from the west. Neither of you is to commence the attack until I arrive, but I desire all your troops to be in position for a massive onslaught."

"It shall be a magnificent pleasure to obey!" pledged hulking, battle-scarred Kroaksmasher. Sparks trailed from his paws and tusks as he smacked his lips, greedily anticipating the slaughter.

"And what of my own legion?" inquired Firetusk, hesitantly. "Shall I, too, turn to the north?"

"Nay. It pleases me to have your kroaks gather against Shalloth."

"Then we attack?" The huge brutox shuddered, releasing a shower of sparks from his shoulders and hands. His hooded eyes gleamed at the prospect of imminent battle.

Reaper's mighty head turned back to the west, and Firetusk waited within another cascade of sparks. If the bru-

tox wondered whether the Lord Minion had forgotten the
question, he was astute enough to wait and see.

"There will be help forthcoming, aid for the onslaught
against Shalloth," murmured the Talon of Dassadec. "So
you are not to attack, yet."

"I assure your lordship," Firetusk offered, standing tall,
prepared to face the Lord Minion's wrath. "My legion shall
need no assistance. The castle of humankind could be razed
within a day!"

"I believe you," replied Reaper, the gentleness of his
response clearly surprising Kroaksmasher and Burner—
who had edged nervously away from the cohort who had
dared to question the Lord Minion's orders. "But, nevertheless, you will wait."

Again his hooded eyes flickered to the west, probing
along that distant horizon. Among the plumes of smoke-
clouds rising from the ruined landscape, he began to discern
a new shape—a darker, denser cloud than even the most
pungent pyre.

"The *Dreadcloud* arrives within another day. It will support your attack, using its batteries to reduce the fortifications of Shalloth. Then, and only then, shall you commence
your assault."

"Aye, Lord," declared Burner, his own eyes alight as
he, too, looked toward the smoky horizon, seeking the skyship of Darkblood.

— 4 —

Bristyn stumbled through the marsh. Her hands remained
bound before her, leashed to the wrist of the massive,
shaggy warrior—the darkman she had dubbed Rat—who
tugged her through the mazelike tangle of the Willowfen.
Perhaps it was the lingering miasma of the tainted spring,
or else simply the dire circumstances in which she found
herself. In any event, the vast swamp seemed like a bleak

and dying place as the file of dark bandits proceeded through the predawn mist.

Again she had no idea where they were taking her. The swampmen moved with very little talking, the long column proceeding quickly along almost invisible pathways. The duchess could only lower her head in an attempt to avoid the lashing of branches, thorns, and vines.

A slight breeze washed her face with the scent of open air, of river water and distant plains. Raising her eyes, Bristyn saw that they had emerged from the thickets into a large clearing. A haze of clouds obscured the stars, but she discerned a rounded hummock of ground rising before her, doming upward into the night sky.

The bandits made their way to the base of this elevation, proceeding upward along a steep and narrow trail. Rat tugged Bristyn unceremoniously onto the incline. Fully alert now, the duchess tried to see through the darkness. A haze of growing illumination lay along the eastern horizon, muted into steel gray by the clouds, but enough light penetrated the overcast to reveal the steep, rocky terrain at her feet.

The trail was cut into the side of the hill, spiraling across the slope at a shallow angle. Bristyn reeled dizzily as the drop to her left became a dangerously sheer cliff. Though the elevation hadn't looked like much at first glance, she realized that it was in fact a fairly substantial knoll.

Soon she could see over the tops of the trees that clogged so much of the Willowfen. As the climbing trail took the file around the back of the hill she got a good look to the east, noting that the tangle of the swampland seemed to end just a few miles away. A band of mist lay across the trees, like a thick serpent of nearly tangible vapor, and she guessed that the fog marked the course of the River Ariak.

Then the swampmen moved around the far side of the hill and the course of that fabled river vanished from her view. Higher and higher they climbed, until at last they crested the summit. Bristyn was pulled along a wide clearing, like an ancient avenue that passed between mossy, ruined walls. Nearby stood a gate of corroded iron, beside the rotted foundation of what once might have been a grand tower.

All around, slopes plunged away to the flat, marshy clearing. Vapors of dawn mist swirled like ghosts among the trees. Rat pulled her along the ancient walkway, then shoved her to the side, through a gap between two crumbling walls. She found herself in a square enclosure the size of a large room. The place was open to the sky above, but the mossy walls reached as high as her head on all sides.

Rat abruptly jerked her to a stop, and the duchess staggered slightly but maintained her balance. Giving her captor a look of disdain, she pulled away to stand by herself, with the rope leash hanging slack between them. Beyond her enclosed space, the band of cutthroats had gathered into a large ring. A hundred faces turned skyward, looking to the east, and at first she wondered if they awaited the first appearance of the sun. She rejected the notion immediately, certain that these were beings who had grown very comfortable with the night. She could think of no reason why they should welcome the arrival of day.

But what was their purpose, then?

Following the gaze of the rapt swampmen, Bristyn saw a smudge of blackness along the horizon. A wisp of dark cloud, thicker and more compact than the overcast that blanketed the skies overhead, materialized in the distance. As soon as she spotted it, the duchess knew that the ominous blob was the thing that had drawn the bandits to this summit.

Though the wind was light, the dark cloud floated closer with surprising speed. Bristyn quickly realized that it was not as large as she had first suspected. In the growing daylight, she saw that it was a mere puffball, though so dense there was no glimmer of illumination passing through it.

Several of the men moved toward the center of the round hilltop. They carried watersacks, and as the cloud drifted toward them they poured the contents of those skins into a smooth, bowl-shaped depression in the rock. By this time the dark cloud nudged against the very side of the hilltop, and Bristyn had to suppress a gasp as she saw something move on the tenebrous mass. A great, hulking figure rose from its surface to utter a barking, guttural challenge.

The assembled swampmen threw themselves to the ground in unison, groveling before this barrel-chested creature as a cascade of sparks illuminated the monster and confirmed Bristyn's first, horrified impression.

Finally the thick, stinking cloud parted and lowered its passenger to the hilltop. The bow-legged monster came to rest on the ground amid the bowing, scraping darkmen. Pounding its chest with both of its massive fists, the beast bellowed aloud, and the men trembled with an emotion like ecstacy.

She remembered the brutox statue as the reality of the minion stalked toward her, and she wondered: How had they known it would come?

SIX

Storms at Darkenheight

Watch the summits and the swales, for the first
tiny leak in the Watershed needs only a measure
of erosion to become a major gap.
—CODEX OF THE GUARDIANS
VOLUME I, GODSTOME

— 1 —

"You stay here and rest, all right?" Awnro Lyrifell said,
nervously twirling the end of his long mustache. "I want
you to promise me that you'll get better."

Anjell drew an exaggerated sigh. "I've told *everybody*—
I'm not sick, so I don't need to get better. I should be
coming along with you to look for a new pass over the
Watershed."

The bard's eyes flickered to Dara, who sat on the other
side of the girl's bed. Anjell felt really miserable—she
knew that her mother had wanted to go along with Awnro,
had wanted to see Halverica again. But now she had to stay
here because she was worried about her stupid daughter,
who couldn't stop herself from fainting and throwing practically the whole city into a panic.

Kerri came over and gave the girl a hug. "We'll find a place you'll like when you see it," she promised, and Anjell found it hard not to cry.

"Be careful!" she whispered, as Awnro and Kerri departed for Shalemont and the Watershed.

"I'm sorry you didn't get to go either, Mama."

"There's nothing wrong with us staying here," Dara insisted. "And you'll be up and about again, before you know it. Awnro's right—just rest."

"All right." It seemed easier to agree than to keep arguing, so Anjell even threw in a yawn to make it appear convincing.

"I'll leave you for a while, now." Dara checked the curtains beside the open window, then left the room, gently closing the door.

A second later a small figure hopped up to the windowsill, looked both ways, then scampered inside. He turned his silver-flecked eyes worriedly toward the girl in the bed.

"Haylor!" Anjell whispered delightedly. "Am I glad to see you! It's really boring around here!"

"Not for long!" declared the young sylve, sauntering over the bed and seating himself on the mattress. He hoisted a small flask and let Anjell hear the liquid sloshing within.

"Guess what?" he said. "And one clue: It comes straight from the Pool of Scrying."

— 2 —

The galyon and its flotilla of sylvan longboats crossed the Auraloch and made swift passage up the narrow, deep fjord Wistan Aeroel had described. Danri spent much of the time missing Kerri, and pining for her, but that only fueled his determination to close up the pass at Darkenheight so that he could rejoin her on the other side of Faerine.

Three days after departing Spendorial, Kestrel found a secure anchorage near a beach that would allow an easy landing of the field army. Before they brought the troops ashore from the *Black Condor*, however, Danri had dispatched Garic Hoorkin and Neambrey to scout the approaches to the pass—and now he spotted a small, winged figure diving down toward the water.

"There he is!" Darret cried, waving wildly. "He's back! Garic! Over here!"

The twissel buzzed like a sparrow above the sparkling water, flying with a speed that even Danri found amazing. The digger stood with Captain Kestrel and Darret on the raised wheel deck of the moored galyon. Dozens of the sylvan longboats had already been pulled ashore on the nearby beach.

Doming overhead was a sky as blue as only Faerine's sky could be. A thick carpet of pines trailed down the steep slopes, plunging into the waters on either side. The little cove where the boats of Spendorial had landed was one of a very few accessible shorelines along this entire passage, and the digger found himself offering a quiet prayer to Aurianth, hoping desperately that the twissel's news was good.

Garic Hoorkin buzzed up to the galyon and came to rest on the rail. Panting, wings drooping, the diminutive Faerine wiped sweat from his brow and drew several deep breaths.

"Well?" demanded the impatient digger. "What did it look like? Can we march into the Darkenheight Valley from here?"

Still gasping for air, Garic nodded. "Steep . . . but Neambrey was right—with a bit of a climb . . . looks like you can make it."

"What about that drackan? Did you see him?" pressed the digger, who hadn't sighted Neambrey since he had winged away on the first day out of Spendorial.

"No, I didn't," Garic admitted.

"Well, we'll find him when we find him, I guess," groused the digger, trying to hide his concern. "Might as well get the army ashore and ready to start."

Danri turned, looking across the crowded decks of the galyon. "Gulatch! Make ready to debark your gigants!"

On the main deck the hulking Faerine warrior nodded grimly. He wasted no time, as Kestrel's crewmen lowered the galyon's boat. Swiftly, three gigants bearing great swords of bronze scrambled down the rope ladder to take precarious positions in the slender hull.

"And it's not a long march," Garic said, in a more normal tone of voice. The twissel hopped down from the rail to stand on the deck, stretching his gossamer wings, leaning forward to work out some of the kinks in his spine. "Like I said, it goes up steep, but once you reach the crest you'll have a clear march into the valley. Best of all, the entrance to Darkenheight Pass is only two days' march away."

"Looks like your water route has paid off," said the digger, clapping the gray-bearded captain on the arm.

"And with their whole army down in the Suderwild, I don't think the minions will be expecting us to show up across their supply line," Wistan Aeroel said hopefully. The lean sylvan warrior, dressed in supple skins dyed a woodland green, sauntered across the wheel deck. His twin quivers bristled with arrows, and the long shaft of his bow—unstrung—was strapped across his back.

"It'll take a few hours to get all the gigants ashore," Danri said. "Why don't we have the sylves and diggers start out? From what Garic says, we'll be taking a pretty narrow trail."

"Good idea," agreed the archer. He signalled to the shore, and one of the sylvan longboats slipped through the clear water, an oarsman steering it toward the anchored galyon.

The sleek vessels of Faerine were too frail to transport the gigants, but within a few minutes the digger and sylvan warriors aboard the *Condor* were on the way to join their fellows on shore. Wistan went in the first boat, intending to organize the head of the column and get the army marching toward the pass, while Danri remained for a few minutes, waiting for the last of the boats.

"Darret, keep an eye on things around here," the digger

said encouragingly, as the youth looked longingly toward the shore.

"Well—can't I come along?" he asked.

"I think your captain needs you," Danri replied. "Remember, we've all got a role to play."

"Aye. And you'll stay here where I can keep an eye on you," Kestrel said, calling down to Darret. The young man sagged with visible disappointment at the captain's command.

"In truth," Danri said seriously, "we want to get up there, make our attack, and see the pass closed. Then we'll throw up a wall to make sure that the minions can't get any Darkblood through."

"And we gigants will hold that wall," Gulatch pledged grimly.

The digger nodded. "The rest of us will march back here on the double quick. Hopefully you can be ready to sail at a moment's notice."

"We'll be ready," Kestrel pledged. "And may Aurianth and Baracan alike watch over you."

"Thanks." With a pat on the sulking Darret's head, the digger clumped down the ladder, crossed the main deck, and climbed down the ropes to the narrow hull of a sylvan longboat. His squire Pembroak and a few more diggers climbed aboard, until the little craft rocked precariously in the placid water.

"It'll be good to feel rock underfoot again," Danri admitted, clutching the gunwales as the boat bobbed slightly under his weight.

"Just sit still, sir, and we'll be there in a minute," counseled the very young-looking sylve who manned the oars.

Glowering, the digger stifled further complaints, and soon he joined the rest of the army on shore. The last of the gigants were completing the transfer as he looked up the steep-sided valley that led away from the water, noting that Wistan Aeroel had already started out with the sylves and some of the diggers.

Soon even the tail of the column was underway, and for

the rest of this day Danri's steps took him into—and up—
the faces of the rugged Bruxrange. With Wistan Aeroel
and the buzzing, hovering twissel in the lead, the file of
Faerine warriors worked its way steadily upward. They followed a trail that evolved as they marched, switching back
and forth across a steep-rising slope or following sheer-
walled ravines and narrow cuts between rocky promonto-
ries. And always it went up.

At one rest stop, as his weary lungs strained for breath,
Danri figured that the army had gained as much altitude in
this one day of marching as they had in a fortnight of
climbing toward Darkenheight on their first campaign. The
ship had gotten them much closer to the pass, but he did
wish there was some way they could have sailed uphill.
Sighing, he turned to the next steep slope, fastening his
eyes upon the high ridge line that formed the Faerine Field
Army's next goal.

By sunset, most of the column had passed the high crest
to work its way into a sheltered, forested valley beyond.
Danri and Pembroak, near the tail of the formation, paused
at the summit and looked at the sun-speckled mountains of
the Bruxrange.

"There it is," Danri announced, grimly pointing to a
notch in the high ridge of the Watershed.

"Darkenheight?" the squire asked, his voice uncharacteristically hushed.

"Aye-uh. The only place the Sleepstealer can send his
Darkblood into Faerine."

"Well, what are we waiting for?" the young digger chal-
lenged, starting along the trail again, long arms swinging
easily at his side. "Let's go let 'em know that this road is
closed!"

— 3 —

For three days the Man of Three Waters guided his Auracloud toward the west, ceasing his concentration only long

enough to get a few hours' rest during the middle of each night. With the landscape of Faerine rolling by underneath, he followed the course of the Aurun River into the foothills and mountains approaching the Watershed. He and Raine were both relieved to see that, once the region around Spendorial disappeared from sight, the wasteland spread by the minion army was nowhere in evidence.

"It looks like they're waiting for Spendorial to fall before they move on," Raine suggested.

"That's a small blessing, anyway," conceded the Iceman. "Something we can be thankful for."

"There's a *lot* to be thankful for." Raine curled beside Rudy in a hollow of the cloud. He welcomed her embrace, and for a time his attention drifted from the skies before them to the woman at his side. Their hands, their lips, their bodies, came together—and the truth of Raine's assertion became crystal clear in the Iceman's mind.

Some time later he yielded to fatigue, warm in the knowledge of his beloved's protective presence. He slept without dreaming, and in a few hours found himself fully restored.

For a while the Man and Woman of Three Waters lay together near the crest of the cloud's billowing tower, clasping each other, sharing their passion or silence or sleep. These moments of closeness, for Rudy, were tinged with a sense of desperation—as if he were subconsciously aware that they would never again share such a benign interlude.

"Do you ever think about what we'll do after the war?" Raine asked once, as they watched the azure sky flow placidly past.

"I . . . I guess I don't. Go back to Halverica?" Even as he made the suggestion, Rudy knew that it didn't sound right, or complete. "What about you?"

"It's too hard to picture, I guess. We've been ruled by this struggle for so long, had all our decisions made for us. I'm not sure I'd know what to do if it was just up to us."

"Until then, let's make the most of these times," Rudy

proposed, stretching out on the cloudy surface and reaching for Raine. "So come here, wench."

She leaned toward him, then rolled away as he leapt after her. Laughing, she turned and tripped the Iceman, then pounced on top of him as he tried to climb back to his feet.

"What was that about a wench?" she asked, pressing her legs together and driving the breath from his lungs.

"I—I love you!" he gasped, struggling in vain to break free. And when she released him, they fell together, buried in the feathery wisps of the Auracloud.

At all times Rudy kept a pair of large waterskins, full of Aura, near at hand. He was obsessive about refilling each sack whenever he took more than a few sips from it. At his side, he wore the artifact of the gods, the sword Lordsmiter—the weapon he had used to slay the Lord Minion Phalthak. Raine bore a gleaming longsword of digger steel at her waist, the blade keen and strong beyond the capability of any human-forged weapon.

The Auracloud itself was a long, slender craft, shaped of the steam from Faerine's magical essence. The Iceman could guide the ship from any position on the puffy, well-cushioned deck, but he preferred to ride on the high tower near the "bow" of the enchanted oblong. The center of the cloud was marked by a bowl-shaped depression, and here the travelers had stored a half-dozen small casks of pure Aura, several barrels of water, and an assortment of ropes and poles, climbing spikes, bedrolls, charcoal, and food.

One other item was stowed aboard—a weapon wrapped in oil-soaked leather, bound in cords, as protection against the elements. Rudy devoutly hoped that the Sword of Darkblood could remain always secured within that wrapping, but a part of him feared—without knowing exactly why—that the black, venomous blade had a role to play in their desperate mission.

By the third day of their journey, the lowlands of Faerine had been left behind—the pastoral woodlands, the streams crossed by rainbow bridges, and the fountain-sparkled glades where twissels played and sylvan Auramasters contemplated the mysteries of their realm. The region below became a rugged land of tangled mountains, bright glaciers, and deep, shadowy gorges. Ribbons of white water and Aura scored channels, spilling from the base of fan-shaped ice fields, surging toward the lowlands with inevitable, world-carving force.

"That ridge . . . is that the Watershed, already?" Raine asked, settling herself beside the Iceman as the cloud surged through air growing rough with swirling updrafts. The sky remained blue and clear, but the winds in these mountainous heights buffeted the flying ship with chaotic, relentless force. Before them rose inky towers of cloud, darkening the sky like an ominous, gathering storm.

"Yes," he replied. Though their elevation was too low to see over the cornice-draped ridge, thunderheads rose as black as night beyond the crest of the Watershed. Staring intently, Rudy sensed the toxic realm's oppressive, menacing presence.

"We'll cross over some time tonight," he announced with certainty. "This might be the last good weather we see for . . . well, for a long time."

"Let's make the most of it," Raine suggested, with a sly smile. She pulled him down onto the cloud and for a time they were borne by the wind, lost in each other's scents and touch, fueled by growing, increasingly desperate love. When the sun set and shadows stretched across the cloud, they remained together, the heat of their shared intimacy keeping them warm.

Finally the Iceman stood, ready for the push across the high ridge. Focusing on the rocky barrier before him, he sent the skyship surging upward with the rays of sunset slanting in from the starboard bow. The Auracloud climbed steadily under the force of Rudy's concentration, until the two passengers could clearly see over the lofty, snow-covered ridge.

Before proceeding, The Man of Three Waters turned back for a last view of the pristine, snow-speckled realm of magic. The rugged ground sprawled luminous and bright

beneath the light of a crescent moon. But that was the past,
and he had to look forward. Across the Watershed, the vastness of Duloth-Trol loomed like a great, black void. Tar-
clouds layered the sky in a blanket so dark that every trace
of moonlight was absorbed. And unlike the snowfields and
glaciers below, the mountains of the Sleepstealer's realm
were cloaked in the sticky goo of tarfrost, an oily black
layer utterly devoid of light.

Rudy squinted, using the force of his mind to push the
Auracloud into that murky air. He felt the resistance like a
physical wall, and the skyship shuddered, straining, groaning to a halt. Feeling the toxic presence of the Sleepstealer's
realm, he tried to rise higher, to press through the barrier.
Creaking and moaning against the pressure of vaporous
Darkblood, the Auracloud scraped forward.

"Go on!" The Woman of Three Waters stood at the
Iceman's side, her arms around his waist. "Push us
through."

Rudy obeyed, leaning forward, feeling the stinging
power of Darkblood against his face, gumming his eyes.

"High Guardians!" Raine warned, pointing to starboard.

The Iceman saw several stone-skinned creatures lumbering with apelike deliberation along the knife-crest of the
Watershed. He tried to veer away, having no desire to fight
the Guardians.

"Hold them off!" he cried, and Raine moved down the
steep side of the cloud, sword in hand.

But when the first of the Guardians reached the edge of
the skyship it didn't try to push them back, or to climb
aboard. Instead, it seized the vaporous hull, sinking bould-
erlike fists into the cloud and pulling. Soon the others
joined, until a dozen of the rocklike figures hauled at the
Auracloud, helping to push it over the barrier of the Watershed.

And then that stinking atmosphere was around them,
smothering like a rot-infested blanket. The Man and
Woman of Three Waters stood side by side, holding hands,
staring into the enveloping murk. The Iceman's eyes stung,

but he blinked back his tears and then he could see. The stench of the place stung his nostrils like ammonia or stale urine, but the air didn't seem to be poisonous. Raine's fingers tightened around his own as she, too, withstood the onslaught without faltering. He pushed hard, straining to part the thick air with the force of his will and his Auramagic.

Raine's gasp spun the Iceman around and he saw what had startled her: A stony Guardian had climbed the flank of the Auracloud, scaling with hands and feet up the sheer side, then pulling itself into a secure position atop the skyship.

"It's making no move to threaten us," Rudy observed curiously.

"No. It's acting more like, well . . . a guardian," Raine replied.

"Maybe he's going to keep an eye on us." The Iceman liked the thought. He stepped toward the creature, which had a face like a craggy rock, and two eyes like patches of dark, wet ice. "Welcome aboard."

Be wary. The creature's thought entered Rudy's mind without speech, and Rudy sensed an element of urgency in the admonition. Unconsciously his hand closed about the hilt of his sword.

Then the smoggy overcast parted and widespread beaks rushed into view. Shrieks echoed through the air as terrions plunged toward the intruding skyship.

It might have been the sheer suddenness of the attack that saved them—that, and the Guardian's reflexive stance. The creature leapt to its feet, raising a stony fist and bashing aside the first of the minion flyers to sweep past the skyship. Rudy tumbled backward in an instinctive evasion, dragging Raine down into a hollow on the surface of the Auracloud. Three winged shapes soared past in the blink of an eye, turning amid the churning murk, already swerving around to attack again.

The Iceman sprang to his feet, Lordsmiter in hand, while Raine stood at his back with her own blade at the ready.

Walls of white cloud rose to either side of them, and Rudy started climbing, looking for more signs of the terrions.

"Stay low, here—we're more vulnerable atop the tower." She pulled him back with her logic.

"Right." As long as they remained between the fore-tower and middle rise of the Auracloud, the terrions could only come at them from port or starboad—or above, Rudy remembered, glancing quickly upward.

And now, once again, they saw their enemies. The terrions were the same gray-black color of the clouds, long-winged shapes rippling in and out of the billowing puffs of darkness, but as they dove closer the wide-winged, speeding shapes stood out clearly against the background murk.

The Guardian stood atop the central pillar of the skyship, and the flyers spread to either side, giving the stone creature a wide berth.

Rudy crouched low, then jabbed upward as the first minion swept past. The keen blade sliced, cutting a long gash in a leathery wing, and the terrion shrieked as it tumbled crazily toward the jagged landscape below.

The Iceman stumbled as Raine fell against his back. He caught himself on one knee, then whirled to see a terrion—and the flashing mirror of Raine's longsword dart forward to tear a long gash in the monster's belly. With a pathetic wriggle, the monster fell onto its back, kicking weakly as it tumbled off the cloud.

Another minion flyer swooped in and this time the Guardian lashed to the side, smashing its wing with a crushing fist. The minion veered wildly past Rudy, and Lordsmiter whistled, slicing the fanged head cleanly from its neck. The remains of that terrion followed the others into the depths, and suddenly the sky was empty of all but the Auracloud. Trembling and jumpy, Rudy looked around, trying to penetrate the overcast, seeking the next threat.

But there was nothing to menace them, at least not at that moment.

"Onward, then?" Raine asked, wiping the gore from her sword on the pillowy surface of the cloud. The gaseous

Aura hissed and steamed, but as the vapor drifted away her blade was once again restored to pristine brightness. "At least, we've picked up an ally," she added, nodding to the Guardian as that creature once again set itself stoically atop the cloud.

" 'Be wary' was right," Rudy commented. "I guess this is our welcome to Duloth-Trol." He looked ahead, trying to picture how many more attacks they would have to face, what obstacles lay across their path to the Sleepstealer's fortress.

And, not for the first time, he wondered if they were mad to try.

— 4 —

"This chute gives a clear road into Darkenheight," Pembroak reported, shouting so that Danri could hear him over the clanging resonance of furious digging, as no less than a hundred miners, pickmen, and shovelers assaulted a nearby rise of rock wall.

"Darkenheight Pass is right past this cliff," Garic Hoorkin explained.

Pembroak and the twissel had just descended the steep slope after scouting the terrain beyond. Now the three Faerines studied the active excavation, where dozens of diggers labored to punch a tunnel through the precipitous wall of stone, the last barrier to their march on Darkenheight. Much rock had already been moved, though more work was still required before the attack could commence. Nevertheless, the field army stood ready, and the miners worked without rest—and, so far, without being observed by the enemy.

"How much farther?" asked Danri. He cast a glance along the trail behind, where sylves, gigants, and diggers advanced steadily. The first company—Wistan Aereol's sylvan archers—was already halted behind the work party.

"Scarcely a mile to the very entrance of the gorge,"

Pembroak explained. "I saw a few brutox there—nothing that would hold up a swift attack."

"Good. Any sign of their bloodwagons?"

"Nothing in sight right now. Still, the road is gouged deep with ruts—and as black as a minion's heart. No question that's where they bring the stuff into Faerine."

"*Used* to bring," Danri corrected grimly. "As of now, the last wagon has passed."

Before Danri's appreciative eyes the mining company created the final link in the road that had carried the Faerine Army through the heart of the Bruxrange. The lead rank, comprised of brawny diggers wielding massive, steel-bitted pickaxes, hacked at the rock surface, swiftly marking it with a spiderweb network of cracks, then smashing it into loose rock. Immediately behind them, several nimble, compact diggers used hoes to scrape the rubble back from the excavation. Next came the shovel- and barrow-men, who scooped the debris and trundled it away—where it was usually used as fill to raise or support a lower section of the trail that was beginning to resemble a road.

"We'll let the troops rest here until the tunnel's open," Danri declared as Gulatch and Wistan Aeroel came forward for a planning session.

"Once through, we attack?" asked the gigant, with a look at the setting sun.

"Should be about twilight or later, when we'll have the advantage," Danri told him. The others nodded, knowing that—because of the many springs spilling bright glimmering Aura across the treeless landscape—the Faerine warriors would not be impeded by darkness. This advantage had been crucial to the army's survival during its first campaign, and now it would give them an advantage on the attack.

"A quick rush to take the pass, then throw up a wall by morning?" asked the woodland sylve, a twinkle in his eye as he posed the question.

"Almost," the digger war chief replied, unaware of Wistan's attempt at humor. "It might take a couple of days, but we'll have a barrier that the minions won't be coming through for a very long time."

"We'll hold it forever, if we have to," Gulatch pledged.

"Hey!" Neambrey cried, gliding to the ground before the huddled Faerines. "You found the way to the pass!"

"And what have *you* found?" Danri asked. "Besides tomorrow's lunch, I mean."

"Tomorrow's lunch? Oh, a joke!" The drackan chuckled appreciatively. "Well, there were some wagons coming up toward the pass, but we dropped rocks on them and they stopped."

"Who's we?" wondered the digger.

"Oh, Verdagon and that other big green drackan, Borcanash, decided to come along after all. They didn't want to miss anything heroic. They're waiting up on the mountain for me to tell them when it's time."

"What does the pass look like?" pressed Danri.

"Well, there's not too many minions in there. Most of them are brutox, though."

Within a few hours the ridge was penetrated almost fully by a deep hole. A thin sheet of rock had been left until the last moment, so that the minions guarding the pass wouldn't be alerted. Grimly determined, the Faerines of the field army formed into a long rank, the sylves in the lead just far enough back to avoid the falling rocks when the diggers collapsed the last section of wall.

"Ready?" Danri asked the question of Pembroak as the sylves fingered their longbows and the gigants muttered deep chants. The digger cum squire raised his pick, nodding affirmation.

"Smash it down!" Danri barked.

A blur of picks whirled against the rocks, battering in a staccato pattern. Dust and chips of stone formed a blizzard in the air, a stinging cascade of debris that the miners completely ignored. The remaining section of wall trembled dangerously, then collapsed with a crash. Slabs of rock smashed downward, splintering into powder, sending an ac-

rid smell through the tunnel instantaneous with the impact
of the crumbling wall.

Even before the dust settled, shovelers and barrow-men
dashed into the breach. Within a few moments they had
scraped a smooth path through the rubble, and with a hearty
cry the archers of Wistan Aeroel's company charged. Long,
graceful strides carried the Faerine bowmen toward any
minions who dared to block their path.

Sparks glimmered in the twilight, marking the position—
and agitation—of the brutox posted at the mouth of Darkenheight Pass. A dozen of the hulking minions straddled
the roadway there, brandishing mighty axes, clearly determined to sell their lives dearly.

"Sylves—halt!" Wistan's cry rang through the still
mountain air, and the line of archers stopped before the
echo could return from the nearest cliff. "Take aim—shoot
them down!"

A volley of arrows showered the line of brutox, killing
all that stood at the entrance to the gorgelike pass. The slain
minions melted and sizzled, their flesh turning to oily gore,
then sparkling into bright, sputtering flames.

Within a few minutes many diggers, too, had swept up
to the dark notch leading toward the summit of the pass.
Still in the lead, the sylves advanced, skirting the smoldering pyres marking the fallen brutox. Once past the acrid
barrier, the Faerines started into the pass at a rapid trot.

Danri jogged along with the leading sylves, diggers, and
gigants, his eyes probing the shadows to either side of the
gorge. Aurasprings were infrequent here, and the darkness
could have masked a significant ambush force. His lungs
strained for air, and he halted long enough to take a drink
of Aura from his flask. Immediately invigorated, he resumed the advance.

Now the Faerines heard bellowed challenges from the
space before them, saw a shadowy line take form across
the gorge floor. Sparks outlined the positions of brutox,
while the hunched, darker forms of kroaks filled in the
gaps.

"Don't stop—show no mercy!" Danri shouted, wielding his hammer and urging his countrymen on.

"For Quenidon Daringer—and the Suderwild!" bellowed Wistan, the sylve's voice surprisingly powerful as it resonated from his deceptively slender chest.

The name of the field army's first commander drove the Faerines into a killing frenzy. The two forces clashed in a cacophony of shrieks and smashes, groans and grunts and curses of pain and fury. Weapons and bones and flesh were destroyed in the storm of violence as, along the entire line, the desperate minions fought with stubborn savagery, unwilling to surrender a single foot of ground.

Danri hammered down a massive brutox, then slashed a kroak with the sharpened pick on the other side of his hammer. Pembroak charged past, his sword slicing into minion bodies with merciless force. Nearby Gulatch roared, smashing kroaks and brutox with his mighty blade, while sylvan arrows whooshed silently overhead, and the screams of dying minions echoed from the steep walls bordering the pass.

When Neambrey and the two elder drackans swept down from the heights, spewing frigid clouds of Aurafrost, the minion survivors broke and ran. The rest of the Faerines charged, overtaking the fleeing defenders, slaughtering the minions with no thought of mercy.

Before midnight the familiar silence had settled over the gorge of Darkenheight. The last of the minions spilled their blood into the deep ruts of the road, while swift-running sylvan scouts probed through the pass, venturing even into the acrid air of Duloth-Trol beyond the barrier of the Watershed. These fleet-footed explorers swiftly returned, reporting no sign of any additional minion garrison.

"Diggers! Set to work!" shouted Danri, as the mining company commanders organized their engineers into two detachments. An hour later, the foundation of the wall began to take shape.

— 5 —

The minion surge fell back again and Roggett Becken
wiped the pick of his ice axe on a rag grown grimy with
use. The slope before him, where the ridge of the Dermaathof swept downward into the valley of Dermaat itself, was
lined with limp corpses and scored by streams of black
blood.

When he tried to think, the weary Iceman could not recall
how many times the horde had swept up this road, had tried
to push through the plug of pikemen that had stood so res-
olutely in Neshara Pass. The quiver of Roggett's crossbow,
sadly, was empty, and he didn't know when he'd be able
to get more quarrels. Until then, he would rely upon his
sturdy axe.

Several of his warriors saw to the wounded, escorting
two men down the road to Neshara. There, in that once-
pastoral mountain village, an emergency hospital had been
established. There, too, was gathered the reserve force—a
few hundred Icemen with picks, axes, and bows, ready to
march quickly, to throw themselves into the defense
wherever they were needed. These men were augmented by
the survivors of the Galtigor company, which had arrived
in Halverica shortly after the breach was discovered. Roggett had heard that it was his old friend and neighbor, Rudy
Appenfell, who had told King Takian of Galtigor about the
threat—and that worthy monarch had hastened to respond.
It made Roggett's head whirl to think about a humble Nesharan Iceman giving advice to kings, but in this changing
era even that wasn't too strange to believe.

"We did it again," Tarn Blaysmith declared, limping
upward along the crest to join the sturdy Iceman atop the
ridge. Tarn's axemen had held the section of ground just
above the pass, and had repulsed numerous attempts by the
minions to outflank the pikemen.

"Aye," Roggett agreed. He saw that the bandage encircling Tarn's thigh was old, the dried blood dating from

before the day's battle. "How many today?" he asked grimly.

"Three killed, and four more who'll never hold an axe again," declared Blaysmith sadly. His brow furrowed in concern as he continued. "And another one of my fellows came down with that fever. We're getting pretty thin down there."

"I'll move my left flank to the edge of the slope," Roggett offered. "Let you condense your front a little." He tried not to show his apprehension, but he knew that two of his own men had recently been debilitated by a virulent, convulsive fever. He dreaded the thought of some sort of plague spreading among these stalwart defenders—but there wasn't anything to be done about it.

"Bringing your men down a bit would help," Tarn acknowledged. For a moment the lanky axeman looked toward distant Dermaat—or, rather, the site where the village once had stood. Now the valley floor was an ugly swath of dark mud and trampled, lifeless ground. The buildings had been smashed to kindling over the weeks of the siege, and the route toward the Glimmercrown, where the tunnel penetrated beneath the heart of the Watershed, was a rutted and stained stripe of corruption.

Roggett knew that his fellow captain was remembering the wife and children who had once awaited him in that peaceful village. He had heard the story over the many dark nights along the front: Tarn had been hunting in the high valleys when the breach had been ripped through the mountain's foundation. He had returned to find his family, his whole town, poisoned. Paralyzed by grief, he had almost been slain by the first kroak to march through the region.

Yet some instinct for survival had saved him. He had killed that initial kroak with a single blow from his climbing pick. Then he had seized his double-bitted woodsman's axe and butchered the half dozen brutes who had come to investigate their comrade's fate.

Only then had Tarn left Dermaat, carrying his weapon and his memories into the hills. He had joined a band of

men, most of whom had lived outside the village, to form
a company of determined warriors. Because of his impressive size and strength—in addition to, though no more important than, his fanatical hatred of the invaders—Tarn had
been elected captain of the little group. Perhaps half of the
orginal number remained, but they were still one of the
most stalwart of the Halverican formations.

Roggett himself had never married—the girl he'd loved
had found another man to wed—but he shivered with horror when he pictured the extent of his comrade's loss. How
the man could function at all seemed a mystery, yet Tarn's
company had proven one of the deadliest in the fight
against the minions.

"Why don't you pull your men back for a day or two?"
Roggett suggested. He knew that the relentless series of
fights was taking its toll on all the men. "We could bring
up a group from Neshara to take your place."

Tarn smiled, but shook his head. "Thanks, friend, but
you know I can't do that. Besides, even if I ordered them
to leave, my men wouldn't go. Dermaat is *ours*. Do you
understand what I mean?"

"I think so," Roggett agreed, not surprised by his comrade's decision.

A commotion from the roadway behind the two men attracted their attention. Several riders galloped up the road
from Neshara. One of them shouted and waved, the urgency
in his voice and bearing manifest even through the inaudible words of his message.

Quickly the two captains scrambled down from the lofty
vantage, meeting the riders in the saddle of the pass. The
leader, a gray-bearded man wearing the mantle of a village
burgomaster, had already spoken to Kristoff Yarden, commander of the pikemen.

"You have to fall back!" declared the older man, the
steadiness of his voice belying the agitation of his manner.
He looked at the two captains, his gray eyes grim and
steely.

"Why?" demanded Tarn, clutching his axe as if he would swing at the messenger.

"We're outflanked! The minions have crossed the ridge farther down, along the Midvales. Already they march up the valley! They'll be in Neshara by tomorrow night—and there's not a damned thing you can do about it from up here!"

SEVEN

Lord Brutox

The gods smite the Watershed with ice and rain,
wind and heat, and a host of other assaults. Of
all immortal weaponry, however, none strikes
with the consuming violence of the lightning
bolt.
—SCROLL OF BARACAN

— 1 —

"We have a sacrifice, Lord Brutox!" declared the corrupted swampman, Rat, who clutched Bristyn's tether. She
spat at him scornfully as he tugged her forward.

The burly minion, faint sparks trailing from the blunt
claws of his hands, leered at her. The acidic stench of Darkblood was strong enough to sting her nostrils, and his red
eyes and slobbery, snuffling jowls reminded her of a very
dangerous bulldog.

"More!" growled the brutox, extending a rough paw toward Weasel.

Eagerly that hunched, shaggy bandit passed him a waterskin filled with Darkblood from the spring, which the
minion hoisted to pour into his gaping jaws.

Bristyn stood at her full height, regarding the hulking

minion with utter loathing. Remembering the word "sac-rifice," she tried to imagine a chain of events that would enable her to take a weapon, to at least die fighting.

The swampmen were all around, gathered like a pack of yelping curs encircling the great, round-shouldered form of the brutox. That black-skinned figure had demanded, and received, a drink from Weasel's flask as soon as he had come to rest upon the ground of the hilltop. The skin was one of many that the bandits had filled from the inky liquid of the corrupted spring. Now the minion eagerly swilled the second container of Darkblood, draining the sack and shaking the last few drops into the moist well of his wide-spread mouth.

As the black stuff trickled over his protruding jaw, the brutox at last pulled the nozzle away. Smacking thick lips, the minion wiped a taloned paw across his face, leaving a trail of sparks crackling and glowing in the air. The spots of fire drifted to the ground as the monster glared at the assembled swampmen with hooded, glittering eyes.

When those eyes came to rest upon Bristyn, she resisted an instinctive shudder that tried to ripple along her spine. Instead, she faced the beast as if her fury could stab from her own gaze and smite him with a whiplash of scorn and loathing.

Throwing back his huge head, the brutox laughed. The sound was like the rumbling of distant thunder, punctuated by sharp claps as the beast repeatedly smacked a callused palm against his bulging gut.

"This is the sacrifice?" inquired the brute, his voice a gurgling growl.

Rat nodded eagerly, tugging on the line lashed to Bris-tyn's wrists. She jerked back, mildly pleased that it was the bandit who staggered slightly—until she was pushed from behind to sprawl headlong in the dirt at the monster's feet.

Her scalp burned from the sparking touch of blunt talons as the minion reached down, seized her hair, and jerked her to a sitting position. His breath was the vile stench of carrion, and she gagged reflexively when he leaned over to stare into her eyes.

"Too good for killing, now at least," muttered the minion. With a hoist that wrenched her neck painfully, the monster lifted the duchess to her feet. He released her hair when she had planted her feet beneath her.

Staring into that hateful visage, she found it impossible to regain her air of aloofness. All she hoped was that her stark terror, an icy ball of fear that had formed in her gut, did not reveal itself in her expression.

"Tell me, human—where is your well?" demanded the brutox, confronting Rat again.

"In—in the swamp, lord. Many miles from here. We have created an altar for your lordship—perhaps you would like to march there, to see it?"

"Nay. I have been journeying for too long. I intend to wait here. Send men to fetch me more of this sweet nectar—and when they have returned, I shall feast. Then we will march."

Bristyn heard the words, understood the meaning. She remembered, vividly, Katlan's horrible fate and wondered if she would be the centerpiece of the next feasting. Again her despair flared into hatred, her mind searching for some way—*any* way—to lash out at these horrible creatures while she still had breath in her body.

No longer did she expect to escape. The events of the last days had battered her hopes to that extent, and this bizarre arrival—a minion of Duloth-Trol, floating from the sky into the midst of corrupted humankind—seemed only to underscore the certainty of her fate. Yet even as she abandoned hope of survival, she resolved that she would not die quietly.

Several of the swampmen dragged her to a sturdy bush. Forcing her to sit, they lashed her to the prickly trunk and, to all appearances, forgot about her. Bristyn sat amid the old, mossy ruins, and tried to picture an earlier time up on this knoll, when peace and good feeling might have prevailed. She was unable to conjure an image of anything except darkness and horror.

A number of the bandits departed at a brisk trot, and she guessed that these had been sent to collect the effluent that was the stuff of life to their new master. Most of the night passed in a numbness of despair and fatigue. Despite her fear, and her belief that these were the last hours of her life, Bristyn eventually fell asleep. She awoke with the chill of a misty dawn soaking through her garments, fingers of ice seeming to reach all the way into her bones. Activity around the hilltop suggested that the swampmen were stirring, and with a bolt of fear she remembered the brutox's announced intentions.

Frantically she tugged at her bonds, but the leather thongs had grown rigid, firmly set by now. She knew that the only way to remove them would be to cut them off.

A figure materialized nearby and she recognized Rat. He made no sound as he reached behind her to slash the ropes securing her to the bush. Jerking her to her feet, he pulled her toward a gathering in the center of the ruins.

The brutox stood head and shoulders above even the tallest of the men. His mouth split into a fang-baring grin as the duchess appeared, and sparks trailed downward from each of his wicked tusks. Again Bristyn tried to master her fear, to force herself to face this hateful creature with the scorn and loathing that one such as he deserved from one such as her.

"Your spirit remains unbroken," the brutox noted, with that growled, rumbling chuckle. "It is good that you show such heart. You will have to walk far today."

At first the creature's words didn't penetrate the veneer of the duchess's haughty courage. Only gradually did she realize that she would not be killed, not devoured by the darkmen.

At least, not here and now.

She smelled the acrid stink of Darkblood, like the mingling of an overused latrine and a disease-ridden charnel house, and saw that the brute's chest and belly were slick with the inky stuff. Obviously, the men had returned with nourishment for their new lord. Indeed, the minion stood with sterner posture and firmer stance than he had displayed the night before. Clearly his strength had been restored.

"Come. We march to the west," he declared, gesturing away from the sun rising through the mists over the Ariak.

When Rat picked up the tether to which Bristyn's wrists were lashed, the brutox snatched it away. "The woman will be in my charge," he snapped, with a drooling display of sparks. Wordlessly, with a deep bow, the darkman backed away.

Bristyn's throat was so parched she could barely speak, but she pulled firmly on the line and forced out the words, "You must let me have water . . . a drink, or I shall be unable to walk."

The monster looked ready to strike her, but then he rubbed his chin with a horny paw. "Very well. There will be water below," he said, gesturing to the swampland encircling the hill. "You may drink when we find some."

Settling for that, the duchess trundled along behind the brutox. The minion took the lead, and when Bristyn looked back she saw the rest of the hideous band, many hundreds strong by now, forming a column behind. They marched down the winding trail from the summit and once again entered the moss-draped shadows of the thick woods. Quickly the Willowfen surrounded them—but then Bristyn corrected herself: This was no longer a mundane, if murky, swamp. It was the Darkfen, now.

True to his word, the brutox allowed her to drink when they came to a small rivulet. Bristyn knelt and greedily sucked at the stagnant water, thinking that nothing she had ever drunk before had been so marvelously refreshing. She was not surprised when none of the darkmen drank any water—she knew now that their thirst could only be quenched by a different draught.

The brutox set a rapid pace, and though he displayed impatience on those rare occasions when Bristyn stumbled or fell, he otherwise took little note of his captive. They

marched steadily throughout the day, passing along a maze
of swampland paths, and by evening had arrived at the
brink of the woodlands. Stepping into the clear, Bristyn was
startled to see the graceful silhouette of Castle Shalloth rising into the sky only a few miles away. The lofty fortress
was oddly lifeless, marked only by torches flaring at the
gates and along some of the highest balconies. None of the
windows glowed with the familiar warmth of candlelight,
though the torches told her that Gandor Wade and his detachment of brave men still remained. The lands around the
castle were empty of humans, and of monstrous troops—
apparently the minions had not yet advanced far enough to
besiege the fortress.

Then her eyes fastened on the skies beyond the castle,
upon a looming shadow of darkness that seemed so thick,
so impenetrably black, that at first she thought an obsidian
mountain had somehow risen from the plain. Only after she
blinked and shook her head did she realize that the towering
shape was in fact a black cloud. The very sight of the thing
turned her knees to jelly and forced her to bite back an
involuntary moan of terror.

"It is the *Dreadcloud*, skyship of my master." She was
startled by the words, then realized that the brutox was
addressing her. "Once I, Direfang, commanded such a vessel. The power of lightning answered to *my* command—
and destruction rained on all of Faerine!"

From the flaring of sparks that dripped from the minion's
talons, she guessed that he spoke the truth—and that this
was a matter of great importance to him. The knowledge
that the scourge of Dassadec had extended even into the
realm of magic did not surprise her, but seemed only to
underscore the futility of resistance.

"Where is your ship?" she asked, hoping to learn more
about his mysterious arrival.

"Wasted . . . destroyed, by the wretched ambitions of a
Lord Minion!" declared the brute vehemently. "He caused
it to drift—and when my beautiful ship flies over water, it
withers. Thus you saw all that was left by the time I reached

here. But know this, my human slave. One day, and it shall be soon, I shall be lord of the skies again!''

Even as she wondered what he meant, the duchess saw that the great cloud had begun to move. Steadily, rumbling with a force of thunderous engines, the huge skyship plowed toward the castle of once-proud Shalloth. Bristyn imagined the sky-borne bolts blasting into her ancestral home, and in her mind the destruction was as real as if the storm had already begun.

— 2 —

''Captain Jaymes has returned from the west, sire.''

Tray Oldar, Takian's loyal attendant, bowed deeply from the door to the observation platform.

''Thank you, Oldar. Send him in. And Tray . . . I want you to know that I appreciate—''

''Say no more, sire. It is my only pleasure to serve.''

In the instant of the man's departure Takian's grief returned with consuming force. Bristyn! She was gone, slain by treacherous humans of her own realm! For a moment, the king's hatred welled into a blazing fire, and Takian needed all of his self-control to refrain from sending his troops into the Willowfen under orders to kill anyone that they found.

In another moment, the broad-shouldered commander of the Golden Lion Company was silhouetted against the interior torchlight. Jaymes bowed, then strode forward to join his monarch on the starlit platform of the high tower. Certainly he sensed Takian's barely contained rage. With equal certainty, he would not let his liege's mood affect his own behavior.

Once more Takian felt weak and foolish, completely inadequate to the massive challenges awaiting him. Angrily he turned away from Jaymes, letting his eyes sweep across the vista to the west. Even against the black night sky, the plumes of smoke, the stinging vapors marking swaths of scorched ground, were visible.

The king thought of the Golden Lions—his own company of hand-picked men. Jaymes had been Takian's teacher of horsemanship and fencing since his youngest days, and had been honored by the appointment to command. All the men of the unit were skillful and brave, willing to sacrifice body and life in following Takian's orders. But what could he tell them to do? How could any force of man stand before this minion tide, this wave that swept onward as irresistibly as the change of seasons?

The captain stepped to the rim of the tower, which was one of the highest in all the marbled city, and cleared his throat awkwardly.

"They are coming, are they not?" asked the king, the certainty of his tone belying the question.

"Aye, sire. The spearhead of the first column will be within twenty miles of the city by dawn."

Jaymes coughed awkwardly, looking at the ground beneath his scuffed horseman's boots. "About the queen, sire . . . I want you to know how sorry I am, all the men are. Any one of the Golden Lions would be willing to ride into the heart of that swamp to find her killers."

Takian waved away the sentiment, even as the same thought took hold of him—how desperately he craved revenge! Forcefully he pushed the matter aside.

"Is there any word from Andaran, sire?" Jaymes asked.

"No—and half the coast provinces have sent word that they won't fight for anyone except the High Prince. I know that other men, too, are wondering if they are yielding too much to Galtigor."

"But you're *here*. And you'll fight—those should be good enough reasons for any man," growled the old warrior.

"How many minion columns are approaching?" the king asked, returning to more immediate concerns. "And are they converging?"

"Only two are coming toward the city, one from the

south and the other from the west. The third seems to be concentrated around Shalloth—we haven't had word on where it's going from there. And of the nearer legions, the southern column is the more immediate threat. The minions there have dammed the Birchcreek with their bovars. Dayr, my chief scout, had a look at their advance from quite close. He rode all night to tell me that the whole force will soon be across—probably is already, given that he took to his saddle six hours ago.''

"The Birchcreek? That's pretty far from the river, right?" Takian asked, trying to remember the local geography.

"Yes, Your Majesty."

"Then it seems that the minions have no stomach for the Willowfen. They're taking a fairly circuitous route, but from the creek I imagine they'll reach the city within a couple of days."

"That's my guess," concurred the warrior.

"And the wing to the west is more delayed?"

Jaymes nodded. "The White Gorge is holding them up. Apparently the bovars have trouble excavating the bedrock—last word, also about six hours old, is that they will need another day to complete their bridge. And even then they'll have a lot of rugged ground to cross before they reach the river bank."

"Let's give their lead wing a proper greeting, then," declared the king, whirling from the parapet so abruptly that Jaymes took a startled step backward.

"Aye, sire!" agreed the captain, clapping a hand to his armored chest in an enthusiastic salute.

Takian entered the keep and stalked through the halls of Castle Carillonn, his steadfast captain hastening to keep up. As they descended stairways, passed through marbled hallways, marched across the courtyards to the stables, it seemed that the whole palace came to life. Servants whispered rumors of the king's sudden animation, while men-at-arms checked their weapons, and turned their own faces toward the unseen enemy in the south.

By the time Hawkrunner, the king's stallion, had been girded and saddled, Takian himself had donned a suit of mail armor. Word had gone out to the captains of two dozen companies, hand-picked for their reliability and quickness of march. Wearing his slender sword of digger steel at his side, the king mounted the steps before the castle keep to address the throng of warriors who gathered in the courtyard within the lofty walls.

The banner of the Golden Lion flew over his head, and enough torches flared within the whitestone walls to light the plaza as bright as day. Takian saw the steel helmets of loyal knights, the bristling pikes of stalwart Halvericans, the bows and swords and lances and axes that formed the weaponry of a thousand brave men. Half of the hundred knights of Carillonn were here, as well as brave Myntarian spearmen and veteran Thutan javelin-casters.

"The enemy is on the march once again," declared the monarch, his tone echoing sternly from the high walls. "There can be no doubt that his objective is our city."

"He shall not have it!" cried one burly warrior, waving a battleaxe over his head.

"He shall not!" echoed Takian. "Nor shall he, on the morrow, be allowed to drive within sight of our walls! We march to the south, men—to meet the enemy under to-morrow's skies!"

The roars of approval rumbled upward from the massed troops, and for a moment Takian felt that emotion as a hopeful thing, a sense of promise that pulled him from the miasma into which Bristyn's disappearance had plunged him.

Then he remembered that she was still gone, and that the hope of these men was for victory in a desperate holding action—a mere prayer that they could delay the onslaught against the marbled city for a day, perhaps two.

And with his memories the night was dark again, and very, very cold.

— 3 —

Gandor—the castle is lost! Flee!

Bristyn tried to send the message silently, to urge the faithful captain to bring his detachment of men from Shalloth while they still had a chance.

Each time she looked skyward, it seemed that the *Dreadcloud* was closer. The huge blob of darkness blocked out half the sky, looming forward and upward as a seething, churning mass of angry vapor. The duchess could see flares of brightness within the cloud, heard the sharp explosion of violent thunder. As yet none of that fury had been directed against the ground, but she had no doubt as to the skyship's eventual target.

Castle Shalloth would be blasted to pieces. Even worse, whoever remained within those walls was certainly, inevitably, doomed. Bristyn saw the fate of those brave men as clearly as if their flowing blood already slicked the ground before her.

Yet there was no way to carry that warning. Still bound to the rope held by the brutox, she stood on a low hilltop several miles away from the fortress. Winds whipped dust from the ground, brushing the matted strands of her long hair across her face—any desperate shout of warning would be lost in the gusts, even before her captors silenced her.

The darkmen crowded the hilltop, apparently vying for the position of honor next to the stinking, sparking minion. Bristyn felt herself elbowed aside, within the limitations of her tether. The sweaty, grimy bodies of the bandits gave off the acrid, gagging odor of Darkblood, but she allowed them to press close, to move past her.

Something jabbed painfully into her side, and she flinched away from a filthy, bearded swampman, fearing he had thrust his weapon at her. He ignored her reaction, pushing past and trying to wedge between a pair of his fellows, to touch the brutox's blood-slickened skin. The duchess realized that she had felt only the hilt of the man's sword, which jutted upward from the scabbard at his waist.

On an impulse she tumbled against him. The bandit, still intent on pushing forward, merely cursed and elbowed her away. When she fell back, the dull steel of his shortsword, blade held low, gleamed in her hands.

Heart pounding, Bristyn dared not look around, fearful of drawing attention to herself. No one, apparently, had noticed her theft. The smelly, hot men pressed forward with growing intensity, and she twisted to the side, slipping behind a burly shoulder.

Carefully, she twisted the blade against the leather strap of her tether, hoping that the bandit had been meticulous enough to keep his weapon sharp. Almost groaning in dismay, she saw that he hadn't—the edge, at first, barely scuffed the leather thong. Slicing hard against the line, she sawed determinedly, using a subtle motion of her wrists, fearing every second that the tugging would draw Direfang's attention. Yet the brutox seemed rapt, almost hypnotized, by the sight of the looming skyship. The darkmen shared their master's awe, still pressing close to his side.

Abruptly Bristyn understood that this agitation worked to her advantage. With men shifting and pushing each other, the tether in Direfang's paw would be subjected to many tugs and pulls, and the brutox would be unlikely to notice her cutting.

She sawed with more energy, catching a loop of the tether between her knees. Holding it tightly, giving herself resistance to the cutting, she swiftly drew the shortsword through the strap. A dozen cuts later the tether fell away— she was freed from the brutox, though her wrists were still bound together.

Hopes flaring, she tried to quell her desperation and formulate a plan. Holding the blade below her waist, pointed straight down, she took a step backward, and then another. The darkmen actually cooperated, surging anxiously from each side, eager to draw closer to the brutox. Steadily she backed away, sliding to the side each time she felt a rough hand on her arm, or a burly shoulder wedging against her back.

She was surprised by how quickly she reached the edge of the circle. Now she dared to look around, seeing only the shadowy overhang of the forest a hundred paces behind her. She remembered something Rudy or Danri had told her—that minions couldn't see in the dark any better than humans, and she allowed herself to hope that she could vanish into those shadows.

Her eyes rose to the castle, where the torches of the watchmen still glowed and flickered at the gates and atop the walls. Again she prayed, silently, for Gandor Wade to take his courageous garrison and flee. Lightning already flared along the underside of the cloudship, seething and billowing, the great dark shape seemed to gather its might directly above the towers of the proud fortress.

Checking that none of the men were watching her, Bristyn twisted the blade around, holding it with her elbows and forearms while she frantically sawed through the bonds at her wrists. Finally she pulled her hands apart, flexing her fingers against the numbness that threatened to deaden her grip on the sword.

Then she turned and fled, sprinting toward the woodland shadows, striving to glide silently over the smooth, but unseen ground. Her efforts carried her for a dozen steps before she tumbled into a brittle bush and fell, with a crackling of dry, breaking branches.

By the time she scrambled to her feet, shouts of alarm had risen to a thunderous chorus behind her.

— 4 —

Twenty hours after he announced his battle plan, Takian's force was in position, blocking the south road into Carillonn—and that road still lay empty before them. The men were emplaced across a low ridge overlooking several miles of the highway, beyond which the route vanished into a gap between two forested hills.

Just past the road sprawled a soggy wetland, a reedy marsh expanding from the center of a shallow, silt-bottomed lake. The road curled around the shore of the marsh and approached the elevation, which was called Mallard Ridge, at an oblique angle. If the minions followed the easiest course of advance they would strike Takian's right flank first, then gradually engage the center and finally the left.

"Maybe they got held up in the bottomlands—a wet road, or tangled timber," suggested the captain of the Golden Lions.

"They'll be here soon enough," the king replied with certainty, nodding at the smoking pyres that marked the enemy's progress through the wooded hills.

"At least the wood's green there—the bastards'll have to work to keep their damned fires going! Now, with your permission, sire, I'll see to my knights."

"Yes, good. You know that your attack is the key."

"I'll be watching for your flag, sire!" With a snapping salute, Jaymes clapped his gauntlet to his chest, then wheeled his great warhorse around. Chain mail, masked by a skirt of golden silks, screened the steed's legs as it cantered easily along the grassy turf. Shortly the captain disappeared down the slope of the ridge, joining the heavily armored horsemen gathered in a dense pine grove. This, too, was part of the plan—the riders, some of them Knights of Carillonn and others the heavy horsemen of the Golden Lions, were to remain out of sight until Takian ordered them into the battle.

The king was well-pleased with his deployments. He had scouted this ground a month before, in the possibly futile hope that the enemy would not converge upon Carillonn in a simultaneous attack from two directions. In fact, he had located a potential battlefield along the west road as well, so that he would be able to strike at the first, careless advance from either direction.

He knew that his battle would not stop the invasion to-day, would not even prevent the eventual siege of Caril-lonn. Yet he hoped that the enemy would be badly bloodied, that the minion commander would think twice before venturing aggressively against the human defenders. Takian's primary objective was to gain time, and he knew that he had a good chance of accomplishing that.

Yet a spark of doubt and fear quickly became a blazing torch, a burning question: time for *what*? There had been no sign, no message, from the High Prince—and it had become increasingly clear that the royal heir of Carillonn was the only leader who could actually unite all the dis-parate forces of Dalethica.

And there was no Bristyn Duftrall. In the dark heart of the king's awareness, he felt an utter emptiness, a void that quashed any attempt to muster his hopes. Determinedly, he pushed self-pity aside, knowing that too much depended on the decisions he would make in the next hours.

"Sire . . . there they are." Randart spoke quietly at Tak-ian's elbow.

Immediately the king focused on the impending fight. He saw the ripples against the morning sky, located the terrions by careful scrutiny. Dozens of his men wielded heavy crossbows, and he knew that their eyes, too, would be turned to the sky.

Even in the distance, the minions on the ground were distinguishable as individual creatures. A series of black dots advanced, spreading into a wide skirmish line and striding through the tall grass with long, gliding steps. These were stalkers, minions capable of treacherous shape-shifting and hypnotizing stares. Though fast, they were also slender and frail compared to the kroaks, and the king knew that the stalkers would move to the sides before the attack began in earnest.

Still, he sensed his enemy's eagerness, now that the min-ions had located the human army. Swiftly the horde of Das-sadec formed into vast, dark blocks of kroak companies, spreading out along the road, facing Takian's line along the low ridge. Several of these dense formations advanced along the roadway, trying to push around the right flank of the defenders' position on the low ridge. A rattle of swords rang out as the probing force aggressively tried to dislodge the heavy infantry and pikemen that Takian had emplaced across the thoroughfare. The king watched with satisfaction as his strong right flank quickly deflected this exploratory advance.

If the minions were nervous about the large, shallow lake to their left rear, they gave no sign. Instead, they advanced en masse, uttering deep bellows, grunting and stomping savagely. The ground shook underfoot as the kroaks, lashed on by brutox overlords, swept toward the men of Carillonn and Galtigor.

Because the ridge curved away from the road to the left, the minions attacking the right struck first, as Takian had predicted. The king watched as, one by one, huge companies of kroaks smashed into different segments of his line, but now they were met by shield walls and the slashing longswords of veteran foot soldiers. The humans held steady as more and more minions roared into the fight.

Soon the enemy closed with the center, which was held by resolute infantrymen of Galtigor. Steadily, relentlessly, the waves of minions pressed forward. The human line held, though shrieks of pain and the hoarse commands of sergeants indicated the desperate fury of the fight. Acrid sparks flashed through the air, and spuming, smoldering piles of dead brutox lay scattered across the ground as, with a sudden rush, the defenders drove back the threat to the right.

From his saddle atop Hawkrunner, Takian finally saw the last of the minion companies engaged with the very left flank of his line—a thin formation, a skirmish line really, of Halverican axemen. They would not be able to hold for long. Even as Takian watched, the mountaineers wavered and began to fall back. Soon the left flank curled inward, men instinctively withdrawing in a faster and faster retreat.

"Now—signal the knights!" Takian barked. Randart

quickly hoisted a standard, a pennant unfurling to reveal the sleek Golden Lion snapping in the wind. The silken flag streamed and sparkled in the sunlight, visible across the field and beyond.

Even above the din of battle Takian heard the thunder of the heavily armored horsemen—at least, he imagined that he did. Soon he saw them, banners trailing from lances, riders galloping into view from the concealment of their grove. As a long, thin line they advanced, lance-tips glittering in the rising sun.

The Halverican skirmishers continued to fall back, and the minions, oblivious to disaster, pressed their perceived advantage. The knights of Carillonn and Galtigor struck the monstrous company in the rear, trampling a hundred kroaks in the first seconds of the assault. Lances pierced the creatures, and hooves crushed and smashed, pounding in with the force of an avalanche. The panic was instantaneous, kroak and brutox breaking ranks together, fleeing the keen steel and crushing steeds.

Like a surging wave, and equally difficult to resist, the heavy knights plowed through more ranks of their enemy. The Golden Lions swerved left, the Knights of Carillonn to the right. Frantic with fear, minions fled in droves, and their terror was contagious, rippling through the enemy army far in advance of the arrival of the deadly knights.

Everywhere the human line advanced, and now the minions reeled, collapsing between converging lines of determined infantry and those implacable, crushing knights. Takian rode at the head of his own bodyguard, slashing with his keen, Faerine-forged blade. Hawkrunner kicked and plunged, breaking kroak limbs, smashing brutox skulls with iron-shod hooves.

Falling back into the marshy ground at the lakeshore, the terrified minions grew more frenzied as they sought to avoid the hated water. But their ranks were too close, the situation too confused, for strength and numbers to come to bear. Panicked kroaks turned and fled from the vengeful humans, pressing their horror-stricken fellows into the marsh and lake—where these wretched minions wailed, thrashed, and died. The men of Dalethica chopped and slashed at the edges of the rapidly diminishing formation, working great slaughter, raising weapons in arms weary with fatigue—but propelled by victorious energy, and the long-awaited chance to work vengeance on the despised invaders.

"Sire!" Jaymes found Takian in the midst of the fight and pushed his charger to Hawkrunner's side. The king whirled, weapon upraised, and the captain recoiled from the fanatical intensity in his liege's eyes.

Slowly Takian's eyes focused on the Golden Lion, now torn and bloodstained, emblazoned across Jaymes's breast. "What—what is it?" demanded the king.

"The second echelon draws into sight," warned the knight, as soon as he had Takian's attention. "We must withdraw—now!"

"Aye—sound the retreat," ordered the king, observing another column of minions marching into view from the gap between the hills. He wanted to offer battle to this foe, as well, but he knew that there was a purpose—however mysterious—to his surviving.

— 5 —

Bristyn didn't dare look over her shoulder. Propelled by raw fear, she sprinted over the dark ground, clutching the shortsword in both of her hands. The crashing footsteps and hungry cries of her pursuers roared terribly near, and at any moment she expected to feel the clasp of a hand on her shoulder, or the tackling grasp of a large, hairy body.

When that touch came, she knew what she would do— indeed, her mind focused on that event with a grim clarity that left no room for hesitation, doubt, or compromise. When the first of the darkmen caught her, she would turn and stab him, aiming for the throat. Then she would fight like a cornered tigress, killing as many as she could, battling until she herself was slain.

A darker shadow loomed ahead and she knew that she had reached the trees. Here she swerved, cutting along the edge of the woods, fearing that the tangled undergrowth within would trip her. Yet the smooth appearance of the ground was deceiving, for she immediately stumbled over a root, catching herself before she fell, then resuming her desperate flight.

The shouts of the darkmen had faded, but a quick glance back showed grim, running shapes just a few paces back, Rat's leering eyes blazing in the lead. A cascade of sparks outlined the brutox, lumbering along in the midst of the bandits. Now the footsteps of her nearest pursuers were audible, a cadence of death knelling in her skull, overwhelming even her rasping breaths.

She was climbing a hill, still skirting the forest. The looming bulk of the *Dreadcloud* rose to the side, and—as if in furious reaction to her flight—that black mass suddenly released a rippling volley of lightning over the castle. Bristyn groaned audibly as she saw the highest tower—the parapet where she had said goodbye to Gandor Wade—outlined in blue fire. In another instant the flames exploded and the tower vanished in a splintering cascade of stones.

She veered around a boulder and suddenly she was in the midst of several stony outcrops. She faltered, leaning against one of the rocks, gasping for breath and knowing that she could flee no farther. Lifting the blade, the dutchess spun around with implacable determination, ready to kill the first of the bandits—and as many more as Baracan would grant her.

Another blast of lightning ripped the night, sparking brightness amid the rocks as Rat leapt into view. The sharp-toothed darkman skidded to a halt, but not before Bristyn's blade hacked downward, carving through his neck and gouging deep into his chest. With an angry grunt she raised the weapon, ready as two more wild-looking bandits surged into view.

But these fell before they reached her, and suddenly she was surrounded by men—*good* men, wearing the breastplates of Shalloth, wielding weapons uncorrupted by the taint of Duloth-Trol.

"My lady!" Gandor Wade's voice was a frantic gasp. "Fall back—we'll handle this lot."

She gave in to a dull sense of relief—the captain had heard her silent plea, had in fact departed the doomed fortress! "Flee!" he repeated sternly.

In the end she fought at their side, and the steady courage and keen steel of loyal guardsmen quickly halted the onslaught of the ragged darkmen. More of Shalloth's men-at-arms appeared, slashing and chopping with grim pleasure, exacting a price in blood for the loss of their castle and their realm. Within minutes the surviving bandits and their brutox master had disappeared into the woods, pursued by several of Gandor's trusted swordsmen.

"How . . . how is it that you're here?" asked the duchess, looking at the castle. Torches still flared from the battlements and gatehouse, while the lightning barrage of the *Dreadcloud* ravaged the keep.

"They burn for a long time," Gandor admitted, with a tight smile. "When we saw that cloud roll in, we knew we were in a hopeless plight. We started for Carillonn after dark tonight—and were just on our way along yonder road when we heard the sounds of your pursuers. But you, lady—why haven't you reached the safety of the marbled city?"

"It's too complicated to explain right now," declared the duchess, still trying to catch her breath. "But let's get on the road—and we can talk as we ride."

EIGHT

Tarclouds

Flying, by wing or Aura, is the ultimate risk—to
attain lofty heights while perched a mere
windgust away from disaster.
—TALLY OF LIVES

— 1 —

"That must be why they call them diggers!"

Neambrey, gliding high in the air above Darkenheight
Pass, was so impressed by the labors of his fellow Faerines
that he voiced his realization aloud. He dipped a slender,
leathery wing and curled around for a better look.

The wall of square stone blocks already rose higher than
a green drackan's length, even if you included the tail! Not
that Neambrey believed that one of the great serpents could
actually balance so outstretched, but it amused him to think
of mighty Borcanesh, or even Verdagon himself, giving it
a try.

Wheeling over the lofty barrier, the young drackan saw
that the wall extended across the full breadth of the gorge
that was Darkenheight Pass. Furthermore, the diggers had

excavated a huge trench on each side of the barrier, and were erecting a battle parapet across the top, protected by a rugged rampart. There was no gate, no aperture of any kind, in the surface of smooth stone.

Several burly Faerines waved at the swooping drackan, and he roared a reply, grateful to see the mighty gigants standing guard. Neambrey, together with Verdagon and Borcanesh, would also remain in this neighborhood, and he felt certain that any minion onslaught would be sternly and quickly repulsed.

Above, a rank of High Guardians sat atop the craggy mountain, stony and patient as they watched the barrier take shape in the pass. Danri had been right, the drackan reflected—the protectors of the Watershed had seemed to favor the work of the Faerines at Darkenheight.

Still, Neambrey had his own job to do. Squinting against the acrid air, the gray-green drackan dove southward along the course of the Darkenheight Road, winging over the Sleepstealer's realm. He had chomped several mouthfuls of snow from an Aura-bright glacier, and was ready to breathe a cloud of killing frost at any minion who dared to show his face. Now the pressure of the Aurafrost swelled his belly with a solid, but not uncomfortable, fullness.

Yet the skies—and even the landscape of Duloth-Trol— seemed utterly empty of life. Neambrey remained alert for terrions, but he knew that Borcanesh and Verdagon had scoured the air of the flying minions at the time of the Faerine counterattack. He hoped, and believed, that he would be safe during his brief reconnaisance.

The stone walls of the gorge were as steep, as rugged and sharp here, as they were in Faerine—but there the resemblance ended. The mountains of Duloth-Trol were draped in slick black goo, the tarry gunk of Darkblood smearing the rugged landscape as commonly as did snow on the other side of the Watershed.

The smell, acrid and rotten at the same time, was overpowering, and when Neambrey took too deep a breath, he choked, gagging out a reflexive cough that almost expended

the Aurafrost contained in his swollen belly. Biting back
the explosion, he blinked, trying to clear the stinging air
from his eyes. When he could see again, he confirmed that
the black scar of the road remained empty of minions or
their lumbering bloodwagons.

He flew far enough to determine that no sinister traffic
moved anywhere along the road leading toward the pass.
Perhaps the Sleepstealer's legions would come in the future
and make a great attack against the digger wall. But as
Neambrey wheeled about and beat his wings, striving to
return to the pleasant air and balmy Aura of Faerine, he
was unconcerned about such an attack. His chest swelled
with martial determination as he pictured himself sweeping
over a rank of kroaks, blasting them with his frosty Aurabreath.

A gush of air suddenly swept around the drakan, sending
him cartwheeling through the skies. Frantically he stroked
his wings, righting himself and groping for altitude as a
huge green shape arced out of its dive to soar beside him.

"Pay attention, Little Wyrm!" Borcanash admonished.
"If I was a terrion, you'd have a bite taken out of your
wing right now."

"No! I'd have ... well, the terrion ... *I* can bite too,"
Neambrey retorted, embarrassed as the big green glided
easily beside him.

"Excuses don't work when you're dead," Borc replied,
grinning wickedly and displaying his dagger-long fangs.

"You're right," the youngster admitted, chagrined. "I
was busy looking at the ground ..."

"No minions here, are there?"

"Uh-uh." Neambrey shook his head firmly. "They're
not even trying to come up the road."

"That's strange, but welcome news anyway. I guess the
three of us gave them a pretty good pounding back at the
pass."

"Well, the diggers and gigants helped." The drackan
half-breed wasn't prepared to accept all the credit for the
victory. "And now they've got that wall up plenty high."

"True enough," admitted Borc, not taking offense. For a moment Neambrey basked in the conversation, remembered that, barely weeks earlier, the elder greens thought of him as little more than a newtling. Now he was a regular warrior—even a war leader, since it had been Neambrey himself who had brought drackankind into the struggle against the Sleepstealer.

"Where's Verdagon?" he asked, as the two serpents winged toward the pass, soaring high above the diggers who labored to finish the top of their wall.

"He's planning to meet us at the Cloud Glacier, after he checks on the minions in the Suderwild."

For an hour the pair flew over the swirling valleys and smooth-sided peaks of the Bruxrange. They skirted the height of Banishment Peak, where Neambrey's wings had first burst forth from their adolescent shell and borne him into flight. Finally they settled onto a frosty promontory beside a coiled, emerald-colored elder drackan.

"It is past the appointed time," Verdagon intoned, glaring at the two new arrivals. "Know that it is written: 'Tardiness is the mark of one who would ever be late.' "

"Sorry," Neambrey apologized breezily. "But we wanted to have a good look along the road." Quickly he and Borc reported on the lack of minion activity.

"Seems like the same thing in Suderwild," Verdagon said. "They're just lolling about in their camps. They must have heard about the closing of the pass, but they're not making any effort to take it back."

"It's because they don't have any Darkblood!" Neambrey declared excitedly. "They can't do *anything* without it!"

"Then we just have to keep a good eye on the pass, and the war is all but won!" Borcanash concluded smugly.

"Correct," Verdagon concurred. "For it is written: 'Without an enemy, one cannot make war.' "

Neambrey nodded, encouraged. Yet as he looked across the mountains, tried to imagine the breadth of the Water-

shed, he knew that there was more to this struggle than
their own little corner of the world.

— 2 —

Nicodareus tore at the wall of black stone, clawing pieces
of rock with his talons, tossing them over his shoulders,
then butting the unfeeling wall with his horned forehead or
crushing a boulder with a bite of his fanged jaws. It pleased
him to imagine that the bedrock of Agath-Trol was the flesh
of the stubborn Iceman. Violently he rent another square
of hardened shale with blows of his taloned paws, then
snapped forward to tear a great shard away with his teeth.
Spitting the boulder to the side, he lowered his head and
once again battered at the rock with his horns.

For a numbing interval Nicodareus labored, digging ever
deeper. He doubled back and created winding loops, excavated deep pits and concealed them with sheets of frail,
gossamer Darkblood that perfectly matched the appearance
of the floor. He created slides that dropped a hundred feet
into pools of Darkblood, and crushing traps of loose rock.
He dug numerous pitfalls, plunging shafts into the darkened
depths of the palace.

At the bottom of one such deathtrap the Lord Minion
was about to turn and climb when a hollow noise attracted
his attention. With driving force he kicked the heel of his
foot downward, and felt a shell of rock crumble away.

He tumbled through the collapsing layer into an open
space, sprawling atop a long shape that was stony hard, yet
not stone. Dry, musty air puffed out of the tomblike enclosure, stale from millenia of confinement. Rearing back, the
Lord Minion prodded at the thing, brushing away dirt and
debris, defining the outline of a large, tapering head and a
squat and scaly body. Four short legs, each tipped with
stubby claws of shiny metal, were tucked into the monster's
flanks.

Stepping to the fore of the beast, Nicodareus saw the

blunt snout, the sharply pointed horn. The whole body was shaped like a giant wedge, expanding to the rear, and a series of armor plates laid one over the other protected the broad back.

Abruptly he realized that this was a Deep Guardian— and he recoiled instinctively from the creature. Guardians of both varieties were the mortal enemies of Lord Minions, and the Eye of Dassadec regarded this one with keen hatred and stiff-winged fear. Yet there was no sign of vitality in this creature, and when Nicodareus looked more closely he concluded that the ancient being was virtually petrified.

His master must have entombed it in this narrow, airtight chamber in some long-ago era, a time predating the Lord Minion's memory. At first, Nicodareus merely wondered how it had come to be here, but further thoughts soon quickened in his mind. He crouched before the mindless beast and examined the crushing mandibles, touched the diamond-hard claws that could excavate through solid rock better than anything in the Watershed.

Stroking his own clawed digits over the single horn, Nicodareus finally pushed and twisted, arousing no response, and even his mighty strength could barely move the wide, neckless head. Yet he felt curiously certain that the creature was not dead. Deep Guardians were ancient, sunless beings, capable of hibernating for centuries on end. This one had merely done so for a very long time.

Passing around to the Guardian's flank, the Lord Minion pulled at one of the steel-hard plates, a shelf of bone tapering over the creature's back. With wrenching force, he found that he could raise the plate slightly. When he used both hands, digging his talons into the bone, he was able to rip the giant scale free. The gap in the armor exposed a small patch of white, stony flesh, and when he touched this wound Nicodareus felt the faint flicker of the Deep Guardian's vitality.

Seized by an idea, the Eye of Dassadec reached upward from the pit and caught one of the ubiquitous trickles of Darkblood that spilled down the labyrinth wall. Cupping his palms, he gathered a small puddle of the stuff, then turned back to the entombed creature.

He allowed a little of the liquid to trickle between his hands, splattering it into the wound he had gouged in the Guardian's back. A soft wail thrummed, growing louder as Nicodareus splashed more of the toxic stuff into the wound, becoming a shriek of agony ringing through the ground. And then the Lord Minion felt the creature tremble and cringe beside him.

When he saw one of the sturdy front legs twitch, the Eye of Dassadec was ready to take the next step. He splashed the rest of the Darkblood onto the stone wall before the Guardian's head, and waited. For a long time he wasn't certain if the thing was moving, but eventually he discerned the sharp horn easing forward. Abruptly the snout, tipped by that wicked spike, jabbed hard, splintering the Dark-blood-spattered rock into a crumbled surface of loose stone.

The Deep Guardian reached forward with stubby claws, pulling the loose rock away, driving the broad body forward with those powerful rear legs. Nicodareus splattered more of the Darkblood against the rock wall, and the monster began to dig in earnest.

Quickly the Lord Minion perceived a great benefit to himself, and he started to guide the creature, splashing Darkblood and goading with pain, forcing the Deep Guardian to excavate new paths for the labyrinth. He directed his slave with cruel glee, designing increasingly intricate twists and turns, making larger chambers than ever before. For a time he had the beast create a series of interlinked, identical five-sided rooms. Then he expanded into wider passages, with deep channels scored down the center to accommodate a steady flow of the Sleepstealer's nectar.

The work proceeded well, and the labyrinth continued to grow. The maze became a winding deathtrap leading into the depths of the great fortress, to the liquid well holding the Heart of Darkblood.

Yet with all his cruel ingenuity, and with the proof of his labors expanding all around, Nicodareus was shamed by the bitter knowledge that, for now at least, he was little more than bait in a trap. It was only small consolation to turn to his Deep Guardian, trickle Darkblood into the festering wound of its back, and let the creature's agonized cries shake the bedrock of the labyrinth.

— 3 —

The tiny figure darted from the cover of an alcove, scooting along the edge of the corridor so quickly that he couldn't be seen, even though two sylvan courtiers strolled right by. In a blur he whooshed around the next corner, skidding to a stop amid the foliage of several decorative fig trees.

Haylor concealed himself among the greenery, drawing several deep breaths to restore his stamina. In a flash he was gone again, whisking around a bend in the corridor, darting and dodging through a room full of apprentice Auramasters—not one of whom even suspected his presence—and then diving out the other side.

Once again he halted, panting, looking around watchfully with his bright eyes. As always, flashmagic was exhilarating, but exhausting. Still, he knew that two more bursts should bring him to his destination.

Again he took off, racing down a wide corridor, past an intersection where several guards flirted with a serving girl. She laughed at some suggestive remark, smoothing the dress that had billowed slightly with the wind of Haylor's passage. In another eye blink he was behind a bench in the hall, restoring himself for the last dash. He took a breath and sprinted down the corridor, diving unnoticed between the two Royal House guardsmen, finally coming to rest in the plant-lined corridor leading to the Scrying Pool.

Here, at last, he could relax. The little Faerine strolled along, relishing the pleasant musk of loam and moss, the dewy scent of fragrant blossoms. Too soon he reached the Pool of Scrying, where he knelt and filled a small waterskin.

He rose to the sensation of movement behind him, and turned to see the Royal Scion, clad in the simple robe of an Auramaster, standing near the shore of the pool. At the sight of the diminutive intruder, Mussrick Daringer's mouth curved into a startled smile, and he tipped his head graciously.

"Hello," he said. "I didn't expect to find you here."

— 4 —

"We're sinking."

Raine's tone was cool and informative, utterly lacking in fear, but when Rudy saw the pillar of black stone sliding past the careening Auracloud, he knew that the danger was very real.

"More Aura!" he gasped. Not daring to look at her, he stared straight ahead into the void of smoky cloud, struggling to concentrate, trusting Raine to hear him and to answer his thirst.

Rise—he turned all the force of his will to the mass of magical vapor supporting them.

Moving with apelike precision on its hands and feet, the High Guardian climbed down from the summit of the skyship. The creature probed silently through the supplies, took a long pole, and steadily worked its way to the bow. Standing like a figurehead, it brandished the shaft in both hands. A jagged, rocky obstacle swept from the murk and the Guardian reached out with the pole, ready to push off, but Rudy's firm guidance pulled the skyship upward before the shaft could touch the rock.

Another spearlike peak appeared, this time off the starboard bow. The Guardian moved across the Auracloud with deliberate grace, clinging to the spongy surface with two feet and one hand, holding the long pole with the other hand. Rudy grimaced in the mental effort of steering, and the cloudship slid serenely to the side again before the Guardian needed to bring its shaft against the rock. With a

shuddering scrape, the spongelike surface vibrated beneath
the Iceman's feet, and he tumbled to his knees. Still he
maintained his tight focus, and the skyship gradually rose,
listing away from the rocky obstacle.

"Stay there," Raine urged. She tossed him a loop of
rope that he mechanically wrapped around his waist as he
continued to guide the cloud with the force of his mental
power.

He was vaguely aware of the Woman of Three Waters
as she kindled a fire in their small brazier. Steam hissed as
she trickled Aura onto the coals, and the Iceman felt the
surging response of the cloud as it was renewed. But still
the skyship was sluggish, and he knew the toxic skies of
Duloth-Trol strove to drag them down.

They pressed on, steadily plunging through the foul air.
For a long time they saw no sign of mountainous obstacles.
They were vaguely aware of full darkness and then a dim
gray that was presumably dawn, but for the most part it
was timeless travel, unmarked by any real sense of day or
night.

Then the Auracloud began to pitch again, and the Iceman
sensed the seething strength of a tempest in the overcast
around them. Slowly, he pulled the white skyship upward.
For several minutes the travelers saw one daggerlike peak
after another jutting from the clouds, bases buried in dark
mists like the foundations of islands rising from a vaporous
sea.

A great summit came into view ahead and the Guardian
raised its pole to push them away from the threatened collision, forcing the skyship sideways and upward. Finally,
once again, they seemed to have left the rocky obstacles
below. The Man of Three Waters dared not relax, but he
was heartened as Raine periodically called out that all
seemed clear around the lone white cloud, and the Guardian
remained on silent vigil in the bow.

For another cycle of black night and gray day they
churned along, pitching and surging and rocking through
the skies, making good progress despite a lashing head-

wind. The smoky black clouds folded to the sides, cut by the blunt prow of the skyship, and the stone-skinned figure of their brooding passenger remained like a fixture on the bow.

Gradually Rudy sensed increasing resistance to their forward movement. His head began to hurt, an ache that grew into a steady throbbing as if a hundred diggers hammered inside his skull, laboring to escape. Mechanically he sipped the Aura from the skins Raine handed him, with no recollection of how many he drained in the course of his striving.

Despite his efforts, the pitching and yawing of the Auracloud gained in violence throughout the day, until they bobbed and bounced like a galyon on a stormy sea. Winds howled, and a stinging rain of Darkblood lashed every exposed patch of skin. The spongy deck rose and fell with staggering force, and Rudy leaned forward in subconscious response to his straining will, finally dropping to his hands and knees for stability.

And still his eyes burned, glaring straight ahead, seeking a path through the black murk that roiled and seethed to all sides. A blistering volley of hail rattled down, bashing and steaming on the surface of the Auracloud, ringing a brutal tattoo against the Iceman's skull. Angrily he shook his head, wiping smarting moisture from his eyes, blinking in a vain attempt to clear his vision.

"Rudy!"

Raine's cry, piercing the chaos with the force of its urgency, commanded his attention. He saw her scrambling toward him, bounding like a panther up the steeply rising slope of the cloudship.

Iceman—beware! The Guardian's warning shot into Rudy's mind, a clanging alarm in the wierd silence of these angry skies.

Suddenly a wall was there—a sheer, seamless surface of dark rock, slicked with tarry snow. Rising until it vanished into the clouds overhead, stretching past the narrow limits of vision to either side, it formed a stark barrier and a deadly menace.

"Damn!" Unconsciously Rudy spat the curse, leaning to the side, desperately trying to veer the ship—all the while knowing it was too late.

The Guardian raised its shaft, leaned far forward to meet the barrier. The impact snapped the pole like a twig, and then the Auracloud churned against the cliff. The bow of the skyship billowed back in steaming wreckage—and the Guardian tumbled down, vanishing between the Auracloud and the mountain.

The collision was a shuddering pause in the white cloud's stately progress. Rudy fell forward, desperately clawing for purchase. In the spiraling arc of his vision he saw Raine slip, rolling toward the edge of the cloud.

She caught herself at the rim as the black cliff loomed beyond. As she looked at him, the Iceman was awed by the serenity on her face—and then the cloud billowed up, burying her in seething vapor.

"Raine—no!" The Iceman's mind fixed on that image as she vanished from sight, and a thousand visions of disaster chilled his brain. All the horror of her fatal plunge at Taywick came back to him, fueling his mind and body with churning energy. He pulled on the rope that connected them, tumbling backward as the end, severed against the rocks, whipped from the murk to lash him across the face. Lurching like the crippled ship it was, the Auracloud continued to pile into the cliff, great sections of the vaporous hull hissing into nothingness from the force of the collision.

"Raine—where are you?" he screamed, slipping farther down the side of the cloud. His only answer was silence, as the black cliff swept past him, sliding eerily upward.

Shuddering, the skyship continued to plunge, hissing and churning as the prow scraped along the precipice. The cliff wall rose through the darkness like a reverse landslide, giving the Iceman a clear and terrifying idea of how fast he was falling. The ship shuddered again, careening against the sheer stone wall. Looking below, Rudy caught a glimpse of the ground, saw that a mass of cracks and fissures covered the barren surface.

The Iceman's last, anguished awareness was a nightmare of despair. Then even that was lost in a blur of rupturing vapor, and steam and Darkblood and Aura that boiled into the air around him.

— 5 —

"Guess what?" Haylor roused Anjell in the dark hour preceding the dawn. She sat up on her bed, blinking and stretching before she saw the little sylve's white teeth gleaming in a wide smile.

"How'd you . . . ?" She started to demand an explanation, then saw the open window overlooking the palace gardens. "Oh."

"So guess, now, guess!" Haylor urged.

"The galyon's coming back!" she said immediately, knowing that she was right—and feeling a giddy sense of relief. "And Danri's not hurt, is he?"

"Goodly guess, girl. Very good. Now tell me, what's the weather going to be like tomorrow?"

Anjell couldn't tell if Haylor was poking fun at her or not, so she shrugged. "It'll be windy if you're around, that's for sure!"

Haylor threw back his head and laughed, and Anjell reflected that this was one of the things she liked about him. He could appreciate a joke on himself better than anyone she knew. Indeed, the days in Faerine had not been boring since she and Darret had met the little sylve.

"What else is going on?" she wondered aloud. Though she already knew the answer, she had to ask: "Has there been any word from Rudy and Raine?"

"Why don't you tell me?" the sylve said, passing a silver drinking bottle over to Anjell. "You can find out, you know."

"I . . . I know that I can," she said, uncertain of why she

was suddenly reluctant. "I have to, I guess. I mean, I think I'm the only one who can help them. Don't you think so?"

"I think you think I think I know the answer, and I do," replied Haylor with an irritating chuckle. "But so do you."

Quickly she made up her mind. "I will."

The Aura was smooth and vibrant, recognizable as the kind Haylor said he got from the Pool of Scrying. She enjoyed the taste, liked the way the tickling pleasure spread throughout her body.

But it was Rudy, she remembered . . . she wanted to know about Rudy.

And then she screamed and twisted in her bed, clasping both hands to her head, thrashing so violently that she fell to the floor. Kicking and crying, she groped for something, *any*thing, but felt herself tumbling into an utter void.

NINE

Milestones

The longest footsteps do not necessarily make
the fastest journey.
—DIGGERSPEAK PROVERB

— 1 —

Takian mounted the steps two or three at a time, reaching
the top of the Rosegate tower as fast as he could, with
Randart trotting right behind. The company of guardsmen
on the fortified battlement greeted him with cheers as he
strode to the rampart and looked across the river.

From this lofty vantage he observed the tail end of his
column as, with many boisterous shouts and whoops, the
men marched across the Rosebridge and returned to the
marbled city. The King of Galtigor could not share in their
celebratory zeal, but he recognized the emotion for the positive sign that it was, knew that these troops had become
stronger, more confident of themselves and their commander.

The victory that the troops were already calling the Battle

of Mallard Ridge had proved they could hurt the enemy, could deliver a sharp setback in the teeth of the minion advance. Hopefully they would realize that their courage and discipline, under Takian's guidance, could succeed against seemingly insurmountable odds.

Suddenly concerned, Takian watched as a company of Myntarians moved through the gatehouse. These weary veterans—a remnant of their devastated western realm's once-mighty army—had been battling the minions longer than anyone. The fighting had taken its toll, visible now to the monarch standing fifty feet above them. Though the company of spearmen had seen only light action in the battle, many of them seemed too weak to walk, and were helped over the bridge by leaning on the sturdy shoulders of comrades. Several wagons full of men trundled beneath the gatehouse, and the king was shocked to observe the red, blotchy skin of these weakened troops.

"Randart—get me word about the Myntarians," he ordered quietly. "Find out if there were more of them wounded than we thought."

"Aye, sire. There was word, in fact, from some of the men . . . something about a fever that hit the company pretty hard," said Randart, then trotted down the stairs.

Critically the king inspected the towers that bracketed the city-side terminus of the Rosebridge. The lofty spires were separated by a short span of space, a lower wall top of battlements that in itself crossed over the mighty, steel-strapped gates. The king had climbed to the very top to get a broader look at his surroundings.

From the elevation Takian looked left and right along the wall. He could see two more bridges, spans of white marble arches crossing the channel of the Ariak. Neither was as broad as the Rosebridge, yet each provided straight access from the west bank to the island, and met the city at a gatehouse as stout and heavily fortified as this one.

Takian made a point of calmly inspecting the local defenses, aware that his example was something these men-at-arms would try to emulate. He saw that this battle

platform, as well as the tower top just across the gate from
here, was garrisoned by a full complement of guards. Arrows, stones, and even bales of oil-soaked straw had been
gathered at each of these strongpoints, ready to rain down
lethally when the enemy made its inevitable attack.

Sturdy gates spanned the gaps between the gatehouse
towers. Though these now stood open to accommodate the
movement of soldiers and refugees, they would be slammed
shut at the first sign of minion approach. Once the mighty,
steel-banded portals were sealed, the entire city would be
encircled by a high barrier of wall and gate.

And the surfaces of the bridges themselves were open to
arrow fire from many of the towers and wall tops. Furthermore, the minions had shown marked reluctance to step
onto any span of wood or stone so long as water still flowed
beneath it. Though Takian hoped that this would prove true
around Carillonn, he was not prepared to take it for
granted—the guards still had orders to close the gates at
the first sign of any threat. If the monstrous warriors refused
to march onto the bridge until the flow of the Ariak could
be dammed, so much the better.

The trapdoor to the tower opened and the king turned to
see Randart climbing onto the battle platform. The sergeant's eyes were grim as he moved to Takian's side and
spoke quietly.

"First word was right, sire. It's a fever, and it came on
fast. Seems to knock the men down, weaken 'em pretty
bad. The physicians are giving them water, but there's not
much else they can do."

"Just the Myntarians?"

"Aye."

"Keep me informed, then . . . and thanks, Randart."

"Of course, sire."

Out of habit Takian turned his eyes to the south, along
the empty road to Shalloth. Soon the advance guards of the
minion army would come along that road, just as they
would advance from the west. It broke his heart to know

that so many realms were lost, half of Dalethica obliterated, vanished . . . like Bristyn.

Again the grief threatened to consume him, rising in a dark tide that set him teetering at the edge of the tower platform. As he had been doing with disturbing frequency, he felt a strong temptation to end his misery, to throw himself to the cobblestones so far below. And as he had done each time before, he banished the notion, telling himself that he was needed—yet still not entirely sure why it was important that he continue to live.

A file of riders emerged from the southern woods, tiny as insects in the distance, and Takian stiffened. All the refugees had abandoned Shalloth days ago—the road had been empty since the last souls had plodded to safety yesterday morning. Yet this movement was curious: not minions, for the distant travelers were clearly mounted on horses. And how could it be that mounted humans were the last to reach safety, when their horses should have moved them faster than the countless thousands of miserable souls trekking on foot?

So who were these mysterious riders?

Angrily he tried to quell the palpitations of his heart— he knew that Bristyn was *dead*, Baracan and all the gods be damned! It was a cruel hope that reared within him, raising his spirits only so that they could again be dashed.

But there . . . was that a banner? A flash of blue, the pennant of Shalloth, sparkled in the bright sunlight, and— surely it was his imagination!—a plume of golden hair trailed from the leading rider. That figure advanced at an impetuous gallop, leaving the armored men of the escort racing to catch up.

Then Takian knew, and his heart swelled with such joy that he felt it must explode.

"Bristyn!" He bellowed her name, scraping his throat with the force of his words, knowing the sound would be swallowed by the wind within a second. He was running then, spiraling madly down the stairway, seizing the handrails as he flew around tight corners. Caution, he told himself—he couldn't break a leg now, because that would mean precious minutes of delay before he held her in his arms.

His stallion was still saddled, tethered to the rail at the guardpost inside the gate. Seeing that the west bridge was still crowded by returning troops, Takian turned Hawkrunner toward the south and in a clatter of hooves the stallion was off, bearing the king along the city streets inside the wall. At the next gatehouse he thundered through the entry and onto the empty Ivybridge. Across the marble span he flew, eyes fastened on the galloping rider. It *was* Bristyn, now clearly visible racing toward him.

Only at the last minute did he pull on the stallion's reins, skidding to a halt as Bristyn's mare drew up beside him. He swept her from the saddle, covering her face with kisses, sobbing with relief into the silken strands of her hair. For a timeless instant he held her, and his world was perfect. She returned his embrace frantically, desperately clinging to him, and he knew that she shared his happiness as Hawkrunner, prancing proudly, carried the two royal riders back to the city.

How she had survived, what had happened to her... these were questions that would remain unspoken, unimportant for now. All that mattered was that she was alive, and that she had returned.

— 2 —

Blackness. Even when he opened his eyes, Rudy was conscious only of the complete, impenetrable darkness of this place. He vaguely sensed that he was lying on his back, and that his flesh and bones were terribly battered. Pain was not merely a sensation—it *formed* him, permeating every fiber of his being.

Agony shrieked through his limbs, slashed and burned his mind, tearing against his consciousness until he could no longer resist. Once more the darkness swelled upward, a merciful blanket, dragging him into the oblivion of blessed relief, burying him for a seemingly endless interval.

Then his nose awakened to the smell—the acrid scent of Darkblood—and he knew that, somehow, he still lived. But he was alive only barely, his body broken, and he was stranded in Duloth-Trol.

Alone . . . or not?

With that thought came full awareness, and a bleak, horrifying remembrance.

"Raine!" he croaked, struggling to sit up. He cried out as renewed pain coursed through him, as if he had been stabbed in the back, or his legs broken by the crush of heavy weights. Rivers of electric, pulsating agony punished him for his reflexive movement, brought a rising surge of bile into his gullet.

He tried to call her name again but his words were choked by a bubble of thick liquid. Gagging, he tasted blood, and he barely had the strength to spit it out, to clear his throat enough to breathe. Now the pain was centered inside him, in the gut and lungs and skeleton of a body still barely alive.

Weakly he reached for the waterskin at his side. Like both his legs, his right arm was broken, and though he gritted his teeth against the pain he couldn't force the fingers to close around the softly sloshing sack. Each effort brought nightmarish waves of agony, but he made himself push through, willing his mind to remain awake.

His left arm seemed intact, though when he reached across his body excruciating pain lanced through his shoulders and down his back. Certainly his spine, too, was broken, but this time his fingers responded to the will of his mind. Clumsily they closed about the waterskin, bringing forth another chorus of vicious punishment as he pulled the nozzle toward his bleeding, gasping mouth.

But when he felt the Aura trickling over his lips, cleansing the blood from his tongue and gurgling down his throat, the Iceman knew that he would survive. The magic of Faerine washed through his system, dimming pain, relaxing the punishing vise that had clamped his chest in such an airless grip. Grimly he clenched his fists, then wiggled his toes, felt them rub against the stiff leather of his boots.

For several minutes he remained still, drawing steadily deeper breaths, feeling the power of Aura knit the wounds of his battered body. All the while he strained his ears, listening for some sound that would indicate Raine was alive somewhere nearby. But there was no disturbance in the bleak surroundings, no wind, no flowing water, nor any sound of life.

Trying to turn his head, he discovered that movement was still punishing, and as a consequence his vision was very little help. The blackness above gradually dissipated into varied shades of darkness, none the least bit heartening. He discerned a sheer cliff face, draped with shiny tarfrost, rising to vanish in the roiling murk of the cloudy skies. Across that sky the overcast pulsed and churned like the inverted surface of a roiling, ink-black stream.

Given the frantic movement of the stratus, Rudy thought it strange that there was no wind scouring across the ground. He felt lightheaded and oddly at peace, until once again thoughts of Raine intruded with the icy grip of fear.

Straining, he turned his head slightly, seeing several large boulders looming nearby, jagged stones jutting upward like a row of sharpened fangs. More significantly, they effectively blocked any attempt to see in that direction. He could only wait for more heartbeats, feeling the excruciating pain gradually fade from his limbs to blend into a dull, lingering ache.

Gingerly he twisted, finally shifting his shoulders and finding them free of pain. Slowly, carefully, he pushed against the ground and this time his muscles responded enough to force himself into a sitting position. He couldn't see much more than before, but now he was determined to keep moving.

Finally, like a newborn calf attempting its first step, the Man of Three Waters rose to his feet. Only then did he turn to encompass all of his surroundings in a sweeping, if slightly unsteady, inspection. He saw a landscape that was jagged, pitted with gullies and outcrops of stone, surfaces everywhere of dark rock or a slick layer of tarfrost.

On one side that sheer cliff rose like a wall. The Iceman had an unfocused memory of a jagged rocky barrier looming out of the murk to gouge his Auracloud, and felt certain that this precipice had been the undoing of his beautiful skyship. Like a great dam, a barrier in the sky, the wall had blocked the Auracloud's flight toward Agath-Trol.

There was no sign of Raine, but he refused to despair. Instead, he staggered to the nearest boulder, a pyramidical block the size of a small house. Using his hands for balance, crawling on his knees, he worked his way upward. His limbs responded with growing agility as the Aura continued to stitch broken bones and torn flesh into a healthy whole.

From the pointed summit of the rock, he saw the nearby wreckage of casks and supplies, splintered boards slick with Aura, glowing brightly amid the foul, black terrain. Steam rose from bubbling pools where the water of Faerine mingled with the caustic and pervasive elixir of the Sleep-stealer. Still there was no sign of Raine, and now fear began to clamor in his ears as he slid down the other side of the boulder, kicking through the wreckage of the doomed Auracloud's cargo.

He took vague notice of one small barrel, still intact amid the rest of the splinters. A coil of rope entangled his feet and he kicked the line away, before advancing to the lip of a deep gully. Fearful of what he might find there, he looked into the shadowy depths.

Slumping with relief, he took in the entire, boulder-strewn floor of the ravine—there was nothing there but rocks and small, stagnant puddles of Darkblood. He could see no body lying on the unforgiving stones, and neither blood nor shred of clothing indicated that Raine had landed anywhere nearby.

Abruptly he stiffened, looking closer, recognizing the battered shape of the High Guardian deep in the shadowy trench. The creature was as motionless as the jagged rocks upon which it fell. It lay on its back, both legs shattered to pieces, leaving a body that ended in a stump at the waist. With a pang of sadness Rudy turned away, nevertheless relieved that it hadn't been Raine down there.

A clattering stone pulled him around, his hand going to Lordsmiter as he looked toward the foot of the precipitous mountainside. With a sprinkling of gravel, a small slide of debris cascaded into view and the Iceman instinctively raised his eyes.

He saw the lithe figure clinging to the cliff face, one foot wedged into a narrow crack, the other dangling free. One of her hands clasped an irregularity in the rock surface, a knob too small for Rudy to see. Her other hand brushed more debris from a small ledge—it was this falling that had first attracted his attention—and then secured a grip.

"Raine—be careful!"

His voice was a whispered croak, taut with fear, as she swung from her left hand, probing with her feet until both were wedged into a narrow, vertical crack. Biting back any further, potentially distracting, exclamation, the Iceman watched in silence, paralyzed by his own horror. He desperately wanted to reach out, to help her, to shout advice. Instead he forced himself to focus on Raine's consummate skill on the cliff wall, and when he did he marveled at her talent, at her keen instinct for every possible option. She stretched and reached with acrobatic grace, clinging to unseen holds like a four-legged spider, working down the cliff inch by painstaking inch.

He tried to imagine what had happened, how she had gotten stranded so far above him. Quickly he concluded that the collision of cloud and cliff must have hurled her against the rock face. As he had plunged to the ground and been smashed into unconsciousness, she had somehow managed to grip the rocks, and now her only hope consisted of descending by strength, skill, and fortune.

For a long time her life was suspended by a fingertip, or the tiniest of toeholds, supports too small for Rudy to identify. He held his breath until at last she reached the relative security of a deep chimney. Bracing her back against one side, her feet against the other, the Woman of Three Waters swiftly lowered herself to the base of the lofty cliff.

They fell into each other's arms, clinging without speaking. Rudy felt his knees shake, tried unsuccessfully to stifle his trembling and his tears. For a few moments, he was full of hope again, determined that their quest for the Heart of Darkblood would continue, would end in success.

Finally Raine stood back, the warning in her expression clear even through the emotion that misted her eyes and flushed the weathered skin of her face.

"Stalkers," she said, pointing north along the vast cliff. "I saw about a half dozen of them, a few miles away. They looked like they were coming toward us."

Rudy glanced again at the mountainside, knowing there was no escape in that direction, short of an exposed climb even more fraught with danger than Raine's perilous descent. A look to the south showed a forbidding ridge of peaks, rising from the rough terrain not a terribly great distance away.

"I found one cask of Aura still intact," he said. "Not enough for another Auracloud, so whatever we do, we'll have to do on foot."

"Any sign of the Guardian?" Raine asked, reminding Rudy of their passenger.

"Yes—I'm afraid he came down in that ravine over there. He's dead."

As Raine shook her head sadly, the Iceman admitted to himself that he, too, would miss the steady presence of the rocklike protector.

"Let's gather what we can of the supplies," Raine said, following him to the steaming rocks, the litter of shattered barrels and scattered rope, charcoal, and provisions. She reached into the wreckage and retrieved the Sword of Darkblood, unwrapping the oilcloth and holding the weapon by its terrion-hide hilt. The midnight blade was concealed by a thin sheath of digger steel.

"Leave it," Rudy said.

"We can't afford to." Raine's tone was as grim as her face.

"Why?"

"It's more than a sword . . . do you remember, when Garamis chased us up the Tor of Taywick, how he used this blade?"

"He appeared damned quickly, that much I recall."

"Well, I *watched* him. He pointed the sword at the place he wanted to go. Then he said the name . . . of the Lord Minion . . . and Garamis was transported to wherever he was pointing, immediately."

"That could be useful," the Iceman admitted, though he was still revolted by the thought of the deadly weapon. "How about if I carry it with the other supplies?"

As he spoke, Rudy knelt beside the lone intact cask of Aura and, with a few slices of his knife, improvised a harness so that he could sling the small but unwieldy barrel onto his back.

"I don't think you should do that," Raine objected. "You don't need the extra weight of the Darkblood sword." Without hesitation, she ungirded her digger blade. "I'll wear it."

Rudy held back for a moment, disturbed, but ultimately forced to admit that she was right. Certainly the blackstone sword was a deadly enough weapon, and she was a skilled swordswoman—more adept than the Iceman himself. Still, the thought of the evil, toxic blade in his lover's hands gave him a fundamental feeling of disquiet.

Raine gathered some of the dried meat, and several of the sacks—some filled with water, others with Aura—that had survived the crash, and bundled the sparse rations into a pack that she could carry on her shoulders.

Meanwhile, the Iceman climbed the large boulder again, creeping toward the crest to avoid appearing against the skyline. Carefully raising his head, he scouted for the approaching stalkers. At first he saw nothing but the expanse of blackened, blasted terrain. Shadowy clouds formed a sin-

ister backdrop, though the only movement visible was the
churning surface of the overcast.

Then a liquid shape slithered through the corner of his
vision and scuttled out of sight. Another, and a third loped
forward, pouncing with catlike grace as they glided from a
gully to concealment behind a large, flat rock. The stalkers
were definitely coming closer.

Perhaps half a mile separated the pursuers from the prey.
The minions advanced on all fours, as fast as racing
hounds, and though Rudy never saw more than two or three
at a time, he suspected that Raine's count had been accurate. Reptilian heads held low, the monsters darted from
one patch of cover to the next, drawing closer in spurts and
sprints.

He slid back down the boulder, already determined on a
plan. Raine looked at him expectantly as she slung a long
coil of rope over her shoulder and shrugged her backpack
into shape, leaning forward to support the substantial
weight.

"I'm thinking that we should just wait for 'em here,"
Rudy said. "They're moving pretty fast. If we try to run
away loaded down with all this stuff, they'll catch us soon
enough."

"I agree, for another reason as well: If we flee, it means
going south," Raine pointed out. "From up on the cliff I
could see that the ground is none too friendly in that direction."

With a quick glance Rudy took in the mountainous bar-
riers indicated by her gesture, and nodded.

"We should ambush them right here," he continued.
"Win, and we're free to go north, without immediate pursuit."

"Good," she agreed.

Quickly the Iceman finished outlining his plan—and this
time it was Raine's turn to bite back a protest in the face
of urgency. "It's our best chance," he insisted. "They'll
be expecting to find someone here—but they can't know
much more than that."

With her mouth set in a tight line of concern, Raine nodded curtly.

"Remember—don't look into their eyes," the Iceman cautioned.

Reluctantly, Raine took shelter in a narrow crevice Rudy had spotted at the foot of the lofty cliff. She was concealed from view within a dozen paces of the Auracloud's wreckage. The Iceman, meanwhile, knelt among the splintered boards to await the minions.

He was not surprised when, after a few minutes, a scaly head rose above the crest of the huge boulder he had climbed earlier. Another joined it, and more, until seven pairs of leather-lidded eyes peered down toward the lone human.

Rudy stood and faced the stalkers, trying to prepare for anything from a sudden rush to a deliberate encirclement. For the moment, he left Lordsmiter in its scabbard—he wanted to look as unthreatening as possible, and he could draw the blade in a second if need be.

The minions scuttled forward, aggressive without being reckless. Walking on their hind legs and armed with long, curving swords, the stalkers stepped down the steep face of the boulder. Rudy noted with chagrin that the monsters' taloned feet gripped the rock easily, even at a pitch that would have sent a cleated climber skidding downward.

The Iceman skirted slowly and deliberately to the side, looking wildly around, staggering in apparent fear and confusion—a frightened victim surprised by attack, desperately seeking any path of escape. The stalkers seemed to buy the ruse, as four of them raced to counter Rudy's maneuver. Their new position placed them with their backs to Raine's hiding place, midway between the man and the woman.

"What are you?" demanded one of the minions, a lanky figure stretching higher than the tall Iceman's head. The words were spoken in a hissing, vile-sounding tongue, yet to Rudy the meaning was perfectly clear.

The bright spots of its eyes flashed, and for just a moment the Iceman saw the dizzying whirl of their hypnotic appeal. Blinking, he refocused on a spot midway between the two groups of minions.

"I am . . . a friend," Rudy declared, not surprised that he could reply in the same sibilant language.

"Liar!" shrieked the stalker, a forked tongue flaring from the fanged jaws. "There are no friends—we acknowledge only masters, and slaves. We can see that you are neither!"

At some unseen command the minions crouched, poised like coiled springs to pounce toward the Man of Three Waters. Rudy drew his blade warily, in expectation of a sudden rush.

But it was Raine who struck first, springing from concealment with silent speed. She cut down two of the creatures with back-and-forth blows of the black-bladed sword almost before the stalkers knew that they had been attacked.

One of the survivors hissed an alarm as Rudy sprang, Lordsmiter gleaming in his hands. The Iceman's powerful blow splintered the sword of the stalker leader, who recoiled in shock at the unexpected attack. The next blow nearly slashed the wicked head from the body.

Before the corpse struck the ground, Rudy flew at the pair of stalkers before him. One of them tried to fight, dying a foolish second later, and he chased the other down in a quick sprint, stabbing it through the back. By the time he turned again to Raine, she had slain another and backed the last of the stalkers against the cliff wall. He ran toward her, but she pierced the monster with a low, rising thrust, pinning it to the rock for a second before she pulled the weapon free.

"Are you hurt?" They asked the question together, answered with a hug of relief.

"If you're still ready, let's get going," Raine said abruptly. "Who knows how many more of these fellows might be on the way."

Under the burdens of scavenged supplies, heavy but not yet crushing, they started along the foot of the towering cliff. They had no map, not even a glimpse of sky to aid with direction, yet they had no choice but to seek a footpath into the dark heart of the Sleepstealer's realm.

— 3 —

Awnro Lyrifell set his brimming mug of dark ale onto the table and meticulously wiped the foam from his curling mustache. With a satisfied smile he leaned back and propped one of his shiny black boots on a nearby bench. Across the small table, Kerri put down her own large mug and did the same.

"Ah . . ." the bard sighed musically. "I've heard Danri sing the praises of this place on many occasions, but even his hyperbole didn't do it justice!"

"The praises of Shalemont, or the Tailings Pub?" asked Kerri with a laugh.

"Both, actually," the bard replied, to a chorus of cheers from the diggers loosely gathered around their large table.

"Both are splendid examples of the best of Faerine," declared a gnarled elder craftsman Kerri had introduced as Hakwan Chiseler.

"With celebrations like no other!" boasted another, to a round of obligatory toasts and a chorus of "Aye-uh."

Two weeks of hiking through Faerine had brought the pair into the realms of the diggers. The arrival of the human bard in the town had, as an event, been overshadowed only by the return of Shalemont's favored daughter and best former barmaid. Quickly a congenial crowd had gathered, and the minstrel had gained material enough for several ballads just from the talk around this table, in this comfortable bar.

The diggers grew pensive as Kerri described Danri's mission in Darkenheight, and many a weathered face turned pale when Awnro told of Rudy and Raine's task— a penetration of the Nameless One's very sanctuary. Other heroes were toasted, and a digger balladeer—whose instrument consisted of three metal drums—rasped a worthy

tale of one Blaze Smelter, a local digger now eulogized as
the Hero of Taywick.

The bard was moved by the ballad, and the ale, and when
he finally wandered off to a bed he slept very well. But the
next morning he and Kerri were off again, this time following rutted paths rather than a smooth road. The weeks of
walking had toughened them both, and though the bard
toted the cask of Aura that had been treated with the Iceman's blood he strode up the slopes with the sturdy gait of
a born mountaineer.

The diggermaid built regular cairns of stones to mark
their path as she led the way through steep foothills, following a variety of paths more suited to goats and eagles
than humans. Nevertheless, Awnro kept up enthusiastically,
remarking rapturously as one after another wonder was revealed.

Each night, now, they camped in the wilderness, each
campsite higher and more remote than the one the night
before. The bard's music flowed as freely as it ever had,
and often he strummed his lute while he and the diggermaid
walked beside a mountain stream or through a flowered
meadow. Everywhere lofty vistas greeted them, but finally
the Glimmercrown itself came into view. That mighty summit dominated the horizon, and they knew that they were
drawing close to the Watershed.

Through these days Awnro sensed that Kerri deeply
missed Danri, but also that hope was alive within her, hope
that was more real than her dreams when she had wandered
through these heights, thinking of Danri digging somewhere underground. Higher still they climbed, Kerri's voice
growing musical with excitement, her steps light and eager.

"This is the place where I remembered that spring," she
said one afternoon, after a long day of steep climbing. The
two of them ambled along a flowered vale above the timberline. High mountains and impressive ridges surrounded
them with an embrace of sparkling snowfields and a brilliant sky of deep azure.

After coming around a shoulder of snow-swept peak,

they entered a narrow swale to find a spuming Aurafall, the water of magic spilling from a spring on a high mountainside, plunging in a long shower to gather in a deep and natural pool below.

"This is a place to start, I think," Kerri said. "A source of Aura, at least. Now, we go down slightly from here . . ."

They followed a path around the side of the ridge, sensing that the Watershed lay just ahead. And then the ridge swept down, and they looked through a saddle in the otherwise precipitous divide. Beyond was a green vista of rolling hills, sloping downward from the summits of the high mountains.

Awnro's throat tightened with the knowledge that he was looking at the Wilderhof—and Dalethica—beyond.

"You were right," he said quietly, unable to master his emotion. "When you walked around up here, imagining your digger under the bedrock at your feet, you were also discovering another pass across the Watershed."

— 4 —

"I just wish everyone would stop worrying about me!" Anjell complained to her mother. "I keep telling you—I'm all right. It's Rudy and Raine who are in trouble!"

Dara, who hadn't left her daughter's side for the last day, remained firm. "When you scream in the middle of the night and I come running in, and I can't wake you up for two hours, then it's *you* I'm going to be watching!"

"But you should be working on your book! You've got to tell the story of the war, of our trip here, before you forget everything!"

"I hardly think that's a danger," Dara replied. She gestured to a quill and sheets of paper on a table across the room. "And besides, I was making some notes while you were sleeping."

"Well, still—Mussrick Daringer didn't have to give me a royal sleeping chamber!" the girl declared. "Someone else needs it—and I don't want to lie around any longer!''

Her mother's inevitable reply was interrupted by the opening of the door, as Cillwyth poked his head in.

"And how is our young maid?" asked the sylvan courtier, poised to retreat should the girl's temper prove as volatile as it had the last three dozen times he had checked.

All at once Anjell felt foolish and petty and guilty. "Please come in," she said. "I'm better." Sighing, she took Dara's hand. "I'm sorry . . . about all my, well—"

"I know." Her mother's smile was warm with relief. "And I want you to know that I *believe* you. It's just that I'm frightened for you . . . and there's nothing we can do for Rudy, except pray, and hope."

"I'll try . . ." Anjell's voice trailed off. In truth, she didn't know how she could avoid having these worried thoughts about Rudy and Raine. For days it had seemed that every time her mind turned to them she felt more scared than the time before—until yesterday's terror-stricken climax, when overwhelming fear had actually knocked her out of her bed.

At least that moment of horrifying darkness had passed. She was certain that her uncle and Raine were alive, somewhere. At the same time, she was pretty sure that something awfully bad had happened to them.

Too, she couldn't let herself believe everything her mother said, about her and her friends not being able to help Rudy. The more Anjell thought about it, the more convinced she became.

There had to be *something* that she could do. She just had to figure out what it was.

Sadly, the sack of Aura that she had kept under the bed was empty, and Haylor had apparently taken his special bottle with him when he disappeared—at least, she assumed that he had sneaked off before her mother came in, because Dara hadn't said anything about him when Anjell awakened. She didn't blame the little sylve for her nightmare any more than she really blamed Dara for making her stay in bed. After all, that was just the way they were.

And of course, Cillwyth was here now, and the young courtier always offered a sympathetic ear and a kindly word. Still, in the depths of her awareness she knew that she had just one real hope.

Only Haylor could help her to understand.

— 5 —

Rock dust trickled from his jaws as Nicodareus lifted his head from the wall of black rock—a wall identical to the surface that had faced him for the countless days since Dassadec had set him to this task. The Deep Guardian paused, sensing its master's distraction, and the Lord Minion casually cut the creature, then trickled more caustic Darkblood into the gaping wound, sending it once more against the unfeeling rock.

The sluggish beast had twisted and changed from the force of the Lord Minion's cruel ministrations. Now the serrated claws of its grinding, scissors-like mandibles gleamed sharp and hard, longer than they had been before, while the wedged body had bloated, scales twisting and curling painfully as the Deep Guardian was corrupted by the poison of Darkblood. Yet it labored as hard as ever, and seemed quite unwilling to offer any resistance to its sadistic master.

Sometimes Nicodareus thought that the presence of the Deep Guardian was the only thing that allowed him to survive. Enslaved by his master, he needed the outlet of a victim of his own—a wretched being he could subject to the cruel whims of his pleasure, and upon whom he could exact vengeance for the multitude of wrongs done by the Guardians to the Lord Minions of Dassadec.

And it seemed that the more pain he inflicted upon the beast, the more diligently it dug. Already the Eye of Dassadec had torn several plates from the arching back. Frequently he spattered Darkblood onto those sores, relishing the sight of the Guardian's suffering. It pleased him to torture and enslave a creature that was conceivably older than the Lord Minion himself.

The labyrinth was already a long network of tunnels, traps, pitfalls and bridges, but still Nicodareus and his slave labored, extending the vast maze surrounding and protecting the sacred chamber and the Heart of Darkblood. The Eye of Dassadec also gathered denizens for the network, vicious and hungry creatures he confined in various portions of the maze. His favorite was a savage killer he called the blutor—this was a hybrid created from the body of a brutox, corrupted and polluted by the blood of the Guardian, and protected by some of that creature's hard, scaly shells. The blutor was released in a large cavern, and it would tirelessly pace there, waiting for the arrival of an actual victim. Until then, Nicodareus amused himself by dispatching kroaks and stalkers into that part of the labyrinth—he derived great enjoyment from the screams of the dying minions, as the blutor toyed with each victim mercilessly before finally administering a killing blow.

But now something disturbed Nicodareus' monotonous concentration, a dim alarm triggered in the recesses of his mind. He snuffled loudly, wiping a paw across his muzzle, alerted by a growing tingle of anxiety. Slowly, like a recovered invalid once again learning to walk, he sent his Sight across his master's realm.

Immediately he located it: a blot of Aura, obscuring the perfect befoulment of Duloth-Trol. The mere presence of the mist was alarming—how could it be that there was such a spoor on this side of the Watershed's protective ridge? The hazy pollution was a powerful stench of magic rising in the midst of the otherwise perfect wasteland.

As always, the liquid of magic masked specific impressions—yet even so, the Eye of Dassadec discerned some very significant things. He saw bodies bleeding Darkblood, distinct images in the midst of magical fog. These were stalkers, and deep wounds proved that they had been slain by weapons. Too, their blood was fresh, trickling from long gashes—indeed, the spoor was so vivid that Nicodareus all but tasted the nectar of his master on his black, dust-coated tongue.

The message of these signs was clear, and it spoke to the Sleepstealer's greatest fear: An enemy had entered the realm, had somehow penetrated far beyond the Watershed, battling and slaying minions on Dassadec's own ground! The invader was on foot, no doubt probing deeper and deeper toward Agath-Trol and the Heart of Darkblood.

And again his master's words came back to haunt Nicodareus. Despite the obfuscation of his Sight, the Eye of Dassadec could have no doubt as to who this intruder might be.

Yet when he thought about it further, it wasn't a portent of doom at all. Rather, it signified a situation of no little potential. When Nicodareus thought of all that might result, the realization brought a resonant chuckle, a gurgling expression of anticipation, welling from the depths of his broad, sinew-encased chest.

TEN

Hail to the Prince

The trappings of monarchy—scepter and
ceremony, robe and crown—can for a time
energize a populace. Still, such symbols have no
more substance than any other illusion.
—SCROLL OF BARACAN

— 1 —

He was the King of Galtigor, regent of High Carillonn and
commander of ten thousand men. She was his queen, a
duchess in her own right, a heroine of Dalethica . . . but on
this night they were a man and a woman in love, sharing
the desperate joy of a reunion that had seemed an impossible hope.

Celebrations in the castle and city roared on without
them, save for a brief appearance by the royal couple on a
high balcony over the castle courtyard. Bristyn waved to a
cheering crowd as people, fueled by the twin pieces of good
news, gave release to long pent emotions. Word of the victory at Mallard Ridge had started the festivities, and the
reports that the regent's bride had not only survived, but

returned to the city safely, charged the carnival atmosphere with additional excitement.

Yet that revelry was only a muted background noise as the couple retired to their apartments. Takian's manservant, Tray Oldar, guarded the outer door, delighted with his instructions: He was to see that nothing disturbed his liege and lady. Alone finally, with quiet delight and gentle, almost disbelieving, wonder, Bristyn and Takian touched, kissed, embraced. The measured hesitation gave way to a frenzied, joyous union. Takian felt all his hopes flaring into passion, and Bristyn cried out in her own jubilation.

Afterward, they talked of pastoral things or lay quietly in each other's arms. Bristyn spoke only a little of her captivity and Takian, likewise, gave few details of the city's preparations for war, or of the previous day's battle.

Only once did the duchess elaborate, telling Takian of the corruption of the darkmen, and of the brutox who had appeared from the sky to lead them.

"But how could Darkblood flow from a spring in Dalethica?" the king asked, grimacing at the announcement of yet another peril.

"Perhaps it's seeping down from the breach in Halverica, traveling underground. Or maybe it was there all along. Gandor Wade comes from the Willowfen, you know, and he says there are lots of old legends about magic lurking there. Even when I was a girl, people used to say that the place was haunted."

"What about the ruins you saw?"

"An old castle stood there once—I think it has a lot to do with the legends."

"You know the stories?"

"Well, the most common one says that an ancient king sought to gather samples of all Three Waters for his collection. He dwelled on a high hill along the River Ariak—there was no marsh there at the time."

"And did he succeed?"

"Briefly. It's said that he had a lovely daughter, and a

brave knight brought him a sample of Darkblood and used it as a bribe to win the daughter's hand. But the king had also been given Aura, by another adventurer, and he thought to use the water of magic to make himself a sorcerer. When he confronted the knight, the reaction of the two waters was enough to destroy his castle and transform the surrounding lands into the fen it is at present.''

''And now there's danger there again,'' Takian reflected grimly.

Yet even the knowledge of one more threat couldn't dampen their joy at their reunion. Alternately serene or giddy, in passionate conjunction or profound communication, they spent the night with little thought of the trials to be faced on the morrow. Refusing sleep, they let the candles burn low and took no note of pale light washing the eastern horizon.

A gentle knock at the door to the royal chambers brought an abrupt return to external concerns, and Takian knew that only something of real urgency could account for the untimely summons.

Still, the king rose from the bed with visible reluctance, and couldn't bring himself to hasten as he wrapped a cape about his muscular frame. Bristyn got up too, robing herself before going to the tall windows as the king grudgingly opened the door.

It was Tray Oldar, and Takian forestalled the man's apologies with a wave of his hand. ''What's happened?''

''The High Prince, sire! Bentram Wayn himself, arrived by galley at the city docks overnight! He's on his way to the castle at this moment!''

Takian's heart soared once more—a third piece of good news in the span of the last half day! He was surprised that the prince was here so suddenly, having expected some sort of advance word. But that astonishment swiftly gave way to his hopes for the aid the royal presence could provide to the city's defense and morale.

''What about troops?'' he asked. ''Any word on a legion from Andaran, perhaps?''

"Word was two galleys in the city harbor," Tray said with a shake of his head. "Though who's to say that there won't be more coming behind!"

"Good point," the king agreed.

"Listen," called Bristyn from the window. She threw open the golden draperies to reveal a sky growing bright with the early dawn, but still sunless. A sound swelled like thunder from the twilit streets. "That's cheering—thousands of people raising their voices!"

"You're right!" Takian stepped to his wife's side, hugging her with a new flush of hope. He turned back to Tray Oldar. "Has the castle been alerted—lords of protocol and such? We should have a proper reception."

"It seems that has been taken care of." Tray cleared his throat awkwardly, advancing into the room and closing the door behind him. "Actually, a party of men dispatched by the prince arrived more than an hour ago. They insisted on taking control of all preparations."

"That's strange," Bristyn said, her puzzlement growing into a frown. "Almost rude, you might say."

"Begging forgiveness, Your Majesties, but you *should* say it was rude," suggested Tray. "They took over with rather more, er, peremptoriness than I thought was called for."

"He *is* the heir," Takian mused. "Still, I thought my communications would have made it clear that we were expecting to welcome him with full honors."

Another knock, this one much more firm than Tray's, sounded at the door. Takian crossed to the portal in three strides and flung it open to confront a tall knight. The man's broad shoulders were draped with a cloak of gold, and upon his chest was emblazoned the head of the High King's white drackan sigil.

"What is the meaning of this?" demanded the monarch, standing at his full height and meeting the man eye to eye. "Surely you can wait until I've emerged from my chambers!"

"King Takian? I'm afraid not. The High Prince will

await you in the throne room. You are to report there immediately!''

Takian flushed, shocked by the man's arrogant tone and bearing. His voice was stern in reply. "I look forward to joining the High Prince as soon as I have dressed."

"He will arrive in the castle shortly. Surely, as regent, you intend to be present to receive him?" The fellow's clean-shaven chin was set firmly as he glared back at Takian.

"It would seem that my services as regent are no longer required, insofar as you have already displayed the presumption to place yourselves in charge of castle affairs." With an effort, the king resisted the urge to hurl other challenges at the man—such as what had taken them so long to get here. Instead, he concluded curtly, "If Bentram Wayn gets to the throne room before I do, then the High Prince can receive *me*."

"But—!" The knight's objection faded in the face of the golden-haired king's glare. "I carry word to His Highness, then," he replied with a stiff bow, before turning on his heel and marching down the hall.

"That is the captain of the prince's Andaran Knights," Tray explained. "Sir Berald, I heard him called."

"I'll see to your robe," Bristyn offered. "It wouldn't hurt to go see him as quickly as you can—Baracan knows we can't afford any further divisions among our own people."

Takian drew a breath. "I know. So many have built their hopes around the prince's arrival. I'll do everything I can to make him welcome."

Yet the ominous feeling lingered as Takian hastily slipped his feet into soft moccasins and shrugged into an overshirt embroidered with the Golden Lion. With his own robe of Galtigor purple swirling from his shoulders, he momentarily considered donning his crown. At the last minute he decided merely to brush his long hair, as usual relying on the majesty of his presence more than the symbols of his reign.

Barely five minutes later he arrived at the throne room which, despite the early hour, was already crowded with courtiers, ladies, messengers, and a few men-at-arms wearing the white drackan symbol. Already new banners had been draped about the room, most of them displaying the coiled drackan outlined in golden thread, with rows of wicked fangs gleaming from the vicious slice of its mouth and leering eyes that seemed to flicker this way and that.

At first Takian had difficulty locating the heir, but, as word of his own arrival was whispered through the room, the crowd parted to give him a path to the throne. Takian stepped forward, increasingly disturbed by the festive air that seemed to pervade the great chamber. He tried to quell his misgivings, knowing that these people needed something to celebrate.

Bentram Wayn had already seated himself in the mighty throne of the High King. Takian's first impression was of a mere boy: The High Prince's face was smooth and beardless, full lips pursed in an expression of tension, humor . . . or fear. Wayn seemed small in his great, golden robe, and his overly large eyes of deep brown darted nervously back and forth around the room before they at last came to rest upon the King of Galtigor.

Takian noticed a tall, silver-haired man standing behind the young prince, and the gold-armored knight, Sir Berald, at his side. Everyone else stood a respectful distance back from the throne.

Now Bentram Wayn regarded Takian with an expression at once anxious and haughty, challenging and curious. The young man's wide mouth creased into a smile as Takian approached, but there was only wariness in the prince's dark eyes.

"Welcome to Carillonn, Your Highness," Takian began, bowing a little more deeply than protocol demanded.

"Thank you," Bentram Wayn replied. "I have been informed that your service as regent has been noble and selfless."

At least the youngster had the good grace to step down

from the throne and incline his head toward the King of Galtigor. Takian grudgingly gave him credit for that, realizing at the same time that his own offended pride was bristling dangerously. He forced himself to remember Bristyn's words, recalling the image of Kelwyn Dyerston, the late High King and Bentram Wayn's uncle. Dyerston had been renowned as a peacemaker, and Takian would not allow himself to betray that legacy with petty bickering.

That memory allowed him to speak graciously. "Your uncle's death was a grievous blow to us all. I simply tried to minimize the damage until you could arrive to assume his place."

"As I have done," said the prince, nodding. He resumed his seat and waved a hand in Takian's general direction. "The time is too soon, by all accounts—I had some years of preparation left before I should have been summoned. But we have learned that events in the world will not always wait until mankind is ready."

"Very true," the monarch replied dryly. "Else this war would not begin for another hundred centuries, or more."

"Quite. And you may imagine that things on Andaran move at a different pace than here in Dalethica."

"I had always thought that Andaran, the island of kings, was in fact a *part* of the realm of man," Takian noted, surprised by the prince's words.

"Certainly it *was*. However, over the centuries, the schisms have grown deeper. Surely my uncle made some reference to the transition when he arrived?"

"Sadly, Galtigor and Carillonn have not been peaceable neighbors until very recently; I did not meet your uncle until he had reigned here for decades."

"Your own contributions to that peace have been made known to me. You are to be commended."

"Thank you, Your Highness." Takian inclined his head. "In view of the enemies of us all, it is well that squabbles among humankind can be set aside."

"Indeed. You couldn't have said that better, eh, Donthwal?" said the High Prince, turning to the silver-haired gentleman behind him. "King Takian, allow me to present my senior advisor, Donthwal. And," he added, indicating the gold-armored warrior, who bowed stiffly, "this is Sir Berald, commander of my knights."

"We've had the pleasure," Takian said coolly. "In truth, any new warriors are welcome, but we can especially use more knights," he added more pleasantly, though the stone-faced Sir Berald gave no indication that he heard the greeting.

"Now, please inform me as to your assessment of the current situation." Bentram gestured to the king with almost insolent casualness.

Again biting back his temper, Takian spoke. "The enemy approaches the city from west and south, in two mighty wings. Perhaps you have heard that we delivered a sharp blow to the southern force yesterday morning, along the heights of Mallard Ridge. It was but a holding action, and we were fortunate to return our own force to the city with very few losses."

"I have been informed. But why hasn't a similar effort been made against the western wing?"

Takian's face flushed, but again he exerted his self-control, reminding himself that this naive prince could have little grasp of what it was like to battle a numberless, tireless foe. He drew a breath and went on to explain.

"Each of these wings vastly outnumbers the entire force available for the city's defense. I dared not risk a pitched battle against either of them. Instead, I chose the ground at Mallard Ridge precisely because it allowed me to concentrate against a portion of the minion army. We inflicted thousands of casualties, for the loss of only a few dozen of our men. Any pitched battle would have resulted in far greater carnage among our people—*your* people. And those are losses that we cannot afford."

"The loss of *Carillonn* is a thing we cannot afford!" declared the prince. "The city of my forefathers must be protected against this scourge—*before* the minions stand on the banks of the Ariak!"

"Ahem," said the silver-haired advisor, Donthwal. Tall and dignified, he looked to Takian like a fellow whose strength was in his intellect, not in his arms.

The prince half-turned with a look of surprise. "Yes—what is it, Donthwal?"

"Perhaps after you have toured the city, seen the preparations that have been made, you will have a better grasp of the situation. It might indeed be wise to delay any peremptory action."

Bentram Wayn scowled, then nodded absently. "Yes, I really should review the troops. Perhaps see some drills, parades and the like? I know it's wartime, but it would only be appropriate to have some kind of display."

"I'm sure that can be arranged," Takian offered, inwardly grimacing at the waste of manpower and time.

But the prince was already moving on, and he addressed the king and regent. "Donthwal has been my teacher for a long time. It could be that he forgets our roles have changed now, that I am at last a noble ruler."

"Forgive me, Your Highness," Takian replied. "But even a king, or a prince, can gain benefits from the counsel of a wise advisor."

"Ah, but life is its *own* teacher. And, to that end, I intend to order an attack against the enemy's western force, as soon as the troops can be mustered! Your minimal success in that ridge battle shall be multiplied threefold or more, and we shall hold the enemy at bay!"

Takian's heart sank—he could think of nothing more foolhardy, or dangerous. Still, he forced his tone to stay relaxed, even friendly. "Surely you want to look around first, familiarize yourself with the city and our defenses."

"It is enough to see this room, to grasp the meaning of my uncle's legacy. As to the defenses, I fear there is too much thinking of defense around here. The key as I see it is to attack!"

Takian despaired at the thought of the butchery that would ensue from Benton's rash plan. "Have you brought legions with you from Andaran?" he wondered.

"Berald commands a company of sixty knights. Their courage and skill shall have a great effect on any battle."

Takian's spirits sank further at the news, then pulsed angrily as the High Prince continued:

"And unlike the warriors of this city, they have not become accustomed to defeat and retreat."

Several of the armed men in the throne room bristled visibly at this remark, and Takian sensed disaster brewing. A fleeting thought occurred to him: He could reject this princeling here and now, and no doubt some of the loyal men of Carillonn would follow his lead. Yet he knew that such a course of action would be mistaken, and almost inevitably disastrous. Unity was the most important thing for Dalethica, and a High King was symbolic of that unity, the force that had allowed mankind to triumph in the Sleep-stealer War of a thousand years earlier.

Now that legacy had apparently come down to this spoiled brat before him. He, Takian, must display an example of cooperation that would give the seed of unity a chance to flourish. Any schism could only give their enemy inestimable aid.

But Takian *could* do his best to see that the plans for the city's defense were carefully prepared, and did not involve potentially catastrophic risks. There had to be a way to protect the army against encirclement, and still give Bentram Wayn the opportunity to win some kind of victory. To this end he replied in cool, measured tones.

"The men of the city have awaited your arrival since the death of the High King. They stand ready, as do I, to follow your commands."

— 2 —

"But it's *insane*!" Bristyn objected, turning away from her husband and stalking to the tall windows of their royal chambers. Beyond, the vista of Dalethica, still green in its nearer reaches, lay shadowed by the massive clouds mark-

ing the extent of the Sleepstealer's advance. "To march out
there, to face a hundred thousand minions on an open field?
You'll all be killed! I didn't come back just to watch you
ride off to certain death!"

"Death is far from certain—or do you have such little
faith in me?"

"Faith in you? To be sure, but you're putting yourself
at the mercy of that . . . that *boy*. Kelwyn Dyerston must be
groaning in his grave!"

"You know we both have duties, things we cannot ignore! Remember that I didn't want you to go to Shalloth—
that I *forbade* you from going?"

"Duties?" Bristyn's tone was scornful. "And where will
your *duty* leave the city? If you're killed, the army destroyed? What then?"

"I won't let the army be destroyed!" the king retorted,
giving vent to the temper that he had so long held in check.
"I can help if I'm there—by Baracan, if it comes to that
I'll take command and order the troops back to the
bridges—"

"But what if that's too late?" Bristyn whirled, her blue
eyes flashing like glacial ice, then melting into raw fear.
"What if I *did* come back only to lose you?"

Takian crossed the room, took his wife by the shoulders
and met her frightened look with a plea from the depths of
his heart. "When you were missing, when I thought you
were dead, I could have fallen in battle and my wounds
wouldn't have increased my despair. Now you're here,
you've come back! But what's the purpose of that, of anything, if we don't stop the minions here, soon?"

"I know we must—but use your brain to stop them, not
just your sword. It's the only way to win!"

Takian sighed, discouraged and exhausted. "How?"

"*Talk* to him! Try and change his mind!"

For a long time the King of Galtigor was silent, face
downturned, brow furrowed. Finally he drew a breath and
raised his eyes to Bristyn's. "I can use the excuse of a
review of the troops, before we start out for the battlefield.

Men are garrisoned all over the city, so he'll have to see
the defenses. The High Prince will surely understand how
strong our position is here!''

She pulled him close, as if even now she would hold him
from battle with the strength of her clasp. Finally, after too
short a time, Takian gently broke free, girded on his sword,
and quietly walked out the door.

— 3 —

Direfang raised his muzzle from the fountain, allowing oily
liquid to trickle over his protruding jaw and splatter onto
the strapping expanse of his barrel chest. He smacked his
lips, and sparks crackled brightly, dropping in bouncing
fireballs from the taloned fingers of his two spade-sized
hands.

The statue was a not unpleasing likeness, he decided. The
blackness of Darkblood fully encircled the base of the stone
block, rising into a dull, murky brown around the crude
figure's waist. Only the shoulders and head remained even
vaguely white, and before long these, too, would be stained
by the Sleepstealer's liquid venom.

Abruptly the brutox roared, a cascade of brittle, fiery
drool spuming from his jaws. He whirled, conscious of the
marble image looming behind his shoulders, rising into the
twilight shadows overhead. Blinking his bloodshot eyes,
Direfang glared at the gathering of darkmen.

He was pleased to see that the company had grown very
large indeed, swelled by a steady stream of new arrivals,
men of weak character and brutal nature who were drawn
by the lure of Darkblood and violence. A sea of swarthy
faces with wild, tousled hair extended the full breadth of
the large clearing, thousands of darkmen spewing frenzied
cheers, glazed eyes fastened with adoration upon their master. As Direfang roared again, the men echoed accolades in
reply. Grunting, clashing sword or sickle or axe against a
neighbor's blade, the corrupted humans raised a cacophony

of ringing steel and guttural, beastlike sounds. They shouted until throats grew hoarse, stomped until the mighty brutox could feel the ground shuddering even through his cleated boots.

Direfang turned back to the statue, bending to drink, slurping loudly, once more allowing the Darkblood to spill from his jowls. The elixir flowing from this well, he had been pleased to discover, was sweet and powerful and pure—as splendid as any Darkblood he had supped in the heart of Agath-Trol itself. How it had come here he didn't know, but its presence was more than a means to save his life—it was nothing less than a tool that would hurl him toward destiny.

He taunted the gathered throng of Darkmen with the sound of his libation, knowing the thirst, the *need*, that must certainly be driving them to a frenzy. And the brutox, natural leader of this ravenous mob, knew that this craving was something he could use to his own advantage.

Finally Direfang rose again, belching with deep satisfaction. He stepped to the side, allowing thirsty men to cluster around the fountain. With himself looming and sparking above, frequently interrupting the queue to requench his own thirst, the brutox watched them drink. He growled ominously when one darkman tried to press ahead of his fellows.

When another man, blinded by frenzy, ignored his master's warning and tried to push through the file, Direfang decapitated the wretch with a swift swipe of his blazing paw. He hoisted the headless body, howling aloud and shaking the gory trophy, and there was no more pushing for place in line, or striking of blows between comrades.

The brutox exulted in his own power. One after another the darkmen knelt and lapped at the fountain, individuals reacting in different ways. Some lurched away, gagging, or fell and writhed on the ground. Others roared like beasts, uttering thunderous cries that shook the leaves on the bleak, weary trees. Hideous fangs distorted some mouths into muzzles, and the eyes of other darkmen squinted in a combination of cunning and cruelty—and always worship, when they turned toward the massive, fiery figure of their leader.

For hours the spring flowed steadily, a suppurating wound in the flesh of the Watershed, and the men swilled and gulped and consumed the vile nectar. Tension thrummed through the milling mob, men growling and pacing until the whole company circled the statue in a restless current, like a vortex of chaos drawing on the pressure of Darkblood.

But only when the last of the band had drunk did Direfang lead the company into the woods, starting along the trails to the north.

— 4 —

"You wished to see me?" Bentram Wayn turned from the windows overlooking the courtyard, where a thousand silver-armored men marched in unison. He faced Takian with his hands on his hips, a tight smile across his youthful features.

The King of Galtigor advanced to stand beside the younger man. "They look splendid, don't they?"

"Indeed. The heavy infantry of the Deltamen. I'm surprised to hear that you didn't use them at Mallard Ridge—do you have reason to doubt their competence?"

Takian shrugged. "Not at all. I simply formed my expeditionary force from lighter units, so that we could fall back to the city quickly. These men are splendid troops, but much slower on the march than others."

"I am reassured. I feared that perhaps you had cause to suspect their loyalty."

"No, Your Highness. For the most part I think that our enemies stand pretty clearly revealed."

"Then you now agree that we should strike them?" Sir Berald entered the room with the advisor, Donthwal. The knight nodded in pleasure as he looked out at the gathering of heavy infantry.

"It would be best to make the decision after the review," Takian replied smoothly.

"Very well—let us begin," declared Bentram Wayn, clearly enjoying the prospect. "Where do we start?"

"With the castle," Takian said, gesturing to another block of men marching into the courtyard that had just been vacated by the Deltamen. "These are Duke Oxnar's swordsmen, renowned for their skill with their interlocking shields. It's said they can form a wall as sturdy as any digger-built stone!"

"Shield walls . . . Your Highness will note the continued emphasis on defense," Sir Berald said, all but sneering at the veterans in the courtyard.

"If you will come this way?" Takian suggested through clenched teeth, wondering how often, if ever, Sir Berald had wet his blade against a real foe.

He led the group over the Kingsbridge, from the lofty vantage pointing out the city walls, the towers and gate-houses that secured each of the six bridges, and the deep channels of the Ariak that divided the city from the main-land.

Bentram reacted with delight to the lofty span, going from one side to the other and looking over the low railing, exclaiming over and over as they reached the high center portion of the bridge.

From the King's Tower, Takian pointed to the Thutan spearmen, who were garrisoned on the surrounding hill. Javelins over their shoulders, these lean troops formed nar-row columns and marched down to the bottom of the hill.

As the king's party was starting back to the castle, Tak-ian was startled to see Randart jogging toward them.

The sergeant saluted, and explained. "Bad news, sire . . . we've had the first reports of fever in the Golden Lions."

"Which units?"

"The foot soldiers, mostly. Heavy and light infantry both, though not the pikes."

"Damn!" Takian turned toward the edge of the bridge, looking over the city and the river. Was there no end to the disastrous effects of this war?

"I'd say that's all the more reason to hurry our attack," Bentram Wayn declared.

"The Knights of Andaran will ride upon your command!" Berald promised.

"But you've seen the walls, the gates! Think about it!" Takian said urgently. "Hold here in the city! If we go, we stand to lose more than the army—the city itself becomes vulnerable! Reconsider your plan!"

"It's too late." Wayn gestured to the west, where the sun had already sunk into the murk of minion smog. "The first elements, led by the Hundred Knights of Carillonn, are already across the bridge. They'll camp in the field tonight, and the rest of the army will join them in the morning."

"How did you manage that?" Takian tried to conceal his surprise and anger. The Knights of Carillonn had been under his command, and that command hadn't yet been officially transferred to Bentram Wayn.

"I sent word that you and I would be riding posthaste, and they were eager to go."

"You used my name?" Takian's voice was cold.

"Of course. We two are their leaders, and our presence gives them the impetus to fight for victory. Now, let us go and lead them to that victory."

"Not until we've tended to the city garrisons," Takian declared, infuriated that the prince's actions had negated his arguments. "We're going to assign an extra detail to each gatehouse."

"But . . ." The prince hesitated, then nodded. "Very well—you can use the Myntarians."

"The Myntarians are staying back, but not for garrison duty. You know as well as I do that four out of five of them are sick with fever! No, it will be the Thutan spears, with the Deltamen as a city reserve."

"Oh, all right!" snapped Bentram Wayn. "The important thing is to get out there and *do* something!"

Flushing, the king stalked beside the prince across the royal bridges, grimly silent as he returned to his quarters and reported his failure to Bristyn. She reacted sadly, but without surprise.

In the morning he went to the stables and ordered Hawkrunner saddled. By the time the first rays of sunlight pierced the dawn mists, he was prepared to accompany the lead elements of the army to the Rosebridge. The High Prince, his advisor, and the captain of the Andaran Knights met the king in the courtyard, and together they rode through a city filled with cheering crowds.

Near the gatehouse they fell in with a grand column of knights, regal warhorses trotting with splendid dignity over the marble span. On the bank of the Ariak, the two monarchs and their attendants rode to the top of the crossroads hill, then turned to watch the rest of the army march out of the city.

The columns that filed over the marble span included pikemen and crossbow archers, sword and axe-bearing veterans, light horsemen and heavy knights. The wide bridge could accommodate a rank eight or ten men wide, and it still took the force many hours just to cross over to the west bank of the Ariak. And if numbers of troops was the determining factor, Takian thought, then this effort must certainly have a greater effect on the minion advance than had the stand at Mallard Ridge. He allowed himself a rising glimmer of hope—with a battle host like this, maybe they *could* prevail.

But how long would it take these troops to cross back, Takian wondered, if the enemy forced them into retreat or, even worse, rout? And would the loss of the army mean the loss of Carillonn? He knew that if the city fell, there was nothing to halt the ultimate tide of darkness sweeping all the way to the eastern coast of Dalethica.

The only way he could answer these questions was to gather more information. Spurring Hawkrunner into a gallop, he left the prince's side, riding through a trampled cornfield beside the marching column of men. Randart rode close behind as the king looked over the distant field, searching—and then seeing the banner of the Golden Lion. He veered toward the fluttering pennant as Captain Jaymes, accompanied by his scouts Dayr and Braxton, emerged from the cover of a forested ravine and urged his own horse into a gallop.

They met near a grove of spindly birch trees, a half mile from the road. Eagerly the king searched his captain's eyes for some sign of encouraging news—but Jaymes's expression was bleak, and guarded.

"What's the word to the south?" asked the monarch.

"The setback at Mallard Ridge did some good," reported the cavalryman. "They lost a lot of minions in that swamp, and the rest are taking their own sweet time about getting back to their march."

"That's encouraging, up to a point." Takian looked to the sky, where the sun was just approaching zenith. "Do you think they'll be marching by tonight?"

"Hard to say, sire. Still, from the looks of things, my best guess would be that we won't have to worry about them until tomorrow."

"Even that's too soon," Takian said with a grimace, looking along the sunspeckled road, the array of bright weapons reflecting like glittering mirrors from thousands of helmets, shields, and blades. The Lancers of Brull were passing now, light horsemen mounted on skittish, prancing steeds of uniform chestnut.

"Dayr—ride to the Lancers. Ask their captain to report to me," Takian said, quickly making a decision.

Dayr, a one-eyed veteran of many campaigns who masked his empty socket with a crimson patch, saluted crisply and galloped away, while Braxton, a loyal young soldier who tried to conceal his age beneath a thin beard of rusty red, waited alertly at Jaymes' side.

A few minutes later the captain of the lancers rode up to Takian. A typical Brullman, he was a stocky fellow of dark complexion, with a bristling black mustache and long, muscular arms.

"You have orders, Your Majesty?"

"Yes. Take your riders along the south road," the King of Galtigor ordered. "I want you to skirmish with the enemy wherever you meet him. Slow him down by any means possible."

"Aye, sire!" pledged the swarthy warrior, before leading his horsemen to obey.

"And Jaymes," Takian said, "take up position with my signalmen. I'll join you later."

Nodding gravely, Jaymes signaled to his riders, and the file of armored men thundered away from the main body. Takian galloped on, and within a few minutes came to the crown prince, who was mounted on his proud palomino stallion beside the road, surrounded by his retinue as he watched the long file of the army pass. Takian counted courtiers, messengers, even minstrels and drummers among the High Prince's men, but precious few—besides Sir Berald—who looked as though they could wield a sword.

"Why did you dispatch those men?" demanded Bentram Wayn. "Surely you know that concentration of force is the major tenet of a military operation. We could use them in the upcoming battle."

"I understand that principle—but you must realize the importance of maintaining an open road to the city. A great victory before us will mean nothing if the army is annihilated by a subsequent attack from behind."

"Once the western wing has been sent reeling," declared the prince dismissively, "I have no doubt but that the other minion columns will share their comrades' dismay. A general retreat must inevitably commence."

"These are not human foes!" declared Takian sharply, his frustration overcoming the restraint he tried to maintain. "They are not subject to fatigue, to the failures of morale that would affect an army of Dalethica."

"They have not displayed those weaknesses, but perhaps that is because they have yet to suffer a serious setback. Be patient—by tomorrow we shall know which of us is right."

Grimly, the King of Galtigor nodded his head. His silent question remained unspoken, but tugged angrily at his mind:

If the prince was wrong, how could there be any hope for this army, for Carillonn and Dalethica and all mankind?

ELEVEN

Journeys of Hope or Fear

To completely understand any voyage, one must
fully consider the places of departure and
destination.
—SONGS OF AURIANTH
VOLUME II, GODSTOME

— 1 —

"For a sylvan city, it looks pretty good," Danri allowed,
as the *Black Condor* coursed across the Auraloch, propelled
by a following breeze. Spendorial's domes were glazed in
the warm light of a setting sun, the eerie shades highlight-
ing the muted green- and rose-colored half-globes of the
Palace of Time.

Wistan Aeroel, standing beside the digger on the raised
deck of the galyon, chuckled wryly. "For one of my tribe,
the walls and streets of *any* city are strange surroundings."

Danri knew that the woodland sylve hailed from eastern
Faerine, where, he had heard—from Anjell, of all people—
that the cousins of Spendorial's sylves dwelled in small
bands, and made their homes in the hollowed trunks of
massive evergreen trees.

His interest in building piqued, the digger had since discussed the sturdy structures in great detail with the sylvan archer, concluding with a pledge that, after the war, he and Kerri would journey to the coast and pass through the realm of forest homes.

"Good thing we're arriving at night," Pembroak said, sauntering over to the pair of Faerines. "Otherwise our general might want to march us right through town and on toward the Watershed. I, for one, won't mind a night in bed."

"And I plan to spare a few hours for the Stone Goblet," Danri acknowledged with a chuckle. Still, he thought of Kerri up at the Watershed beyond Shalemont, and knew that his own impatience would compel a departure with the dawn.

The last traces of daylight still glowed in the western sky, a lingering memory of aquamarine fading into violet and black, when the passengers of the galyon were ferried to shore by a flotilla of sylvan longboats. Together with Wistan, Pembroak, Kestrel, and Garic Hoorkin, Danri hastened to the Goblet.

Enlivened by the triumphant strains of a sylvan balladeer, the companions drank many toasts. Their joy was muted by the knowledge that another campaign awaited, and by the memory of absent companions—many a glass was drained with a nod to Gulatch and Neambrey, who remained in charge of the protective force left at the pass.

With Pembroak's active accompaniment, Danri told the tale of their battle at Darkenheight before an appreciative crowd that included virtually every shape and size of Faerine. The digger saw gigants scowling in appreciation as he related Gulatch's charge against the brutox, watched twissels recoil in imagined horror when Garic Hoorkin stepped forward to describe the discovery of the pass's approach.

When Danri gave his account of the excavation through an intervening mountain, the numerous diggers in the audience gave him a hearty round of applause. And Wistan

Aeroel's modest descriptions aroused proud—if dignified and restrained—emotions among the gathered sylves. Completing the feeling of unity, a table of drunken sartors toasted every tale, and a large buck even bought a round of pitchers for the crowded tavern.

Danri learned that the horned Faerines were veterans from the Suderwild campaigns of Wattli Sartor. They told of their own attacks against the minion encampments—fast, hit and run strikes that had infuriated the minions.

"We couldn't get right into the middle of everything, you know, so we could work some real slaughter, 'cause they'd all start to wake up then," one sartor explained. "Still, I think we kept their minds off Darkenheight Pass!"

Near the end of the recounting a stir arose at the doorway, and the throng parted to allow passage to Mussrick Daringer, accompanied by Dara Appenfell. The Royal Scion paused to murmur quietly to the digger innkeeper. That worthy merchant beamed and immediately brought forth additional refreshments with the whispered news that the Royal House sylve was covering the tab for all the festivities.

"Dara!" Captain Kestrel rose and embraced her, then backed away to regard her with concern. "But weren't you going to Shalemont, with Awnro and Kerri?"

She told Kestrel and Danri about Anjell's affliction, but tried to soothe their worries. "I don't know what it is . . . it doesn't seem to be wearing her down, wasting her . . . she'll be up soon. I *know* she will."

"Darret and I will come by to see her first thing in the morning," the captain promised, as Mussrick Daringer joined them at the crowded table.

"News spreads quickly," Daringer said, inclining his head toward Danri and Wistan so that he could be heard above the sounds of celebration. "So Darkenheight is closed to the minions now?"

"Aye-uh," affirmed Danri. "Now it's off to the Watershed on the other side."

"Do you think your maid found a place for the canal?"

"I'm expectin' she did—maybe with Awnro's help. He's got a good eye for detail, and she knows those mountains. And if they've found the place, I have the troops to dig a trench!"

Danri spoke with no false bravado, but a full measure of confidence. "I saw these diggers cut a tunnel through a mountain over one night. They should be able to make a little ditch without too much trouble. Now, how 'bout another pitcher?"

Mussrick agreed, but gradually the mood became more somber as the Faerines and their human guests turned their thoughts to friends and comrades they would never see again—Quenidon Daringer, and Kianna Kyswillis, and Blaze Smelter . . . too many names for Danri to recite. Yet he held a thought for them all, and made a silent pledge that their sacrifices were not made in vain.

Finally the weary celebrants retired to rooms in the spacious inn, and despite his fatigue Danri rested uneasily, acutely conscious of the lake breeze with the taste of sea wafting through the big windows that opened onto the Auraloch. When he slept it was lightly, and his dreams were troubled by images of battles, of violence and pain and too much death. It was with relief that he greeted the sunrise, and the chance to take further action.

He stopped at the palace, to see Anjell, but was told by her mother that she was still sleeping. Asking Dara to pass along his best wishes for her daughter's health, he accepted her kiss on his bushy cheek, and murmured an "Aye-uh" to her good luck wishes.

Shortly after dawn, the warriors of the Faerine Field Army made a measured march through the streets of the sylvan capital, accepting the accolades of thousands of Faerines. The side streets and ramparts, open gardens and courtyards, the balconies of the highest buildings, were all lined with sylves, diggers, gigants, and sartors, while twissels buzzed through the air above the troops and around the pastel-colored domes.

All the Faerines waved and cheered the army that had

closed the enemy's road at Darkenheight Pass. Sylvan and digger maidens rushed forward with tankards of wine and ale, and these Danri enjoyed for breakfast.

For a few minutes he allowed the celebration to elate him. With a victory at Darkenheight to fuel his hopes, he was ready for a new challenge. They would find a place and dig the canal, allowing Aura to flow into Dalethica and provide the means at last to turn the tide of the war.

And even farther into the future, he pictured the inn where he and Kerri would spend their days, and their years, together . . . the place would be perfect, he knew, for her judgment was the same.

Then the woodlands of Norwild surrounded them and the march began in earnest. The long column of diggers, accompanied by an escort of twissel scouts and woodland sylves, started through the digger realms, moving toward the very crest of the Watershed.

— 2 —

"We *have* to fall back across the Klarbrook—it's the only way we might still hold the town in the morning!"

"No! By Dunkar Kalland himself, we'll stand and die here before we retreat like cowards!" Kristoff Yarden's jaw jutted forward like a mountainous shoulder of granite. He faced Roggett Becken astride the dirt track leading through Neshara Pass, as if daring the Iceman to make him move.

Instead, Roggett drew a deep breath and spoke respectfully. "The courage of your men is legendary, my friend— no one would dare to call them cowards."

When the pikeman spoke again, his tone had softened, but nothing eased the glaring stubbornness of his posture. "How can I ask them to leave? Twenty of my men have *died* here—and you're sayin' we should give up the ground bought with their blood?"

"Their blood bought more than this ground, Kris! They gained us time, forced these minions to spread twenty miles

down valley to get around you!'' His arguments justifying
the retreat rang hollow in Roggett's own ears, but he had
to keep trying. ''Your company can fight again, and *win*,
if you'll just get them across the stream! And furthermore,
you'll give Neshara a chance of holding.''

''How'd they get around the flank?'' demanded Kristoff,
turning to look down the valley of the Klarbrook on the
Neshara side of the pass.

''They crossed the ridge closer to the lake, somewhere
past the Midvales. A company of lakemen was holding on
the flats, but word is they fell to the last man.'' Roggett
couldn't hold back a hint of rebuke. ''No one's calling *them*
cowards, either.''

The pikeman captain looked stricken, and shook his head
in apology. ''I had that coming . . . Aye, there's no lack of
courage along this line—just too damned many of those
minions! And who knows, maybe those poor bastards in
the Midvales just got sick. Baracan knows that fever seems
to be spreading everywhere.''

''Same thing in Neshara—half the houses are serving as
hospitals. Every company that's spent any time on the line
has lost half its men to the fever.''

''How about the ones evacuated, to Zollikof and the
lake?'' asked Yarden.

''Word is a good number of them die. Those that survive
just stay sick—there doesn't seem to be any getting better.''

Kristoff spit into the side of the road. Roggett could tell
that the man was furious about this new insult—one more
menace that seemed to obliterate all hope of success.
''What about the minions, then? The ones that got past our
flank?''

''Our last reports have thousands of them marching up
the valley behind us,'' Roggett explained. ''Most of the
men are already down off the ridge. And I know this: If
we don't have your pikes standing at the bridge, I wouldn't
give my village more than a day of hope.''

''We'll be there—but still, it's not right, by Baracan!''
fumed Kristoff, absently twirling the end of his waxed mus-

tache. "To run away without ever losing a battle!"

"It's not runnin'!" Roggett insisted. "And if you have the sense to get your men into a good position, it won't mean losing a battle, either!"

For a moment the Iceman felt tremendous sympathy for his fellow captain, who had been a hog farmer a few months before. Kristoff Yarden sighed, and the slump of his shoulders was a heartbreaking sight. "Aye, my friend. I know yer right. . . ."

"And I know your men will fight just as well in the valley as on the ridge," Roggett replied softly, clapping the courageous man on the shoulder.

"Stand about, troop!" Yarden called, summoning his pikemen from their bivouacs in the brushy woods to either side of the pass. "Form column—we're going to give 'em a fight from somewhere else."

The Iceman was impressed by the rapid response of the doughty veterans. They formed a bristling column, quickly proceeding down the winding road toward Neshara— though Roggett knew that every one of them hated to abandon their pass.

An hour later the Halvericans plodded grimly past the Black Bull Tavern, over the Klarbrook bridge, and took up a new position on the village side of the stream, just outside the cluster of chalets that was Neshara.

"Put some men down the road toward the Midvales, to make sure you get warning of the first advance," suggested Roggett. "I'm going to see to the rest of the town's defenses—but I'll be back."

"You'll find us here," growled Kristoff. Though still surly, he wasted no time in sending out the pickets the Iceman had suggested.

Roggett, meanwhile, walked up the once-pastoral main street of his little village. He saw walled yards that had been converted into forts, with crossbowmen posted in silos and atop roofs. Many chalets had been boarded up, while others—chosen for stout shutters and steep foundations— were garrisoned with dozens of armed men.

Also within those buildings, he knew, were the dozens, even hundreds, of the sick. Many more men had succumbed to fever in the last few days, and now the defenders simply lacked the manpower to evacuate them.

"Hey, hold up there!"

Tarn Blaysmith called to Roggett from the door of the village wainwright's barn, where the Iceman from Dermaat and his company of battle-scarred axemen had taken position. The complex of barns and a large mill building on a raised foundation overlooking the stream was planned as one of Neshara's premier strongpoints. Now Tarn jogged between the open, iron-girded gates to speak to his fellow captain.

"If any of 'em try to cross here, we'll be waitin' to throw 'em back into the water," pledged the grim widower.

"Aye, my friend, I know you will." Roggett patted the tall man on the shoulder, before moving on to the southern terminus of Neshara.

Here he found another company of veterans who had stood without faltering on the Dermaathof. Like the pikemen, they were ill-tempered, resentful of the retreat caused by no failure of theirs. Now, to the last man they vowed their grim determination to make a stand on the village outskirts. Young Karlsted—still a pimply boy to Roggett—declared that they would not surrender one garden, or one sidewalk, of the mountain village.

"Roggett! Roggett Becken!"

Bekker Staylton, panting after a long run, found Roggett as the Iceman was making his way back through the town.

"The minions are coming up the Klarbrook valley, fast," Bekker reported, as soon as he had caught his breath. "Maybe two miles out by now."

"How strong?" asked Roggett.

"Thousands, easy. With plenty of brutox. I've already warned the pikemen you had down by the bridge."

"Good."

Roggett looked around. In addition to Kristoff's company of pikes, he had a few hundred brave axemen, most of them native to Neshara. Nearby were a company of crossbow, as well a band of unarmed but stalwart youths who had volunteered their services wherever they might do the most good.

The only natural obstacle to the minion invasion of the village was the stream that curled in a semicircle around the chalets and yards of Neshara. The defenders were deployed in a long line arcing along the bank of that stream, and stood ready to repulse any attempt at a crossing.

Roggett was on his way back to the bridge by the Black Bull Tavern when he again encountered Tarn, jogging along the road toward the village with his face locked in an expression of dour concern.

"What is it?" asked the Nesharan.

His fellow captain, the man who had lost his entire family in the wasteland of Dermaat, looked at Roggett grimly.

"In the last half hour, the flow of the Klarbrook has dropped by half."

Tarn didn't need to say anything more. "A dam," Roggett guessed. "Somewhere upstream."

"It's got to be," Tarn agreed. "They've come around the base of the Glimmercrown and got themselves next to the headwaters. There's lots of places where it wouldn't take much to stop up that creek."

"Then we've got to be ready for an attack from any direction."

"Aye. I've sent half my men into the woods uphill of the village. They should give us some notice if the bastards try to come down from the glacier."

"Good. I have a feeling it won't be long."

The words had no sooner left his lips than the two men heard a low, resonant horn wail from the lower village.

"Nope," Tarn agreed laconically. "Not long at all."

— 3 —

"How she doin'?" asked Darret, sidling past Dara Appenfell to look into the sleeping chamber. The woman put down her paper and quill and stepped after the boy to take a look.

Anjell's room was in a sunlit wing of Spendorial's domed palace. Through the glass window the Auraloch sparkled, viridescent gems under the bright daylight. Above stretched a vista of green trees and puffy clouds.

But she had been here for *days*, and she was getting quite sick of it. Of course she was glad that Darret was back. The lad, for his part, had declared himself happy that his friend didn't have a view of the minion camp and the ruined shoreline of the Suderwild.

"I keep telling her—I'm fine!" Anjell insisted, sitting up in the bed and glaring at her mother. "Except I'm about to die of boredom! She won't let me do anything, or go anywhere! I can't even eat anything fun." Naturally, she neglected to mention her spells of unconsciousness.

"Too bad," Darret muttered—without as much sympathy as Anjell would have liked to hear. "But what about them dreams 'n' stuff? You sleeping okay now?"

"Well, sure," she replied crossly. "I *never* had any trouble sleeping! It's just that I . . . when I think about Rudy . . . I just get so scared!"

For the first time her belligerent façade cracked slightly, as Anjell felt her lower lip start to quiver. Darret sat beside her and took her hand.

"What about those minions out there across the lake?" Anjell asked, with a disgusted wave at the open window. "Like you pointed out, I can't see *anything* from here!"

"Not doin' much," Darret admitted. "Just sitting around over there, waiting for Darkblood."

"Well, it's not coming!" Anjell declared sternly. "Neambrey and Gulatch will see to that." She sniffled, once again feeling sorry for herself. "And I didn't even get to go to Danri's celebration!"

"Well." Darret nodded noncommittally. "I wish you wouldn't worry so much about the war and stuff. Just get better, okay?"

Dara rose from the chair she had occupied for most of

the last week. "I'll go tend to some things," she said, "as long as you can keep her company for a while."

"You bet." Darret agreed, with a braid-bouncing nod of his head. "I'll keep an eye on her, too," he promised, before turning to scowl at Anjell. "You gotta stop scarin' everyone with this stuff, fainting and tellin' us about Rudy and all!"

"I'm scaring myself," she admitted meekly, but then set her chin firmly and met the boy's level gaze. "But I can't stop thinking about what I know! And it's even scarier *not* knowing."

"It's *good* not to know some things!" Darret insisted.

"No . . . did you bring me some?" Anjell asked, after leaning out of the bed and looking into the corridor, making certain that her mother had disappeared.

"Well . . . yeah, I did. But I dunno . . ." Darret scowled, his hand closing protectively over the waterskin concealed beneath his shirt.

"Come *on*!" Anjell would have stomped her foot if she'd been standing. As it was, all she could do was twitch in irritation beneath her quilted blanket. "I need to know what's happening with Rudy!"

"It's just that you gotta get better . . . and, I dunno, maybe it's not good for you to drink this stuff alla time."

"I told you—I *am* better!"

"Hey, hi—howzat girl?" chirped a voice from the window as a diminutive figure skipped over the sill and leaned casually against the wall. Those silvery eyes blinked sagely as the handsome little sylve grinned at the two humans.

"Haylor! I'm glad you came by!" Clapping her hands in welcome, Anjell swiveled in bed to turn her back on Darret. "I bet *you'll* be nice to me!"

"And someone isn't?" The little sylve sauntered over and cocked a curious eyebrow.

"Tell Darret to let me have my Aura!"

"Bosh!" sniffed Haylor. "You can get it yourself!"

"How can I?" she demanded.

"Call it . . . *think* about how much you want it."

Skeptical, she nevertheless turned to Darret and squinted in concentration.

"Hey!" the boy squawked as his waterskin slipped from beneath his shirt and flew through the air, straight into Anjell's hand. "How'd you . . . ?" His objection trailed into silence.

"I don't know." Anjell was puzzled, but quickly became rather pleased when she began to think about it. "But thank you just the same." She uncorked the nozzle on the sack.

"Don't drink that!" Haylor cried in mock alarm.

"What?"

"Take this, instead." Removing a small flask from his pocket, the tiny sylve handed it to Anjell. "Right from the Pool of Scrying!"

"Really?" The girl took a sip, then gulped down several swallows.

Darret sulked for several more minutes, but with the inevitability of sunset following day he eventually yielded to Anjell's cheerfulnesss. Finally, he even laughed, though it looked as if he were trying to ignore the cloud of seriousness that had suddenly come into the girl's eyes.

"Any dreams lately?" asked Haylor casually.

"There's one I keep having. It's like I see a giant jigsaw puzzle, where all the pieces are black. But there are white lines between the pieces, and I have to balance on the lines."

"Or what?"

Her lower lip trembled and she couldn't help it—she was afraid!

"Or I die—and not just me, but you two, and Mama, and Captain Kestrel too."

"Just remember, my girl, that puzzles can be solved," Haylor said as Anjell abruptly drifted off to sleep.

TWELVE

The Darkest Wasteland

Remove sustenance, rest and comfort from a
man's surroundings, and you are left with the
seed of his determination. The success of any
great endeavor requires that this seed germinate
and take root in his soul.
　　　　—SCROLL OF BARACAN

— 1 —

The darkness was a shapeless void, a place without bound-
aries, lacking even a sense of up and down. Rudy saw nothing, smelled nothing . . . his fingers groped, his arms flailed,
and yet no substance, not a single sensation, came within
reach of his touch, his nose, or his eyes. There was only
that infernal, repetitious sound, a thudding, pulsing cadence
that struck his ears as noise, but also as crushing pressure,
the air itself pounding and quailing in rhythmic response.

He woke with a stark, terrifying feeling: He was lost,
and had no way to find his way home. Afraid and helpless,
he wrapped his arms around his chest, feeling the ribs beneath his fingers, staring into a shade of gray that was
brighter than utter darkness, but no more heartening.

Only then did his olfactory sense come alive with stinging proof in his nose and throat: This was still Duloth-Trol. A moment later his hand confirmed that Raine slept here beside him. He touched her back gently, before he quietly rose to his feet and moved away. Sleep had been too precious a commodity, lately—he would let her enjoy it as long as she could.

Plumes of fire rose from many places across the plains, spewing from irregular cracks and fissures. As always, this place was nightmarishly active, alive—yet at the same time lifeless. He wondered if it was daytime, and he felt a weary hopelessness when he looked at the clouds and tried to remember the sky, unwilling to believe that the lack of sunlight could be so utterly, terribly oppressive. Recalling the darkest, stormiest winters in snowy Halverica, Rudy realized there was no comparison. The stratus of Duloth-Trol was nothing like the gray blanket of overcast that had frequently shrouded Neshara and the rest of Halverica for weeks or months at a time. Even on those days of eternal grayness, there had been the certainty that sooner or later the sky would again be blue, the rays of sun would eventually sparkle across the peaks and lakes and glaciers. Here, it was easy to imagine that the pure light of day was only a distant memory, a thing banished forever from the face of the Watershed.

Forcing his doubts and weariness aside, Rudy reminded himself that they had reason for hope, as well. In fact, the Man and Woman of Three Waters had not only survived for many days in this hostile environment, they had trekked for hundreds of miles, finding a way around every obstacle. And each exhausted rest had been followed by renewed determination and progress.

Since departing the site of the Auracloud's crash, the pair had spent two days seeking a route around the massive cliff wall that had claimed the skyship. At last they had skirted the end of the barrier, which was a straight precipice plunging from the cloudy heights into the rock-studded plain, as abrupt and sheer as the mountain's entire face.

For a measureless time, then, they had plodded onward.

When the massif had vanished behind them they held to a
straight line by mutual consent, neither of them quite sure
of why they felt the vague sense of direction.

During their trek they had twice more been forced far
from their path—each time in search of passage around
deep, fire-filled gorges. Otherwise they hiked in a generally
straight line, through regions of gullies and ravines, over
rolling hills of black bedrock, or—rarely, but with some
relief—across featureless plains of dust and gravel. Bright
crimson swaths of cloud, they had deduced, marked open
lava on the ground—the caldera of a volcano, or perhaps
an entire lake of infernal fire. Blistering waves of heat in-
sured that they gave these obstacles a wide berth.

The realm of the Sleepstealer had proven to be virtually
devoid of life. Although this was not a bad thing, the
strangely birdless skies, grassless plains, and slopes barren
of trees or flowers or shrubs made for oppressive surroundings in an apparently endless trek.

The only thing they had seen even faintly resembling a
plant was a lichenlike layer of leafy crust that coated many
places elevated above the cracked plains. The stuff seemed
to prefer vertical faces of rock, and was so brittle Rudy half
suspected it was inorganic mineral. Despite its strangeness,
the Iceman had begun to seek the leafy encrustations when
he crossed a ridge of rock, or climbed a high promontory
for a look around.

There was just such a spire of jagged rock beside their
barren campsite, rising like a darkstone tower toward the
clouds. The top would certainly provide a good vantage, so
the Iceman decided to ascend while Raine still slept. He
scrambled up a series of large, square-edged boulders at the
base and in ten minutes had reached a face of worn, weathered bedrock. His hands were already coated with the sticky
dew of Darkblood—a substance, he and Raine had discovered, that actually improved a climber's grip.

One horizon of cloud had brightened from black to gray,
and he guessed that the sun was rising over the rest of the
Watershed. Hand over hand he climbed the stairlike shelves

within a wide gully, finding the walls coated with the brittle leaves. The stuff broke to dust upon the slightest touch, but even then it provided excellent traction for fingers or boot. Finally the ravine narrowed into a chute, becoming a chimney that ran as a groove all the way to the top of the fanglike spire. The Iceman ascended quickly, but with care, and soon pulled himself onto a flat summit no more than a dozen paces across.

Even up here he could feel the pull of direction that had carried them so far. He looked along the course of their upcoming trek, relieved to see no obstacles more serious than a few short, gaping fissures. The plain was also dotted with many rocky spires similar to his current perch, but these were narrow enough that they could merely walk around any that stood in their path.

His inspection completed, he spent a few moments studying the roiling clouds. Terrions, as always, were their greatest worry, though they had seen no minions at all since their battle with the stalkers. He was relieved to see that this morning seemed to be running true to form.

Retracing the route of his ascent, he found Raine standing up and stretching as he jumped down from the last of the boulders at the spire's base.

"Any sign of . . . well, anything?" she asked.

"Not a living thing," replied the Iceman. "I guess not even the stalkers and terrions like it out here."

"Can you blame them?" Raine looked upward, surveying the vast, roiling layer of dark stratus that blocked any view of the sky. Rudy was startled to observe the sharp angle of her jaw, the gauntness that seemed to draw in her cheeks and ribs.

He hugged her, remembering his earlier feelings of despair. "It's something to be thankful for—even if it's the only thing."

Through his fatigue, through the numbing ache in his gut that was constant hunger, Rudy tried to embolden himself with some optimism, but so complete was the embrace of the Sleepstealer's lifeless realm that utter hopelessness often seemed like the only possible emotion he could feel.

"Water?"

Raine's question brought Rudy back to the present, to the task before them and the need for action.

"Yes." Gratefully the Iceman took the proferred skin and drank long swallows, following the drink with a few sips of Aura.

He turned to his own backpack. Pulling out a strip of hardtack, he tore it in half and gave a portion to Raine. For a while they chewed the tough bread, relaxing and stretching the sore muscles of shoulders and hips. Finally, reluctantly, the Man of Three Waters hoisted the cask which was still suspended from his back. The small barrel was mostly full, and he ruefully reflected that this was a mixed blessing. He shrugged his shoulders through the straps and leaned forward into a position that had grown habitual.

Raine, too, strapped on her own sloshing, bulging bundle. Watching her, the Iceman was shocked by the weariness of her steps, by the harsh, almost papery quality of her skin.

"Which way do we go from here?" she asked, turning to regard the rugged range of hills that broke up the terrain across their path.

"Straight ahead." The Iceman pointed to a gap between two of the nearest spires.

"Just what I was thinking," she confirmed with a grim shrug. Side by side they started plodding forward once again.

Many hours passed in timeless fatigue, broken by occasional rests for sips of water and Aura. Night curled around them with a subtle shift in illumination, and once again the fiery flares from deep crevasses and lava lakes cast a hellish glow across the ground. For more hours the pair trekked through a small range of hills, following the valleys between the outcrops. Occasionally a long elevation loomed in their path, and then they marched upward, picking a route between pillars of rock and steaming fissures.

It was at the top of one of these hills that Raine slumped against a rock. Rudy saw her drawing deep, ragged breaths, and for the first time recognized his own fatigue.

"Why don't we rest, try to sleep for a while?" he suggested.

Mutely she nodded. They had neither bedroll nor blankets, but at least the air was warm. Curling together on a flat piece of ground next to a sheltering outcrop, they closed their eyes.

Rudy sensed the distant pulse through his skin, a throbbing in the ground that reached him from afar. The rhythm originated before them, from the direction in which they were traveling. Jerking upright, he came fully awake—and still the cadence continued. He remembered the pounding he had previously sensed only in his dreams, and he knew.

The Heart of Darkblood was the driving force of this bleak realm, the steady meter of Dassadec's grim presence in the Watershed. For a long time that pulse had been the summons that drew them on, brought them from sleep after they had spent a few uncomfortable hours on the ground, lifted them to their feet again after each all-too-brief and unsatisfying rest stop.

Yet now he could hear it, and the knowledge excited him in a deep and fundamental way. Certainly it meant that they were getting closer—indeed, even more significantly, it proved that they really *had* a destination, a target.

The Iceman felt the warmth of his companion as an abiding vitality. He wrapped his arms around her, and she turned to face him, inviting his embrace, needing his touch as badly as he needed hers. Under the glowering skies of the Sleepstealer they shared their passion with a straining desperation, as if neither of them believed that they would ever have the chance to be together again.

Finally they slept, and for the first time in many days the Iceman's dreams were untroubled by monsters, minions, or fears.

— 2 —

Tears stung Danri's eyes as he came over the verdant ridge to see the familiar slate roofs of Shalemont clustered in the pastoral valley. The rainbow arches of numerous bridges spanned the Bluerun, soft in the bright sunlight, while sparkling Aura laughed and splashed on its way down from the heights. Smooth hillsides, bright with blossoms of red, purple, orange, and yellow, marked the flanking valleys where the mines and smelters were located, and when the digger drew a deep breath he tasted the familiar, pleasantly tangy scent of melted copper and burning coal.

Shalemont was far more peaceful, so much more beautiful, than he had remembered. Embarrassed, he turned away from his companions.

"It's only right that it move you," Wistan Aerel murmured. "It's been an awfully long time since you've seen it."

"Aye-uh," Pembroak agreed. "Nicest town in all Faerine, and anyone'll tell you so!"

Danri cleared his throat gruffly. "There was a time when I never thought I'd see this view again," he admitted. "And, to tell you the truth, I didn't know how much I'd missed it."

"It is a fitting place," declared Wistan, taking in the vale of Shalemont with an approving smile. "Where you are upon the Watershed, but *of* it, as well."

"Well, it's different from Spendorial, that's for sure," Danri allowed.

Indeed, the rainbow bridges over the Bluerun seemed brighter, more vivid than any such spans he had seen in lower Faerine. And the stone houses, roofed with great slabs of dark slate, struck him as more perfect, more beautiful in their setting, than were the artificial domes and towers of Spendorial along their splendid lakeshore.

Danri chuckled with a realization. "You know, I was getting awfully tired of pastel buildings. I forgot how nice a plain stone wall can look."

"And flowers don't have to be planted in a garden to please the eye," Wistan added, taking in a hillside bright with columbine and firebrush blossoms.

"See the old cave across the valley?" Pembroak asked slyly. "Do you remember who used to work there?"

Danri saw the Tailings Pub—the entrance, anyway, since the tavern itself was buried in the accumulated rock of many centuries' excavation—on the rocky hillside across the Bluerun.

"Seems there was a waitress . . . kind of a flirtatious wench, if I recall. Cute as a button, though." His throat tightened as he remembered his first farewell to Kerri. Unconsciously his fingers touched the beaded waterskin he still wore on his belt, the gift she had given him before his departure under the spell of Digging Madness. Even Pembroak's good-natured punch into his shoulder couldn't lighten the strong emotion that blurred his vision and thickened his voice.

"Someday we're going to have a place as good as the Tailings, maybe better," he murmured, willing his thoughts to Kerri across the miles. "Just you keep looking for the spot."

The Faerine Field Army marched down from the hills, the column approaching the town along a wide road paved with smooth stones. Diggers swarmed through the streets, cheering in warm greeting, forming crowds to flank the road as Danri and the others led the file into Shalemont.

"Up into the hills, this road is just a dirt track," Danri explained to Wistan as the sylve marched with the leaders of the digger company. "But here in the valley we tried to make it nice."

"Splendid workmanship," the archer noted approvingly, skipping over joints between the paving stones that were so tight as to be almost invisible. "Of course, I would expect nothing less—when it comes to stone, you folks are the masters of the Watershed."

"We can do a pretty good ditch, too," Pembroak pointed

out, as he caught up. "And a good ditch can make a good canal."

Wistan was about to reply when the young squire shouted and waved at one of the diggers who had emerged from the town to watch the field army's approach. "Uncle Hakwan! It's me, Pembroak!" he cried.

"Hakwan Chiseler!" Danri shouted. "You old mountain goat—by Aurianth, it's good to see your whiskers again!"

A sturdy digger, his long gray hair and beard each tied into twin braids, stepped forward to embrace Danri, and to chuck the young squire under the chin. With his arm around Danri's shoulders, Hawkan joined the procession through the town.

"That twissel came through a few days ago, told us you'd be coming today. Said you had plans to dig a canal! I had to see for myself, naturally."

"What digger ever believes what he's told?" asked Danri with a twinkle in his eye, then quickly turned serious. "Have you had further word from my frien—er, the twissel?"

"He flew on up the valley, looking for Kerri and that human fellow, right after he came by here. Hasn't been back, yet."

Danri tried to hide his disappointment. After all, he hadn't really expected to find his diggermaid waiting for him in Shalemont. He would be up there soon enough—and in the meantime, it was admittedly good to see the old homes again.

"I've taken the liberty of laying on a little feast over at the Tailings," Hakwan said. "I was hoping that you'd want to spend the night in town."

Danri turned to his old friend. "There's still good hours of daylight left . . . but I know these diggers will march twice as far in the morning if we let them have a little celebration tonight. And besides, I haven't been home in too many years not to stop and say hello to old friends."

"And new recruits," Hakwan noted, steering Danri—and thus, the entire column—toward the rainbow bridge leading across the Bluerun to the Tailings Pub. ''Three or four hundred from Shalemont alone. And lots more from the hill towns. Word went out as soon as we heard about your plan, but you'll have to wait here overnight for most of 'em to get here.''

''Too many good reasons to stop,'' Danri agreed with a chuckle. When he thought about it honestly, he was glad to have the excuse to spend some time in Shalemont. It startled him to realize that his biggest worry was that, come morning, he wouldn't want to leave.

Then he thought of Kerri, somewhere up near the divide, and he knew beyond any doubt that he'd be ready to march with the dawn.

As it turned out, though, he didn't take the time to go to bed. Borith Leadvein, owner of the Tailings, pulled out all the stops to welcome back his best former customer. Danri and his companions were given the table of honor—midway between the fireplace and the bar—and the innkeeper's staff kept food and drink coming in plentiful quantities. Naturally, only a small portion of the field army could squeeze into the dark, cavelike tavern, but the rest of the diggers and their sylvan allies spread through the city, welcomed in all the inns and most of the homes. Throughout the night, fires burned low on countless hearths, and many a wine cellar was repeatedly raided for prized vintages and fresh kegs.

Yet when dawn paled the sky, Danri was ready to leave. If anything, the addition of Hakwan and many other old friends gave him fresh energy for the task before them. First light showed a long file of diggers marching down the road from Pumice, with others reportedly on the way from Silverhill and Placer. Satchels on their backs, picks, shovels, and other tools slung over shoulders, the stocky Faerines arrived with enthusiastic offers to help build the canal.

Thus, it was a much larger column of diggers that, weaving only slightly, departed Shalemont in the morning, following the track into the rising and increasingly rocky foothills. By the end of the day the horizon of mountains had closed around them, leaving Shalemont but a memory. That night they found the first of Kerri's cairns, a small pile of rocks oriented to guide them on the next leg of their march.

All the next day Danri's steps were light and eager. Every few hours they reached a new cairn, proving they were on the right trail as they approached lofty valleys that few diggers had ever seen. The reinforcements at Shalemont had swelled the field army to an astounding size, and recruits and veterans alike proved willing to march up the winding slopes at a steady trot.

For more days the column of Faerines climbed, traversing deep valleys where eternal snowfields lay in the shade, moving from patches of timber through mossy tundra, into lands too high for trees to grow. Once they spotted a herd of Auragoats grazing on a high precipice. Sensing the movement in the valley below, the billy and his ewes leapt into space, spreading their leathery wings to carry them in a controlled dive around the shoulder of the peak.

The Faerine Field Army moved into still higher reaches, with the Crown of the World frequently in view to their left. That massive summit, streaked with dazzling snowfields and lofty cornices, pierced the clouds in the one place where the borders of Dalethica, Duloth-Trol, and Faerine all came together. Because of the massif's proximity, Danri felt certain that they must be drawing close to the Watershed.

"The Wilderhof—that's the first part of Dalethica I saw," Danri explained. "And the Crown rises over it as well."

"With luck, you'll be strolling into that same Wilderhof before long," Wistan offered encouragingly. They were distracted then by a shout, looking up to see a diggermaid sprinting toward them, down from the heights, following the course of an Aurabright stream that spilled from a gorge to the right.

"Kerri!" Danri's voice was choked with joy as he raced forward to sweep her into his long arms.

"You made it—you found me!" she cried, her voice echoing across the valley.

Lifting the diggermaid off her feet, he whirled her through the air until both of them were winded, grinning like fools and gasping for breath.

"But there's more," Kerri exclaimed. "We've found a place! It's right near here, and there's plenty of Aura!"

"A pass? For the canal, you mean?"

"Yes—we'll start it at the spring!" the diggermaid explained excitedly. "It's gushing pure Aura, and Awnro's surveyed a route. He says you won't even have to dig a tunnel!"

Danri's hopes flared, firmly underlaid by his happiness. "Well," he declared, gesturing the field army forward, "let's go have a look."

— 3 —

"We've got to sail to Duloth-Trol."

Anjell made her announcement bluntly, straining to keep her nervousness under control. Once she had spent a little time thinking about it, the answer became perfectly clear.

Carefully she looked at Dara, Kestrel and Darret, the trio she had arranged to meet in this lakefront grove. Since she had figured out the mystery of her mazelike dreams, Anjell had been alternately excited and frightened. Now that it was time to tell the others about it, she had difficulty forcing herself to remain calm.

She was relieved when none of her listeners shouted or exclaimed. And, truth be told, she wasn't surprised to see that the two adults had gone pale as ghosts—after all, it was only to be expected. She, herself, had been terribly frightened when she at last realized what they had to do.

But now that she'd made the big decision, she wasn't scared anymore. She could only hope that the grownups would be as adaptable.

"Perhaps you could explain." Kestrel was the first to

speak, and Anjell was heartened to hear that his tone was gentle, even encouraging.

"It's the only way," she explained frankly. "Otherwise everything we're doing, and whatever Danri and Takian and everybody else does too, won't mean a thing."

Dara reached out and pulled Anjell close. Though the girl could feel her mother's heart hammering, Dara said nothing, and her silence emboldened Anjell to continue.

"You mean, to sail on the Darksea?" Kestrel was skeptical, but apparently still willing to listen.

"Yes! That's the jigsaw puzzle I kept dreaming about—only it's not really a puzzle at all. It's an ocean that's mostly deadly, but there are ways to sail through it!"

"Ways that you can see?"

"I've learned some things after drinking Aura," she admitted. "But mostly it's just common sense. . . ."

Steadily, with growing confidence and conviction, Anjell began to explain.

— 4 —

The trek across Duloth-Trol seemed a timeless thing, a journey without milestones, lacking even the rhythms of sunrise and sunset to give measure to our days.

A sky of eternal black was our blanket. A land of splintered rock, smoldering fire, and tarry plain formed the road beneath our feet. Perhaps there was life on the fringes of our path, but we remained unaware of its presence or intentions.

In light of later events, I am forced to wonder if the Nameless One was toying with us, even observing every step of our journey. It may be that he held his minions at bay, allowed the toxic atmosphere and landscape of Duloth-Trol to be our sole enemy. Even so, it was a deadly foe, one that sapped our strength on a daily basis, constantly threatening to destroy both flesh and spirit.

We had only our Aura, and each other. During these

eternal days we subsisted on the water of magic, sustained by a shared determination that had grown beyond our love and our duty, that far overshadowed the insecurities of our earlier travels. It was as though we journeyed toward the end of the world, toward the finality of time.

Carefully we rationed our precious Aura, but our reserve inevitably dwindled as the days—and the miles—passed. Rudy's cask was nearly emptied, and we each carried a pair of waterskins with our remaining supply. Neither of us voiced the obvious conclusion: Though we had enough Aura, perhaps, to reach Agath-Trol, we would never be able to get back home again.

Our countless steps merged into countless miles, numberless hours giving way to a limitless succession of days. How many? Naturally I have learned, since that trek, of events in Carillonn and Faerine, of developing campaigns and desperate battles. By comparison, it seemed that we spent perhaps ten weeks on this desperate, endless march—yet in all those days we had no real sense of time passing.

There came a time when Rudy despaired, collapsing in utter defeat, unable to force himself to rise. I begged and cajoled, struggling to lift his lean frame, finally kissed him with unrestrained desperation. Kneeling beside him, whispering into his ear, I finally brought him to a pulse of vitality that was not quenched—indeed, was only fueled—by our feverish coupling. This, too, went beyond love. It was as though we fed each other, gave to one another nourishment and sustenance from our very flesh. On another occasion it was myself who faltered, and then it was my Iceman who revived me, who restored my own strength with the physical expression of his passion.

Always we continued, summoned by the distant pulsation of Dassadec's foul heart. In the time since Rudy had first recognized the sound, my own awareness gradually awakened. For a long time the sensation increased, until the sound actually became audible. At times it was maddening, but on other occasions it was almost seductive, alluring.

Until at last we came to the canyon, a yawning gulf extending an unknown, unimaginable distance to left and right. Miles across, it was deeper than the greatest gorge of mountainous Halverica. From the vast gulf rose acrid smoke, and we saw the seething torrent of a lava river scouring the bed of the plunging chasm.

It was this sight that killed our hopes, for—even if we could have climbed down the sheer cliffs and ascended the other side—we could see no way to cross that flaming stream.

And there, finally, both of us collapsed, together falling to our knees and yielding to a rising wave of purest despair.

From: *Recollections*, by Lady Raine of the Three Waters

THIRTEEN

A Campaign of Bentram Wayn

The line between catastrophe and triumph is
thin, often defined by nothing more than a
stroke of luck for good or ill.
—SCROLL OF BARACAN

— 1 —

Banners fluttered along the field, a colorful flock of streaming pennants crowning rounded heights, demarcating positions across grassy meadows. Bentram Wayn had arrayed
his army across a broad plain, with several strongpoints
anchored on steep hillocks. Spearheads, helmets, and
shields sparkled like diamonds in the sun, and a succession
of trumpet calls rang out, signaling the arrival into the line
of yet another company. Horses whinnied in nervous excitement, and wagons carrying extra arrows, water, and
bandages rumbled back and forth.

How many men were out there? Takian wondered, with
no accurate idea of the answer. One thing he was certain
of, however: No matter how many human troops they put
on the field, there were sure to be many more minions.

At least he had convinced the High Prince to rest his right flank on a marshy lowland where an open-water creek still flowed. The stream provided a relatively secure protection from attack against that terminus of the miles-long line. Yet the King of Galtigor was gravely concerned, for from his own command post he could see the other flank of the vast army trailing into open plains.

True, the companies there had been pulled slightly back from the main line, positioned to repulse an enemy attempt to encircle the defenders. And, too, the Knights of Carillonn, silver armor shining even in the far distance, stood ready to counter any threat to the left. But Takian had seen the tidelike advance of the enemy, and he knew that no regiment, no matter how elite and well-equipped, could stand for long against overwhelming odds. If the minions swept too far around that end of the line, there would be no stopping them.

More than a mile away stood the command post of Bentram Wayn, his retinue of nobles and advisors, and the sixty Knights of Andaran on their sleek palominos. The pennant of the white drackan marked the highest hill of the several elevations in the line. It was a natural strongpoint, save that it stood a hundred paces back from the crucial juncture of the human line.

For his own part, Takian had placed his signalmen on a high, steep-sided hill, midway through the right wing of the army. The banner of the Golden Lion snapped and fluttered in the breeze, marking the spot as a strongpoint. Swords and shields blocked the front slope of the hill, with the Lions' archers and light horsemen poised to turn back any assault against the sides. Leaving Hawkrunner's reins in the hands of an attendant, the king paced the circle of the grassy elevation, checking his deployments and looking across the battlefield, and into the skies beyond.

Around the army of humankind, from widely spaced directions, two distinct pillars of smoke spumed into the air. Each marked a wing of the minion army. The nearest was the western legion, with the smoldering proof of its destructive swath churning into a violent cloud just a few miles away. Gusts of wind periodically wafted acrid smoke over the field, leaving many of the human warriors red-eyed or coughing.

To the left, some ways to the south of Bentram Wayn's position, the plume had expanded like a glowering haze, not as dark nor as thick as the other. In fact, the cloud resembled a natural, albeit angry and threatening, overcast, and had shown no sign of advancing since the sharp setback at Mallard Ridge. Takian allowed himself to hope that the minions of that wing were still smarting under the sting of the earlier holding action. Most of the fires in that area had burned themselves out, no doubt because the fuel had been expended and the lack of advance kept the minions from reaching untrammeled woodlands.

Yet, despite the imminence of the western wing, Takian was most concerned about the force that still lay many miles to the south. If that vast legion made a sudden and precipitous advance, there was a very good chance that it could come between the army of Dalethica and Carillonn—and if that should happen, the scope of the disaster was unimaginable.

"Sire . . . looks like things are about to get underway." Randart broke into the king's concerns with a deceptively gentle announcement.

Takian turned to see that the first enemy troops had come into view two or three miles away, tiny black figures emerging from the cloaking woodland where the West Highway broke onto the plains. The minion column immediately expanded into a broad front, flowing like an endless river, swelling in a slick of darkness across the flatland.

The monsters emerged from the forest not as a single, thick flowage along the highway—though a broad column did arrive from there—but as a trickle from each of hundreds of small pathways, even from thickets where there *were* no paths. They seeped like liquid through the filter of the dying woodlands.

Smoke marked the fringes of the mass, a billowing cloud

darker than any storm front, here and there rippled by the shimmering forms of terrions. The flying minions wheeled back and forth above the front of the army, and their shrieks were the first, distant sounds of approaching chaos. Wisps of thick smoke swirled around the advancing companies as the minions formed into great blocks, moving forward, ranks expanding even more as thousands upon thousands of the monstrous troops came into view.

The battle cries of the minions reached human ears not as a chorus of shouts, but as a steady, rolling din, like surf pounding along the length of a rocky shore. A growing storm, the sound swelled and rumbled and shook the air itself, erupting into a forceful, building crescendo. The stench of Darkblood was strong and acrid, carried to the humans in increasing strength by each teasing whisper of wind.

The charge began almost imperceptibly, the black stain creeping forward no faster than a shadow advancing under the late afternoon sun. The speed of the advance increased markedly as the distance closed, until finally the massive front—kroaks and brutox shoulder to shoulder for as far as Takian could see—swept forward like an inrushing wave of seawater.

The clash began at a rocky hillock set slightly forward of the Dalethican line. There the Deltamen—the heavy infantry Takian had declined to use at Mallard Ridge— formed a wall around their tiny crest. Minions swarmed up the steep incline, meeting the swords and shields of the defenders at the front of the hilltop. The first wave fell back immediately, but other minions pressed through the shattered ranks, rushing forward to enclose the ring of humans.

From his vantage Takian watched hundreds of brutox and kroaks tumble backward, slain or knocked down by the solid troops, but the heavy losses had no effect on the fury of the advance. The clash on that lone hilltop resonated loudly, audible violence that carried across the entire field and echoed the thunder of the advancing charge.

A line of pikemen to the right of Takian's hill was next

to meet the wave of minions, facing the tide with steel-tipped spears, breaking the momentum of the charge with weapons anchored firmly in the ground. As the kroaks surged to left and right, seeking a way around the porcupine formation, many of the monsters swarmed onto the hill held by the Golden Lions. Now the men of Galtigor showered arrows into the mass, then met them with sword and axe as the charge quickly exploded from scattered clashes into a savage melee along the entire front.

Brutox swept around Takian's hill, and more men of the king's own regiment met them with sword and shield. Slashing blades into minion bodies, sending up showers of black blood and a crackling haze of sparks, they absorbed the first brunt of the assault, then shouted in hoarse triumph as the brutes staggered back down the slope.

Growling, bristling, sparking, the minions stomped and snapped, restoring spirit for another charge. Some waved great, serrated blades, while others bashed bare paws together with thunderous force. Then the mass of brutox advanced, this time slowly and deliberately, until again the two forces clashed. Individual minions swiped against two or three men at a time, the humans dodging and diverting, striving to protect themselves and deliver a blow with razor-edged steel.

Though the Golden Lions continued to hold, in other places the line bent, even ruptured—but wherever the minions poured through, human reserves charged forward, meeting breakthroughs with infantrymen's pike and sword and axe, or the keen lances of light cavalry. Arrows showered from the hilltops, falling with deceptive silence and grace among the teeming horde. Hailstorms of these deadly shafts washed across entire enemy units, slowing the momentum of a charge here and there. Yet though their killing was real and extensive, the missiles seemed to make no lasting impact on the numberless horde.

For a long hour, then two, men fought and died in a valiant effort to stem the onslaught. Fresh companies marched forward to join the line, and in many places the

minions reeled backward. But in other locales the defenders
wavered, threatening a disastrous breach until another formation of cavalry or jogging axemen arrived to plug the
hole. Though the line of battle remained stable as the afternoon hours bled by, Takian saw more and more minions
advancing across the pounded plains, the tide unabated
since the appearance of the first wave.

The vast front of battle expanded until the minions
pressed as close as they dared to the wetland on the human
right. A few scouts, keen-eyed archers, harassed the enemy
from the safety of the marsh, without any real effect on the
battle. Still, that flank remained secure, anchored so firmly
that the minions would never turn it.

When the brutox once again tumbled away from the hilltop, Takian looked through the dust and smoke to the far
left, seeing that the black stain had spread far. In the distance he saw horsemen moving against the probe, and
thought he recognized the silvery armor of Carillonn's
knights. The valiant surge turned back the probing assault,
at least for now.

To the rear the spuming smoke of the southern minions
had moved, though not terribly far. Yet the advance was
steady and inexorable, and would eventually create a fatal
trap for Bentram Wayn's army.

And still the rivers of minions flowed onto the plains.

— 2 —

Bristyn paced anxiously across the bridge from the King's
Tower to the castle, acutely aware that a week earlier her
husband had done very much the same thing. No doubt,
too, he had been racked by the identical combination of
distressing emotions. Chief among these was wrenching
fear—the consuming dread that she would never see her
mate again, or that her next look at him would reveal a
bloodied and lifeless corpse.

Yet other feelings stormed within her as well. She felt a

barely contained fury toward the High Prince, cursing aloud as she remembered his arrogance, the untested confidence that likely as not would get his entire army destroyed—and lead, as night follows day, to the loss of this city's towers and bridges and people.

And she knew despair, as she imagined the inevitable advance of Dassadec's horde, to the very banks of the Ariak. How long could the city last? Her eyes rose to the pastoral views eastward, to rolling hills and forested swales, realms of people, lands of water and rain. If the City of One Hundred Bridges fell, what would be the fate of the rest of Dalethica?

Complete, utter doom, she knew. Mankind might survive in remnants, on the islands off the coast of the Watershed, but the world would belong to the Nameless One.

Her crossing carried her to the Rivergate tower on the upstream end of the island. She looked at the aquamarine waters parting so far below, trying—and failing—to imagine a force that could blockade one of these deep, wide channels. Yet when she raised her eyes she was confronted by the vast, smoggy darkness of the western skies. The whole horizon was masked by haze, the two pillars of smoke still emerging from their distinct sources. South, where Takian had won his battle at Mallard Ridge, the swath was distant and somewhat diffuse, growing broader instead of closer.

North of that was the nearest smoke cloud, and she knew that battle raged at its foot. She mumbled silent, unconcious prayers to Baracan and Aurianth, praying for the success—and lives—of the men who tried to stem the minion tide there.

In anguish Bristyn whirled again, but something to the south caught her eye. Suddenly tense, she squinted in the direction of ruined Shalloth. A great forest burned there, and from her lofty height the duchess caught glimpses of flame licking along the trees, saw the smoke belching into the sky from its very source.

Yet when she raised her eyes she beheld a greater dark-

ness, a towering presence looming higher and far more terrifying than even the most virulent blanket of smoldering
vapors. The mass was pure, vaporous evil, seething with
pulses of internal lightning, churning and expanding in a
roiling surface of cloud.

It was the skyship of Darkblood that had destroyed Shalloth—the *Dreadcloud*. Bristyn immediately saw that the
vessel had grown significantly larger since wreaking that
destruction. Staring intently, she determined that the vaporous menace was not currently moving, though it seemed
to expand at a pace visible to the naked eye. The black
skyship crouched like a bear over helpless prey, devouring
meat, sucking blood—and then she understood.

The *Dreadcloud* was reabsorbing the vile essence of its
master's blood, gaining power, building force in clear preparation for . . . what?

In a flash of clear thought she knew, and before her gasp
of alarm could echo back from the parapet she had raced
across the bridge in a return to the castle. Servants and
courtiers whirled to stare as, skirts flying, she dashed
through the halls, across the courtyard, and into the stable.

"I need a horse," she announced to the startled stable-
master, snatching the reins of an animal tied to a nearby
post.

"Take Spitfire, by all means—but don't give him his
head, or you'll go where he wants to take you."

She hiked her skirts and swung herself into the saddle.
Pawing as if he sensed her urgency, the gelding turned toward the door and bolted like a shot. Bristyn ducked low
and let the horse carry her through the gate and over the
drawbridge in a thunder of hooves and an eye-blurring
force of wind.

Wrestling, she pulled to the right and the steed obeyed,
clattering down the stone-paved Roseway toward the city
gate and the long, wide bridge. Since the army was in the
field, she encountered few obstacles on the street, in
minutes closing on the arched gateway leading to the white
marble span.

Suddenly a man-at-arms stepped into the roadway, holding up a hand and loudly shouting at the horse to stop. Bristyn shook her head angrily and dug in her heels as the gelding skidded to a halt.

"Get out of the way—I've got to warn. . . ."

She recognized Gandor Wade only after she had begun to scream at him, her voice shrill and foreign even in her own ears.

"It's the *Dreadcloud*, Gandor—it's gathering power, waiting to move against the army. I've got to tell Takian and the High Prince, get them to fall back to the city, behind the river!"

"*I'll* tell him," Gandor replied sternly. "I didn't see you safely to Carillonn only to let you ride out the gates and straight into danger."

"Takian's out there!" insisted Bristyn.

"With ten thousand good men at his side. And—not to put too fine a point on it, Your Grace—the king didn't go riding off with such a clatter of hooves, and not even wearing a riding cloak."

Abruptly Bristyn realized the irrationality of her own plan. Shamefaced, she swung from the saddle. "Take Spitfire—he's fast, and fresh."

"Not as fresh as Thunder." Gandor pointed to a lanky chestnut warhorse, already saddled and pacing in a corral beside the gatetower. "You'll need your gelding to get you back to the castle. And Your Grace, may I say that your king is lucky to have a queen such as you."

"Thank you, Gandor—but *go*!"

Bristyn remounted in agitation as the captain swung himself astride his horse. She watched him gallop along the wide marble surface of the Rosebridge, and only when he had disappeared amid the copses of timber on the far bank of the Ariak did she turn and let the spirited gelding carry her back to the castle. This time she let the horse choose the route, as her mind was elsewhere, once again praying to the gods of men and magic.

— 3 —

All afternoon the fighting raged along the front. When the hilltops proved too well-defended, the minions struck at the sections of line stretched across the flatland between the heights. Several fronts threatened to buckle, until King Takian or the High Prince shifted weary reserves to counterattack. For a short time the minions streamed away, or fell between the prongs of vengeful human companies. No sooner was each breach repaired, however, than did the monstrous horde make a new surge, or two, or three, and the grim cycle was repeated.

Except that each time there were fewer men to form the reserve—while, as always, the minion numbers seemed infinite, unaffected even though many fell for every human lost. The landscape was dark with the corpses of kroaks, and stained puddles marked the places where brutox had been slain. On some killing grounds, arrows had felled the monsters in great swaths, black bodies lying like shocks of corn scythed down in the field during harvest.

Yet the toll on the human side of the line was terrible as well. Never in the course of this long and bloody war had there been so *many* dead. Wearily seated astride Hawkrunner, looking across the field, Takian felt his heart breaking at the extent of carnage, as if he suffered the wound inflicted upon each and every man.

Even now, hours after the first clash, the bodies lay where they had fallen. The survivors were too busy fighting for their own lives to form burial details for slain comrades. The king had heard reports of fever running rampant through a dozen more companies, weakening men as they stood in line of battle. How many had died, Takian wondered, because they had been too sick to defend themselves?

The sun neared the horizon, and still the onslaught showed no sign of easing. Troops of dark figures came out of the smoke, steadily flowing across the plain, replacing whole legions of slain minions—and *still* the enemy numbers kept swelling. Men fought like automatons, chopping axe or wielding sword for the thousandth time, raising shields or crouching behind battlements in evasions practiced against countless foes. In each instance, the penalty for momentary hesitation or slight miscalculation was death.

During a brief lull, Takian dismounted and found Randart sitting on the ground. The sergeant was bandaging a gash on his forearm, but shrugged away the king's question as to the severity of the wound.

Unsurprised by the man's stoicism, Takian told him, "I'm going to find Bentram Wayn. I need you to keep an eye on things here, make sure that we hold all the way around."

"Aye, sire," grunted the sergeant, the glint of determination in his eye undimmed by the ongoing strife. "But be careful."

"You, too."

Swinging back to the saddle, Takian wheeled Hawkrunner, intending to let the stallion pick his way down the rear of the steep hillock.

It was then that he noticed the lone rider approaching from the rear, from Carillonn, marking a line toward the banner of the Golden Lion. The man wore the blue and brass breastplate of Shalloth, and he lashed his lathered horse until the steed gave every reserve of strength. The animal all but staggered up the hill as it brought its rider to King Takian's command post, where by this time the monarch had recognized Gandor Wade. Mustache bristling with alarm, the captain of Shalloth saluted the king.

"What is it? Is Carillonn surprised by attack?" Takian demanded, conjuring a mental picture of catastrophe.

"The cloud, sire—the skyship that destroyed Shalloth. It approaches!" Gandor drew a breath while he pointed to the south, where the murk of smog obscured half the sky and the entire horizon. "The queen identified the threat, Your Majesty, which is now plainly visible from the city. She rode to warn you, and only when I insisted that she remain within the walls did she dispatch me instead!''

Shock and relief mingled in Takian's mind. "Thank you for that—and compliments to your courage. But how near is the danger?''

''The cloud was growing monstrously, sire . . . I can't say how long it will take to move against you, but the time is certainly not great.''

''What about the city—perhaps that's the target?'' The king felt another jolt of fear. Bristyn had briefly described to him the destruction of Shalloth, and he shuddered to picture the white marble towers, the graceful bridges, under the heel of such crushing destruction.

''The river should protect the city—at least, the queen seemed to think that it would. For now, it's the army that's in danger!''

''I see that—but I've got to convince the High Prince! Ride with me!''

Without a backward look, Takian pressed the spurs to Hawkrunner. The stallion leaped down the steep hillside and raced across the field, powerful hooves kicking up clumps of sod. They streaked along the rear of the army, veering around clumps of wounded men, dodging weary warriors who had slumped to the ground to catch a precious moment's rest. Glancing back just once, Takian saw that Gandor's lathered steed had somehow managed to keep up with him.

They reached the site of the prince's command post and here Hawkrunner burst into the lead, exploding up the hill, arriving at the crest sweating and heaving. Takian immediately saw Bentram Wayn amid his entourage—the High Prince rode his prancing palamino, and was garbed in a silken shirt and golden breastplate unmarred by battle.

Turning at the sound of the approaching king, Bentram tried to offer a smile of encouragement—but the strain of the day showed in the hollows of his cheeks, the dark circles that had formed under his eyes.

''We're holding them, eh?'' the prince said in a tone of forced heartiness.

"Yes, we are—for now," Takian admitted, then shook his head. "But I've had word of another threat—one unseen from here, but capable of destroying our army."

"Surely you don't mean the south wing?" declared Bentram Wayn. "That smoke cloud is fifteen miles away if it's an inch."

"I don't mean that, though your sense of direction is accurate." Briefly, sternly, Takian told of the *Dreadcloud*'s threat as Bristyn had described it to him. Gandor nodded in agreement when the king announced that it was already visible from the city, and could move to intercept the army's return.

"Her Majesty would have ridden here herself; it was only with difficulty that I stopped her," the guardsman of Shalloth informed the High Prince. "The cloud could move at any time—there's no telling how long we have!"

In another moment Bentram Wayn's expression hardened, and he fixed his sparkling eyes on Gandor Wade. "But it wasn't moving, you say?"

"Your Highness!" snapped Takian, the force of his voice bringing the High Prince up short. Pointing to the skies, the king continued:

"The danger is *there*, and it could move at any time."

While he argued the battle raged, the armies locked like wrestlers in a death grip. And when the king had finished he could see the fear in Bentram Wayn's face, but also knew that the young ruler couldn't admit that he had been wrong. Instead, Bentram whirled in the saddle, shouted to one of his signalmen.

"Send in the knights, Garton! I see another place where the line is beginning to break!"

— 4 —

Reaper circled among the lofty pillars of smoke, the dark, scaly surface of his body blending into the blackness that fouled the sky.

The humans were stubborn, surprisingly so. The Lord Minion suppressed a growl of rage, reminding himself that the force of numbers would eventually, inevitably, prevail. Yet it was so difficult to be patient.

He had seen the *Dreadcloud* fully fueled, ready to be unleashed. Though at first he had cursed Burner's failure at Mallard Ridge, now it seemed that that small setback might have been a blessing in disguise. It had served to lure the human forces out of the city, and onto the field where they were vulnerable to so much of Reaper's power.

For a time he watched as those golden knights once again charged from the hilltop with that vexing banner, the pennant displaying the image of the white drackan. And once more the minions fell back, leaving countless dead on the gore-stained field. Too often that had happened, across the entire battlefield—but especially at this one irritating point.

The Lord Minion was reluctant to lend his own weight to the fray. The humans could do him no real harm, of course, but the inevitable shower of arrows that would meet his approach was bound to prove irksome, their stings uncomfortable—and from Reaper's point of view, it was far better that ten thousand minions lose their lives than that he should be subjected to discomfort.

But finally the Talon of Dassadec could contain his rage no more. The battle had continued too long—it seemed possible that the insolent humans might even hold up his advance! He bellowed a furious cry, tucking his wings, arrowing toward the fight. Those knights of gold would be made to suffer.

If the lesser warriors were failing, it was up to the master to show them the way.

— 5 —

"Hold firm there!" cried the High Prince, his tone shrill with triumph. He turned to regard Takian, who remained at Bentram Wayn's command post. "We're stopping them!

Now do you see the rightness of this fight?"

"My young lord—the trouble is in the rear," the King of Galtigor insisted. "The *Dreadcloud* can cut us off from the city!"

"Bah—you think too much of retreat!" declared the prince. "We'll turn to that threat after we send this army fleeing back to Duloth-Trol!"

"They won't run—look at them, still streaming onto the plains!"

"Ah, but closer—see here!" Wayn's voice was loud, his eyes wild. He gestured past the Knights of Andaran as his company completed a spectacular charge, sweeping through the minion ranks, scattering line after line of kroaks and brutox. "Look how we drive them back yet again!"

"Only to regroup!" the golden-haired monarch replied. "Don't fool yourself into thinking this legion will retreat from us! They can lose ten thousand warriors and still win the battle."

"Allow us to make another charge, my prince!" demanded Berald, riding up on his lathered horse. The knight's armor was gashed, and his eyes were bloodshot. "We can get them to run!"

"Your Highness!" Donthwal broke in, his voice stern. "The King of Galtigor is right—there is too much at stake for you to remain here!"

"We can win!" cried the prince, clapping his knight on the shoulder. "Go, Berald! Put steel to them!"

Takian wanted to grab the young ruler around the neck, to try and throttle some sense into him. He looked across the field to the hilltop held by his own company, saw Randart's gray helm bobbing along the rank of shield men, still holding the hill. Yet the line between the strongpoints was thin, and growing weaker. Behind the entire front the king saw weary men, warriors collapsing in groups where exhaustion—and, increasingly, fever—dragged them down.

Abruptly a shadow darkened the ground as a massive shape emerged from the clouds to soar overhead, an image of serpentine wings and tail and legs, all purest black. The

sight of the beast sent a gut-wrenching tremor of fear
through Takian, and he heard a wail of despair rise along
the entire length of the human line. Those great wings
spread wide enough to encompass the entire hill as the
monster plunged toward the command post.

Berald shouted and raised his sword, rallying his sixty
horsemen. "Charge!" he screamed, his voice a shrill command.

And the Knights of Andaran responded. Lances raised,
the heroic riders spurred their horses over the crest of the
hill, confronting the beast even as their horses reared and
panicked. But those stout lances snapped like twigs against
the monster's scaly breast as the irresistible body crushed
downward from the air.

This was Lord Minion Reaper, a fearful voice whispered
in Takian's mind—the Talon of Dassadec. The king could
only watch in horror and despair as the monster landed
amid the brave men, lashing to all sides with talon and tail,
claw and fang.

"Berald—look out!" cried Bentram Wayn, terror ringing in his voice. The prince drew his sword, would have
lashed his stallion toward the knight's side except for
Donthwal grabbing the reins, holding the bucking horse
back. "Let me go!" shrieked the heir to the High Kingship.

The Lord Minion smashed the captain of knights and his
horse to the ground, casting the mangled corpse aside in a
single contemptuous gesture. The mighty head darted forward, jaws tearing more men from their saddles, while that
sinuous tail lashed across the ground to crush a whole rank
of signalmen.

Quickly Reaper leapt back into the air, the downdraft of
a broad wing nearly blowing Takian from his saddle. By
then Hawkrunner had turned, ignoring the king's efforts to
haul back on the reins. The stallion galloped headlong
down the hill, fleeing in mindless panic along with every
other living horse and man of the prince's command post.

Terror swept like a gale wind through the surviving men
of Dalethica. In moments the well-ordered line, a formation

that had stood for six hours under black steel and scorching sunlight, broke and ran. Screams of raw fear and pain rose from the mass, swelling into a roar of panic.

Routing troops stampeded like cattle from the hills and plain of the battlefield. Men clawed their comrades out of the way in desperation to reach safety, pulled riders from saddles to steal the mounts and flee that much more quickly.

A few veteran companies managed to maintain some semblance of order. Courageous archers showered the first of the pursuing brutox with arrows, stemming the onrush slightly. A band of pikemen formed a wall of bristling steel, blocking a great horde of kroaks—until Reaper settled into their midst, snapping weaponshafts like sticks, wiping them out to the last man.

The valiant infantry of the Deltamen, too slow to outdistance the minions all around, made a stand on their hill, heroically fighting to the last as darkness closed in—from the sky and on the ground.

And by then the army of humankind had flowed away like water, once-brave warriors fleeing with no thought but for their own slim prospects of survival.

FOURTEEN

Watersheds

The greatest treasures in the world are neither
rarest metal nor perfect gem—rather, they are
those prizes entailing the highest effort, the
deadliest risk, in the gaining.
—CREED OF THE CLIMBER
BY DUNKAR KALLAND

— 1 —

The work on the canal began immediately, as two thousand
diggers marched off under Awnro's guidance, ready to begin the channel that would mingle the waters of Faerine
and Dalethica. The remainder of the diggers set to work on
the construction of a massive encampment, choosing the
shelter of a cedar forest near the timberline for their lean-
to shelters and massive, rock-lined firepits.

Wistan Aeroel took his sylves into the hills and mountains around the sprawling camp with a dual mission. First,
they were to hunt the deer and Aurasheep that were common at these heights, augmenting the bland trail fare of the
army with fresh meat. Secondly, the woodland sylves
would form a picket line several miles away from the canal.
The archers had readily agreed to the precaution, sharing

Danri's opinion that the canal should be kept secret from both minions and humans until the work was completed.

After seeing to the deployments of the Faerine bivouac and assigning captains for the next shift of workers on the canal, Danri slipped Kerri's arm through his and started along the proposed route of the ditch. She showed him the spring itself, which was just beyond the perimeter of the mountain camp. The digger looked up, admiring the natural spout as it gushed a steady stream of pure Aura from a gash in the rocks midway up a sheer cliff.

"If we start here," Kerri explained, "we can run all the way to the new pass at a gentle downhill grade."

The two of them stood beside a boulder-lined bowl at the base of the cliff. The diggermaid pointed to the pool, which had a natural flowage through a gap in the far side.

Danri was impressed. "We can stop up the other side, and channel a ditch along here."

"That's just what Awnro thought."

"What about the Guardians?" wondered the digger. "Have they made any move to resist?"

Kerri shook her head. "Awnro's idea was a good one. As soon as we fixed the general location of the canal, he took the cask of Aura that had been mixed with a little of Rudy's blood and sprinkled drops of it along the two sides of our route. We haven't even *seen* a Guardian."

As the diggermaid gestured toward a path of double stakes laid out in a sweeping curve around the base of a grassy, rounded elevation, Danri pictured the course of the canal. Arm in arm they followed along the route, which the bard and the diggermaid had carefully marked with the white birch posts. Quickly the couple encountered a crew of diggers breaking up the bedrock on a section of smooth trench.

"The Watershed itself is just around that mountain," Kerri shouted above the clamor of picks and shovels. She pointed at the pastoral knoll. "Believe it or not, the ridge of the Watershed swings pretty low here. We won't have to do any pumping—or tunneling."

"Good," approved Danri. The capacity of any canal would have been greatly limited if they had been forced to lift the water over a ridge—and the project would have required much more time if they had to bore through any thickness of rock.

Together they continued on, approaching the smooth saddle that the diggermaid had described. More Faerines labored before them in rhythmic waves of rising and falling pickaxes, the line of the project clearly delineated by those birch posts. A tall figure, kilt swirling, turned from the excavation and waved as they approached.

"This is perfect!" Awnro Lyrifell exclaimed, spreading his hands to encompass everything from the workers to the mountains and the sky. "Your diggermaid has found another pass over the Watershed!"

"As easy as Taywick, maybe easier," agreed Danri. "Do you know what lies beyond?"

"That's one of the best parts." The bard strolled along with them, gesturing to the large, triple-peaked mountain that came into view as they moved through the pass. "The Crown of the World, of course. At its foot lies the village of Dermaat."

"Where the first breach occurred?"

"The same. Once the canal reaches this valley, we can use a natural ravine to save ourselves quite a bit of digging."

"And where will the Aura come down?" Danri was becoming increasingly intrigued by the prospects of the canal.

"It should flow right down into Dermaat Valley. We've sent some scouts ahead, led by Garic Hoorkin, to see exactly what we can expect."

"Good—I just hope he can stay invisible if he runs into any minions." Danri was pleased by the twissel's mission, even as he winced at the thought of the peril involved.

"He knows the danger. I'm sure he'll be careful," Awnro said somberly.

"There's one more thing I want to show you," Kerri

said, as Danri pondered carrying their reconnaisance farther into the Wilderhof.

"Oh?" With one look, he knew that his diggermaid had additional news—exciting news. Her round face beamed like the sun, apple cheeks flushed to a delightful rosy shade. The sparkle in her eyes, as those eyes found his own, sent a stab of anticipation through him.

"What is it?" he asked.

She nodded coyly to Pembroak, Awnro, and Hakwan Chiseler. "Will you excuse Danri for an hour or two? I have to show him something!"

"Of course!" the squire replied, while the bard bowed graciously, his eyes sparkling as he winked at the diggermaid. Hakwan merely looked at the couple with a knowing, slightly wistful gaze.

"It's not what you think!" Kerri said, her blush deepening. "At least, not just that."

Danri cast a look toward the sprawling campsite. The diggers of the night shift were already marching toward the canal. The day crew, two thousand strong, was in the process of stacking picks and shovels at the conclusion of their stint on the project.

"Guess they can get along without me for a while," the digger concluded.

"My, aren't *we* important," Kerri teased. "Of course they can get along without you! It's not like you're digging the canal single-handed!"

"I'm helping out," Danri huffed. "Besides, someone has to worry about guarding the camp and . . ." His voice trailed off as he realized that she wasn't listening. Instead, Kerri forced him to hurry just to keep up, leading him at a rapid walk along the course of a sparkling stream, then through a smooth cut between a pair of low bluffs. The fragrance of countless blossoms was a rich perfume on the breeze, and the sky seemed a blue more perfect than flawless turquoise.

Midway through a climb up the shoulder of a wooded summit, they paused to sit on a sunlit boulder which afforded a view of the canal excavation below. A hundred picks rose and fell in unison as a column of diggers proceeded along the opposite mountainside, gouging a channel that descended at an almost imperceptible angle.

"That ridge there," Kerri said, pointing to a saddle at the base of the opposite elevation. "That's where the canal will cross the Watershed."

"It's perfect—it *is* an easier crossing than Taywick, even without the illusions," Danri replied. "It's amazing you could find a place where the ridge dips so low."

"It beats digging a tunnel through the mountain—though I think Hakwan would've done that if it was necessary."

"I know that I would have, too," said the digger, as Kerri rested her head on his shoulder.

She chuckled, kissed his beard, and murmured into his ear. "I've come to realize that you're one stubborn digger—if you want to do something, well, you're going to figure out how to get it done."

With a sigh of utter contentment, he stretched his long arm around her shoulders and allowed several minutes to pass in warm silence.

Abruptly Kerri rose, extending a hand to help him to his feet. "C'mon. It's not too much farther."

They came over a low saddle and Danri halted, surprised and impressed. Before them lay a sheltered valley framed by high peaks dusted with snow and Aurafrost. A small lake, more of a pond really, reflected the dazzling skyline, while pines of a green so dark they were almost black softly blanketed the ground. The surrounding meadows were bright with flowers of every color, and trout too numerous to count jumped and splashed in the waters of the lake. Danri held his breath as a mighty stag, proudly bearing a branchlike rack of antlers, grazed easily along the shore.

"It's beautiful," he declared softly. "Almost as beautiful as you."

"Why, you digger," Kerri said with a blush. She tightened her grip on his hand. "I'm glad you like it—and I think it's beautiful, too."

"Is that why you brought me here?"

"Actually, there's something else."

He looked at her in silent query. Kerri faced him and took a deep breath, drawing both of his hands into her own.

"Like Awnro said, we've discovered another pass here, a place to cross the Watershed between Faerine and Dalethica. . . ."

"And?" He regarded her quizzically.

"And . . . I've decided that this is where we're going to build our inn."

— 2 —

"Rudy . . ."

Raine's voice reached the Iceman through a fog. The barrier was not the haze of mist drifting through the air, even though vaporous Darkblood was everywhere, sticking to skin and clogging nostrils. Instead, his thoughts were obscured by a blanket of fatigue and hunger, and the voice at his side seemed to come from far away.

Reaching out, he clasped his hand around Raine's, drawing comfort and strength from the physical contact as they plodded numbly along. They would have to drink Aura again, and soon—but they had to go farther, keep walking! He looked to the side, conscious of the great canyon yawning in the ground, feeling the abyss as an almost magnetic thing, a pit that urged him to leap in, to end this hopeless quest.

How long ago had they first encountered that immense chasm? Rudy remembered only that discovery of the barrier had threatened to bring their quest to a halt—indeed, they collapsed at the brink of the precipice, overwhelmed by the impassable, inescapable expanse.

Only after many hours of motionless oblivion did Raine move a hand, taking the Iceman's fingers in her own. And then, drawing on some unknown reserve, Rudy found the strength to rise, and Raine came to her feet beside him. By silent agreement they changed their course to the south, attempting to skirt an obstacle that might very well extend to the far end of the Watershed.

Angrily he shook his head, disabusing himself of that fear for the hundredth time. He felt the Heart of Darkblood pulsing from somewhere beyond the far side, a distant summons, weaker than before—and even when he sensed it, the rhythm was mocking, a reminder of the unattainable goal that a fool had set for himself.

Thirst tightened his throat and he unconsciously reached for the nearly empty skin at his side. His sense returned with the touch of his fingers to leather and, acutely conscious of their dwindling supply of Aura, he lowered his head and trudged on with brute determination.

"Imagine we're climbing a mountain," he mumbled, nodding vaguely at the flat wasteland before them. "We've got to get to the top . . . can't stop, can't turn back here."

When Raine didn't reply, he turned to look at her—and was shocked by the blank weariness of her face. There were deep grimy circles under her eyes, and her once lush hair lay matted about her cheeks and shoulders, black strands clinging limply to her skin. He could only imagine what he himself looked like, and with that thought he scratched at the beard that had begun to layer his face. As always, his hand came away sticky with Darkblood—the stuff drifted like mist in the air, and caked their hair and their clothing with relentless insistency.

"Rudy . . ."

Before he could reach out, the Woman of Three Waters stumbled and fell, slamming face first onto the hard, flat ground. She lay there as if dead, not moving even to turn her head to the side.

"Raine!" Panic swept through the Iceman as he knelt and touched her gently. Feeling no response, he eased her onto her back, leaned down, and kissed her parched, partly open lips. "Can you hear me?"

Gingerly he stroked her cheek, seeing that her eyes were closed but that she breathed, albeit weakly. With shaking

hands he lifted his Auraskin, dribbling a few drops of the
precious liquid onto her lips.

"Come on! You've got to get up—please!" he begged.

She showed no sign of consciousness, not even the
slightest awareness of his presence. Slumping in dejection,
Rudy tried to think.

As he leaned back, the cask he bore on his back sloshed
hollowly against the ground. Remembering his depleted
waterskin, he carefully refilled it and his spare. By the time
he had filled Raine's canteen, the cask was empty.

"I won't leave you, ever," he promised softly, taking
Raine's unresponsive hand. Lifting it to his lips, he kissed
her fingers and her palm. "Just rest for a while."

A little while later her eyes flickered open, and she
pushed herself up to a sitting position with a groan.

"Wait," he urged.

"What for?" she asked.

"Just . . . just for me." He pulled her close and she held
him tightly. Rudy felt himself growing stronger, and when
she broke away and rose to her feet he knew that she felt
stronger too.

"Let's go," she said, and this time it was the man who
followed the woman beside the endless canyon.

— 3 —

"It *is* a beautiful spot," Danri agreed heartily. "But I always pictured an inn as having, well, you know . . . customers. Perhaps you hadn't noticed, but up here we're in the
middle of wilderness."

"Oh, really?" Kerri's tone was droll, but the look she
gave Danri convinced the digger that she was absolutely
serious. "While we're talking about noticing things, I wonder if you'll remember that canal we looked at a few
minutes ago?"

"Of course! You can practically see it from here—how
could I forget?"

"Well, that 'trench,' as you call it, is going to change the Watershed. Or did you think that the Aura would just stop flowing when this is all over?"

"No—well, I don't know. I suppose you're right—it's going to keep on flowing unless we stop it."

"Think about it, Danri. This is a new pass, one that could have people coming back and forth over the divide for a long time."

"You might be right," he admitted, once again letting himself admire the splendid lake and lush forest of the setting.

"And Danri . . . about those customers. It'll be all right with me if some of the time we're, well . . . we're alone."

The digger of Shalemont felt emotion swelling his heart. "This was a perfect choice," he said thickly. "I just wish I could start building it right now."

"There'll be time for that. But I don't think it should be built, so much as dug. You know, kind of like the Tailings."

"Sure—and it'll blend in better, too. Folks'll come over the ridge and not even realize there's an inn here—unless we want 'em to know!"

Arm in arm they crossed back through the narrow saddle, pausing to inhale deeply the sweet scent of the pines. They strolled easily, following a woodland game trail until they came out in the clearing where the diggers were encamped.

It was with a sense of wonderment that, over the next days, Danri hurled himself into the project, lending his pick as often as giving orders. Kerri aided Awnro in insuring that the canal remained on course, and periodically marked their path against interference by the Guardians.

Sweating and exhausted, covered with mud or dust depending on the weather, the digger watched the trench snake its way around the mountain and through the saddle of the new gap—Kerri's Pass, he had taken to calling it privately.

After a week the canal was nearing completion. At its terminus in the Wilderhof, it would be channeled into a natural ravine that would carry the Aura directly into the valley of the first major stream. A short plug had been left at the source of the canal, so that the trench would stay dry during its construction.

Finishing his shift of excavating, Danri was feeling invigorated and alive. He found Kerri and asked her if she wanted to take a walk. She agreed, but they had barely started out when they were met near the Auraspring by a beaming Hakwan Chiseler.

"We're going to get quite a flowage!" Hakwan declared proudly, gesturing along the length of the deep, stone-sided ditch.

Danri inspected the work critically. He could see that when the time was right a dozen diggers would be able to rechannel the entire stream with a few minutes' work.

"What about the other end?" he asked.

"We're already across the Watershed, into the Wilderhof." Hakwan's pride stood tall in his voice—and with justification. He had been the one to supervise the diggers on the day shifts through the course of the excavation. "We've reached a point where it can join an existing stream channel—we get a few miles out of that. Right now, Awnro's with the crews in the Wilderhof, supervising the digging on the last stretch."

"Then it'll run right into Dermaat?" Danri questioned, trying to picture the Halverican wilderness that had been the site of his first experience with Dalethica, and humankind.

"Should take it down into the stream that flows past the minion camp," Hakwan reported. "At least that's what Garic Hoorkin tells us. None of the diggers has risked going that far ahead."

"Good." Danri nodded. The twissels, with their ability to become invisible for short periods of time, were the ideal scouts for the army. "No sense risking discovery—until we're ready to call attention to ourselves."

"And we're almost there!" Hakwan Chiseler declared.

Danri smiled, pleased. "You know, I swear that I can almost smell the Glimmersee!"

"If all goes well, we'll be through in just a few more days," Hakwan replied. "Pembroak's up there with Awnro, keeping an eye on the head of the ditch."

"Let's go see how they're faring," Danri suggested, in a mood for further good news. With Kerri and Hakwan accompanying him, the digger strolled along the completed section of the canal. It was still dry, so they could see the smooth bed and slick, well-sculpted walls. The channel was about a gigant's height in depth, and as wide as four or five diggers could span with outstretched arms. The gentle descent of the canal would cause Aura to flow steadily, but not in a great rush, toward the Watershed, and through the easy grade of the saddle across the divide.

"Ho, my digger friends!" Awnro Lyrifell's voice hailed them from the summit of a low hillock. The bard, kilt and lute bouncing, jogged down a steep slope to join them.

"What are you doing—stealing a nap?" teased Danri as the huffing human caught his breath.

"Stealing my share of a view, in truth." Awnro's jaunty mustache curled even farther from the width of his grin. "And, best of news, I'm sure that our canal has reached Dalethica. I recognized the mountains just past this ridge, and we're coming past the Wilderhof, somewhere high in Halverica!"

"That's wonderful!" Kerri exclaimed, giving the minstrel a hug, then taking Danri's arm in a tight clasp.

"Aye-uh," the digger agreed, his throat tightening with strong emotion. He felt a little light-headed, knowing he was witness to an occurrence unlike any other in the history of the Watershed.

The bard fell into step beside the diggers, pointing along the course of the finished, though still dry, canal. "Garic has gone ahead to mark the course of the stream, to have a look where the Aura's going to flow. He should be back any minute—and we'll be able to see into the valley for ourselves from just up here."

As they approached the ridge, which here was little more than a round-crested, grassy swale, a winged figure buzzed into sight over the lip of the hill.

"Garic! Garic Hoorkin!" Danri waved to his old campaigning comrade.

"Danri! Awnro! Guess what?" The twissel buzzed up to the party, so excited that he hovered above the ground, meeting the bigger folk eye to eye.

"What is it?" Danri asked, sensing Garic's urgency.

"There's a bunch of minions and humans having a battle over there! Right now!"

"Where?" Awnro asked sharply. "Can you describe the place?"

"Well, it's not in the big valley where the minions have trampled everything. I saw them marching out of there and decided to follow them. I hope you're not mad."

"That was very brave," Danri acknowledged, waving away the twissel's apology before it could be made. "Tell us—what did you see?"

"The minions went over that ridge and now they're attacking a village in the next valley."

"That would be Neshara—Rudy's town," Awnro deduced immediately.

"Well, it's going to be *nobody's* town!" interjected the twissel. "Unless we can get over there to help!"

— 4 —

The High Guardian was a being of stony visage and deliberate, even glacial cogitation, yet it was well capable of feeling pain. Indeed, for many days pain was the sole focus of its awareness, the only means by which the creature knew that it had not been killed. Great, tearing wounds had mangled the stonelike flesh, and rivers of throbbing agony prevented any attempt at movement.

Only gradually, over the space of this long time, did the creature make a more detailed appraisal of itself and its surroundings. First, it discovered that both legs were gone, splintered to gravel from the force of the fall. Amazingly, however, those legs had borne the full brunt of the damage, and the torso, arms and head of the Guardian seemed to function normally. The slate-gray eyes could still see, and slowly the powerful hands proved that they could still grasp.

Over the course of a day and a night, the creature turned itself around and fastened those stone-fingered hands to the cliff wall overhead. Slowly, deliberately, the great body began to climb, pulling relentlessly upward, rising out of the deep gully where it had fallen.

Finally emerging from the crevasse, the Guardian hauled itself onto level ground, flinty eyes sweeping a landscape of darkness and a sky of black and angry cloud. The Watershed was very far away, and the skyship was gone, destroyed.

And with it, probably, all hopes for the future of the world. This was something the creature knew on a deep and instinctive level, part of the knowledge that had caused it to climb onto the Auracloud in the first place. It was like a duty, and the Guardian knew all about duty.

Regret, however, was an unfamiliar emotion. Swiveling about, the heavy body moved by swinging on the two rock-like fists, then pivoting on the stump where its legs had been. Each pace caused unspeakable pain, but the creature was content to be able to move. In one direction, countless leagues away, rose the heights of the great divides, the High Guardian's natural realm, and there was a strong temptation to go there.

But from the opposite direction came a different spoor, a beacon sensed by the creature on some deep and fundamental level. And it was this summons that the Guardian followed, lurching awkwardly at first, then creating a rhythm of movement as it loped from fists to stump across the trackless plain.

— 5 —

"Can we fit any more barrels in the hold?" Anjell asked, frowning down at the crowded main deck.

Beside her on the wheel deck, Kestrel glowered, visibly straining to bite back an outburst. "Nay, lass," he declared, his voice a growl. "We're low enough in the water as it is. And if we run into trouble, I need to be able to jettison some of this Aura and lighten our load."

"Well, okay I guess."

"You *guess*?" The seamaster's temper slipped another notch. "Look, girlie. We're embarking on a voyage like none ever done before, and we're doin' it on your suggestion. Now, I don't mind that—but if this is going to work, you've got to let me take care of my own ship!"

"I'm sorry," Anjell said, meekly casting down her eyes. "I know I haven't been easy to . . . it's just . . . well, I promise I'll try to do better."

"You're already doin' more than most of the rest of us put together," Kestrel admitted, his manner softening. "And I'll try to go easy on you as I can:"

"Oh, I know I can be a pest," the girl said seriously, sniffling as her eyes grew moist. "Rudy used to tell me that all the time."

"Aye . . . well, I know the lad loves you like his own sister," the captain replied, awkwardly clearing his throat. "Er, I'd best see about hauling the anchor. Seems that we're all aboard."

Darret and Dara worked their way through the maze of barrels on the deck, greeting Kestrel at the foot of the stairs, then climbing to where Anjell stood before the helm. Dara leaned against the rail, her eyes wandering across the rippled, colorful expanse of Spendorial, then rising to the green hills of Norwild.

"What's the matter?" Anjell asked, as Darret slouched over to the rail and looked toward the bustling docks.

"I couldn't find Haylor . . . din't even get to say good-bye," the boy said dejectedly.

Anjell felt a strange sadness as she, too, thought about the diminutive sylve. After a moment, however, she realized that the emotion was kind of forced. "I think we'll see him again," she declared seriously, ignoring Darret's shaking head.

"Hey, lad, up to the mainmast!" cried Kestrel, drawing the boy to his chores. Darret swung into the rigging and quickly pulled himself to the top of the ship's central mast.

Anjell crossed to Dara's side and took her hand. "Are you thinking about home?" she asked.

Dara laughed softly, sadly. "Yes, I am . . . about Neshara and the Glimmercrown . . . and your father."

"I think about him, too. How he died on that mountain . . . I think that's one reason I hate the minions so much. Not that it takes extra reasons to hate them."

"It's just . . . I've lost the person who once meant the most to me in the world. And now, I . . . I worry that it's going to happen again."

"Don't be afraid, Mama."

"I can't help it," Dara replied, pulling Anjell close. "Being afraid for you. It started before you were born, and it'll continue as long as we're both breathing."

"You think this is the right thing, don't you? I mean, sailing to get Rudy and Raine?" It suddenly occurred to Anjell that although her mother had agreed to sail to the Darksea, it was important that she *believe* in their task.

"I do, sweetheart. And that's part of why I'm afraid— because I'm admitting that you see things the rest of us don't. *Impossible* things, things that mean you've changed very deeply. And it's not a change I can understand."

"Well, sure I've changed," Anjell pointed out. "I mean, a person can't fight minions, and meet kings, and see battles and watch a city blow up and sail to Faerine and *not* change!"

"You always were wise beyond your years," Dara said, and her gentle laugh was bittersweet.

"I can't wait for what's next! You know, we might be the first human people—I mean, besides Rudy and Raine— to see all three realms! I don't mind if we just see Duloth-Trol from the ship, though. I don't mean we have to go walking around there."

"That's a relief," said Dara.

"Haul anchor," Kestrel's voice called out from the main deck. Immediately the creaking of winch and chain rang over the deck, and the galyon trembled underfoot as the massive iron weight was raised from the bed of the Auraloch. "Make sail, lads—I want full sheets catchin' the wind!"

Anjell watched Darret control the descent of canvas as the huge main sail was unfurled. The wind had freshened out of the west, and by the time Kestrel returned to the wheel deck and took the helm, the sails had snapped taut and the galyon surged eagerly through the crystalline waters. The *Black Condor* knifed across the placid surface of the Auraloch as if the ship was eager to reach a sea of open brine.

Still standing at the railing with Dara, Anjell watched the domes of Spendorial fade into the hazy distance. She felt a curious sense of detachment, as though she knew that she was doing the right thing—but at the same time was well aware that she could do anything she wanted.

For a while she thought of Haylor, of the special Aura that he had given her. She still had a flask of it, tucked under her vest. She had already decided that she would save it for some instance when she really seemed to need it.

The sun sank toward the place where the city had disappeared. Kestrel announced that they would sail through the night, relying on the full moon to guide them safely along the Auraloch's broad estuary. The shores of green became shadowy outlines in the darkness, brightened by occasional flares where Aura flowed from springs or fountains on the land. Anjell was startled that she could see this Aurabrightness, just like Uncle Rudy.

The wind remained strong and the galyon fairly leaped

ahead, leaving a phosphorescent wake expanding, then fading, on the smooth waters behind. Dara went to bed, and so did the sailors who didn't have to stand watch. Anjell visited with Darret until the boy climbed to the crow's nest, ready to take the lookout spot for the darkest hours of the night. Kestrel, meanwhile, maintained his steadfast vigil at the helm.

Around midnight Anjell moved to the bow, taking a long drink of Aura from one of the casks on deck, trying to picture the course that lay before them. For long moments she stood still, staring across the twilit waters, her thoughts traveling far faster than the galyon. She flew through the air more swiftly than any falcon, with keener senses than the most sharp-eyed eagle. Riding wings over three realms, she bore her perceptions across a checkerboard of dark squares.

Only one image came into her mind, and it frightened her beyond words—not so much for herself, but for Rudy and Raine, and for her mother and Darret and Kestrel and all the crewmen who sailed, as the captain had described, under her "suggestion."

For that image was an encircling cloak of utter, absolute darkness.

— 6 —

Rudy dared not take a drink of Aura—and not only because he only had a single skin of the precious elixir left. More to the point, he was certain that if he stopped walking he would never be able to start again. Even the revitalizing effects of Faerine's draught would prove inadequate against the consuming weariness, the bleak loss of hope, that threatened to drag him down. Instead he shambled on, scuffling his feet through the black goo or powdery dust that alternately coated the flat plain of Duloth-Trol.

It seemed that he and Raine had been walking for a lifetime, yet he had very little sensation of movement. The vast

canyon remained a fixture to the right. They followed a
pathway several hundred paces away from the precipitous
edge, since closer to the brink numerous gullies and ravines
would have forced long inland detours. Every so often he
and Raine did approach the edge, looking into the smoldering distance ahead in a hopeful effort to see some kind
of end to the barrier. Always the canyon continued, as deep
and wide as ever. Nor was it uncommon to catch, in the
distant depths, a glimpse of fiery flowage as a stretch of the
lava river came into view around a shoulder of plunging
cliff.

For countless days the rest of the horizon had been barren of any feature, any ridge or elevation or butte that could
provide some point of reference. They might have been
walking across an eternal plain, though the Iceman con-
soled himself with the reminder that visibility in Duloth-
Trol was the equivalent of a gray and foggy day back in
Dalethica. There might have been a mountain range rising
five miles to his left and he wouldn't see a single foothill.

The only alteration had occurred overhead, where the sky
had closed to a roiling overcast of black, smoky cloud. Day
and night were unnoticed variations in the passing of time,
and only the pulses of fiery eruptions cast illumination
across the wasteland.

The Woman of Three Waters marched like an animated
statue beside him, a machine made from stone, incapable
of fatigue. Raine was silent, but held the pace steadily,
showing no further signs of the momentary weakness she
had suffered several days earlier.

They passed around the end of a gully that cracked into
the plain, stepping over a ditch barely a footstep across and
twice as deep. Looking toward the chasm, Rudy saw the
channel grow deeper and wider, snaking through a sinuous
pattern until it spilled from the lip of the gorge, a deep
notch scored in an otherwise perpendicular edge.

"Let's have another look across the canyon," he suggested.

Raine nodded apathetically, following as he turned toward the lip of the chasm. He skirted the path of the gully until he stood barely a footstep from the brink, where the world toppled away into a gulf so deep and broad that it might have been infinite.

Having an Iceman's view of heights, Rudy found nothing disconcerting in his proximity to the cliff. A fold of lower canyon hid the lava river from his view, but he could see the deep gash of the central channel, saw the hint of crimson illumination glowing in the depths. His main interest was southward, along the length of the chasm, where he sought any sign that the canyon walls drew closer together, an indication that the obstacle might be coming to an end.

Instead, he saw a bridge.

He blinked and shook his head, suddenly alive to hope—and to dread. The span appeared to be a natural arch, a curve of stone that emerged from a sturdy bulwark on this side, narrowed to an impossibly thin shaft of rock, then expanded to merge with a similar support on the far side. Mists of green vapor seethed and roiled in the depths below the bridge, the murk apparently rising from the lava river that gouged the canyon's deepest channel.

"Do you see it?" asked Rudy, shaking his head in a fog of disbelief.

"Yes—I do. It must have been obscured by the haze the last time we looked."

"It can't be more than a few miles away.

"Do we dare to cross there?" Raine asked.

"Do we have a choice?" The answer seemed obvious to the Iceman.

Slowly, Raine shook her head. "Let's go."

Conscious of his trembling knees, Rudy took a step backward. Then he was advancing in a running shuffle, careful not to lose his balance or to leave Raine behind.

As the bridge emerged more clearly from the murk, his observations did more to enhance his dread than his hope. From this distance it was still impossible to tell exactly how thick the stone arch was through its tenuous middle portion, but it clearly presented a frail and dangerous path.

He reached the point at which the span began. Stepping down on the tops of a few jutting boulders, the Iceman climbed onto the surface of the arch. Raine came behind and, for a moment, they locked fingers and thoughts in a silent prayer.

With a single, carefully placed step Rudy started outward, releasing Raine's hand so that they wouldn't unbalance each other. Hearing her follow, he didn't take the chance of looking around. The upper surface of the stone bridge was reasonably flat, though it dropped away precipitously just a step or two to either side.

"Give me a chance to get out ahead—we won't concentrate our weight so much," he suggested.

"Okay, but first tie yourself on."

Raine tossed him one end of the line and, after a moment's reluctance, he lashed the rope around his waist. She played out the length as he continued on, until she started to follow at a constant distance, holding the rope just taut enough to keep it from dragging on the rocky surface of the bridge.

The stony bridge narrowed, seemingly with each step, and Rudy became acutely aware of the space yawning below. It was easy to feel as though he were walking on air, so vast was the gulf that opened to either side. Though in younger days he had traversed many a knife-edged Halverican ridge, never had the threatened fall been so far. And even the sheerest cliff of a mountain had some slight outward sweep to it, while here, beneath the shaft of rock upon which he stood, there was absolutely nothing.

He looked down as he moved farther out, saw that he was approaching the deepest cut in the center of the canyon, where the lava river blazed and churned. For a moment the Iceman imagined he could hear the roaring surge of its passage. Listening more carefully, he felt the dull rumble through his feet, and knew that his audible sensation had been correct.

Finally he was standing on the narrowest part of the bridge, where the stone span was no thicker than a good-

sized tree trunk. Thankfully it remained sturdy and un-
bending, even as he felt gingerly for any sign of weakness
or collapse.

The blast of heat hit him as a physical blow and he staggered, lurching to the side. Instinctively he fell to the
bridge, spanning the stone with his chest and belly while
his legs and arms dangled over opposite edges of the gulf.
For the longest heartbeat of his life he waited for the stone
to break, the arch to crumble away from him. He heard
Raine gasp and for a brief, mad moment he considered
slicing the rope that held them together, knowing that his
fall would almost certainly result in her death as well. Only
the precariousness of his position prevented him from
reaching his knife and making the frantic cut.

And then his heart beat again, and he knew that the
bridge wasn't going to collapse. Carefully he rose to his
feet, surprised by the weariness, the grogginess that fogged
his mind—he must have landed harder than he thought, he
told himself.

"Watch out for the heat," he called back in warning.
"It took me by surprise—don't let the same thing happen
to you."

"Be careful!" she shouted, her own voice strained to the
breaking point.

Again he pressed ahead, but now each step was like
pushing through murk. Was the air thicker here?—why did
this require such effort? Looking back, he saw Raine following determinedly, watched as she weathered the shock
of the powerful updraft and stumbled along after.

He was weaving, he sensed, and forced himself to sit
down on the narrow span of stone, drawing deep breaths
in an attempt to recover his senses. Yet each inhalation only
made him more dizzy, clouded his thoughts with a heavier
blanket of confusion.

Then he knew: It was the air! Poison fumes rose from
the combustion of rock so far below, and they were sapping
the consciousness from his mind. He struggled, trying to
get to his feet, but could only crawl on his hands and knees.

He moved forward, but felt resistance against the rope.

Awkwardly turning his head, he saw Raine sprawled insensate on the narrow span of the bridge. Face down along the length of the lofty shaft, she lay without moving, right and left limbs drooping over opposite sides of the span.

Rudy tried to turn, feeling a crushing wave of dizziness. A sudden idea flared in his mind, and his numb fingers fumbled with his waterskin, trying to pull at the cork. But it might as well have been glued into place, for he couldn't get a hold, couldn't even force his fingers to pry at the stubborn plug.

When he fell onto his face, he barely had the presence of mind to sling his wrist through the strap on the precious sack of liquid.

Then his eyes closed, and the only blackness more complete than that layering the sky was the blissful unconsciousness that crept into his mind and swiftly gathered him into an all-encompassing embrace.

FIFTEEN

Last Rout

There is more honor in the performance of a
simple duty than in the greatest of individual
attainments, if the performance of the duty
results in the good of the many while the great
deed counts only for the gain of one.
—CODEX OF THE GUARDIANS

— 1 —

The Klarbrook had been reduced to a muddy ditch, a series
of puddles and rivulets interspersed with slick boulders
bleached white by exposure to air. Roggett was relieved to
see that the channel of the creek still remained wet, but he
could only hope that the remnants of the flow would be
enough to prevent the minions from trying to cross.

His heart sank as he looked across the valley, saw the
stain of minion troops plodding steadily over the Dermaathof, blackening the track through Neshara Pass. Here on
the road following the valley floor, the brutox tromped in
unison alongside the Klarbrook, sparking and growling as
they drew closer to the bridge.

The Black Bull Tavern and several farmsteads stood on
the other side of the stream. These had been abandoned,

though not until Kristoff Yarden had been forced to order the innkeeper, Barton Bull, physically hauled away by a trio of burly Icemen. Now Barton clutched a battleaxe and paced angrily behind Kristoff's company of pikemen. Farmers and their grown sons had armed themselves similarly, while the women and younger children had fled across the next ridge to the tenuous shelter of Zollikhof.

Roggett felt a tug of sadness as he observed how small the ranks of the pikemen had become. He knew that more men had been lost to fever than to battle, but the overall total had reduced the formation by more than half.

Roaring and stomping as they approached, the leading brutox brandished their weapons—blades straight and curved, axe and sword, spear and halberd, all having in common one feature: They were huge and heavy, capable of inflicting deep, maiming wounds with no more than a casual flick of the wielder's wrists.

Flames crackled beside the road, and Roggett winced at the sight of the Black Bull ablaze, the wood-shingled roof yielding with flaming, hissing intensity. Barton uttered a strangled yell, but the Iceman was pleased to see the innkeeper clench his hands around the haft of his weapon and grimly wait for the minions to advance. Watching the cascading sparks, the billowing cloud of smoke, Roggett couldn't help recalling numerous pleasant hours in the fire-warmed great room of the comfortable inn. Sharing Barton's grief, he vowed to kill an extra brutox or two over the affront.

Still moving along the road, the monsters crept closer, rattling weapons, stomping feet, raising a chaotic range of animal-like howls and barks. A hundred paces away they halted, growling and smashing weapons, the din of battle frenzy growing to a relentless roar.

Kristoff Yarden's company stood at the bridge, blocking the road into Neshara with a hedgehog of bristling steel. The men were packed shoulder to shoulder, the front rank kneeling with long-shafted spears anchored, angling upward from the ground. The second rank stood, with pikes jutting straight ahead, and the third, also standing, arrayed their weapons at shoulder height.

The mustachioed captain flashed Roggett a fierce grin. Obviously Kristoff had gotten over his bitterness about the retreat from Neshara Pass—the prospect of a new and desperate battle was all that it took.

Despite their hulking size and monstrous ferocity, the brutox advanced slowly toward the bridge. Roggett suspected that more than a few of these minions had met the pikemen at Neshara Pass. Certainly, they now showed great respect for the bristling formation.

Some of the brutes picked up rocks and clumsily hurled the missiles toward the defenders. Others barked and growled, pounding fists against barrel chests or sweeping talons through the air in spark-trailing swipes. They worked themselves into a still greater frenzy, bellowing, clashing, and sparking. Abruptly the leading brutox charged the bridge in a thunderous explosion of sound and movement, the rest of the band howling close behind.

The pikemen met the assault with the discipline and steadfast courage displayed during their weeks on Neshara Pass. The first of the brutox howled and wailed, stumbling backward, pierced and gashed by steel blades, spilling black blood from numerous punctures. More of the minions pressed, knocking shrieking comrades off the bridge, but they couldn't break the steely array of pikes. In less than a minute the assaulting monsters reeled away, grunting and shouting fiercely but showing no urgent inclination to make another attack. Roggett knew that they'd be back, but every moment of respite was more time to solidify the village's defense.

To that end, the Iceman started jogging through the woods, heading toward the thin line of Halverican mountaineers watching the approaches toward the southern end of Neshara. The ground was rough there, and well-watered, but if the minions could block off a few tributary streams they would have little difficulty working their way through forested foothills.

A sharp *crack*! echoed through the woods, the sound of a rock striking another rock. The noise was repeated, several times, and Roggett immediately deduced its source—and knew that the village faced a new danger. Unslinging his crossbow, he slowed his pace to a crouching walk, advancing silently toward the near bank of the stream.

From concealment behind a large evergreen he saw a brutox on the other side. The minion hoisted a large rock over its head, then tossed the boulder into the channel of the Klarbrook, where it clattered onto a pile that had obviously been started a short time earlier. An impromptu dam grew quickly, choking the stream's flow even more.

Sizing up the situation, Roggett knew that within a few minutes the minimal trickle passing under the bridge held by the pikemen would wither entirely. The Iceman eased forward, now concealed by the leaves of a lush fern near the creek's bank. He watched another brutox step past the first. This one also had a large rock, and Roggett raised his weapon, taking careful aim as the monster hoisted the boulder for a toss into the stream.

The *clunk* of the heavy crossbow echoed through the woods as the powerful, steel-headed bolt punctured the monster's chest, just below its jowly chin. With a gurgle of surprise and pain the brute fell backward, dropping the stone and pawing frantically at the deadly missile. Within seconds the burly minion arched its back, then melted into the grotesque, oily blaze of its death throes.

Ducking to the side, Roggett sat and pressed his back against a heavy tree trunk. Bracing the weapon with his feet, he recranked the crossbow and prepared another bolt while several rocks smashed through the trees to his right in clear proof that the surviving brutox hadn't located their adversary.

Carefully the Iceman leaned from behind the trunk, sighting beneath the low-hanging needles of the evergreen. When another brutox swaggered up to the stream bank, he aimed and fired, killing this one with another well-placed shot to the chest.

Once again Rogett ducked low, crawling to the shelter of a large boulder. Here he repeated the reloading process, and then popped up to slay another of the hulking minions. Readying still another missile, he whipped into shooting position only to find the far bank barren of targets. Apparently deterred by the hidden sniper, the minions had abandoned their efforts.

Relieved, the Iceman hoisted his weapon in both hands and started through the woods again. He broke into the mill yard in a dozen steps and halted, shocked at the vacant eyes, the reddened and ravaged skin of the twoscore men who lay within. The sick covered the ground, lay on pallets, blankets, and straw mats along the high wall. Some raised a hand in greeting, others just stared at him with empty, haunted eyes.

"Hello, Captain," said a young man, emerging from the house with a pitcher of water and a ladle. He looked around sadly. "Just givin' 'em more water. It's about all we can do."

"Good luck . . . good luck to you all," Roggett said softly. Shivering involuntarily, he passed through the yard and jogged on toward the village's main street—when he heard a shout that propelled him into a full sprint.

"We're under attack! From the *south*!"

The cry, vibrant with panic, rang through Neshara. Roggett raced toward the end of town, his hands tight around his crossbow as he hastened under the impetus of growing fear.

The mountaineers had formed a thin line at the edge of the village, staring nervously uphill, along the sparsely wooded slope.

"I saw one—up there!" Young Karlsted shouted, pointing toward a clump of cedars.

"Stand firm!" Roggett ordered, bellowing like a mountain horn above the shouts and blows, the rising chorus of battle. "Watch the woods there. Be ready, now!"

Even as he spoke, a massive brutox lumbered into view, bashing small pines aside with powerful, crushing fists.

Kroaks rushed in the monster's wake, a strike force lunging from the woods above Neshara.

Roggett charged, ice axe raised in both hands, his impetuous attack bringing the advancing brutox to a skidding halt. The huge minion raised a broadsword, ready to meet the foolish human.

Forgotten were the Iceman's countrymen, his village, his home. Roggett's entire being focused on the face of this hideous monster as he feinted, allowing the heavy sword to slash through the air before him. In the next instant he swung, driving the pick through the brutox skull.

Several kroaks rushed Roggett, then fell under the deadly quarrels of Halverican crossbows. Dozens of men rushed in their captain's wake, slaughtering more kroaks that emerged from the cover of the trees. Nevertheless, the howling mob advanced like an avalanche, stinking of Darkblood.

Hacking viciously, cutting down one minion after another, Roggett fought his way to the forest's edge. He chopped to right and left, clearing a wide front—and the rest of his men surged to expand the position. In moments the minions were driven back into the woods, forced from their foothold on the village outskirts.

But when Roggett looked back, he saw more and more of the minions spilling toward Neshara from the lower woods, and over the stream. By the time the Iceman raced back to the town, smoke was spiraling from a half dozen doomed buildings.

— 2 —

"Leave that wagon, you fool! Pull it out of the road! Now, or by Baracan, I'll cut you down!"

Takian's voice was a roar. Hawkrunner reared in the path of a laden supply wagon, causing the team of draft horses to whinny and kick as they were about to pull their creaking conveyance into the gravelly bed of a shallow stream.

The ford was narrow, flanked by muddy silt on either side, and one of the unwieldy wagons had already capsized in the creek bed. The stream of fleeing troops parted around the obstacle as men splashed and lurched and stumbled in their haste to get through the watery barrier. On the far bank the irregular mass re-formed, driven by mindless terror, propelled through the night only by the desperate desire to escape.

Hawkrunner's rearing fury startled the wagon's driver out of his panic. The man recoiled with a whimper as the King of Galtigor drew his sword. Takian wore his golden crown, and on the prancing stallion his presence alone quelled the driver's protests. The wretched fellow hauled on the reins and whipped the hapless steeds, his eyes wild as he sought a way around the enraged monarch.

"There!" Takian pointed to a patch of trampled ground, blocked by trees so that it remained clear of the stream of fleeing troops. "Pull the damned thing off to the side, cut your horses loose, and move on!"

With a crack of his whip, the man did as he was told, urging the team off of the crowded track. The wagon lurched into the muddy ditch, canting dangerously to the side until it was mired up to the axles.

Casting a frightened look at the king, the driver slashed the leather harness, freeing both of the snorting horses. He tried to catch the bridle of one, to haul himself onto the animal's back, but the steed's fright was too intense and it thundered away, dragging the miserable driver through the mud until a hoof crashed down on his skull.

Takian turned away, anguished at the man's death—despite his obvious cowardice. After all, if evidence of fear was reason to condemn a man, then virtually every able-bodied warrior in sight should receive a mortal sentence.

Around him the army of Dalethica was a sea of terrified humanity, men clawing over each other as they tried to flee. Routed by the Lord Minion, their exhaustion was subordinated to utter panic, a mad scramble toward the imagined safety of the city walls.

The fever had claimed more victims already this day, and these weakened souls were shunted aside by the healthy. Many lay in the ditches, too weak to move. Shamefully, many able-bodied warriors had cast aside their weapons, and more than once Takian had seen an armed man use his blade against former comrades in an effort to aid his own escape. In these instances, the king's justice had been swift and merciless—and fortunately, the example of a few swift executions had quelled internecine violence in the retreating army.

That was the case, at least, among those men who were within sight or sound of Takian. Yet the king knew that there were many who were beyond reach of his authority or his example—some who had no doubt already reached the city walls, and others who were, for all he knew, being massacred by the minions harassing the withdrawing army's rear.

By the time Takian had reached this ford full night had fallen, and the shallow streambed had become clogged with troops. Dozens had already perished, trampled and drowned amid the press, while others floundered in the deep mud, their pleas for help ignored by the hysterical mass that churned so close beside them.

The king had donned his crown immediately, then pushed Hawkrunner into the mob, the force of his voice focusing the men on a single objective—moving with a semblance of order and discipline. He had inspired the strong to help the weak, and now the file moved without the violent chaos that had marked it a minute earlier.

Even with the steady progress, Takian knew that the chances of most of these men escaping depended on their vanquishing their fear. They had to reach the city, but they had to do it without battling each other. For now, the king concentrated on seeing them across this stream, knowing that the shallow barrier might hold the pursuing minions up for an hour or two.

Urging Hawkrunner out of the shallow water and onto the muddy bank, Takian looked around, spotting in the moonlight a warrior in the tattered cloak that had once marked a prominent nobleman. The captain's helmet had been lost and his bald head, slick with sweat, gleamed like a skull in the darkness as, in a voice hoarse with use, he exhorted the warriors in the file to move steadily, taking little note of Takian as the king rode up to him.

"Have you seen the High Prince?" the monarch asked, recognizing the eagle symbolizing a legion of eastern pikemen emblazoned on the captain's chest.

"Word is he passed here long ago, him and a couple of those gold-plated knights of his," replied the man sourly, before looking up to notice the crown of Galtigor on the golden-haired rider.

An edge of defiance crept into the man's eyes. "That is, with all due respect, Your Majesty."

"Of course—and keep up the good work," Takian declared, before spurring his stallion toward a knot of men bottlenecking a nearby intersection of roads.

Still, the king was surprised to learn that the High Prince was already on his way to the city. Certainly Bentram Wayn had displayed his share of faults, but Takian hadn't suspected that cowardice was one of them.

— 3 —

Atop the now-familiar watchtower beside the city's Rosegate, Bristyn recognized the sounds of disaster long before the first of the fleeing men came into view. A swelling tide of noise rumbled from the west, like the crashing of a waterfall with steadily increasing flowage.

Of course, coming as it did out of the murky darkness of the night, the resonance could easily have been thunder from a lowering storm. Yet the duchess was certain that she heard sounds made by men—terrified, panicked men. Vividly she imagined thousands of voices raised in shrill screams, shouts and cries and pleas blending into a white wave of sound.

Occasionally the shriek of a fear-crazed horse, a bellowed command, or the splintering sounds of a crashing
supply wagon emerged from the roaring background. More
and more of these audible clues signaled that the first of
the escaping men were drawing close to the city, and Bristyn had no trouble imagining that the pursuing minions
would be close behind.

Even before she was certain, she took action. Racing
down from the tower, she climbed the stairway spiraling
around the outside of the white marble tower. The dark
waters of the River Ariak surged far below, but her eyes
were fixed upon the alabaster stone spans that connected
the western bank to the walled city. The Rosebridge, wide
and straight below her, was the closest, but she could see
the Ivyway and Grainbridge to the left and right along the
river, the white marble standing out clearly in the moonlight. All three spans connected the island city to the western bank of the Ariak.

She entered the gatehouse at the Rosebridge and ran
through a garrison room, bringing a dozen startled men-at-
arms leaping to their feet. Many of them rushed protectively
after her as she descended to the street in time to meet the
stampeding vanguard of the retreating army.

First to cross the Rosebridge were numerous horsemen
and several supply wagons, the latter hauled by frothing
horses lashed by wild-eyed drivers. Some of these bore a
full complement of fleeing warriors, men-at-arms clinging
to seats and posts, even hanging from the chains of the
tailgates. Other wagons were empty, driven by fear-stricken
men. The first raised his whip as if to lash Bristyn when
she stepped into the road before him—and fell dead,
pierced by a bolt from a guardsman's crossbow.

"These cowards," the duchess declared to the commander of the gatehouse guard detail, gesturing scornfully
to another pair of men who had fled with empty wagons.
"Clap them in irons—they can face the king's justice when
Takian returns."

"Aye, my lady!" declared the man, his own lip curled

into a sneer of disgust as he observed the flight. Quickly he urged his men into the crowd, and several more manic wagoneers were hauled from their benches.

"Pull them in here—get them out of the way!"

Bristyn ordered the lumbering wagons parked in a court-yard outside the protection of the city wall. With the streets freed of the ungainly obstacles, the stream of men flowed more freely through the gates.

She encountered a group of clearly weakened men, brawny warriors leaning on the shoulders of comrades, all but being dragged into the city. One of these hapless wretches turned his face to the duchess and she was shocked by the flaming blotches, the glazed, feverish eyes.

"These men—what's wrong with them?" she asked.

"It's the plague fever, Your Grace. It took the whole company just today," grunted one of the men.

"Well, here." Her voice rose to a shout, ringing through the packed column. "Bring the sick in here, into these houses and stables. You guards, there, bring water and clean blankets! Hurry!"

"Yes, lady!" The men in the city and on the road reacted quickly, and soon those stricken by the fever were being moved into makeshift hospitals that had been set up just inside the Rosegate.

Only then did the duchess again ascend the wall arching over the entry. She stood at the rampart between the spires of the two lofty gate towers. Hundreds, thousands of fleeing troops were gathering on the far banks, slowed by the bot-tleneck at the Rosebridge. She could see little detail, as the men were packed so closely together, striving to push their way onto the marble span, but she knew that she had to help.

She rode first to the Ivygate, leaving strict orders with the garrison there that the bridge remain wide open until the last of the army had crossed, and that all obstructions to traffic be removed from within the gates. She designated several buildings to serve as resting-houses for the sick, then raced through the city at a gallop, riding along the base of the wall, pushing her way to the north, to the Grain-gate and its attendant bridge. Already some of the men were crossing here, and she knew that many others would soon follow.

An hour later she had seen that all routes were open, and that the men were guided into different quarters of the city once they arrived.

She returned to the Rosegate in time to see a slight figure, spurring on an exhausted horse, pressing through the crowd. The High Prince himself, accompanied by Donthwal and a few of his golden-armored warriors, reached the safety of the gatehouse and pulled into the courtyard. Several of the knights were battered and bloody, being supported in their saddles by comrades. Nevertheless, they waited stoically as Bentram swiftly dismounted and climbed the gate tower.

The prince, ashen-faced in the flaring torchlight, emerged onto the battle platform, but took no notice of the duchess as he stared to the west, where tendrils of smoke wafted above the heads of his demoralized forces. Donthwal trailed him, and Bristyn was struck by the weariness and dejection in the stolid advisor's posture.

"Prepare to defend the city against attack!" Bentram Wayn shouted to the captain of the gatehouse garrison, who had come to ask for orders. "Be ready to close the gates!"

"No!" shouted Bristyn, her tone so sharp that the gateman turned from his capstan, eyebrows raised in question. "There are thousands of men coming across this bridge, fleeing the minions! You've got to let them across before you close it."

The prince whirled upon the duchess, his face white with fury. "How dare—"

"Your Highness!" declared Donthwal, drawing a deep breath and placing a hand on the infuriated prince's shoulder. The advisor's gray eyes, fixed upon the much younger face of his liege, were hard as steel.

Bentram stiffened in visible tension, but was unwilling

to meet that metallic gaze. Abruptly his shoulders slumped and his angry features relaxed.

"Very well," he declared curtly, turning to face Bristyn. "You can wait here until the army has passed—then you shall give the order that the city gates be sealed."

"My husband still rides among that army, no doubt somewhat closer to the enemy than we are right here," she replied, her tone scathing. "You do not have to give me orders—I would have stayed here anyway, until his return."

"Do that, then!" he barked. "I will go to the castle and . . . and make a plan for the city's defense!"

He spun and spoke again to the gatehouse captain. "I want regular updates on the status of the retreat. Send messengers to the castle every quarter hour, if not more often. It may be that I will send them back with further orders."

"Aye, Your Highness," declared the man, though his eyes regarded the young liege with barely concealed loathing.

Apparently Bentram Wayn was prepared to ignore the hint of insubordination, for he retreated back through the tower door, descending in a hurry.

Donthwal waited behind, clearing his throat awkwardly. Bristyn fixed him with a look of scorn, but he met her glare firmly and spoke.

"Your husband, the king . . . he was unwounded when I last saw him. He is lending his presence and authority to the rear of the retreat."

"No doubt he will be one of the last to cross the bridge," Bristyn replied sharply. Even so, she was heartened by the news. "Thank you . . . for telling me that."

Donthwal looked down into the courtyard where Bentram, trailed by his wounded knights, mounted and spurred his horse into the crowded Roseway, fighting his way toward the castle.

"It's a tragedy, in more ways than you know," the advisor observed pensively. Bristyn said nothing, her silence inviting him to continue. "He is much too young . . . was called here too early, far ahead of schedule.''

The silver-haired diplomat shook his head and faced the duchess squarely. "His whole life he has been inculcated with the sense of his own superiority, the rightness of his destiny to rule. Yet though he has learned of his legacy, he has not had the time to develop the corresponding responsibility. Did you know that normally the High King, when he is called from Andaran to assume the throne in Carillonn, is at least forty years old?"

"And usually there is no war waiting to greet him," Bristyn observed. Her manner was curt, for she had little interest in hearing the reasons behind the High Prince's failure. As the royal advisor started back to the castle she turned her eyes to the west, seeking some sign of the Golden Lion banner, and the king—the *man*—she so fervently prayed would return.

— 4 —

The darkmen moved through the swamp like ghosts, following the tireless pace of the padding brutox. The shadowed corridor of marsh-bound trail veered around tree trunks that were broader at the base than the span of Direfang's arms. Tendrils of moss dangled from low hanging limbs, but the powerful minion merely bashed these aside or flamed them into ashes with a sparking touch of his talons.

Direfang felt bold, capable, and very dangerous. Though he bore no weapon, he knew that his hands were killing tools greater than any man-wielded blades. Occasionally he bulled aside a small tree, or crashed through a thicket just to savor the destruction, yet he became increasingly anxious to vent his power against a more sentient foe.

To that end, he led his ragged army on a march of several days, following by instinct along the network of verdant paths. Occasionally, passage of a clearing or vista from the edge of a grassy swamp or watery pond gave him a clear look at the sky, and he followed the progress of the advancing smoke clouds with interest.

Direfang himself was surprised by his own endurance, considering that several times the path had carried them through eddies of muck, or even shallow water. Yet the liquid had not burned his skin, hadn't filled him with nameless dread as it should have. Perhaps the taint of Darkblood had spread throughout the swamp, he reflected—or even into the realms beyond.

His darkmen, too, seemed tireless, plodding through the night with only brief rests. During these intervals, the men were not so likely to sleep as to seek out a source of black swampwater. Gathering like wolves around a kill, the shaggy, growling denizens of the swamp lapped at the liquid, swilling the stuff until their bellies were swollen and their eyes bright, intense, and fanatical.

The mighty brutox had only the vaguest idea of his location in relation to Carillonn and Reaper's armies—yet even with such a dim idea, the course of his action was clear. Taking advantage of the knowledge among the darkmen, he sought descriptions and maps. His warriors informed him that they followed a general course toward the City of One Hundred Bridges. From the blue skies yawning over their destination, the brutox knew that the minions had not yet laid claim to the human capital. Indeed, the vast swath of destruction visible off to the left clearly marked the progress of Reaper's horde, and from that proof Direfang deduced that his own advance would bring his force into the attack from a completely different direction than the minion army, not only south, but east of the fabled city.

By the third dawn of the muddy trek, the darkmen had drawn close enough for Direfang to catch an occasional glimpse of marbled tower or white-walled hilltop through the thinning trees. The minion advanced at a lumbering trot and his men jogged relentlessly behind, their pace steadily growing until, as the plains of the river bank finally brightened before them, the darkmen and their hulking commander were charging in an impetuous rush. Toward what or who the brutox still didn't know, yet his monstrous heart surged at the hope of imminent battle.

When he broke from the cover of the tangled darkfen and saw a broad plain before him, a swath covered by the panicked throng of fleeing humankind, Direfang couldn't believe his good fortune. The roadway was choked with disorganized men, driven apparently by chaos and fear toward the imagined safety of the marble bridges.

Waving his brawny fist in the air, the brutox let a cascade of sparks trail behind him, a battle pennant that inflamed the hearts of his bloodthirsty warriors. A rumbling bellow of anticipation roared from his muzzle, echoed from a thousand throats. Inflamed by the prospect of massive butchery, Direfang led his screaming darkmen toward the flank of the ruined, defeated army.

— 5 —

Hawkrunner snorted and reared, hooves thrashing the air. Takian rode back in the saddle, feeling the stallion's urgency, as if the warhorse would kick the troops of the fleeing army into even greater haste.

"They're going now, old boy—these fellows have got the idea."

Bobbing his head, Hawkrunner allowed the king to guide him farther off the side of the road. Takian watched the men streaming past in the dawn mist, relieved to see that panic was no longer epidemic, the way it had been through the middle of the night. Many brave veterans cast worried glances backward, and the pace of the retreat was as swift as the crowded road and muddy ditches could accommodate—but, too, there was also order in the marching ranks, and many of the wounded or exhausted men were being supported between a pair of healthier comrades. Those who had succumbed to fever, too, were being helped along by their fellows, no longer cast aside to die.

Nudging the stallion forward again, Takian allowed the

powerful horse to churn through the marshy ditch, passing the slower moving foot soldiers. As he moved onto a gradually rising stretch of road, the terrain underfoot dried and Hawkrunner was able to trot, then canter. Recognizing the place, Takian gave the steed his head, and they rapidly ascended the gentle hill. This was the same height where he had watched for Bristyn, where the great avenue of the West Highway forked before the city bridges. The king knew that in the brightening daylight, he could view from the top all three roads leading into Carillonn—and the surrounding terrain from the Willowfen to the river bluffs north of the City of One Hundred Bridges.

Reining in at the crest, Takian was relieved to see the army filing in columns toward each of the three bridges.

"King Takian—Your Majesty! There you are!"

"Eh?" He turned to see Gandor Wade, also mounted, now guiding his horse across the hilltop to join the golden-haired monarch. "By Baracan, man, I'm glad to see you! Hawkrunner tore away when the Lord Minion came down, and I feared you were lost."

"Aye, sire . . . Thunder did the same. But, with respect, could it be that that's what saved us all? Look, Your Majesty—they're going to make it!"

"Wise words—I hadn't considered that, but you're right. Our only chance for the army to survive was to leave the field immediately."

"Now half the men are in the city already, and the rest're lined up in good order waiting to move onto the bridges."

"Good—it looks like they're using all three bridges."

"Aye. Word is that Queen Bristyn has organized the traffic in the city; she's got them moving to different quarters, putting the best troops into positions on the walls and gates."

Takian nodded, not surprised by the news. "What of the High Prince?"

Gandor turned to spit, then met his king's eyes. "He was among the first back to the city, they say. Supposedly he's gone to the castle—and that's good news, I guess. At least, he can't do any more damage there."

The loyal captain looked to the west, where the spuming clouds still billowed into the sky, and Takian knew that the man was remembering the image of black, winged death that swooped from the sky, taking so many valiant men. Though Sir Berald of Andaran had done nothing to endear himself to the king, it grieved Takian to remember the loss of that brave warrior who—even in the face of the most monstrous foe imaginable—had raised his lance and died fighting. Which was more than could be said for Berald's liege, the High Prince.

"What word from the rear, sire? Is the minion pursuit aggressive?"

"Their vanguard is not quite a mile back," replied the monarch, his brow furrowed by concern. "It seems that the stream held them up for an hour or so. We can only be thankful—that's all that bought us the little time we have."

"Aye, my lord. And may I suggest we move across the hilltop toward the east, here. You'll have a better view of the bridges and the approaches."

Takian nodded, still concerned. If the pursuing enemy caught up to the men trapped on this side of the Ariak, panic and massacre would be the inevitable results. Hawk-runner followed Gandor's lathered warhorse, pushing through the wide column that now spilled from both sides of the road. The king crested the very top of the rise and cried out in delight.

"Randart! You're alive!"

"Sire!" The sergeant, who had been seated on the ground holding the reins to his blood-spattered horse, leapt to his feet, then knelt and bowed his head before Takian.

The king swung down from his saddle and swept the weeping man into an unabashed embrace. "By Baracan, I was certain you'd fallen!"

"Nay, sire—though far too many of us were left upon that hill."

Looking around, Takian recognized a few of his warriors, battered and gashed armor still worn proudly by battered and gashed men. They knelt in unison as the king walked among them, Takian touching a shoulder here or offering a word of praise and condolence there.

The remnants of his Golden Lions occupied the top of this low crest, and true to Gandor's claim and the king's memory, the elevation offered a good view in every direction. Barely a half mile past the junction of roads rose the marble gate towers of the Rosebridge, the widest crossing leading into Carillonn.

Swinging back to check the south, Takian scrutinized the dark line of the Willowfen. Numerous figures had emerged from the thickets and advanced toward the intersection of roads. Though these newcomers were nowhere near any of the minion spearheads, the king felt a chill of apprehension.

"Those men—who are they?"

He pointed to the long file emerging from the tangle of the Willowfen. He hadn't been aware of a garrison in that direction, though the retreat could accommodate a few more men if that's what this new arrival meant.

As the thought flitted through his brain, he knew that his first guess wasn't the case. The advancing men didn't march as a road column, but instead spread into a wide front—a line of battle, ready to charge the crowded intersection.

"Where did they come from?" Takian demanded, even as he knew the answer was irrelevant. The important fact was clear: These troops were aligned with the enemy.

A glint of illumination rose from the middle of the broad front. Takian had battled enough minions to recognize the sparking trail of a brutox, and when he remembered Bristyn's tale of the minion that had floated into the swamp, he knew the answer to his question.

A roar rose from the rank of newcomers, and that knowledge was little comfort as the charge swept closer, thousands of fresh enemy troops striking at the vulnerable point where the whole army was tangled and congested, men hoping only to reach the bridges to safety.

SIXTEEN

Halls of Light and Darkness

A general with a ten-to-one advantage can lose
five warriors to each enemy casualty—and still
attain a magnificent victory.
—TOME OF VILE COMPULSIONS

— 1 —

"Get those pikemen up!" Takian shouted to Randart, gesturing to a company of troops who had retained their long-
shafted weapons through the chaos of the retreat. A minute
earlier the king had watched the weary veterans, many
wrapped in stained and muddy bandages, move off the road
for a rest on the grassy slope of the hill. "Move them into
line—*hurry*, by Baracan! I want them on the right flank!"

"Up, you men!" the sergeant bellowed, riding his prancing gelding through the startled pikemen, sending them
scattering and cursing.

A brawny fellow snatched up his weapon in reflexive
resentment, whirling the steel tip toward Randart—but the
horseman arrested the motion with a fiery stare.

"Look lively there—we're attacked!" Pointing, the sergeant directed the foot soldier's eyes to the south.

By the time Hawkrunner had broken into a full gallop, the company had responded to Randart's commands. Pike tips bristled and bobbed in the sunlight above gray metal helms as the men formed their three-rank line with the precision born of long drill. Hafts anchored in the soft dirt, the weapons soon formed a steely barrier that protected the crest of the hill and extended halfway down the slope to the road.

The king's stallion raced back to the crowded thoroughfare, where some of the fleeing men had noticed the tiny figures emerging from the Willowfen. Like Takian, they were at first uncertain about the newcomers. The troops muttered and whispered nervously, loath to accept the possibility of attack from a supposedly secure direction.

Approaching a group of captains who huddled like lost sheep beside a fleeing flock, Takian drew Hawkrunner to a skidding halt.

"Sire!" cried one of the company leaders, a gray-bearded elder wearing the plumage of a northern barony. At the word, the rest of the men knelt in unison.

Takian barked his words. "We're attacked again, my captains! One more hurdle to cross before the bridges."

He looked over the little group, fixing his eye upon a burly sergeant major whose eyes had glowered angrily at the king's assertion. Takian pointed at the fellow, knowing that here was one who would still show some fight.

"You! Get every man you can find who has a shield. Pull them out of the column and bring them into line to the left of yonder pikes!"

"Aye, sire!"

Takian swept his gesture across the others. "Split up and get busy. Gather everyone who can shoot a bow, or a crossbow! Put them behind the shield wall and start shooting as soon as you've got good targets!"

One of the captains, a sturdy, red-bearded swordsman at the rear of the group, turned a longing eye toward the marble towers rising so temptingly near—and Takian's temper snapped.

"Do it *now*—or by Dassadec I'll run you through!"

The name of the Sleepstealer drew an audible gasp from all the men within earshot—but it also propelled them into instant action. Shouting and gesturing, even physically tugging at arms and shoulders, the commanders pulled retreating troops out of the column. The recently defeated human fighters responded with alacrity, several shouting lustily, urging their comrades to haste, and Takian sensed the army's fighting spirit once more.

"Another batch of the bastards, men—get them out of the way and we're home!" he cried.

By the time Hawkrunner wheeled away, the king had seen a strong defensive line begin to take form. The position extended from the hilltop and screened the highway all the way to the crossroads, with the archers behind and more men rushing to fill the ranks.

Again Takian stopped beside the road column.

"Those things over there—!" His voice was a roar, thundering along the length of the line. "They're not men— they're bastards of the Sleepstealer. And they look to stand between us and the city walls!"

Mutters of fear and anger rippled through the rank, and the king was heartened to hear an increasing resonance of the latter.

"You, and you—and you!" He barked out the words with a finger pointing at various men—not chosen for the epaulets on their shoulders, or the plumage of their helms. Instead, the Golden King selected warriors with glowering eyes, with chins that jutted in unbowed determination.

"Get these troops into line. Send all archers back to the hill! *Move!*"

Once again Takian left a bustle of activity in his wake as he spun Hawkrunner around, ready to fly along the column, bringing more and more men into his impromptu defense.

"Sire—Your Majesty!"

The king halted as the summons, accompanied by the sound of pounding hooves, rang from behind. A dozen horsemen raced to catch him, and even through smudges of blood and inky grime he recognized the golden breastplates of their light armor.

"Braxton, Dayr!" shouted the king, greeting his Golden Lion riders. His heart soared at the knowledge that a few more men remained from his once-proud company. "By Baracan, you men are a sight to warm my heart!"

"So the day's work's not done?" inquired Dayr, staring intently with his good eye. He had lost his patch, and the scar underneath was red and inflamed.

"What are your orders, sire?" asked Braxton.

"Stand ready, men," Takian replied. For the first time his strong voice broke—he desperately wanted to send these brave riders on to well-deserved safety in the city. Yet they were the only horsemen in sight since, not surprisingly, the cavalrymen had for the most part concluded the retreat ahead of their foot-bound comrades. "For now, follow me!"

With the remnant of the Golden Lions in close pursuit, the King of Galtigor continued down the line, finding now that the troops themselves had discerned the danger and were already anticipating his command. Looking back, he saw arrows and crossbow bolts flicker in the sunlight, then settle amid the ranks of the darkmen who swept across the base of the grassy hill.

Reaching the crossroads at last, Takian drew up before a man he recognized—the captain who had been so useful at the fording of the stream behind the battlefield. Still without a helmet, the man's bald head gleamed in the cool morning. He had been pulling swordsmen out of the file, gathering several hundred in a clearing beside the road.

"We've had word, sire—another attack on the way?"

"Yes—and good work, again. You need to hold this crossroads at all costs!"

"With my *life*, Your Majesty. I will turn them away." Even as he spoke, the captain gestured to his swordsmen.

Quickly the troops formed a skirmish line, advancing through the field toward the onrushing swarm of darkmen.

Takian looked back to the hill, seeing that pikes bristled along the front, beside a shield wall that extended for a hundred paces. The men of Dalethica shouted their defiance while the attackers responded with a swelling chorus of whoops, barks, and howls. A shiver passed along Takian's spine as he realized that the darkmen sounded more like animals than humans. When he thought of Bristyn's brutal captivity among them, a haze of red fury fell across his eyes. For too long he had merely watched the fighting— now he would shed blood.

"Stand firm there!" cried the king, encouraging the men who had formed a line along the length of the road. "Lancers—*charge*!"

Takian wheeled Hawkrunner through a circle, and the men of the Golden Lion fell in beside him. Drawing his sword, the monarch felt the wind lashing his long hair, stinging his eyes. A kind of exhilaration came over him, and he raised his blade, feeling the stallion surging with the same battle fury.

The horsemen of the Golden Lion, riding their fleet but unarmored steeds, thundered toward the force approaching from the Willowfen. Lances leveled, the small band drew into a line abreast, wind lashing manes into battle pennants, streaming hair and beards back from gritty faces.

A darkman shrieked, pierced by the first lance as the riders swept into the midst of the teeming horde. In seconds the humans were surrounded by leering, hairy creatures— beasts that bit and clawed and snapped. Takian slashed his blade into the mass, carving a gory path as Hawkrunner pitched and kicked. Clawlike hands scratched at the king's leg and he cut down a lupine form, gagging at the thought that this brute might once have been a man.

A stench of acrid smoke stung Takian's nostrils and he whirled his head, seeing a corona of sparks, then spotting the brutox through the melee. The stallion sensed Takian's intent, and snorting and bucking, drove toward the minion through the howling mass of darkmen.

But a fierce-looking figure, hulking and knob-skulled almost like a kroak, lurched into Takian's path brandishing a huge battle axe. Hawkrunner reared, driving a sharp hoof into the fellow's forehead—but by the time the wretched creature fell, the surge of battle had taken the brutox out of the king's sight.

Not to say that there was an absence of foes. All around, darkmen howled like wolves, striving to reach the riders by weapon or tooth or talon. Whirling like a tornado, Takian drove the digger blade down on the right, then the left, then back to the right again.

A clash of arms sounded nearby, and he saw that the helmetless captain now led his skirmishers forward, into the flank of the darkmen. The savage attackers whirled against this new foe, swarming around the outnumbered humans on foot, as the valiant leader pulled his troops into a circle, fighting bravely, diverting the attention of the mob from the crossroads. Takian groaned aloud when he saw the man fall, sword flailing against the foe until the bestial warriors swarmed completely over him.

Yet the attack had freed the lancers of the Golden Lion, and Takian shouted at his riders, gathering them to his side, leading them in an impetuous flank assault against the milling darkmen. This time the foe reeled in momentary confusion and disarray, and the King of Galtigor pressed the advantage, slashing against cringing creatures on all sides. In another moment the monstrous troops streamed away, still jabbering loudly—but the brunt of their charge had been broken.

A glance showed Takian that the bridges to Carillonn were still crowded. Even now the troops moved across in good order, but how long could that semblance of discipline last? The crossroads was secured, and already the troops of Takian's impromptu defense force were filing away, withdrawing from the field of their desperate victory.

Atop the nearby hill a stain of darkness blackened the

ground where the pikemen and archers had held. Soon the
vanguard of kroak and brutox were trundling down the
slope, over ground that minutes before had been the scene
of battle. The darkmen too, rallied by the brutal roars of
their minion master, advanced—but now the bottleneck had
broken, and the men of Dalethica trooped to safety beneath
the gates of Carillonn.

Takian was the last rider across the Rosebridge, and as
he looked up at the gate tower he saw the golden plume of
his queen's hair streaming in the wind. As soon as Hawkrunner was off the bridge, she raised her hand, and the great
gates swung closed.

— 2 —

Neambrey shivered, not so much because he was cold, but
because shivering was something to do. About the *only*
thing he could do, he reflected with a sigh, as long as he
was sitting on this mountaintop, watching over Darkenheight Pass.

And really, there wasn't much to watch. The few probing
minions who had tried to force their way through the gap
had been easily turned aside by the gigants manning the
high wall. It had been more than a week since any of the
Sleepstealer's creatures had dared show its snout down
the smoldering valley.

Finally the young drackan spread his wings and flew,
determined to go someplace where something was happening. An hour's glide brought him to a sheltered valley in
the high mountains, where two sinuous green shapes lay
coiled along the shore of an emerald lake. Verdagon raised
the wedge of his great head, squinting suspiciously as the
younger drackan settled to the ground and carefully folded
the long membranes of his gray wings.

"Have you guys seen anything interesting?" Neambrey
chirped, as Borcanash, alerted by Verdagon's "Harrumph"

of greeting, opened a leathery eyelid to scowl at the new
arrival.

"By 'interesting,' I presume you mean deadly and dangerous," the elder sniffed disdainfully. "Therefore, I am
relieved to answer in the negative."

"Me either," Neambrey said, moping. "There's *nothing*
moving along that road!"

"That's exactly why we closed it!" growled Borcanash.
"So that nobody would cross Darkenheight anymore."

"Well, yes, but . . ." The drackan crossbreed wasn't satisfied with that answer. Still, it was hard to think of an
appropriate rebuttal.

"And," said Verdagon, "Know that it is written: 'An
enemy who fears to take action is no enemy at all!' "

"Well, sure—but there's still *lots* of minions around!
And we're just sitting here, wasting time and not helping
anybody."

"This is our part of the plan—you told us so, yourself!"
Borcanash growled.

"Yes, but—"

"No buts! A plan is a plan, and a task is a task," Verdagon declared huffily. "And you helped make the plan,
and we have our task!"

"Maybe . . . maybe this task doesn't need all three of
us!" Neambrey blurted, before either of the adults could
interrupt him. "Maybe you two can keep an eye on the
pass, and I'll go look for some minions that are causing
trouble!"

"Suit yourself," growled Borcanash, shrugging.

Verdagon seemed about to protest, but he merely shook
his head and looked over the sparkling lake.

"And I'll be back in, well, sometime!" the youngster
promised helpfully.

Before either of the big males could think of some objection, Neambrey spread his wings into the steady mountain gusts and pounced into the air. In moments he had left
the valley behind, relishing the freedom of flight, the pris-

tine beauty of the Bruxrange expanding in a panorama below.

He flew over the mountainous heights, above the foothills, past the bleak wasteland of the Suderwild. He wondered if the minions there would be turning around, perhaps trying to march up to the pass to break through the wall from this side. Instead, they seemed to be camped as listlessly as ever—without their Darkblood, the enemy warriors seemed quite incapable of mustering an offensive in either direction.

So Neambrey kept flying. He glided up the valley of the majestic Aurun, soared above the bright stream of the Bluerun, over the villages and mines of the diggers. Smoke churned from the foundries and smelters, and life seemed to be going along pretty much as normal.

Then he was again over high mountains, though the swales were greener, softer than in the Bruxrange. The Crown of the World loomed off to the side, and he craned his neck to admire the peak for so long that he almost lost his balance and went into a spin.

Finally he saw the extent of the long gouge, the canal excavated by Danri's diggers. Soaring along the winding channel, he didn't even realize that he had crossed the Watershed. Though the lakes and snowfields of the Wilderhof consisted for the most part of mundane water and not Aura, they made for a splendid view, reflecting sunlight from dazzling, wind-rippled waves and vast sheets of white.

He was still skirting the lofty, triple-crowned mountain, the central summit rising higher than the drackan cared to fly, and it gave him a thrill of pleasure to know that he was looking at the Crown of the World.

Only when he saw the blight that had been Dermaathof did he understand that the minion scourge had spread here as well. And when he soared over the next ridge, saw the teeming army of darkness swarming against the human village from two sides, he finally found what he was looking for: that is, something to do.

But first he would stop on the ridge of that high mountain, the one called Faerimont, and have a bite of snow.

— 3 —

Brutox rushed shoulder to shoulder up the main street of Neshara. Arrows showered the road from chalets and shops to either side, while a racket of clashing steel rose around the periphery of a walled farmyard at the village's outskirts.

Roggett knelt in a sturdy shed beside the feverish form of Kristoff Yarden. The pikeman's face was marred by red pox, and he shivered uncontrollably despite the double blankets the Iceman had draped over him.

"G-go," stammered the ailing captain. "There's too few of us left to fight as is."

"I will," Roggett promised. "But I'll be back to check on you."

"Kill one of the bastards for me, will you?"

"You bet."

Roggett stepped from the shed, crossed the yard to the street, and immediately saw a wave of minions charging along the lane. His crossbow was once again slung from his shoulder—this was a situation that called for the ice axe. He met a lunging brutox and killed the creature with a pair of vicious blows, then stepped back to avoid the spuming vitriol of the minion's death throes. He ducked the blow of another brutox, saw that the street was filling with the monsters—and barely sidestepped a spark-spewing attacker from the right.

Knowing that he couldn't halt the tide by himself, the Iceman darted into a side street—a narrow lane, actually—and stood between a tree and a small shed. For a minute he held there, killing another brutox and several kroaks that tried to rush him. Only when the shed's roof started to smoke did he retreat farther.

Looking up, he was startled by the sight of a familiar house. The Appenfell chalet, like so many buildings of Neshara, had been boarded up when the family departed for the Glimmersee following the discovery of the breach. Yet Roggett remembered many pleasant evenings inside the comfortable, sprawling home, drinking beer with his friends Rudy and his brother Coyle, or planning expeditions and learning about the high mountains from Rudy's other elder brother, Beryv. The Iceman remembered Coyle's wedding, in particular, for the man had married the girl Roggett had been too shy—and too slow—to approach with a declaration of his own affections.

He was startled to see that despite the planks nailed over the windows and front door, one of the side doors of the chalet had been pried open. Though it seemed like none of the minions had penetrated to this part of town, Roggett held his ice axe ready and crept into the house.

Advancing through the kitchen and front room, he saw much dust, and nothing to suggest that any intruder was present. He continued a quick exploration, and nearly bumped into a sword-bearing mountaineer as he turned into the front hall.

"Whoa, there, friend," said the man as Roggett instinctively raised his axe. "I'm just looking for a place to get a view of the action."

"Upstairs should work—there's a high balcony." Roggett took in the man's scuffed and battered clothes, noting the denim trousers. "Are you from one of the Midvale companies?"

"No, Zollikhof," the man replied. "Lars Larsman."

"Roggett Becken," said the Iceman, leaping up the stairs to the second floor with Lars behind him. Moving through the master bedroom, he saw that the windows of that room had been left unboarded.

From this vantage, Roggett and Lars could see across the village, getting a full view of the raging battle. The minions had broken the line of the Klarbrook along much of its length, and the Icemen defending the approaches from the Glimmercrown had been driven back to the village on their end as well.

For all practical purposes, Neshara was surrounded—and now this company of sparking brutox dared to charge right through the streets, bashing against the houses and gates as they passed each strongpoint.

A howl of animal fury rang from the entrance of the wainwright's shop, and Roggett saw Tarn Blaysmith burst into view. The axeman slashed a brutox practically in two, then turned to confront another pair of the monsters. Tarn's eyes were wild, his mouth locked in a grin of crazed intensity. And all the while he uttered that wailing cry, an unworldly scream that sent a chill along the watching Iceman's spine. Roggett imagined that each slain minion represented one more measure of the blood debt for Tarn's family—a debt that would never be fully repaid.

The brutes backed away from the fanatical human as Tarn whirled through a circle, decapitating one minion and gashing another. More figures rushed from the barn, a dozen axes shining in the sunlight as the men of Dermaat came to their captain's aid. Leaving many comrades writhing or smoking on the ground, the surviving brutox turned and fled along the street, toward the safety of the kroaks still massing along the streambed.

"Good work, to be sure," Roggett observed.

"But how long can they last?" queried Lars.

A roar thundered from up on the mountain ridge, and more kroaks spilled down like a black avalanche. Swiftly they encircled an outlying farm—a place Roggett had ordered abandoned over the frantic pleas of the owner. Now he saw the doors and windows kicked in, watched flames rise from the roof as the black tide darkened the ground all around the house.

By the time these minions reached the chalets at the edge of town, the farmhouse, barn, and outbuildings were fully engulfed by flame. A wind off the great mountain blew the smoke down the valley, the plume lying like a shroud over poor Neshara.

Something clattered, startling Roggett with its proximity. He listened carefully and heard a noise behind the closet door. "Wait here," he cautioned Lars, then stepped across the room with his hand on the hilt of his axe. When the noise was not repeated for several heartbeats, he flung open the door.

A small, startlingly pretty face greeted him, and he stepped back in astonishment, taking in the long strands of hair, tangled with burrs and branches, and the weather-stained cloak enwrapping a slight figure.

"A girl!" he gasped, before his face darkened into a frown. "But you should have been gone from here weeks ago—when the breach—"

"This is my house!" Despite her waiflike form and disheveled appearance, the girl—or was she a woman?—spoke with a determination that would not be denied. Rogett started at the sound of her voice, tugged by a vague sense of recognition. "At least, it was my husband's house, until he perished on the mountain," she concluded firmly.

Suddenly she moved, raising a hand, splashing something—water—across Roggett and Lars. The Iceman cursed in surprise, then saw the other man reel backward across the room, screaming.

"Get him!" cried the young woman, and Rogett pounced, bringing down his ice axe as the figure of Lars Larsman, already shifting back to its stalker's body, tried to writhe away across the floor. Reptilian claws reached for the windowsill, but two quick chops were enough to kill the creature.

When the childlike figure emerged from the closet and glared defiantly up at Roggett, he could see by the set of her chin and the maturity of her eyes that she was clearly an adult. "Thank you," she said primly. "That was quick thinking."

"Quick acting, anyway. I guess you did the thinking." The Iceman's mind whirled with memories, awareness that caused his heart to skip a beat. "Payli Appenfell! Coyle's wife, er, widow, aren't you . . . ?"

"The same. Greetings to you, Rogget Becken."

"And Coyle died at the start of all this, didn't he? I'm sorry, my lass."

"As are we all," she replied, holding her head high.

"But how do you come to be here? Surely you went to the Glimmersee with Dara!"

"I chose to return," she replied in a resolute tone. "And I'm tired of hiding—give me a weapon, and I will fight for my village and my home."

"But . . . come here." Roggett led her to the window, where the stain of charging kroaks spread through the streets, isolating each strongpoint from the neighboring fortresses. Smoke already rose from many of the buildings, and it seemed as though the black shroud he had earlier imagined was being drawn tightly over Neshara.

"Look! The village is lost. Try to slip out the back, get up the mountainside. You should be able to make your way to Zollikhof."

"What's that?" Payli stepped boldly to the window and pointed into the cloud. A long wing slipped into view for a moment before vanishing in the thickness.

"Terrion!" cried the Iceman, snatching the woman back by her shoulder. Crossbow raised, he peered through the murk, looking for another sign of the flyer.

"No!" insisted Payli, tugging at his arm. "Look!"

Roggett stared as a serpentine shape dropped from the blanket of smoke. He saw the pointed wings, like a terrion's, but that was where the resemblance ended. This creature had a long tail, four legs, and a supple, snakelike neck.

And a head that displayed gaping jaws, and a mouth that expelled a blast of white cloud through the minions massed at the end of Neshara's main street. The vapor swept into the monsters with explosive force, mist hissing and churning while the dark bodies trapped within screamed and writhed—but only for a second. Other minions, beyond reach of the gaseous expulsion, turned and fled in whichever direction offered the most direct route away from this serpentine creature.

The flyer swept along the street, roaring savagely, powerful wing strokes pushing the vapors along the ground. Stretching those long membranes, the monster glided easily into the air, rising above the level of the buildings to wheel over the panicking minions at the village outskirts.

Behind, in the once-crowded street, the cloud wafted away, leaving walls, trees, and minions coated with frost, a white tableaux of what had been a raging charge.

"It's a drackan! A drackan from Faerine!" Payli cried.

"It *can't*—" Roggett didn't try to delude himself, for the evidence in front of his eyes was incontrovertible.

"And look, the minions are running!"

It was true—the figures of kroaks and brutox could be seen scrambling out of the village. The drackan dove again, quickly leaping on several minions, crushing them as they fled. The Faerine serpent pounced and bit and clawed like a mountain cat enjoying the slaughter of field mice.

Again the shrieking of the battle-maddened Tarn Blaysmith echoed through the town, and the axeman emerged from the fortified barn with his company charging in his wake. Cutting down dozens of kroaks who were scrambling through the dried-up streambed, the men of Dermaat wildly pursued their enemy into the woods beyond.

Icemen broke from other buildings as well, slashing and shouting and hacking into the fleeing minions. Roggett raced down the stairs and joined his own company as the men rushed from surrounding chalets, adding their throaty yells to the din of triumphant humankind.

Only after he had run down the street to the edge of town did he see that Payli had found a large cleaver somewhere. The slight woman raced along as quickly, and as savagely, as any of the charging warriors. Her face was white, her jaw set determinedly as she shouted after the fleeing invaders.

With whoops of triumph the men of Neshara pressed their advantage. Stampeding back toward Dermaat, thousands of minions fled in terror from the vengeful Halvericans.

The slender, gray-green drackan flew along, shrieking and biting and killing minions and apparently having a wonderful time.

— 4 —

The Heart of Darkblood pulsed in its deep well, thrumming a cadence throughout Agath-Trol. When the Deep Guardian, still guided by the spatters of Darkblood cast by Nicodareus, broke through the wall of that subterranean enclosure, the Lord Minion knew that his task was done.

He looked with loathing upon the mutated creature that had labored so mindlessly to obey his commands. The Guardian's body was bloated and grotesque, and the head darted back and forth in reflexive seizures. On its snout, the spiraling horn bobbed here and there from the monster's aimless tremors.

There remained one final task. The Eye of Dassadec again scored a talon through the tender flesh of his slave's back, and when the ringing shriek echoed through the chamber he knew that he had the Guardian's full attention. Only then did he splatter more Darkblood, this time on the floor.

"Dig!"

He directed the blind, mutilated creature to excavate a trench in the shale floor. Nearby, a vat of Darkblood, contained by a sturdy sluicegate, seethed and bubbled, ripples flickering across the inky surface in time with the monster's excavation. The hole grew deeper, the Deep Guardian working its way into the depression it was creating. When it was sufficiently deep, Nicodareus opened the gate and allowed a flood of Darkblood to spill into the excavation.

A wail pierced the air at a pitch that would have shattered any mortal eardrum. Nicodareus stood atop the grave and chuckled, then laughed aloud at the beast's death throes, which continued for minutes after the Deep Guardian was fully immersed in its vat of Darkblood. Gradually the wail faded and grew still.

Nicodareus stalked through the tunnels of his maze, gliding over the deathtrap pits, admiring the ferocity of the growling, claw-rattling blutor. Finally he immersed himself in a stream of black liquid until he once again rose onto the floor at the connecting passage to the Sleepstealer's vaulted throne room.

The Lord Minion raised his head from the high, arched entryway, flexing the wings on his wide shoulders. He faced the wide stairway leading up to his master's throne room, and dared to hope that he would once again be allowed to mount those steps.

Return to your labyrinth. I shall summon you when the desire moves me.

The words emerged from the chamber of might to crush his hopes and his spirit. Nicodareus crept back into the maze, fully reminded that, in his master's eyes, he remained a failure.

Yet at one thing he had succeeded. The Heart of Darkblood was now surrounded by a network of stone corridors, all hewn from the bedrock of Agath-Trol. The Eye of Dassadec had incorporated subtle shifts in elevation, secret passages, trapdoors, and other deadly snares within the network of lightless halls. Darkblood flowed and eddied throughout, sometimes in little trickles, in other places through deep troughs in raging torrents. Any intruder would be forced to wander for miles—and to confront threats like the blutor, countless traps, even immersion in Darkblood—before having even a remote chance of stumbling across the pulsing vessel at the center of the maze.

Even within the limitations of his Sight, Nicodareus knew that the Man of Three Waters was coming closer, and that the woman, somehow, had survived with him. His earlier dread had become anticipation, for he knew that he was ready, understood that his chance for redemption would come when he had smashed the life from the human, had scattered his blood across the floor of his master's lair.

The Eye of Dassadec dared to use his Sight to sweep the bleak plains of Duloth-Trol, grateful that his master had restored that power—even if it was only to taunt him with a view of the world, the realms he might never again prowl. He was startled at the image he quickly discerned on the bridge arching over the great canyon: two motionless bodies sprawled on the bar of stone. He could *see* them!

But they were not moving, to all appearances dead, and suddenly Nicodareus saw a cold and frightening truth: Without an enemy, he could never have his redemption. With a bellow of pure rage he recognized the ironic fact that the defeat of the Man of Three Waters outside the walls of Agath-Trol meant that the Lord Minion was doomed to languish within.

— 5 —

Rudy's eyelid cracked open, but still he couldn't see. He felt a hard pull, realized that he was in the painful grip of some creature. Struggling, he grunted as a stony tentacle closed more tightly around his belly. His captor lurched along, awkward and slow, until abruptly the Iceman was flopped unceremoniously onto the ground.

By the time he had sat up and cleared his eyes, he could see the legless Guardian going back for Raine. The creature moved with deliberate precision across the bridge, anchoring its body with one hand while pivoting the other forward. When it clutched the stone, the surface of the rocklike hands actually seemed to merge with the bridge, clearly providing a very solid hold.

"You, old pal . . . I'm glad to see you," the Iceman muttered groggily, not at all clear on how the creature was still alive, or how it had come to them without legs. Yet there could be no doubt that this was the stowaway on the Auracloud, the being that had smashed to the ground upon the skyship's destruction and lost its legs in the fall.

By the time Raine had been carried to the edge of the

canyon, Rudy was able to stand up and walk around. He couldn't detect any lingering effects from the noxious gas, and as he knelt beside his beloved he was relieved to see her eyes flutter open, her lips part to draw deep breaths of the comparatively fresh air.

"What happened?" she asked hazily, shaking her head back and forth to try and clear her mind.

"The Guardian . . . *our* Guardian," Rudy said. "It must have followed us, come up to the bridge. Who knows how long we were lying there?"

Raine turned to regard the creature, whose slate-cold eyes were right at the woman's level. "Thank you, my friend."

Rudy was suddenly anxious, unaware of how long they had been unconscious, or of how many hundreds of miles they had to go to reach their objective. But the canyon was behind them and they had been joined by a new companion—it seemed like a good time for renewed hopes.

"Come on," he said urgently. "Let's get going."

Nodding, the Woman of Three Waters fell into step beside him, with the Guardian rolling along behind, swiveling from knuckles to trunk. In silence they moved up the slope of the gradual ridge that rose from this rim of the canyon. Rudy felt a growing urgency, hurrying unconsciously until he was jogging toward the crest of the elevation. Beside him Raine, too, trotted tirelessly.

At the top of the hill they stopped, looking across a broken plain, scarred by fissures and smoking craters, marred by spires of blistered rock and canyons of apparently bottomless depth.

But neither of them had eyes for the obstacles before them. Instead, they looked toward the massive pyramid of black stone that rose beyond the valley—the greatest mountain Rudy had ever seen. The massif loomed upward from a base as broad as any Halverican canton, culminating in a single pinnacle that was nearly lost in the scudding blackness of the overcast. Craters pocked the shoulders of the mighty peak, and smoke spumed from these, as well as from gaps and fissures that scarred the rough slopes.

They had found it, he knew: Agath-Trol, fortress of the Sleepstealer's legions, and guardian of his iniquitous heart.

SEVENTEEN

Gates of Darkness

One must be willing to make tools from
whatever materials lie at hand.
—CREED OF THE CLIMBER

— 1 —

"It makes me long for the times when we thought this place was abandoned," Raine said wryly, whispering even though the nearest minions were a mile or more away.

Still, after weeks of empty, lifeless vistas, a mile was uncomfortably close. The two humans and the legless Guardian had just flattened themselves, all but hugging the rocky ground as they watched a long file of kroaks emerge into view and march along the rim of a winding ditch. Brutox plodded nearby, cracking whips in spark-flashing explosions of sound, bellowing and kicking and bashing their sullen charges along.

Rudy crawled to the shelter of a broad, flat-topped boulder, one of many obstacles amid the broken, jagged wasteland that scarred the ground around the massive bulk of

Agath-Trol. The Woman of Three Waters moved deliberately behind him, her dark eyes flashing at the sight of the
objective that had drawn them for so long. Pulling itself
with its powerful hands, the Guardian also dragged itself
out of sight behind the large mass of rock.

Poking his head up cautiously, Rudy observed the column of minions while Raine lay on her back and scrutinized the sky for terrions. Though it had dominated their
view for several days, the vastness of Agath-Trol still
stunned the Iceman, and he found himself craning his neck,
ignoring nearby dangers to gape in awe at the imposing
massif. Today the summit was lost in the roiling clouds,
and trails of black vapor wisped around the mountain's
lofty flanks. In many places currents of inky liquid flowed
down those slopes, forming rivulets and streams that spilled
off the great mountain from twoscore locations in Rudy's
line of sight alone.

Remembering his immediate concern, the Man of Three
Waters looked along the ground, watched the tail end of
the kroak column disappear between two large blocks of
stone. He and Raine remained silent for another hundred
heartbeats, making sure that more kroaks—or stragglers
from the first column—wouldn't amble into sight.

"Let's go!" the Iceman finally said, satisfied as much as
his patience would allow.

The couple dashed from the cover of their low ridge,
ducking low as they scurried along. The Guardian came
behind, moving steadily but more slowly in its swinging,
hands-to-torso gait. Clumps of rock and other irregularities
provided occasional concealment, and Rudy chose a path
that took them from one piece of cover to the next. He felt
acutely conscious of the black massif, the impossibly huge
mountain rising before them, so awe-inspiring that he felt
like a mere bug in its shadow.

Ducking through the worn trench of the minion road, the
pair scrambled up the waist-high bank on the opposite side.
Casting a look to the left and right, Rudy saw no sign of
movement along the twisting route—though the tremor of

the plodding column still echoed, receding slowly in the distance. Behind them, the Guardian approached the road in its rolling progress, the awkward-looking lope that must have carried it over countless miles.

A hiss of warning from Raine dropped the Iceman to his belly with Lordsmiter in his hand. He looked around, saw that she had rolled onto her back with her eyes locked onto a point in the sky. Rudy squinted against the seething cloud.

"There," she whispered, gesturing with a slowly moving fingertip.

Now he saw it: a shimmering underneath the black cloud, like a heat mirage casting a reflective gauze over the scene. He picked out the terrion's narrow wings, though the head and tail remained invisible no matter how hard he looked.

The minion was flying toward them, though apparently without urgency. The Iceman froze, waiting for the telltale shriek of recognition, the cry that would bring a thousand kroaks charging toward them from the nearby road. Twisting slowly, he dared to look for the Guardian. At first he couldn't see their unique companion, but finally he spotted it, frozen as motionless as any other rock to blend with the surrounding terrain.

Turning back to the sky, Rudy saw the crocodilian snout then, and the sinuous neck wheeling grandly back and forth. The terrion swept closer and the Iceman wondered: How can it *not* see us? Abruptly the wings tipped and the graceful creature dove, veering away from the two intruders on the ground. Flapping its wings with visible urgency, the flying minion soared between a pair of rocky knobs and disappeared.

Scarcely daring to breathe, Rudy followed Raine as she bent low and sprinted toward several boulders that jutted from the ground a hundred paces away. Soon more outcrops of rock surrounded them, and they darted into a gulley with walls reaching higher than their heads. At last they stopped to rest, stretching out the cramps from their long, hunched dash.

"Here, let's take a sip of this," Rudy said, pulling his

waterskin off his shoulder. "There's about enough for each of us to have a taste."

While he drank, Raine checked her own Aura supply. "Not much more than that in here. It's a good thing we don't have to walk much farther."

He chuckled wryly, passing her the leather sack so that she could quench her own thirst. Still neither of them voiced the rest of the inescapable truth: that without Aura, they had no hope of reversing their trek and reaching the Watershed. They would never come out of Agath-Trol alive.

After she drank, Raine raised herself high enough to look from the gully over their backtrail. "Here he comes," she whispered, and in another minute the stolid Guardian had pulled itself into their shelter.

Despite the creature's lack of speed, Rudy was grateful for its presence—even here, when they had been forced to run and hide for the first time since the crash of the Auracloud. The Guardian had saved their lives on the bridge over the canyon, and, too, possessed a quality so quietly competent, so eternally wise, that its mere company was a comfort.

Remaining low in the concealment of the gully, they again moved toward the great mountain fortress. Eventually the trio drew near to the gaping entrance they had seen in the base of the massif. Crawling to the lip of their sheltering gully, the two humans cautiously raised their heads above ground level to scrutinize the yawning aperture.

The roof of the cavern was a cave mouth vaulting high overhead. Rudy imagined that a large building—or, perhaps, Captain Kestrel's galyon—could have been placed within, and would have failed to approach the curved apex of the ceiling.

"Look." Raine's warning was a bare whisper of breath against the Iceman's ear. He followed the flicker of her eyes, saw a troop of dark figures marching along the ground, following the course of the gully and plodding toward them.

The humans scuttled downward, hugging the wall of the
ravine as heavy feet tromped closer, then rumbled past directly overhead. The three intruders pressed against the side
of the gully, not daring to move as, for a long time, the
horde of kroaks marched by.

Only after the last footsteps plodded into the distance did
they draw breath again, but still they remained silent for
many minutes. Finally Raine turned and, as carefully as a
stalking cat, climbed the gully wall to peer over the rim.

"We can't go in here." She dropped back down and
spoke grimly. "Even when there's not an army marching
through the gate, I count at least a dozen brutox standing
guard."

This way.

The Guardian's soundless words reached them both and
they saw it start moving, reaching and swinging along the
ravine floor.

"Might as well let him choose the path for a while,"
Rudy said with a shrug. Raine nodded, and they fell in with
their stony companion.

The winding gully curved around to reveal a bridge of
black slate spanning it at ground level. Rudy lifted his head
for a quick look and slid back with an "all clear." Quickly
the trio dashed to the bridge, pausing for a moment in the
chilly shadows underneath the span, then racing onward
until another bend in the ravine moved them out of sight.

Now the massif loomed large, visible even from the
depths of the trench, and Rudy was seized by an odd
thought—which he voiced when they paused again to catch
their breath.

"Did you ever think about it—we're probably the first
humans to see this place?"

Not first . . . one was here in a time before Guardians.

"That's comforting," Raine said wryly, while Rudy
looked at their companion in surprise. Then the woman's
face grew serious. "Though Pheathersqyll did tell me a
story once . . . about the Heart of Darkblood. And I'm certain there was a human there."

"There have to be a few interesting stories in this boulder of a head," the Iceman murmured, looking without success for a flicker of response in the gray slate eyes.

They moved on again, and within a few minutes came around another bend to discover the end of the ravine—and a shadowy niche that apparently merged into a lightless tunnel.

"It might be another entrance," Rudy said, indicating the crack where the gully abruptly terminated.

Carefully they crept toward the opening, studying the dark outline which came more fully into view as they approached. Suddenly a flicker of light flashed in the gap, and the trio froze. Staring, Rudy made out the shape of a great brutox hulking just inside.

"Stay down here," he whispered, his voice a bare puff of air. "I'm going to work my way up to the right. I'll try to take it in a rush."

Raine's face displayed her fear at the notion, but she nodded grimly, having no other alternative. The Man of Three Waters backed out of sight of the aperture, then climbed up to ground level. He found himself in the midst of a boulder field, which provided useful cover as he crept over the rocks along the rim of the gully. The mountainside swooped upward from just ahead, but fortunately there seemed to be no other minions in the vicinity.

At the end of the gully he drew his sword. With a fluid gesture he leapt down to the floor of the ravine and lunged into the tunnel, Lordsmiter gleaming hungrily in his hand. Slashing quickly, he sought the flesh of the brutox that had been standing here—but his blade found no target. Only when he had advanced a dozen steps, probing into the shadows with the tip of the deadly sword, did he realize that the minion was gone.

By the time he had jogged back to the entrance, intending to wave Raine inward, she and the Guardian had advanced to the tunnel mouth. "I saw that brutox disappear just after you started up. I couldn't tell if it was waiting, or if it had wandered away."

"As far as I can tell, it's gone," Rudy replied. "Let's move on before it decides to come back."

Together they peered inside. The aperture was about Rudy's height, and led to a tunnel penetrating straight under the mountain.

"Looks like our way in," the Iceman said.

"I don't think we'll see a better one," agreed Raine.

Swiftly they started inward, advancing through the darkness. Both of them were surprised by how quickly the murky illumination of the world outside disappeared from sight behind them.

— 2 —

Neambrey relished the pursuit. He flew in a short spurt, then pounced on another throng of his enemies, slashing and biting against the fleeing minions—until a brutox raised its long, jagged-edged sword and scraped a deep gouge in the drackan's belly. Howling in shock and outrage, the supple Faerine twisted his neck and chomped down on the brute's leering face. Casting the corpse aside, Neambrey tried unsuccessfully to spit the vile taste of Darkblood from his mouth. Shaking his head, he jumped back into the air, concluding that the unpleasant aftertaste was a necessary accompaniment to this kind of entertainment.

Actually, even when he just flew above them, the minions seemed to retreat pretty well on their own. The drackan had already chased them up the long, forested ridge that overlooked the town. Of course, he would freely admit that the humans had helped some too—the Halvericans had thrown themselves into the pursuit of the enemy with a vengeance.

Allowing himself a brief time away from the battle, Neambrey flew upward, straining with all the strength of his wings toward one of the high ridges of Faerimont. Settling to the snowy cornice, he looked around until he saw the rainbow swath that marked Aurasnow. Craning his neck, he took a massive bite, allowing the frosty stuff to trickle from his jaws, gulping down enough that he began to feel the pressure of deadly frost building within his belly.

Wings spread, he launched himself from the high mountainside, arrowing toward the battle raging in the forested ridges below. The river of minions flowed backward now as the monsters fled from Neshara toward the source of their breach, in Dermaat. The young drackan came to rest amid this stream of monstrous troops, spreading his jaws and spewing a white cloud of chilling frost into the faces of panicked kroaks. A hundred of the brutes fell under the frigid blast, and dozens more limped off the trail, even threw themselves from the precipitous summit in order to avoid the deadly serpent.

Throngs of victorious humans raced through the woods beside the fleeing minions. The Icemen moved like ghosts, emerging from the trees to strike a company of kroaks as the minions scrambled up a steep outcrop, or showering deadly crossbow bolts against a file of brutox lumbering along an exposed stretch of trail.

Hopping and pouncing amid the enemy warriors, Neambrey dodged the occasional blow directed at him, as often as not slaying overly aggressive minions with a single chomp on the head, or a slash of his claws. For the most part he fought alone, quickly leaping away if too many minions charged him. After one such evasion, however, he looked around to see a trio of brutox make a sparking attack at two humans. One of the pair was a large man who wielded an oversized ice axe, and his partner was a waifish woman slashing fiercely—but armed only with a large cleaver.

"Let me help!" the drackan offered, charging head down like a bull, tackling one brutox and then wrenching it into a twisted corpse while the woman herself cut the other one down with a cleaver slash across its bulging belly. The big Iceman pulled her back as she would have thrown herself further into the pursuit, and Neambrey took to the air with a quick leap, avoiding the bronzed spear tip of another lumbering brutox. That minion, in turn, fell beneath the Halverican warrior's sharp ice axe.

Banking through a sharp curve, Neambrey dove to the trail as the pathway arced over the grassy summit of the ridge. He snapped at a brutox and sent the beast tumbling over the edge while his forepaws raked a pair of kroaks that were too slow to dive out of the way. Before the invaders could do more than slash wildly at his hard scales, the young drackan had leapt again into the air, soaring beside the ridge as he sent more kroaks tumbling with sharp jabs of his forepaws.

Now the minion flight degenerated into a mad dash, as brutox bulled the lesser kroaks out of the way. Most of the Halvericans halted at the crest of the ridge, but sent plunging arrows and tumbling boulders after the retreating horde.

Neambrey glided over the deep valley, distracted by movement along the far ridge. The minions gathered like a pool of ink in the low ground that had once been Dermaat, while a file of warriors, sunlight glinting on their steel helmets and weapons, came into view in the wilderness beyond the ruined town. Many thousands of the Sleepstealer's monsters clustered alongside the black stream. Sparks flared from the brutox among them, but even those hulking brutes seemed to show no inclination for rallying the horde.

Deciding that the danger was over, for now, the drackan soared over to get a better look at the newcomers.

"Hey, look!" Neambrey bugled in delighted recognition. "The diggers are here!"

— 3 —

"Can you see?"

Raine whispered the question as the Man of Three Waters squinted through the murky darkness.

"Barely. But we've got to keep moving."

Raine's reply echoed his own opinion, despite the fact that—barely a hundred steps into Agath-Trol's narrow tun-

nel—the pair had been forced almost to a halt. He shuffled
forward gingerly, probing the rocky floor with his foot to
insure a secure step. The Woman of Three Waters kept
pace, and the Guardian thumped softly behind.

"Try Lordsmiter," suggested Raine.

Drawing the weapon, the Iceman immediately sensed a
lessening of the darkness, like a thinning of once-
impermeable fog. There was no visible luminescence to the
blade, but now he saw the nearby walls, realized that a
ceiling arched overhead higher than he could reach.

"It seems to be getting a little better," he said, encouraged by the growing definition he discerned in the narrow
passageway before them. The corridor swerved to the left,
gradually expanding in width.

Mutely, Raine nodded, and once more the Iceman proceeded carefully along the winding passageway. Now he
could see the knobby outcrops of rock, and he picked up
his pace correspondingly. Fortunately the floor was smooth,
and they were able to glide along silently without stumbling—and the Guardian's gait, as always, was virtually
noiseless. A tight curve in the corridor took them into a
gentle climb and Rudy held the sword high, looking up.

"Hey—what—?" he gasped in surprise as the floor gave
way and he dropped straight down. He skidded down a
steep ramp, struggling to hold Lordsmiter aloft, away from
himself and Raine. Abruptly he smashed onto a flat, stone
surface, instinctively scrambling out of the way just before
Raine, and then the Guardian, tumbled after.

"What happened?" Raine asked, holding her head and
slowly sitting up. Behind her the Guardian, having landed
flat on its face, slowly pushed itself up with its arms, un-
blinking and stoic as ever.

"The floor fell away, turned into kind of a slide. But can
we get back up there?" wondered the Iceman.

A quick inspection, with Lordsmiter raised overhead,
showed that the chute had plunged them into a deeper cavern, depositing them through a gap in the ceiling.

"I don't think we can even reach the end of the slide,"

Raine declared bluntly. "Not that we could climb it in any case."

"Well, let's have a look around down here, then. Looks like a dead end behind us, so I vote we go that way." Rudy pointed along the one route available.

Once again the Man of Three Waters led the way, this time following a long, smooth-walled corridor. After a hundred paces the passageway led to a room that had been carved from the bedrock in the shape of a pentagon. In each of the five walls an identical tunnel mouth offered shadowy passage toward the unknown.

Shrugging, the Iceman chose one of the corridors at random and the trio continued on. After another hundred paces, they reached an identical five-sided chamber, and this time they paused for a conference.

"I get the feeling we're in some kind of maze," Rudy observed grimly.

"Can this be the same room?"

"I don't think so—the tunnel from the other room ran straight all the way, so we couldn't have doubled back."

"Let's take the first choice on the right, then," Raine suggested.

For a long time they explored, finding more pentagonal rooms, once crossing an arched bridge, following a series of curving tunnels and long, straight halls in an apparently endless maze. They came to another junction of featureless corridors, a nameless intersection in a series of similar choices. With no guidance other than his own instincts, Rudy again turned down the nearest right hand passage, hearing Raine's padding footsteps whispering along the floor right behind.

Ducking to avoid a low ceiling, the Iceman moved along in a crouch. Abruptly the walls and ceiling came to an end and the floor became a straight bridge, a stone span suspended above a gulf of darkness. He heard sounds of gurgling flowage below, imagined the Darkblood coursing along in a great canal beyond the range of his vision. The black liquid seemed to be everywhere in this palace, pulsing and flowing and dripping through each corridor.

Like blood through a body, the Iceman thought—and he knew this blood would flow so long as its heart continued to pump. An increasing sense of urgency hastened his step, until he moved along at a trot. He cast a glance back, saw that Raine was following him across the bridge, her own black sword poised to slash against any attack that materialized behind them.

The span ended at a tunnel into a smooth, dark cliff, and once again they proceeded along a lightless passageway bored from the bedrock of Agath-Trol. They came to a junction of two corridors and Rudy turned to the right, picking up his pace again until he was striding along.

Yet once more they entered a five-sided room, and again there were five choices, each identical, each apparently boring deeper into the endless maze.

— 4 —

Danri stood on a ridge of the Wilderhof, looking down into the mass of minions concentrated in ruined Dermaat. Huddled in the shadows beneath the slopes of the massive Glimmercrown, the tiny black spots that were kroaks and brutox flowed down the opposite ridge. When he squinted, the digger could see flashes of arrows in the air, and he sensed the pressure of the human troops across the valley— obviously, the Halvericans had driven the invaders back with a sharp counterattack.

He recognized the place, too, for it was very near the location at which his tunnel had emerged when he had gouged through the Watershed under the influence of the Digging Madness. The massive summit of the Glimmercrown, draped with dazzling glaciers, looked to have suffered not at all from the breach that had been driven through its base.

The same could not be said for the valley, however. Everywhere the stain of minion occupation was a blight across the ground. The stream itself flowed with black sludge, a canal of pollution that carried the effluent of Darkblood toward the Glimmersee.

"Oh . . . poor Halverica," Awnro Lyrifell said sadly, marking the course of the toxic stream.

"Aye-uh—but we'll be giving a bit of it back to the bastards," the digger pointed out. "As soon as that canal starts flowing."

"Aha—and I see our drackan friend has been busy," the bard noted.

A large shape pounced into the air from the opposite ridge—the elevation called Dermaathof, Danri recalled—and Neambrey soared above the deep valley. The drackan pitched his wings, feinting a dive against the gathered minions, and the mere threat of his swooping flight scattered a thousand kroaks that had only moments before gathered, under the lashes of the brutox, into a semblance of formation.

Grinning delightedly, the drackan flapped his wings, climbing back to the ridgetop height and then coming to rest on the promontory beside the digger commander.

"Did you see them run? Like they can't wait to get back to Duloth-Trol! C'mon Danri—why don't you diggers and everybody attack now, too?"

"I did see that—and it was a nice piece of work," chuckled Danri. "But I've got a better idea."

"Better than attacking?" Neambrey's long snout drooped, but then he brightened as a small figure buzzed into view. "Hey, Garic—have a look at this!"

"Just a minute." The twissel hovered high enough to see into the valley, but turned to Danri with important news. "Hakwan Chiseler says that he's ready to cut away the plug. Do you want the canal to start flowing?"

"No time like the present," the digger agreed readily. He looked back along the course of the straight-sided trench, trying to imagine the flowage before it began. "It should spill off this bluff here, and run right down into

Dermaat. When it hits that black stream, we'll see some
results.''

"Righto." Garic took to the air, disappearing in a blur
of wings as he darted back along the course of the canal.

"So we just wait?" Neambrey asked, bobbing anxiously
between his forepaws as he looked longingly into the en-
emy-occupied valley.

"Actually," Awnro Lyrifell said, placing a long arm
around the drackan's supple neck, "there's something I
need you to do."

"Tell me—ask me anything!" Neambrey nodded eagerly. "I'll do it!"

The serpent's enthusiasm dislodged the minstrel's arm
and knocked him off balance, but Awnro continued
smoothly.

"How'd you like to be an ambassador—from the Faerine
Field Army to the bold defenders of Halverica?"

— 5 —

When the narrow tunnel he chose merged with a wider
cavern, the Iceman didn't exactly feel relieved—but at least
they had found something other than a pentagonal room.
Still, though there was neither sound nor sight of any denizens within the massive, descending cave, the air itself
made the back of his neck prickle with alarm. The flow of
Darkblood was a good-sized stream, gurgling along a
trough at one side of the passage.

"Listen!" Raine's warning hissed through the air like an
electrical shock. A clatter of stones followed the word, dull
sounds echoing for long moments.

"There—behind us!"

"I think I see it." The Iceman did discern motion in the
darkness, and he clearly heard another crunch of stone. For
several heartbeats the movement had no shape, no context,
beyond a shifting of darkness, a gradual oozing of black,
stonelike wall. Only as he drew a ragged breath, felt the

hilt of his sword buzzing in his hand, did the Iceman begin to see the thing as a creature. A hulking shape, taller and broader than a gigant, rocking forward on two massive legs, emerged from a shadowy alcove that the intruders had passed unaware.

"What is it?" whispered Raine, her voice hushed by awe.

"I don't know—but it sees us!" Rudy couldn't contain his astonishment, nor his dismay.

The monster rumbled forward on two massive, gnarled legs, each of them braced on a paw stubbed with blunt claws. Looming in a stooped, hunchbacked posture, the beast growled, baring tusks longer and sharper than any brutox's. Hard plates angled downward from the shoulders like a crude suit of mail, and the arms that lashed out from beneath that protective shell were long—and so supple as to appear boneless. They writhed like tentacles, slashing toward the man and woman.

"Run!" hissed Raine, as the Iceman, sword in hand, wavered on a course of action. "We can't fight this!" she pleaded.

The pair stumbled along the cavern floor beside the trough of Darkblood, dodging around stalagmites that jutted like black fangs from the ground. Rudy held back a step, spinning to get another look at the looming giant. He saw the creature lumber past the motionless shape of the Guardian. The flailing tentacles slashed through the darkness like whips—the Iceman could hear them cracking in the air before he whirled and sprinted after Raine.

Lumbering on its sturdy legs, the monster pursued with astonishing quickness. Rudy looked back again as it lunged around a spire of stone, saw the lash of a long, snaky tendril lash out after him, nearly slicing his ankle as he stumbled to the side.

Backing away, he raised the sword Lordsmiter, trying to anticipate the next, shockingly quick attack.

"Look out!"

Raine seized his collar and pulled the Iceman onto his

back. Scrambling to his feet, he saw that the passageway had ended, that they were perched at the brink of a ditch. Some ten feet below flowed a thick sludge of impermeable dark liquid—and beyond rose a sheer, unclimbable wall.

EIGHTEEN

Seas of Dark Water

Stray not toward the seas of Darkblood,
helmsman, for naught but doom awaits there.
—SONGS OF THE SAILOR

— 1 —

The Faerine Sea was as idyllic, as perfect and placid and smooth, as it had been during the *Black Condor*'s arrival in the realm of Aurianth months earlier. Again Anjell spent days at the rail, fascinated by the denizens of the sea—coiling serpents, flying fish, and spuming leviathans—that enlivened the days with their spectacular, though unthreatening, leaps and antics.

Yet this time she wished that the wind would blow a little stronger, that the ship could improve on the stately grace with which it coursed the idyllic waters.

She drank Aura whenever she wished, which was often. Her mother seemed to understand the necessity of this, for Dara no longer disapproved. Certainly she was frightened, but then, so was her daughter. Anjell was pleased to see that Dara was working on her book again. Her mother had started her journal of their adventures when they departed for Faerine, yet following the departure of Awnro Lyrifell she had rarely touched quill to paper. Now it heartened Anjell to see Dara sitting in the sun on deck, pages clipped to a writing board as she compiled sheet after sheet of notes.

Finally the balmy sea gave way to a sterner ocean. The wind howled through the rigging, pressing the three-masted vessel hard to port as Kestrel steered ever southward. Dara took her writing to the tiny desk in the cabin she and Anjell shared, but the girl still preferred to spend her days on deck. With endless patience she watched the horizon roll along, a thin dark line above gray waves. Those waters seemed to darken—or was it merely her imagination?—as they drew ever nearer to a realm of eternal night.

As the trip progressed, Anjell found herself unable to sleep, though she often recalled, vividly, her earlier dreams. Especially she pictured that puzzle of broken fragments that she had envisioned so many times.

And finally the darkness was the horizon before them. Black clouds rose into stormy thunderheads over a surging sea. The ocean heaved, dark waters breaking into foaming crests that were a rusty red in color, a churning mass of inky liquid with the consistency of water, but the appearance and stench of poison.

Anjell took a place in the forward rigging, with Darret by her side, and looked over the expanse of angry sea. Stinging spray lashed at her, and she pulled herself higher, out of the rising waves.

And then she saw it—the jigsaw puzzle that had been in her dreams. She could tell that much of the black water was pure, sucking doom for any ship. Those awful places were the pieces of the puzzle, and she could see them, recognizing their implicit peril. Conversely, the interconnecting lines were wide swaths where the ocean still churned and stormed, but consisted mainly of actual seawater. The gal-

yon could float on these passages, sailing onward by finding
the paths *between* the pieces of the puzzle.

Calling out directions that were instantly relayed to Kestrel at the helm, Anjell guided the ship onto the first safe
lane between the seething swaths of pure Darkblood. They
rode a ridge of seawater, the water sloping away, vanishing
into a black abyss barely an arrow's-flight away to starboard and port. But the current was favorable, and the ship
bobbed and rolled along, swiftly passing both plunging
chasms.

Before them loomed a mountainous summit of inky liquid, Darkblood swelling higher and higher into the sky.

"Right—starboard!" Anjell yelled, seeing by the waves
that the current was veering that way. Kestrel steered and
the *Black Condor* swept around the curve like a raft in a
rapids.

There was danger on every side, yet the ship managed
to score the maze of pathways between the hazards. The
crew glared fearfully at the boiling sea—and, sometimes,
they regarded the golden-haired girl with like expressions.
Yet they couldn't deny the efficacy of her guidance, as the
Condor coursed through the vast darkness of the Sleepstealer's Sea.

— 2 —

"Wait a minute," Roggett called, grasping Payli by her
wiry arm at the top of the Dermaathof. The woman, ready
to start down the trail into the valley, turned on him in a
flash, her face locked into an expression of ferocity that set
him back on his heels.

"They're running!" she cried. "Let's finish the job
while we can!"

"At least give the rest of the men a chance to catch up!"
insisted the Iceman, gesturing to the hundreds of Halvericans who still scrambled up the Neshara side of the Dermaathof. "And look down there—you see the monsters

forming companies, getting their order back?''

"Yes."

"Well, they'll be a lot harder to hurt now they're ready for us. We got a break when that drackan came over and started 'em running. But don't you think we've tried to knock them out of there over the last weeks?''

"Now's the time to *do* it!" she said stubbornly. "Before they can re-form!''

Roggett was struck by an irrelevant thought: Payli's determination, the flush in her cheeks and the angry glower in her eyes, only enhanced the woman's fundamental beauty. When he had pined after the pixie-like girl of a few years earlier, he never suspected that her prettiness and femininity concealed this kind of fire.

But he knew that the men were too weak to continue the attack. He wiped a hand across his own face and it came away damp with sweat. Suddenly he felt woozy, swaying drunkenly until he leaned against a tree for support. *Fight it!* He willed himself to resist the sickness, even as he sensed the fever, the plague, locking its talons into him.

"Look—across the vale!'' someone shouted. "Here comes that flying ice-breather!''

The man who'd called out was pointing, and the Iceman turned to see the grayish drackan leap into the air from the high bluff of the Wilderhof. The creature soared toward them with powerful strokes of wide, leathery wings.

"There's people over there," Payli said, her tone low but excited. "Where the drackan came from.''

"Stand ready!'' shouted another Iceman, and Roggett saw a number of crossbows come up as the jittery warriors watched the drackan fly closer.

"No—don't shoot!'' he cried, pushing aside several of the weapons as he fought his way to the edge of the cliff. "He's on our side! You all saw that!''

Nervously the crossbowmen watched the serpent approach. At the last minute the humans scattered back from the cliff, allowing the drackan to perch on the rocky promontory. Tail lashing and neck curved upward, the Faerine flyer blinked serenely, tucked its wings, then dipped its head in a passable imitation of a bow.

"Greetings, humans," declared the drackan in deep, musical tones. "I come to announce the arrival of the Faerine Field Army."

"Army?" gasped Roggett, his heart soaring with hope. Looking across the valley again, he saw that, indeed, the throng of warriors was growing steadily larger on the far ridge.

"I'm just an ambassador—Neambrey is my name," declared the wyrm, settling his yellow eyes on the tall Iceman. "Do *you* have an ambassador I can talk to?"

"Yes!" At first Roggett was about to step forward, but then he remembered the course of the fight, and the determination he had witnessed.

"Payli Appenfell will speak for us," he announced, to a chorus of agreement from the men within earshot.

"We're grateful for your help," the young woman declared, smoothly approaching the drackan and bowing. "I think your attack saved Neshara."

"And there's more. Danri—he's that digger over there, though I guess you really can't see which one he is—says it's time to start the canal. The diggers are going to spill Aura down there, onto the minions."

Roggett, still wrestling with encroaching fever, wondered if he was imagining this conversation . . . Aura in Dalethica, flowing over the Watershed. It was the stuff of dreams, not real life.

"Then he thinks we should attack them together," Neambrey continued. "That is, if you think it's a good idea."

"It is!" Payli agreed, and a shout of assent rippled along the whole line of men gathered on the ridgetop.

"Look—there it comes!" shouted someone, and Roggett turned in time to see a silvery gush emerge along the lip of the opposite precipice. The canal spilled its contents into the ravine on the side of the Wilderhof, and that channel carried the flow directly toward the polluted stream that had been Dermaat Creek.

"Better cover your ears," warned the drackan, as the silvery torrent drew near to the vast stain of Darkblood.

As the first spray of Aura reached the streambed a violent hiss erupted, and black steam boiled into the air. The hiss became a roar, the eruption growing in violence, as more and more of the silvery flowage spilled down the ravine. A steady explosion rumbled like distant thunder from the first contact of the two waters, the sound swelling as more Aura flowed into the town, until it sounded as though the thunderstorm raged directly overhead. Smoke and steam billowed outward, obscuring ruined Dermaat in a haze of angry vapors—and everywhere minions scattered, trying to escape the growing convulsion.

"Charge!"

Payli's voice, echoed by a thousand throats, rose above the din and the vengeful men of Halverica swept down the long ridge face. Roggett, reeling dizzily, stumbled along behind, determined not to miss the culmination of a grand victory.

Across the valley the Faerine Field Army surged into view, sunlight glinting from the polished steel of countless weapons. Thousands of stocky warriors marched sternly down the slope, while lithe forms glided through the woods to either side, launching a deadly rain of arrows into the panicking minions.

The site of Dermaat was a seething, smoking inferno. Explosions rocked the ground, even broke boulders loose from the surrounding heights. Minions scattered everywhere, though most tried to flee back up the valley, toward the breach underneath the Glimmercrown.

Roggett knelt and sighted his crossbow, drawing a bead on a jabbering, sparking brutox. His hands trembled so much that the shot was low, the shaft plunging through the monster's thigh. Fortunately, a short, bearded Faerine warrior came by and killed the minion with a stab of a sword.

Vaguely the Iceman realized that he was seeing a digger for the first time.

Though he tried to prop his crossbow, to recrank the weapon, Roggett found that he lacked the strength. Sitting on the ground, doubled over by stomach cramps, he could only watch helplessly as the few healthy Halvericans—and the horde of vengeful Faerines—put the minions to rout.

"Roggett! Here, don't try to get up." Suddenly Payli was there, her hand blessedly cool on his forehead. He was having trouble seeing, and wondered if she had suddenly grown wings.

"It's a twissel," she said gently, gesturing to the Faerine beside her. "He saw you fall and came over here."

"Hi—here, have a drink of this."

The little fairy handed the Iceman a small bottle and while Payli supported his head, he took a swig of the cool liquid within. Immediately he felt the stuff seeping through his body, vanquishing the disease more quickly than it had set in. Like a miracle, the cooling balm soothed his flesh, driving away the ache that had barely begun to settle into his limbs. In a few minutes Roggett was sitting up, shaking his head in wonder. He would have thanked the twissel, but the creature had already flown off to tend to other sick humans.

In less than an hour the last of the minions had fled up the valley, with Halvericans and diggers chasing after to make certain they vanished into the tunnel. Roggett saw one of the diggers shouting orders, assigning a work party of skilled stoneworkers to follow the retreating invaders, with instructions to seal up the entrance of the breach with a sturdy wall.

"That's Danri," Neambrey explained, as the stocky Faerine clumped over to Payli, Roggett, and Tarn—the Halverican commanders who had not yet been felled by fever or battle. The Iceman was surprised to see a kilt-wearing human, bearing the lute of a master bard, striding among the Faerines. "And he's Awnro Lyrifell. He's from Dalethica, you know."

"The twissels were saying there's a lot of sick still in Neshara," the bard mentioned to Danri.

"Pembroak!" shouted the digger. "Get some Aura—take a party over the ridge. Get going!"

Soon the humans were mingling with sturdy, bearded diggers and lean and graceful sylves. Roggett clasped hands with Danri, who squinted when the Iceman was introduced.

"Neshara, huh? Know a fellow named Rudy Appenfell?"

"My late husband's brother!" Payli gasped, clapping a hand to her mouth. "Rudy disappeared from the village almost a year ago."

"He was my good friend," Roggett added. "We'd heard that he traveled pretty far."

Danri's face flickered with a shadow of sadness as he looked to the south, toward the dark region beyond the Glimmercrown. He sighed as he turned back to the humans.

"You don't know the half of it."

"Where is he? Is he well? Do *you* know?" Payli pressed, white-faced.

"I'll tell you what I can," the digger said. "Is there a place we can talk?"

Shortly the Faerine and Halverican captains, with Awnro Lyrifell, Neambrey, and a twissel called Garic Hoorkin, had gathered in a pastoral clearing above the stench of ruined Dermaat. Someone built a fire while others pushed together some fallen tree trunks, and a unique council began as the small blaze crackled into life.

Danri looked around, making certain that he had the full attention of the gathering. He cleared his throat and spoke with determination.

"Let's make a plan for winning the rest of this damned war."

— 3 —

"We've got to fight!" Rudy declared, seeing no way around the monster. The shadows were thick, but he

guessed that the tentacle-like arms were easily long enough
to span the cave and block any attempt to escape past the
beast.

Raine's black-bladed sword flashed, striking a heavy,
lashing appendage. The force of the blow knocked her
back, and Rudy grabbed for her with his free hand, catching
her fingers, balancing precariously at the edge of the ditch
while he slashed with Lordsmiter.

The silvery blade struck another tentacle, slicing the re-
pulsive flesh with a hissing cut—but two more of the supple limbs flew out, emerging from below the first pair on
the monster's sides like a second set of arms. Rudy rocked
to the side, grunting as his shoulder was bashed.

Then the Guardian was there, loping up behind the creature, reaching out with its long arms, pinning the flailing
tentacles. The monster roared and thrashed, whirling back
and forth in a frantic effort to escape, toppling onto the
Guardian and grinding the sharp plates of its natural armor
into the floor. But still those powerful arms remained
clasped, like straps of steel.

Rudy lunged, seeking to strike with Lordsmiter, but the
end of a tentacle smashed him hard to the side. Only
Raine's quick grab of his arm saved him from tumbling
into the trench.

*You are the Man and Woman of Three Waters. Go—do
your duty!*

The message was a stern admonishment in Rudy's mind.

"No!" the Iceman protested, unwilling to leave the loyal
ally. He raised his blade and lunged again.

"We *have* to!" insisted the Woman of Three Waters,
pulling him back from the limited reach of another tentacle.
"Run!"

He cried his grief aloud as he followed her, as they once
again lost themselves in the endless passages of the labyrinth.

— 4 —

Takian urged Hawkrunner up the broad avenue, but for
once the proud stallion seemed reluctant, even afraid, to
obey his rider's will. Perhaps it was the press of feverish
men, lined along the curbs and between the buildings. Some
of them moaned or thrashed, while others lay silent, or
shook terribly, racked by uncontrollable tremors.

"Go!" snapped the king, his simmering temper giving
way to a rolling boil. The stallion clattered forward like a
rocket, racing up the hill, charging over the castle drawbridge at a full gallop.

In the courtyard Takian dismounted, leaving his horse to
willing attendants as he stalked through the doors to the
keep, then through the vast, silent throne room, and finally
to the entrance of the royal chambers beyond.

A nervous man-at-arms tried to stand in the path of the
stalking monarch.

"The High Prince is in seclusion—"

"Out of my way!" roared Takian, and the fellow scuttled
aside. Bashing the door to the apartments with his steel
gauntlet, the king took some faint pleasure in the creaking,
splintering sound of the wood. The oaken panels flew open
and he marched through, his riding cloak still flapping from
his shoulders.

He found Bentram Wayn seated in one of the soft chairs
before the fireplace. If the prince was surprised by Takian's
entrance, he gave no indication, instead looking up with an
expression of desperate pleading.

"Is there news . . . ?" he asked tremulously.

"Of course there's news—all of it bad!" growled Takian, standing before the cringing youth with his hands
planted on his hips. "Get out there and see for yourself!
Better yet, try and *do* something!"

"I . . . I can't . . . I'm not ready," blubbered Bentram
Wayn. He gained control of himself with an effort, glaring
up at the king with a trace of his old hauteur.

"I want to go back to Andaran!" he declared.

"*This* is your realm!" Takian roared. Impulsively he reached down, grabbing the prince by his shoulders and hoisting him to his feet. "I don't care if you're not ready— you'd better *get* ready while you still have a city to protect!"

"But—I can't . . ." The prince broke free and fell back into the chair, burying his face in his hands as his shoulders shook with convulsive sobs.

For a split second Takian's hand twitched toward his sword. It would have been very easy to draw the weapon, to run the blade through this sniveling pretender. The act of impulsive violence would, in fact, have felt pretty good.

Instead, the king spun on his heel and stalked from the royal chambers. Disgusted with his own failure as much as Wayn's pathetic display, he pushed past the gathered attendants, and stalked through the halls to his apartments. He found Tray Oldar there, and the servant informed him that Bristyn had gone to the West Tower.

He climbed the castle keep to a high bridge portal, and started across the span. The stench of burning and soot, tinged with the acidic taint of Darkblood, was a miasma on the evening breeze, and the smoggy air obscured all but the easternmost swath of sky. Still, he relished the lofty vantage, the muted sounds of the city below, and the freedom to take his long strides without interference or delay.

The bridge ended at the base of the westernmost castle tower, and when he ascended he found Bristyn alone there. Together they stayed through thickening twilight, watching the far shore of the River Ariak grow dark. On the ground it was as if a stain of ink spread inexorably along the bluffs of the river bank, though this stain was a collection of individual, malevolent blots of darkness.

Throughout the night the city of white marble was ghostly and silent, brightened by a full moon until the silvery orb was obscured by the billowing cloud of pollution that continually surged into the western sky. Dawn came as a murky affair, with a blanket of smoke lying in the valley of the Ariak, obscuring the water and leaving the island of Carillonn like a city afloat on a very dark and menacing cloud.

Everywhere the western bank was darkened by minions, two great legions converged from west and south, rank upon rank of kroak and brutox drawing up along the marbled bluff. Stalkers had seized the far ends of the three bridges, which the humans had made no effort to defend.

"The water still flows . . . they won't try to cross until they can stop the river," Takian declared with assurance, after a gust of wind cleared the vaporous blanket for a short time, bringing the Ariak into sight as it coursed past the foundation of the city's battlements.

"How can you be sure?"

"That's how it was at Myntercairn, at every place they've invaded. I don't know why, but they won't cross a bridge over water, flowing or stagnant. Instead, they have to build a dam or a dike, and only cross when the flow has been completely stopped."

"We have that time, then—but how long will it be?" Bristyn looked to the south, trying to imagine the course of the great river as it flowed from the mountains and the Glimmersee. "And besides, the Willowfen is already corrupted—who's to say that they won't spread that plague across the whole river?"

"I've got scouts along the bank for a hundred miles," the king replied, taking her anxiety as a chance to review his own preparations. "At any sign of . . . well, of anything out of the ordinary, they'll send word—both by horseman and rivercraft."

Takian sighed, knowing that there were still other threats, things he couldn't begin to address. "We can hope that the marble bluffs along so much of the river will make it hard for the bovars to excavate material for their dam. We can hope Duke Beymant arrives with his ten thousand corsars. Other than that, we can use the time to train, to heal, and to prepare."

— 5 —

Reaper glided through the thick smoke, drawing deep and pleasurable breaths through his wide, smoking nostrils. The Lord Minion had flown for a full day, circling around the rear of his army, insuring that the precious trains of Dark-blood rumbled steadily forward. Having learned from Phalthak's mistake—when a sortie from Spendorial had destroyed the Lord Minion's bloodtrain and paralyzed his army—Reaper had gathered his great reserve of Darkblood on a stretch of plain far to the south of the battlefield at Carillonn.

Firetusk and his minions had bulled through the shattered wasteland of Shalloth. The huge brutox led his legion toward the end of the Glimmersee, where the North Shore Wayfarer's Lodge marked the scene of a thousand-year-old battle—a legacy of failure that, shortly, Firetusk would avenge tenfold. Indeed, one reason Reaper had placed his Darkblood reserve so far to the south was to insure that Firetusk's rapid advance had adequate support.

Immediately south of Carillonn, Burner was on the move again following his delay of a week earlier. West of the city Kroaksmasher had pressed relentlessly, and now his minions were gathered along the river bank, controlling the terminus of each of the city's three western bridges.

Idly, the Talon of Dassadec wondered if his master would be pleased with his progress. Undoubtably not, though perhaps the Sleepstealer would have praised Reaper as further insult to Nicodareus. The Lord Minion had a startling awareness: He did not relish a return to Agath-Trol, to the ready interference of the Nameless One's pleasure. He liked this instead, the independence to freely command his legions, to make his decisions without an overseeing presence.

Finally Reaper was ready to fly back toward Carillonn, content with his dispositions. Yet one voice of warning still reared its hissing head, whispering in his ear, reminding

him of those precious wagons. They were screened by three
legions, but still there was that south flank, where the
ground was too wet for his minions. The terrain was desolate swampland but, after all, humans had proven to be
unpredictably dangerous in the past. Perhaps he should take
steps to guard the present, as well.

Spurred by this nagging voice, he summoned a flock of
terrions. Five of the winged minions answered his inaudible
cry, emerging from the smoky sky to circle around their
master's gliding form, cackling and hissing their abject
worship of Reaper's might.

"Fly to the south, my winged ones," commanded the
Talon of Dassadec. "I wish you to watch the shore of yonder lake. Glide there day and night, back and forth above
valley and ridge. Should you see any sign of human movement, you must fly to me at once with word."

"Yes, O Mighty One!" pledged the terrions, in their
guttural, beastlike tongue. With a veering of sinuous bodies,
a curving of slender wings, the swift killers soared toward
the Glimmersee, fully bound to obey their master's commands.

— 6 —

A vista of black smoothness stretched to the far horizons,
an infinite reflection of heavy overcast. The sails of the
Black Condor, stained almost to the color of the bleak sea,
hung in limp and listless sheets, drooping without the
slightest hint of movement. So far as Anjell could tell, the
vessel sat utterly still on the trackless ocean, apparently in
the exact same place it had been when the wind died some
days earlier. The ship was becalmed, without wind . . . and
without hope.

The girl paced restlessly on the main deck, trying to con-
sole herself with any kind of positive thought. After all, at
least the pattern of deadly seas had been broken. Now the
whole ocean merged into a kind of black slickness that

seemed patently unhealthy, but at least did not threaten the instant destruction that had loomed with the seething pockets of Darkblood closer to the Faerine Sea.

Two crewmen, slumping with weariness, all but dragged themselves into the forward cabin, and Anjell wondered why they were so tired. So far as she had seen, nobody had done much work since the wind had died. On deck, a few men slumbered in open air hammocks, but there was really nothing happening.

She climbed to the wheel deck, shaking her head in a futile attempt to ignore the stench that lingered in the air, that seemed to permeate everything from her hair to her skin. Other, more important things claimed her attention, as she reflected on a conversation she'd had with her mother earlier in the day. Dara had seemed distracted, as if she was having a hard time concentrating. Furthermore, Anjell hadn't seen her so much as get out her writing materials in several days. She decided that she would go check on Dara in the cabin as soon as she said hello to Captain Kestrel.

As her eyes rose above the level of the upper deck she gasped, bouncing up the last steps to sprint to the man slumped over the spoked wheel of the galyon's helm.

"Captain Kestrel! Wake up! What's wrong?"

"Eh . . . who's 'at?" Swaying drunkenly, the seaman fell away from the wheel. Anjell threw her arms around him and lowered him to the deck as gently as she could.

"Mama! Darret! Help!" Anjell cradled the captain's head, shocked at the way his eyes rolled back in his skull, tongue drooping loosely from his slack jaws.

"What's wrong?" Darret raced up the ladder and quickly knelt beside the girl and the moaning, restless figure of the sailor. "Captin! Whatsit?"

"Aura!" Anjell saw the solution immediately. "Here—hold his head for a minute. I've got to get him some Aura."

"Hurry!"

The girl raced down to the main deck and scooped a clay jar of Faerine's water from an opened cask. Taking care not to spill any of the precious stuff, she climbed back to the raised stern deck and poured a thin trickle into Kestrel's mouth.

In a few moments the grizzled seaman groaned and shook his head. When he struggled to sit up, however, his arms buckled beneath him and Darret lowered him once again to the planking.

"Just rest a bit, Captin. We'll git you up soon enough."

"Where's Mama?" Anjell looked around worriedly, surprised that Dara hadn't raced to see what was the matter. "Stay here, okay?"

Darret nodded and she bounced down the ladder, noticing with a tingle of alarm that there was still no activity on the deck. The crewmen lying in their hammocks slumbered on, but she saw no sign of anyone polishing planks, mending sails, or braiding ropes—unusual inactivity, for a ship whose master generally kept his sailors busy.

In the cabin her alarm grew to real fear, for she saw her mother sleeping on the bunk—and Dara didn't respond when Anjell called her loudly.

"Mama—wake up!" The girl threw herself onto the mattress and rocked her mother back and forth. Dara groaned quietly, then shivered and fell still.

There was Aura in the cabin, a pitcherful, and Anjell wasted no time in gently drizzling some between Dara's lips, until she gasped and coughed, thrashing reflexively.

"Sit up, Mama! Listen to me—something's wrong." But Dara only slumped backward, drawing a deep breath but showing no sign of awakening. Anjell nudged her a bit, but quickly realized that her efforts would not be successful. She dashed back up to the wheel deck to find Darret, seated beside Kestrel, swaying woozily. He looked up, squinting at the sound of her voice, as Anjell knelt beside him.

"Here—you drink some of this," she said soothingly extending the ladle. Darret understood, and took a long drink. When he lowered the empty cup, his eyes were clear—and his expression full of alarm.

"Are dey all sleepin'?" he asked, gesturing around the ship.

"I think so."

Anjell checked the men in the nearest hammocks, and was not surprised that they didn't awaken. Trying to stem the trembling of her hands, she gave each of the sailors a few sips of Aura and made certain that they were breathing.

"What can we do wit' no wind?" asked Darret, trying unsuccessfully to conceal the fear that quavered in his voice.

"I don't know." Once again Anjell allowed her eyes to take in the sweep of dark, placid liquid. It was hard to think of it as an ocean or sea—the expanse of Darkblood seemed more like a sheet of glass, or a mirror reflecting a vault of shrouded, starlit skies.

But it was a liquid, very much like water. The prow of the galyon had parted the surface easily, and while the wind had lasted, the ship made good time. Anjell had avoided thinking about the fact that they were sailing into uncharted waters, seas that humankind had perhaps never visited before.

Kestrel had kept the landscape of Duloth-Trol as a grim smudge on the northern horizon. They had never sailed close enough to see any details, though the captain had been insistent about keeping the Watershed in sight. For a time they had been very hopeful, coursing rapidly, under skies that remained overcast, but never threatened them with thunder, lightning, or other stormy aspect.

But then the wind had died, and now all the grownups had gone to sleep so soundly that they couldn't be awakened—not even with Aura. There was no breath of air, nothing to propel the ship, and no one to ask for advice or to help solve this complicated problem.

"What are we goin' to do?" Darret asked. His dark eyes studied Anjell, his voice lacking any sense of accusation or despair—but the display of confidence frightened Anjell more than any outburst or tantrum might have.

"We have to *think*," she replied, certain that this was

the right answer. Unfortunately, she didn't understand what they were supposed to think about.

"Hey there—howzit?"

The familiar voice brought Anjell bouncing to her feet, whirling in a blur while Darret gaped in surprise. Haylor ambled into sight, sauntering from behind one of the large water casks.

"Haylor!" gasped Anjell. "Where did you come from?"

"But—how—" Darret stammered in his own astonishment, and Anjell sensed that only Kestrel's head cradled on his lap kept him from leaping to his feet and embracing the young sylve.

So she hugged Haylor instead. "Boy, this is a good time for you to come along. We've got a problem." She pulled back and looked at him, suddenly squinting appraisingly. "Hey! How *did* you come along, anyway?"

"I've been here all along," replied the sprightly fellow, pointing to one of the large casks. "It was getting a little stuffy in there, so I thought I'd come out."

"But why? Maybe you don't know it, but we're *stuck* here," Anjell explained.

"I know that you *think* you're stuck, but there are things that *you* don't know. Like, you can move any time you want to."

"What do you mean?" Anjell suddenly felt very, very serious, and a little frightened—as if her stomach were filled with large, fluttering butterflies. "Does it have something to do with the water from the Pool of Scrying?"

"That might be a place to start."

The girl looked down at the flask that was her constant companion. Gingerly she hoisted it, possessed by a strange sense of uncertainty regarding the liquid that sloshed within.

"Try it, human child. Try it, and find the power to move."

Anjell took a deep drink of the pool's Aura, then another. She swallowed the elixir of Faerine until she felt as if her stomach were about to explode, until she felt the magic of the enchanted realm rising in her gullet, flowing outward from each of her pores.

She looked at the sails, still limp and lifeless, stained by the inky mist. Haylor and Darret watched her silently, and she felt very aware of the grownups slumbering throughout the ship, unknowing and helpless.

Drawing a deep gulp of air, she pursed her lips . . .

And gave breath to the wind.

NINETEEN

Dams and Tunnels

Neither attack nor flee, but stand like the rock
that is your father.
—CODEX OF THE GUARDIANS

— 1 —

"I think we should rope up," Raine whispered through the darkness. The monster in its lair had been left well behind, but they had found no indication of any obvious path through the maze of tunnels. "There's too many tricks and traps in here."

"Good idea," the Iceman replied. In moments they were secured by their supple line. "Give me about ten paces," he suggested.

They wandered for a long time, through a natural cavern and then back into a tunnel that had been bored through the rock. Emerging from this into a wider, square-walled corridor, Raine's foresight was proved wise as the floor suddenly dropped away from Rudy's feet. He shouted a warning and grabbed at the rope with his free hand. In a split second it snapped taut, burning through his hand and jerking hard against his waist. Still clutching Lordsmiter, the Iceman held the blade out. The dim glow showed him only blackness yawning below.

Sheathing his sword, he hauled himself up the rope to find that Raine had thrown herself flat on the floor to maintain the difficult belay of a climber heavier than herself. Grunting and straining, he finally pulled himself over the edge and flopped onto the floor. They both sat up, backs to the wall, and allowed their breathing and heartbeats to settle.

"What happened?" she asked.

"I don't know. I was walking along, the floor felt normal as ever. Suddenly it vanished from under both my feet at once. I'm certain of that—I didn't step off the edge! The floor was there one second, and gone the next."

"Great—magic," Raine said with a groan. "Monsters, poison, and now sorcery. What else do you suppose we'll find?"

"Nothing, if we just sit here. Let's get going."

They saw that the pit was a circular shaft plunging through the floor. Crossing one at a time on the narrow ledge between the hole and the tunnel wall, they resumed their exploration of the trackless maze.

One corridor looked like the next, and none of them offered the Man and Woman of Three Waters any hope of escape, even any reason to believe that they were making progress through the labyrinth. When they wandered into another in the series of five-walled rooms, Rudy cursed aloud at the sight.

"How many of these damned things are there?" he rasped, his voice quiet even in the face of his frustration.

"Maybe we're backtracking," Raine suggested. She took her sword and scored a mark on the floor of the room they had entered, then gouged another to indicate their departure.

"The Guardian . . . ?" Raine asked softly as they explored the next long corridor. "Do you think it's still alive?"

The Iceman sighed and shook his head. "I don't see how it could have beat that thing—or run away from it, either. And I'm surprised how much I miss the big fellow."

"Me too. Somehow, I keep expecting to see him come along behind us."

The floor gave way beneath Rudy before he could reply. Catching the rope in his hand, he prayed that Raine could make another successful arrest—but then he slammed into a sloping surface. The rope coiled past and he knew that his companion was falling as well. Together they tumbled down a long, smooth chute of stone, the Iceman twisting frantically to keep his sword from cutting either one of them or the rope.

His back burned from the friction of his skidding slide. He tried to claw for purchase with feet and hands, but his speed was too great. Then there was nothing except air as the chute dumped him into a void. He felt himself falling, dreading the unknown landing below. Feet downward, he prayed to Aurianth for a smooth surface.

From above he heard a muffled gasp, and knew that Raine came right behind.

— 2 —

"That should seal up the tunnel, at least for the time being," Hakwan Chiseler explained. "We set a plug in for a good hundred paces, interlocking shale. Of course, they can dig through it in time, if they really want to, but I'll be with a detachment watching the outside. We'll keep an ear to the ground—and I'll be certain to hear if we've got a threat from that direction."

"Good." Danri praised his old friend's work, even as his mind turned toward their next challenges. "I'm going to get together some of the diggers and talk to these humans, see if we're ready to get moving."

He found Kerri overseeing the finishing touches on the canal. The sparkling Aura was already scouring clean the previously fouled channel of Dermaat Creek, and the diggers and humans alike hoped that it would soon begin to restore the brackish Glimmersee.

"Where's Pembroak?" Danri wondered aloud.

"He might still be sleeping. He had a bedroll laid under that pine tree over there."

Muttering about the laziness of the younger generation, Danri clumped over to the tree and found his squire, indeed, snoring loudly on a soft bed of needles.

"Get up, you slug!" barked the digger captain, giving Pembroak a good nudge with the toe of his boot.

By the time the squire yawned, stretched, and then— recognizing Danri—hastily stumbled to his feet, Awnro Lyrifell had sauntered over. The bard was accompanied by Kerri, the Iceman Roggett Bekken, and the young woman Payli Appenfell.

"Awnro has told us what you've done," Payli explained gravely, taking Danri's hand in hers. "Both about the canal . . . and in looking out for Rudy. There's no way we can thank you enough."

"As to that Iceman, I'll admit he did as much watching over me as I did for him. And for the rest, well, I'm thinkin' the job's not quite done yet."

"Not done—but we've won a victory here for the ages!" Roggett declared, glowering toward the Glimmercrown as if challenging the minions to once more spill out from the mountain's base. "I daresay they won't be comin' back this way."

"You all gave them quite a chase," Danri acknowledged.

"And Payli was using a kitchen knife," Kerri said with a chuckle. "I guess these men wouldn't give her a sword."

"It worked well enough," the human woman said with a shy grin, displaying the rather hefty cleaver.

"Hmmm." Danri found himself liking this young woman, sensed the way her spirit inspired the men around her. "It may be that we could find you a replacement."

"Here!" Pembroak said quickly, drawing his digger

blade. He extended the grip toward the woman, who took the splendid weapon with a look of awe. At Danri's raised eyebrow, the squire explained. "I've decided to try something new, a little more traditional, I guess you could say."

For the first time Danri noticed the hammer carried on the youngster's belt. Blunt head at one end, dagger-sharp spike at the other, it was a match for Danri's own. "Good choice," he said gruffly, pleased.

"And . . . and thank you," Payli said, sheathing the weapon, then drawing it again to look at the silvery blade in wonder.

"How're all those men back in the village?" Kerri asked.

"Better, almost every one of them. That Aura is, well . . . it's magic!" Payli declared.

"Aye-uh," Danri chuckled. "We should load as much as we can to take with us. Even though we're marching beside the creek, the flowage will become diluted by water soon enough. We'll be wantin' some pure Aura with the army."

"Good idea. We'll have to use mules, though," Roggett explained. "The mountains of Halverica aren't much for wagon roads."

"That'll do," the digger agreed. "Let's get barrels, two for every mule, and get them loaded."

"We'll do it!" agreed the Iceman, as Tarn Blaysmith and the newly healthy Kristoff Yarden joined them. "We've got the men forming up in Neshara, and marching over here as fast as possible. I'll send word to have 'em bring every barrel in the town."

"Good start," Danri said. "I'm thinking we'll have quite a force at our disposal—sort of a Combined Field Army. Now, we'd better make some more detailed plans."

"We've got to attack!" Tarn growled aggressively. "Word is that there's minions moving toward the North Shore Wayfarer's Lodge. What better place for a fight?"

"How accurate is your information?" cautioned Awnro Lyrifell, paling at the news of the threat to the establish ment he had so proudly managed in the years before the war.

"I came from the Glimmersee just a few days ago." Payli said. "So all my news is that old. Still, I was down by the shore for quite a while—before I decided to come back home. There's a lot of traffic on the south shore. Every ferryman and fisher has brought his boat there, bringing word of invasion to the north."

"How far have the bastards gotten?" asked Tarn Blaysmith.

Payli drew a deep breath, her waiflike features aging in the instant of remembrance. "I talked to a man who saw Castle Shalloth destroyed, blasted to pieces by the lightning from a huge black cloud—"

"The *Dreadcloud*." Danri muttered the word under his breath and it came out as a curse.

"And that same storm moved toward Carillonn. There's minions everywhere on the plains, and nothing but smoke and ash to the west. One army came through Shalloth— that's the one Tarn was talking about. It's moving against the Wayfarer's Lodge, now. The rest are supposed to be concentrating against the City of One Hundred Bridges."

"But the city still stands?" asked Kristoff Yarden.

"Word was, yes. But for how long?" Payli looked around the circle, from human to Faerine and back again. "And what can we do about it?"

"Do? Against a million minions? Not much that I can see," growled a weary, bloodstained axeman.

"But do we have to fight all the legions?" It was Awnro Lyrifell's question, and he posed it lightly—as if it was a puzzle being offered for his listeners' amusement.

"No!" Danri barked. "It's not the minions that we have to destroy—"

"But the Darkblood!" Kerri cried in sudden understanding. "At least, that's how they were stopped in Faerine."

"Good idea—but there's no Darkenheight Pass to shut down between here and Dalethica," Roggett pointed out regretfully. "They come across the Dry Basin, so far as I

can tell, and that's hundreds of miles across. Not to mention
that it would take us half a year to get there.''

"We don't have half a year—and besides, for all we
know they've already got plenty of the stuff here already.''
Danri scratched his beard, deep in thought. Abruptly he
continued. "If they've called up a *Dreadcloud*, then they'll
need a base somewhere, a place where they can gather their
wagons and boil Darkblood, fuel the skyship.''

"Then that's the point at which they're vulnerable—but
how can we find it?" asked Roggett.

"I have an idea," Neambrey ventured. "Maybe I should
fly for a while. I could get a pretty good look around, and
I always like to see a new part of the Watershed.''

"A part that hasn't seen a drackan before, to boot,"
Awnro Lyrifell agreed. "I think that's a good idea. But
don't fly too low—you don't want some sharp-eyed cross-
bowman to mistake you for a terrion!''

"I'm *always* careful—at least, I try to be," the drackan
asserted, before flexing his wings and soaring into the air.
Within a few minutes he was out of sight of the warriors
gathered on the ground, gliding down the winding course
of newly enchanted Dermaat Creek.

—— 3 ——

Reaper was distracted, feeling vaguely uncertain. He was
worried about his concentration of Darkblood, though it
seemed well protected by the three legions. Still, there was
a hundred-mile gap to the south of the bloodwagons,
screened only by a few terrions, that continued to loom
large in the Lord Minion's mind. Nearing Carillonn, Reaper
came to rest on the wide battery deck of the *Dreadcloud*,
allowing the spongy vapor to absorb his weight while the
stalkers at the great lightning-throwers prostrated themselves to pay homage to their army's master.

"Rise," declared the Talon of Dassadec. "And summon
your captain!''

One of the hissing, fork-tongued minions scuttled into the skyship's shadowy hull, while the others returned to the rumbling pillars of black vapor, the death-dealing piles that rose in a hexagonal pattern from the jutting forward prow of the great black vessel. The serpentine Lord Minion allowed his eyes to wander across the landscape revealed below. The *Dreadcloud* was currently tethered by a great column of darksteam, bitter vapors rising from a great, bubbling cauldron of the Sleepstealer's nectar. The ship's captain had secured the vessel well back from the city and the river, which was wise—the Lord Minion knew that if the cloud drifted over a large body of water, great portions of the hull would be dissolved by the presence of the mundane liquid.

Swiveling his vast head, the Talon of Dassadec looked to the south, across the sweep of ruined plains. He could see his bloodtrains on the horizon, hundreds of wagons gathered in a vast concentration. They were screened from the human defenders by all three of his legions, as safe as they could possibly be. Still, Reaper had made a decision that would make it even safer—and that was the reason for this meeting.

The captain of the skyship, a burly brutox, emerged from the hull and bowed deeply, genuflecting before the mighty wyrm amid a cascading shower of sparks.

Reaper raised a curious eyebrow, eyeing a second brutox that had followed Captain Sharptusk. That minion, too, bowed with a properly honorific display of sizzling, fiery scintillas.

"This is Direfang, master," declared Sharptusk. "I have drawn him from the battlefield via the darkwind, as you commanded."

The Talon of Dassadec regarded the hulking brutox. "I have heard that you brought troops through a swampland—something no minion should be able to do. Is this true?"

"Yes lord, it is." Direfang's response emerged from a cloud of sparks. "For my troops are not minions, but humans that have been transformed by our master's nectar."

"And you struck at the fleeing humans after the battle. I shall forgive your failure to destroy them—you displayed commendable initiative."

"Thank you, lord," declared the brutox, shuddering in relief, and bowing with a proper display of obeisance.

"Now, how have you worked this transformation of humans?"

"It was a gift of Darkblood from a spring in that same swamp," replied the brutox. "The taste has corrupted a great company of darkmen, creating in them a craving for the elixir. In me, it seemed to provide a means to traverse water, even to wade through the stuff when there was no other way around."

"I will send more of my minions to sup from this spring," Reaper declared musingly. "But in the meantime, I have a task for you."

"Your commands will be obeyed to the limits of my strength and power!"

"Good. Take your company, these darkmen, and follow the course of this mighty river up to the lake called Glimmersee."

"I know the place, master, having seen it from my own cloud."

"Once there, you must place yourself to guard the bloodtrains against any attack from the south—it is the only place my army's flank is vulnerable. Because there is so much water there I cannot guard it with my minions. It seems this is a task fit for your darkmen."

"It shall be my pleasure to obey!" The brutox saluted in a chest-thumping cascade of sparks.

"Splendid."

Already the second brutox was forgotten, as Reaper turned back to Sharptusk. "Now you will send word to Kroaksmasher and Burner. As soon as they have finished their replenishment, the attack against Carillonn must commence."

— 4 —

The black cloud seethed and grew, piling high over the west bank, rumbling and flickering with the threat of massive destruction. Meanwhile bovars hauled load after load of gravel and boulders, bearing the fill on the great, scooplike plates of their foreheads. Takian watched in furious impotence, knowing that the growing dam would choke off the city's main line of defense. But he and all the humans of the garrison were helpless to counter the efforts of the relentless minions.

The endless file of elephantine beasts dumped the material into the gorge, and though each load was only a grain of sand in a ditch, the grains kept coming. Silt tainted the blue-green river to a muddy brown in the west channel, where the flowage churned through the narrowing gap beside the dam. Of course, clean waters still circled the island to the east, but this was on the opposite side of the island and no help in the city's defense.

For an endless week, then two, the beasts kept coming, the channel growing more and more obstructed. The file of bovars continued day and night, each massive creature arriving at the bluff on the far bank and pouring its fill onto the slope of rubble that crept outward across the channel. The top of the dam was soft and irregular, but because of Carillonn's bridges the minions wouldn't need to cross on the barrier—they merely needed to stop the flow of water.

During all this time, the High Prince remained in seclusion in the royal apartments of Castle Carillonn. On the second day after the retreat Bristyn remarked, acidly, that he wasn't missed, an opinion shared by the king—and most of the rest of the population, as well.

Even though the humans were for the time being protected from actual contact with minion troops, the feverish ills contracted by the veteran companies had spread throughout the army. Many had died, and countless more remained debilitated. As always, the only treatment seemed to be plenty of water—sick men who went thirsty for more than a few hours almost always perished.

Bristyn saw that many of the ailing were evacuated to the eastern quarters of the city, on the far side of the island—across Whitestream, the brook that bisected the island. She used her royal authority to requisition houses, manors, warehouses—any building where a number of sick men could be sheltered and tended to. Many of Carillonn's citizens had fled to Galtigor or other eastern realms, so the duchess was able to set up the makeshift hospitals without displacing much of the populace. Even so, too many had been stricken, and hundreds of feverish men remained in the western districts of the city.

Takian saw to the defense of the castle district, which included the two hills west of the brook. He enlisted every healthy man he could find, but because of the rise in illness, these were becoming fewer and fewer in number. He had sent another missive to Duke Beymont, though too much time had passed for him to hold much hope out for any timely arrival of the Corsars. Some recently arrived Coast-men had yet to succumb to the disease, and the king also ordered the last of his reserves from Galtigor to ride to the front. If Carillonn fell, he was convinced there would be no hope for his homeland or any other realm to the east.

The battle would have to be won right here, or it would never be won at all.

And still the bovars kept hauling, and the western channel withered and died.

— 5 —

Rudy slammed to the ground with stunning force. He heard the snap of bone as pain shot through his ankle and leg. Rolling, he aimed Lordsmiter to the side and absorbed the rest of the impact with a jar that knocked the wind out of him. The sword, casting its pearly light, remained clutched in his hand as he lay gasping on the floor.

At least that floor was flat. A moment later Raine landed on her feet in the place Rudy vacated with his roll, tumbling in a different direction, then bouncing to her feet with the Sword of Darkblood in her hand.

"My ankle's broken," Rudy gasped through teeth clenched against the pain.

"Here." She slipped the Auraskin off her shoulder and handed the pathetically empty sack to the Iceman. "Take what's left."

He started to object, but then realized they had no choice. Crippled as he was, he represented only a liability to them both. Gratefully he sipped the trickle of Aura that remained, then drew several deep breaths as the throbbing in his ankle faded, cracked bones fusing into a whole.

"What do we have for options? Any way out that you can see?" he asked, when he could talk without grimacing.

"Backtracking's out," Raine replied, pointing up as she made a circuit around the chamber.

Rudy saw that the chute had deposited them through a hole that was twelve or fifteen feet overhead. The ceiling arched downward into a large room, so, as Raine had said, there would be no climbing back up.

"I don't see any doors, either," she declared—with remarkable lack of emotion, when Rudy felt his own despair rise up. "Just a pool—of Darkblood," the Woman of Three Waters concluded, indicating a trench of inky liquid along one portion of the wall.

"Then that's the way out," he said, rising and walking over to the dark and sinister channel.

The slick liquid reflected the light of his blade like a sheen of oil. The pool was very still, though occasionally a faint pulse of ripples would spread across the midnight-black surface.

"What if . . . ?" Raine started to object, then fell silent for a moment. "I'm coming with you."

"I'm glad," replied the Iceman, sheathing his sword.

He didn't allow himself to think any more about his plan as he stepped into the pool. Feeling for the bottom with his

boot, he found that it was barely knee-deep with the first
step but got rapidly deeper as he slid carefully down to the
slippery, sloping bottom.

The sensation of the Darkblood on Rudy's skin was neither pleasant nor unpleasant. The temperature was tepid,
though the liquid seemed to have a more oily consistency
than water. When he lifted his leg to take another step, his
trousers remained slick, with very little of the stuff dripping
back to the pool.

In a moment he was floating, and with deliberate strokes
he swam to the cavern wall where it descended to the water's edge.

"It's solid on top," he announced, running his fingers
along the stone surface. But when he kicked with his feet,
they met no resistance, and he realized that there was some
kind of indentation below the water level.

"There's something down there," he announced. "At
least a cave, and maybe a tunnel."

"Did you see those ripples on the surface before?"
Raine asked.

"Yes—what about them?"

"I think they indicated some kind of current passing
through here. And if so, that means there has to be a tunnel,
doesn't it? Some kind of connection to somewhere else?"

"It's a good bet. Wait here for just a moment—I'll be
right back."

Diving, he stroked along, feeling the walls of a tunnel
around him. After twenty strokes he stopped, turning to
start back to the chamber—but as he pivoted he heard a
gurgling, splashing noise ahead, and the sound gave him
hope as he pulled back to the chamber below the trap.

He rose before Raine and drew a deep breath. "I can't
say for sure," he reported. "I heard some current up ahead.
But there's no saying there'll be air."

"What other choice do we have?"

"Right. Well, take a deep breath . . ."

"Rudy?"

He paused, touched by the tenderness in her voice. "I'm

grateful that you . . . used the sword, back at the Tor of Taywick.''

''So am I . . . you know I never would have made it here, if it hadn't been for you,'' he replied.

''Well, we're not done yet.'' Raine's voice was suddenly stern, her face masked by an expression of determination.

''Let's go,'' the Iceman agreed.

His dive was clean, and he pulled along, following the course of the tunnel. He felt a current tugging at him, sweeping him farther, and very quickly he had passed the point of possible return.

And still the tunnel continued, lightless and endless—and airless.

TWENTY

Horizons of Darkblood and Doom

Any person of skill and endurance can climb a
lofty peak, given favorable weather, terrain,
equipment, and companions. The master Iceman
is that rare climber who, ropeless and alone, can
overcome precipice and blizzard to reach the
summit.
— CREED OF THE CLIMBER

— 1 —

Neambrey saw the terrion as the monster glided through a
scrap of cloud and momentarily shimmered, the scales of
its winged shape adapting to the brown and dusty plains
below. The Glimmersee was an azure swath behind him as
the drackan banked, using a wisp of high, white cumulous
as cover.

Only as he swept back did he see that there were two,
no *three*, of the flying minions. It was a good thing he had
learned to be careful, Neambrey reflected smugly—a less
experienced drackan might have soared into battle upon
glimpsing the first, shimmering terrion.

Before he completed his self-congratulatory reflections,
a sharp beak slashed into his right wing and he uttered a
squawk of indignant surprise. Almost belching out his bel-

lyful of frosty Aurabreath, he veered away from the terrion that had dived from the sunlit skies overhead.

"Hey!" The drackan half-breed pulsed his wings once, hard, and arrowed after the vicious flyer. The wound throbbed, but the bite had gashed only a small portion of his wingtip—it seemed that he could fly as fast as ever.

And that was faster than any terrion, at least in a dive. Swiftly Neambrey swept after the creature, reaching out to snatch the whiplike tail in his forepaws. With a sharp tug he jerked the monster backward, then broke its neck with one sharp bite.

But the trio of lower minions had been alerted. Squinting, Neambrey saw one of the creatures as it flickered around to the east. The serpent of Faerine growled in frustration when he realized that he had lost sight of the other two terrions.

He flew toward the monster that he could see. That one veered away from the drackan, but was apparently unwilling to fly any closer to the skies over the great lake. Neambrey swiftly closed the distance, pumping his wings with measured force, slashing toward the minion at an oblique angle.

The flyer turned at the last minute, jaws gaping in the face of the onrushing drackan. Neambrey's dextrous forepaws grasped the monster's neck, just below the head, and for a dizzying second the two winged creatures tumbled downward, locked in a ball of raking claws and snapping jaws. Once more the drackan's fangs closed around a terrion throat, and with a pathetic shriek the minion's life was ripped away. Dropping the limp corpse, Neambrey pulled out of the dive, still seeking the other two terrions.

But they seemed to be nowhere in sight. The drackan strained for altitude, casting his head back and forth, seeking some sign of movement, some flickering irregularity in the sky that would identify his enemy. Only when he leveled off and, in bafflement, swept his vision across the panorama of the plains, was he rewarded by a suggestion of his enemy's location—and the news was not good.

The remaining pair of terrions were already far away, flying toward the looming clouds of tarry smoke that lay like smog in the northern sky. As soon as he spotted them, Neambrey understood that it would be disastrous to let the two survivors get away. Tucking his wings, narrowing his body into a spearlike shaft of slate gray scales, the young drackan dove after the fleeing minions.

He squinted until he clearly saw both of the creatures. Neambrey thought it strange that they declined to fight, but the conclusion was obvious: They were going to report on his presence to someone.

Wings scooping and pushing at the air, Neambrey flew through the whistling wind of his own momentum, leveling off, straining to drive himself a little faster, to narrow to his sleekest possible shape. Never before had he flown with such exhilarating speed. Miles swept by as the foothills became grasslands below him. The shimmering shapes of the twin terrions grew in definition, rippling through the air in favor of speed over camouflage. Nevertheless, it seemed to the drackan that he was painstakingly slow to close the distance.

Once, one of the minions turned a snakelike neck to look backward. Uttering a squawk of alarm, the monster dove toward the ground, seeking to increase its speed. Because it was almost sunset, Neambrey momentarily lost sight of the minion against the landscape.

The remaining terrion surprised him by looping about and arrowing in to the attack, beak widespread in that familiar, threatening grin. Obviously the monster was willing to sacrifice itself in order to give its comrade a better chance to escape.

The drackan's jaws gaped in fierce imitation of his enemy's expression—but Neambrey struck just before the two flyers collided. His breath exploded in a cloud of frost, a white sphere of vapors that surrounded the terrion with a deadly chill. Silently the minion tumbled from the sky, wings frozen in outstretched posture, jaws still locked in that leering grin. The corpse flipped and cartwheeled, now utterly graceless as it spun toward the unforgiving ground below.

It was late twilight by the time Neambrey caught the last of the flying minions. Surprised by his own ill temper, the young drackan slew the monster quickly, taking no pleasure from the single, fatal neck bite. As the terrion fell he grimaced and tried to spit the taste from his mouth.

The ambush of the minion flyers irritated him, but it also made him think. They were far from the main concentration of the Sleepstealer's horde. The shore of the Glimmersee blocked any combat below, so these terrions were not likely searching out a route for the next attack. Rather, it seemed likely that they were protecting something, that they had been assigned by their Lord Minion to insure against attack from this backward, unprotected direction. And in the drackan's mind, there was only one objective that would cause the enemy to watch his rear with such vigorous defenders.

Hopeful now, Neambrey flew into the night, certain that he was on the track to the enemy army's store of Darkblood.

— 2 —

The twissel darted low across the aquamarine waters, watching his reflection flicker over the waves as the humming wings carried him toward the western bays of the great, mountain-flanked lake. For days he'd been busy with his assigned task, and each stop had proved more interesting, more exciting, than the one before.

Soon Garic Hoorkin saw another one: a sheltered anchorage, deep waters well-protected by steep ridges and a forested shoreline. Though the broader surface of the Glimmersee was marked by whitecaps and a rolling swell, within the sheltered confines of the bay it was placid, even mirrorlike. A few wooden houses clustered beside a spindly dock, and a muddy track seemed to be a sort of main street.

More important to the twissel, no less than a dozen boats bobbed serenely atop the nearly waveless waters.

Experience had taught Garic a thing or two, and so he blinked out of sight, gliding invisibly up to the prow of the largest of the lake boats. Many other craft were lashed to either side of the big hull, but this vessel was clearly the centerpiece of the aquatic gathering.

The broad-beamed craft seemed to be some kind of ferry, for the hull was lined with row after row of bench seats. A half dozen oars were shipped along either gunwale, and a portion of the interior was sheltered by a canopy of canvas nailed over a wooden frame. Under this protection a score or more of humans had gathered, huddled around a puffing woodstove to talk in low, nervous tones.

Garic settled to one of the benches just outside of the canopy, trying to decide on a course of action. He had already spoken to four or five such groups, and each time it had been his initial appearance that had provoked the most consternation. Still, experience had shown that it was best to be blunt—and besides, staying invisible for very long was a real strain on his endurance.

Letting out a deep sigh, he popped into sight, standing on the bench with his wings fluttering slowly. If the men reacted poorly, the twissel could spring into the air in the blink of an eye.

"Eh? Who's that?" asked one burly human, a bearded fellow who lowered a bottle to the deck and stood unsteadily, peering into the shadows concealing Garic.

"I'm a messenger—a friend," the twissel proclaimed smoothly. He hopped down to the deck and strolled into the lamplight of the gathering. "I'm a twissel. You know, from Faerine."

"By Baracan, so you are!" declared one pot-bellied sailor with a hearty laugh. "And a great bit more welcome you are than the lot across the lake!"

"Well, thanks," Garic replied politely, stepping closer so that the men could get a look at his wings. He smiled disarmingly as the ferrymen and sailors made a place for him on one of their benches.

"Eh—what kinda host are ya, Rupert!" called another seaman. "A beer for our guest!"

The pot-bellied man gaped in mock horror. "Me manners are sunk to the bottom! What'll it be, twissel? A beer, or would you like rhum?"

Garic knew what beer was, which was more than he could say about rhum, so he took the safer course. "A beer would be very nice."

Captain Rupert gave him a large bottle, then settled to his bench with a fresh beer for himself. "A messenger, you said? Well? What's yer message?"

"Well, I've been flying around this edge of the lake, talking to all the boatmen I can find. You see, the Combined Field Army needs your help. . . ."

— 3 —

Just when Rudy was certain that his lungs would explode, that the airless tunnel would go on forever, his flailing hand felt a gap above him. Pushing upward, he broke the surface and drew a deep, ragged breath. He was in some kind of alcove, and sensed a larger torrent rushing by just ahead.

"Raine! Where are you!"

He felt her slip past his legs, still underwater, and then she vanished into the surging current of the bigger channel.

"No!"

He shouted frantically, his voice ringing with desperation as he dove into the flowage after the Woman of Three Waters. He saw a slender hand flash above the churning surface of the Darkblood, realized that a fast current bore them along. Kicking, he pushed himself through the murk, drawing a breath as he saw Raine floating before him. She, too, swam with her head above the surface.

The side of the ditch raced past with startling speed as, with long strokes, Rudy drew closer to Raine. He was relieved to see that she was not only conscious, but swimming strongly.

"I'm sorry . . . I couldn't stop," she gasped despairingly.

"We're out of there and alive—far as I'm concerned, it was a good escape," he replied, shaking his head, spitting drops of almost tasteless Darkblood from his lips.

Here was another aspect of their transformation: The Man and Woman of Three Waters were apparently immune to a toxin that would have killed any normal human.

But Rudy's relief was tempered by another realization, as he heard a dull pounding, which was getting louder and louder. The current was fast, and whooshed down a pipelike trough with very little air space over their heads. Looking through the darkness, the Iceman saw the end of the channel rushing toward them.

Yet he knew that the flowage continued on, for the force of the current grew stronger and stronger—and then he felt the drain, as they were pulled through a tight spiral, whirling downward with disorienting speed. He tumbled free, floating in the air, surrounded by Darkblood, and plunging toward a landing unknown distance below.

The impact came with the shattering force of a landslide, driving out the little bit of air that remained in Rudy's lungs. He coughed and gagged, choking on Darkblood, instinctively clawing toward the surface. The torrent pushed him hard and he felt himself tumbling, head down, then spinning to the side. He couldn't get his head free, couldn't get his mouth up for a precious gulp of air.

But he was still *breathing*. Hard as it was to believe, even when the vile liquid fully buried him, he didn't suffocate. Instead, he found that he could swim, and tried to pull himself through the Darkblood with strong strokes, laboring in the liquid with his mind focused on one raging terrifying question: Where was Raine?

Had she been killed by the impact of the long fall—or almost as bad, knocked senseless and then carried away by the surging flow? Frantically he groped and thrashed, cursing the darkness that blinded him so thoroughly.

Then he felt a leg kick against him and he knew that she
was still alive. A hand flickered past his face and he lunged,
grasping Raine's fingers as she slipped through the Darkblood. Pulling and straining, he wrapped an arm around her
and held tight, trying to locate some kind of solidity in the
midst of the raging torrent.

The black fluid around them moved with noticeable pulsations, surging, then settling, then surging again. The Man
and Woman of Three Waters were carried along in the airless tube, and Rudy could feel from the answering pressure
of Raine's arms that she, like him, was surviving in the
noxious stuff. They swirled around a tight bend and now
the pulsing liquid carried them downward, deeper and
deeper into the Sleepstealer's fortress.

Rudy's feet struck rock, and then he was standing, letting
the Darkblood flow around his waist. Bracing himself on a
slippery floor, he pulled Raine into his arms, feeling her
deep breaths as she, too, rose from the murky flowage.
Staggering, he pushed through the fluid, seeing a shelf of
black rock just a few steps ahead. Raine followed, and in
moments the man and woman had dragged themselves from
a deep pool and knelt, dripping and trembling, on a stone
floor.

"Where are we?" she murmured.

Rudy tried to see something farther away than Raine or
the pool of black liquid. A ceiling of stone, with numerous
dangling stalactites, domed far overhead, and through the
center of that dome a huge shaft rose upward. He couldn't
be certain, but the Iceman thought that he saw black clouds
scudding past the end of that lofty chimney. The pool of
Darkblood where they had emerged was wide, but broad
shelves of dry rock fully encircled it.

"Do you hear that?" Rudy froze, sensing a cadence so
deep and resonant that he wondered if it came from within
himself.

"The Heart of Darkblood—it's pounding, louder than
ever!" Raine whispered.

A shiver of tension rippled down the Iceman's spine as

he sensed the summons, a silent plea that penetrated his mind and pulled him onward. It was as if someone were calling his name in a cruel, mocking tone.

"We're near . . . very near to the heart," he replied. "But there's something else . . . some kind of cry. Don't you hear that?"

"No." Raine shook her head, staring at him intently.

It came again, and it was more than the beating of a foul, monstrous heart. It was a call to Rudy himself, a challenging mixture of danger and promise.

"Nicodareus!"

He whispered the name, knowing that his old enemy was very close.

"But he's dead!" Raine objected, shaking her head determinedly. "You killed him under Lanbrij, remember?"

"I . . . I thought so, too. But it's like I recognize his voice. He's in here somewhere, and he's drawing us toward him."

"You *hear* him? But—"

Raine stopped as another voice, deep and growling, rumbled from the darkness of the cave.

"You feel me, Iceman . . . for I am here."

— 4 —

"I can ride, sire . . . just need a little help getting to the saddle. Please—let me come with you!"

Captain Jaymes spoke boldly, but the crimson flush to his skin, the palsied trembling of his hands belied the words. The knight lay on his back, struggling to rise. With a groan he failed, slumping downward again.

"Not this time, my captain." Takian took the man's hand, feeling the skin dry as parchment and burning with an internal fire. He was heartbroken by the sight of this valiant warrior, struck down by a pernicious and unseen foe.

"You get your strength back, be ready for the nex

fight,'' Takian said, desperately wishing there were some grounds for hope. Yet he knew—and, certainly, so did Jaymes—that those stricken by the racking plague were weakened to a bedridden state—and showed no sign of getting better. Those already debilitated when stricken, whether racked by wound or thirst or hunger, seemed likely to die by the time the fever entered its second week—and even the previously healthy victims were utterly drained and enfeebled by the virulent plague.

Leaving the infirmary, the king stalked through the castle, ascending to one of the western watchtowers to get another look at the minion dam. From the promontory he couldn't see into the channel as well as he could from the towers on the city wall, but he was tired of riding back and forth, of observing from here and there and never being able to do anything. And always overhead, towering above the minion army, there was that great, dark cloud, growing and pulsing and rumbling with barely contained violence.

''Your Majesty?''

''Yes, Donthwal.'' He greeted the advisor from Andaran, feeling a twinge of sympathy for the silver-haired scholar. Donthwal had dedicated his life to the preparation of Bentram Wayn for kingship. Since the prince's abysmal performance and subsequent, self-imposed seclusion, Takian knew that Donthwal had placed a great deal of the blame for that failure on himself.

''There's word from the river,'' Donthwal informed the king. ''Best guess is that the channel will be dry by morning.''

''Well, we'll be as ready as we can. I have strong garrisons at each of the three gatehouses. If they break through the gates, though, we've got trouble.''

''Not enough men?''

''With this damned fever dragging down nine out of ten, that's the problem. I spent most of the night scouring the city, trying to come up with enough healthy men to form a reserve.''

''It's not much, but I want you to know that my sword

is at your service." The elderly dignitary drew a heavy cutlass with a blade of engraved steel. "I knew how to use it, in my day."

"I'm sure you did—and thank you. Perhaps you'll meet me at the Rosegate with the dawn? That should be where things start to happen first."

"It will be an honor." Bowing, the man of Andaran departed.

Takian had one thing left to do. He found Bristyn in the castle commisary, supervising an inventory of provisions. He walked with her into an empty hallway, then turned and faced her seriously.

"I want you to be ready to flee to the east bank if the city gates fall. I don't want you getting caught in the castle, if the minions get onto the island. We could be besieged here, maybe for a long time. In any event, things could get very bad."

"No, my king . . . I won't."

Drawing a deep breath, Takian groped for a response, but Bristyn touched a finger to his lips and continued. "Here, in Carillonn, is where it will end, one way or another. You and I both know that. And I'm staying here with you."

A rush of love rose within him and he pulled her close, kissing her for a long time. When he broke away, he felt as fragile as a glass figurine, and wanted only to fall back into her arms.

Yet the king was on the tower of the Rosegate with the dawn when the first wave of minions started across the span. White marble vanished beneath the crushing wave of darkness, brightened by the sparks of two hundred brutox leading the swift onslaught. The *Dreadcloud* loomed in the sky, close to the river bank, lightning flickering and crackling underneath the glowering skyship's black hull. With a growl of powerful thunder, the great cloud began to move, pushing slowly over the dried river channel.

Takian thought fleetingly of Corsari, of that walled city standing against another minion onslaught. Duke Beymont and his countrymen had been the recipients of a miracle when the Man of Three Waters had laid his Auratrap for the Lord Minion. Looking at the cloud, at the swath of darkness on the far shore, Takian knew that here, today, there would be no miracle.

The king's attention was pulled back to the present with violent force. The far end of the bridge was invisible beneath the press of trampling boots, and now the sky was blacked out by the vast skyship. The *Dreadcloud* pushed closer, seeming to grow wider and taller with each passing minute.

In a moment of dire prescience, Takian saw that this gatehouse, these lofty towers and this graceful wall, were doomed. He remembered Bristyn's descriptions of the ruin of Shalloth, picturing the inevitable assault here, and realized that his men would only be uselessly sacrificed if they waited exposed on the walls and towers.

"Go! Off the walls, down from the towers!" he cried, turning to both sides and bellowing the commands at the top of his voice. "Re-form in the street beyond the gatehouse!"

The defenders of the Rosegate, with the shadow of the *Dreadcloud* growing darker by the second, obeyed with alacrity, streaming down the stairways and out the doors, every man knowing he was running for his life. Takian, the last down from the tower, felt his hair stand on end in anticipation of the first destructive bolts.

The sinister cloudship darkened an expanding swath of sky, pressing across the channel of the drying riverbed. The billowing forward deck of the vessel loomed over the city wall, and the king saw the black holes gaping in the underside of that prow, again recalling Bristyn's vivid descriptions of Shalloth's destruction.

Then the first blasts of lightning snaked down, striking the high towers of the Rosebridge gatehouse. The white spires glowed red for a brief instant, outlined in fire, trembling under the force of destruction. A cascade of shards exploded outward as additional spears of sizzling energy, one after the other, blasted into the lofty structure. Stones flew over the city and tumbled into the river channel, and the smell of rock dust and char was everywhere. The air itself shuddered under the explosive impacts, staccato booms blending into a drum roll of thunder. More stones fell, obliterating the parapets of both towers, scoring a deep crack through the stonework running down the side of one.

After dozens of monstrous blasts, the twin towers of once-white stone had been reduced to blackened stubs of their former glory, like the splintered stumps of blasted trees. Any man trying to stand there would have been killed as certainly, and as uselessly, as if he had hurled himself from the parapets into the minion ranks.

Next the batteries turned their destructive power toward the gates and the arching wall. Blast after blast shivered into the white stone, exploding carefully jointed parapets, casting rubble for hundreds of feet in every direction. A section of the wall crashed, and within the ruins the frame of the iron portcullis glowed red, then yellow, until it melted away, liquid metal flowing into the pile of ruins.

When this bombardment finally halted, the echoes took a long time to fade—but they yielded to a stillness that was not utterly silent. Even through his ringing eardrums Takian heard them, thousands of iron-shod boots tromping over the marble bridge. Soon the dark shapes and glowing trails of advancing brutox could be seen pushing their way through the wreckage. Sparks flashed and crackled amid the piles of shattered, smoking stones, and then a line of brutox came out of the smoke, brawny shoulders brushing together with hissing explosions of energy.

Takian looked across the street. He saw a block of pikemen there, long spears angling toward the entryway, a hoarse-voiced captain urging them into position.

"Stand ready, my brave fellows," the king murmured. "You're our wall, now."

The gatehouse ruins were a tangle of howling, flaring brutox. The captain of the pikemen ordered his men forward, and the minions roared into a charge, hurling themselves at the hedgehog of spears. The lead rank impaled itself, brutox dying in gory waves, but then the second wave came on—and behind pressed a third, and a fourth, and more stretching into the distance.

— 5 —

The column of diggers and Icemen spilled out of the gap in the foothills, and as they descended a long, gentle slope Danri took in the broad expanse of placid waters that spread to the right and left horizons in the sun before them. The smell of rotten fish reached them more than a mile from the shore of the Glimmersee, and despite the bright sunlight, the surface of the water had a filmy look of murk and decay.

"It's suffered," Danri observed sadly. "Not like the first time I saw it. Then, this lake looked like something worthy of Faerine!"

Kerri squeezed his arm. "It must have been beautiful."

"Aye-uh—and it will be again, now that we have the breach plugged up. You can see that the Darkblood flowing down here was pretty hard on this lake."

In contrast to the water itself, the setting of the Glimmersee lay revealed in rare glory, with a deep and cloudless sky kept clean by winds prevailing from the high mountains, holding the pollution of the Sleepstealer's blight at bay.

"Do you think Neambrey got through? Or Garic had any luck?" asked the diggermaid, her delight tempered by the fact that the drackan and twissel had been absent for several days.

"There's one answer," declared Awnro, strumming a soft ditty as he strolled along with the column of diggers. "Look at all the boats."

"By all three gods!" gasped Danri, whose attention had been focused farther out on the water. The shoreline below them, where the Klarbrook flowed into the lake, was marked by a small fishing village and sheltered harbor.

That anchorage now teemed with vessels of all sizes. As the Halvericans and their allies from Faerine tromped toward the shore, more boats came into view around the point of the village breakwater—a pair of large flatboats, and several sleek, twin-masted schooners.

"Danri! Kerri!"

Garic Hoorkin buzzed into sight, scooting out the door to the village inn. "I got you some boats."

"And the timing of our drackan friend couldn't be any better," Awnro said, pointing to the sky above the lake.

Neambrey flew just above the water, wings pulsing through long strokes; neck, tail, and legs angled as straight as an arrow. With a final series of beats, he pushed himself into a climbing glide, rising over the masts of the hundred or more ships bobbing in the harbor. The drackan banked slightly, soaring over the docks, then coming to rest in the middle of the village street—causing an immediate, shrieking panic amid the hapless residents of the lakefront town. Fortunately, the confidence of the Halverican troops, who had seen the drackan fight at their side, greatly restored the equanimity of the lakemen.

"That's the reason they didn't send Neambrey to talk to you captains," Garic explained to a pot-bellied boatman who regarded the drackan with appraising eyes.

"What's the word on the wagons?" Danri asked, as soon as the startled human populace had been persuaded to return to the village.

"I found them on the plains." Neambrey, trotting beside the lead diggers, continued his explanation. The drackan's wings were tucked against his lean flanks, but he seemed as tireless on the ground as he was gliding through the air.

"Anyway, I saw those big wagons up ahead. They're a ways past the end of the lake, but the Glimmersee flows into a bay that kind of goes in that direction. You know, kind of like the fjord did up toward Darkenheight. D'you think that helps?"

"I think it could make all the difference," Danri admitted with a grim nod. "Just show us the way."

TWENTY-ONE

The Darkest Shore

The culmination of a contest comes after
peripheral battles have been forgotten, pawns on
both sides fallen in uncounted (and
unimportant) numbers. When the two opposing
lords face each other in the ultimate test, the
victory for one is triumphant, the defeat of the
other, catastrophic.
—TOME OF VILE COMPULSIONS

— 1 —

In the shadows across the chamber, where the plunging wall
met the smooth, slick floor, something moved . . . something large and winged, with twin eyes burning from the
darkness like the coals of an infernal forge.

And Rudy knew that Nicodareus was alive.

''This time the Man of Three Waters comes to *me*.''

The voice bubbled like an explosion from a lake of lava,
rolling into Rudy's face, shivering his bones. The jolt of
fear penetrated to his heart and his soul, threatening to turn
his will to jelly. But in the next moment that terror was
gone, replaced not by rage, but by a cool and calculated
appraisal of his enemy and himself. When Rudy spoke, he
chose his words for the effect they would have on the Lord
Minion.

"And the dog of Dassadec waits, leashed beside his master's hearth."

The black shape swirled from the base of the chamber's arching wall, roaring toward the two intruders in a bluster of flapping wings and clattering talons. Rudy saw a feline grace in the long pounces—and a demonic hatred in the fanged visage, jaws gaping, twin horns curling back from the monstrous skull. Eyes of vengeful fire expanded in the rush as the Lord Minion swept like a hurricane across the cavernous chamber.

Lordsmiter flared in Rudy's hand, a sudden wash of light brightening the vast darkness. The Iceman was ready, even eager to meet his enemy. He crouched, blade extended, bracing himself to meet the full brunt of the Lord Minion's attack.

But Nicodareus, enraged though he was, retained a vestige of the patience he had bred over millenia. Wings taut above his shoulders, he glided into the air, then circled to land on all fours, crouching with back arched, head swaying close to the floor. He growled, a long, deep, rolling sound that shook the very bedrock of Agath-Trol. Black strings of drool dangled from the Lord Minion's jaws and he shook his head furiously, casting the strands into the darkness, then glaring at the Iceman from just beyond the range of the gleaming sword.

"You dare to insult me?" The Eye of Dassadec's tone rumbled as deeply as ever, but he sounded genuinely surprised—even shocked. "Know that my mercy can mean the difference between a swift death, and an eternity of torment for you—or your beloved."

Those glowing, hellish eyes turned to fasten upon Raine, whose sword was also drawn, and for the first time Rudy's confidence was banked by a glimmer of cautious fear. Still on all fours, the Lord Minion padded to the side, forcing the woman to pivot and the man to step forward. Side by side, blades extended, they faced the horror.

"Remember, I tasted her blood once—and found it sweet." Again the Lord Minion's chuckle shook the stony floor beneath the Iceman's feet, and Rudy's fear erupted anew. Sidling a few steps, he moved to screen Raine—but was frustrated as she countered his maneuver so that the pair continued to face their enemy side by side.

"I see you have the Sword of Darkblood," observed Nicodareus. He rose to standing height, wings flaring behind him as he seemed to grow before their eyes. "It is fitting that you bring it here before you die—it is far too fine a weapon to remain in human hands."

The Eye of Dassadec swelled still more, looming above the intruders, sneering down at them.

"It's an illusion!" Raine suddenly exclaimed. "He's not growing—he's the same size as he was when Pheathersqyll tricked him, and when you defeated him under the land bridge."

With a roar the monster swept a paw toward the woman, but her swipe with the blade of midnight-black drove his talons away. Seeing a chance, Rudy lunged, driving the tip of Lordsmiter toward the Lord Minion's belly. The Eye of Dassadec pounced backwards, returning to all fours as he paced like a monstrous tiger, circling his two enemies.

"Is this where you have been sentenced?" Rudy asked, keeping his tone cool, almost conversational. "Does your master keep you here, to serve his pleasure?"

Nicodareus froze, the embers of his eyes flaring brightly—as if someone had turned a bellows onto the coals. Rudy sensed his enemy trembling, poised at the brink of control, and goaded him again.

"I'm surprised to find you alive. Even if you lived through the Aura in Lanbrij, I would have thought that your many failures would have earned you nothing less than the Sleepstealer's condemnation."

The roar exploded from Nicodareus like a thunderous avalanche. The Eye of Dassadec again stood tall, and the Iceman staggered backward from the force of the sound. Yet he smiled grimly, knowing that his barb had struck deep into Nicodareus' prideful being.

"Your trickery and good fortune were not enough to

destroy me!'' bellowed the Lord Minion. ''And now you must face me without the luxury of elaborate traps, without an ocean of Aura!''

''Perhaps—but this sword was not named Lordsmiter because it beheaded a kroak.''

The Iceman felt another flush of satisfaction as Nicodareus roared and swelled, pounded his chest, stretched his wings into a stiff, menacing arc over his horned skull.

''Attack him—now!'' Raine's voice was an urgent whisper at his shoulder.

Then Rudy was a bull charging a flag of fiery red. Lordsmiter burned in his hands, leading him, and the Man of Three Waters shouted aloud. It was not a cry of challenge or even of fury—he recognized the sound as his own pure, unadulterated joy. He lunged, stabbing at the figure of swirling wings and pouncing, sleek muscle. Raine rushed from the other side and the Lord Minion whirled, dodging between them.

The Iceman saw his chance, Lordsmiter darting for the patch of skin beneath the monster's arm. Rudy stabbed, driving the weapon home with all his strength, surprised by how easily it penetrated the hateful flesh.

Then, abruptly, all was darkness. He slashed the sword and it came free of his hand, sucked away, vanishing into the murky shape that had been the Lord Minion. At the same time, the Man of Three Waters realized that Nicodareus was gone. Liquid flowed past his knees as the hulking image dissolved into Darkblood. Frantically he kicked through the goo, but found no sign of his sword.

And Rudy knew at once that this had not been the Eye of Dassadec—an illusion, a decoy, had fooled him. It had been a clever fake, an image crafted from Darkblood.

But where was Nicodareus?

A clang of metal sounded across the chamber—Rudy recognized a sword falling to the floor. He heard a gasp from Raine, followed by a horrifying second of silence.

Then, from out of the darkness came the deep, mocking laugh of the Lord Minion.

"No!"

The cry was an instinctive wail as the Man of Three Waters whirled through a circle. Frantically he groped through the murk of the cavern, stumbling toward the place Raine had been, trying to deny the truth that his ears, and his touch, confirmed. His foot kicked a sword and he picked it up, realizing that it was the Sword of Darkblood—the weapon his lover had carried.

But now she was gone, silenced and taken by the vengeful Lord Minion.

— 2 —

"Hold the first crossroads—don't let them out of the waterfront!"

Takian directed the city's defense from a street corner on the Roseway, several blocks back from the fallen gatehouse. The sun was high, though clouds of smoke cast this entire area into shadow. The minions had progressed through the gatehouse on their first push, but now they struggled against fresh human defenders, and that rush finally sagged to a bloody halt. The King of Galtigor had less than two hundred men to hold the Roseway, but he stretched them across the street and rode among them with his own sword extended, using his example to inspire the troops to contest every foot of ground.

The avenue before him thronged with kroaks, minions pressing through the shattered gate in an endless river. They swarmed like ants over ruined buildings, already chopping apart the two stately inns that had stood near the Rosegate. Even closer, Takian saw a three-story manor tumble down, literally bashed to pieces by the press of invading monsters.

Randart had vanished into the smoking chaos of a side street, where a file of stalkers disguised as men-at-arms had been reported. Takian could only hope that the sergeant's mission was successful—otherwise, this company could hold the wide avenue for the rest of the day, only to lose the fight when the minions moved up the hill via an un-defended parallel route.

And there were simply not enough men to hold all the streets. The castle district uphill of this spot was full of makeshift hospitals, each crowded with the sick and dying, men racked by fever and weakened by plague beyond the point where they could even rise to flee. Every time the minions advanced another block, more of these makeshift hospitals fell—and the shrieks of the helpless victims as they were tortured to death cast a sickening pall over the entire city.

Lightning hissed and exploded in the background, and more of the outer wall crumbled. Flames crackled from wooden buildings, while the great stone edifices of the gate-house and waterfront had been reduced to smoldering, shapeless mounds of splintered marble.

"Takian!"

Bristyn's voice sent a jolt of fear through the king, who had thought his wife safely atop the hill, within the walls of the castle. He whirled, Hawkrunner skittering back from the line, in time to see a flash of blue gown and golden hair. The Duchess of Shalloth stood in the entryway of a walled manor house—one of the places where the sick had been quartered.

"What are you doing here?" he demanded as the stallion dashed across the street to Bristyn. The king saw several large wagons drawn up within the square courtyard, and suddenly he understood.

"I'm taking these sick men to the castle, or to the east bank of the Ariak. And any others we can fit!" snapped the queen in confirmation. "And I need your help!"

"Of course—but how . . ."

"The *road*!" she cried, gesturing to the avenue of the Roseway. Several files of weary troops streamed down the hill, blocking any passage upward. "Give me a few men on horseback, enough to open the path."

Takian spotted more of the freight wagons rumbling down the avenue in the midst of the reluctant reinforce ments, and knew that his wife's plan might be able to save hundreds, even thousands.

"Get them loaded—I'll see you can get back up the hill," he promised.

Hawkrunner clattered back to the crossroads, where the king found a few of the city's knights. With sharp orders, he sent a half dozen men riding up the hill to help evacuate the wounded.

The sudden shadow that darkened the bloody, chaotic scene was like a curtain drawn across a bright window. The shade was accompanied by a chill of falling temperature colder than any winter gust. Takian quailed at the sight of a massive inky blot of cloud, saw the billowing, pulsing skyship of the Lord Minion rolling over the shattered gatehouse, looming above the City of One Hundred Bridges.

In the street the minions sensed the movement as a heartening reinforcement. The roaring of brutox echoed from stone walls, and once again the ground shook underfoot from the cadence of thousands of charging, booted warriors. Lightning stalked along the rooftops, creeping closer— then assaulting in a splintering barrage the house Bristyn had just evacuated.

"Stand firm, men!" cried Takian, urging Hawkrunner forward to take a position in the center of the line.

"Back, sire—please!" cried a captain.

Several swordsmen moved to take the stallion's reins, but the king curtly gestured them away. "Let me blood my blade, men—and do the same with yours!"

They obeyed as the charging minions rushed closer, and then battle surged along the compacted front. Men were packed tightly across the avenue, holding the line with shield and sword. Hawkrunner reared, bashing his forehooves into the minion horde, while Takian laid about to the right and left, quickly smearing his digger steel with the vile black fluid that pulsed through minion veins. Soon the monstrous invaders fell back, brutox roaring and kroaks panting, milling in the street just a stone's throw away from the human defenders.

The raging sounds of explosions gave way for a moment, but in the sudden, eerie stillness Takian heard other, equally disastrous noises. The clangor of battle had passed up the hill on both sides, as minion spearheads broke through the blocking forces on the flanking side streets. Already they were past the king's force—and in another minute or two Takian's detachment would be surrounded.

— 3 —

"I see somethin' . . . I think . . ."

The shout from the masthead broke Anjell's concentration and she looked up to see Darret perched in the crow's nest. For a long time she watched him stare toward the forward horizon—and then he pointed in a direction just to starboard of the bow.

"It's a mountain!" Darret's voice cracked and he waved wildly. "A black mountain—and it's *big*!"

Anjell's heart rose with hope, but she kept her tone serious as she shouted across the decks. "Keep an eye on it— I'll point us over there. Haylor, be ready to trim the sail."

Using both hands to pull down on one of the big spokes, the girl slowly turned the massive wheel of the galyon's helm.

Darret, meanwhile, swung through the rigging, releasing a line to the *Black Condor*'s foremast midsail—one of only two sheets of canvas deployed to catch the wind that had steadily propelled them for the last few days. Balanced on a high boom, he ran to the end of the long timber, playing out one line, then backtracked to pull in another. On the main deck, Haylor, too, ran back and forth, unspooling a rope so that Darret could turn the boom, then securing additional lines to a stanchion, insuring that the sail remained fixed to catch the breeze.

Fortunately, the wind had remained steady since, some days earlier, it had risen as a current of relatively fresh air from the trackless ocean to the south. Until that time, Anjell's breath had been the only force propelling the *Condor* through hundreds of miles of the Darksea.

The girl had stood for all that time, feeling the power of Auramagic in the wind that whirled from her lips, and in the endurance that allowed her to maintain the sorcery for all those days. She had wondered at the power, analyzing it, trying to understand the transformations that were occurring within her. When the first gusts of air had swirled around her, she had been surprised and a little thrilled— but not overwhelmed. In fact, it was as Haylor had suggested: She *knew* that she could do things like that. It was just a matter of learning how.

And she had wondered about Haylor, too. At first she'd had lots of questions that she had been desperate to ask, but she learned that, naturally, a person can't talk much while blowing a hard wind. Instead, Haylor had kept her supplied with Aura, while Darret had anchored a lone mainsail. For days and nights Anjell had puffed, pressing the ship forward like a skiff in a fresh wind.

While she had maintained her unsleeping vigil, the boys had given Aura to the sleeping adults, all of whom seemed to breathe steadily, to all appearances slumbering in an apparent state of peace. They didn't get any better or show signs of awakening, but at least they didn't seem to be getting any worse.

When the following breeze had freshened, the miasma of stale air and thick, filmy seas had broken as well. As the galyon leapt forward under nature's power, Anjell had limited herself to steering the ship, while Darret made the multitude of adjustments necessary to keep even minimal canvas aloft. Haylor had been very helpful, doing whatever they asked of him—though he showed no aptitude for the mast and ropework at which Darret excelled. Usually the little sylve carried Aura to his two companions, or helped make the rounds of the sleeping passengers.

Sustained by the water of magic, none of them dozed more than a few minutes at a time, and together they brought the great ship steadily along the coast of Duloth-

Trol. Anjell maintained their course, with the land usually a bare smudge on the right horizon, visible only from the masttop lookout. The waters were dark and rough, but not stormy. Fortunately, this deep ocean showed none of the turbulent vortices of Darkblood that had made the merging with the Faerine Sea so treacherous.

The air still smelled bad, but Anjell had kind of gotten used to it. She wondered if it had been the smell of Darkblood that had made her mother and all the crewmen get sick—but if that was true, why had she and Darret and Haylor been spared? Of course, Haylor was a Faerine and therefore different, but it *still* left questions about Darret and herself. And she had questions for Haylor, too, but they were different questions.

Once she had tried to talk to the others about this, but Darret had scampered into the rigging, muttering about bad luck. Haylor had turned away with a strange sparkle in his silvery eye, and when Anjell pressed him for explanations the sylve claimed to have none. She wasn't sure she believed him, but for once she'd been thwarted in trying to get someone to talk.

Throughout the voyage, Anjell's visions of Rudy had been uncertain, but frightening. When she thought about her uncle, he was a strong presence before them, and she was relieved as much by the confirmation that he still lived as by their growing proximity. She found real hope in the knowledge that they were getting much, much closer to him. But frequently her mental images were obscured by an ominous darkness, or—even worse—distorted by vague, but very frightening and dangerous, threats.

Now this mountain had risen from the horizon, and she knew they were closer than ever to her uncle and Raine. She couldn't see the black massif from down here on the deck yet, but it seemed at least possible that the place was Agath-Trol. And she knew that was where Rudy and Raine had been going. All they could do was keep on sailing as they were, hoping for landfall. She hadn't figured out what they'd do after that.

Haylor hoisted himself nimbly up the ladder and perched at the top, leaning on the railing at a rakish angle. "Arrgh, matey," he growled in his deepest sea-dog tones, "let me handle that wheel, thar!"

Anjell laughed, her fears momentarily dispelled. "Okay. I'll go have a look at Mama and the sailors."

Waiting long enough to see that Haylor held to their course, Anjell descended to the main deck and filled several Aurasacks from one of the barrels. Starting with the forward crew's berth, she went to each of the sleeping sailors, carefully trickling Aura into the slack-jawed, snoring mouths. She checked to see that each man breathed comfortably, adjusting a pillow or hammock when she thought it would help.

Crossing to the rear cabins, she first tended to Captain Kestrel. Though he, too, slept without visible distress, the girl was worried by a thinning of his features, a further graying of his already salty beard. She made sure he had a good drink of Aura and plumped up his pillow as much as she could before she crossed the tiny hallway to the cabin she shared with Dara.

She sat beside her mother for as long as she dared, holding her hand and taking some comfort from the silky skin and the familiar warmth.

"I know you'll wake up when we get out of here, Mama," she said, and for just a moment her voice faltered. "I *know* you will." Trying not to sniffle audibly, she kissed Dara's cheek and rose, propping the cabin door ajar as she returned to the deck.

By then she could see the mountain Darret had spotted from the rigging. The blocky pyramid was so dark, it stood out like a stain of ink against the smoldering gray sky. Angling to a point, the massif sloped steeply downward to right and left. Though they were still a long distance away, Anjell realized that she was leaning backward to look at the summit. No stranger to high mountains, the girl felt a glimmer of awe as she realized the truly vast proportions of this massif.

And Rudy was there! She came to know it gradually, as she stood and stared at the mountain. This knowledge *did* thrill her, but it frightened her, too. Grimly she climbed back to the wheel deck, telling herself that she was merely sobered by the sight of the place that had to be Agath-Trol. She reached for her Auraskin and took a long drink.

"That's it, then . . . we've sailed to the very end of your dream," Haylor murmured, his voice startlingly deep.

"No . . . it's only a wayside for us, not the end . . ." Anjell whispered softly, her words a prayer to the gods as much as a reply to Haylor.

Then she took the wheel, making a minute adjustment to move the prow of the galyon into line with the massive, dolorous mountain.

— 4 —

Bristyn Duftrall, with Gandor Wade at her side, stalked to the door of the royal apartments and pushed past a guard who tried to stop her.

"No—you can't—!"

The man's objections were quelled by Gandor's hand to his throat. "The Queen of Galtian has business with that useless wastrel you're protecting," growled the captain of Shalloth.

Despite the sweat beading his forehead from the early stages of fever, Gandor's grip was firm and his eyes hard. The guard made a move to draw his sword and the captain took the weapon, casting it down the hall. "You might hurt someone if you're not careful," he declared. "Best leave it over there until we're done."

Helplessly the guard watched the queen and her captain stride into Bentram Wayn's private chambers. The High Prince was huddled before a blazing fire, though the room was uncomfortably hot. When he looked up to see Bristyn, he flinched, then apathetically shrugged deeper into his chair.

"Who let you in here?" he demanded sullenly.

"I came here on my own—whether you want me here or not is irrelevant. *You're* irrelevant, damn you!"

The sting of Bristyn's words jerked the prince's head up, and he glared at her without speaking.

"You've helped to bring on this disaster—you know that, don't you?"

"No! I just wanted to . . . to see—"

"To see what? A pretty army marching for you? Well, here's something to look at!" Bristyn stalked to the window, pulled open the drapes with a furious gesture, then whirled to confront the cringing prince. "Take a look at a city, the whole hope and future of Dalethica, dying! Look out the window—*there's* something to see!"

"I don't want . . . it's too late!" Bentram Wayn's voice was a pathetic wail.

"No, by Baracan—it's not too late! Not yet, though it will be soon. Get out there and *do* something!"

"What? It's hopeless to fight! Anyone can see that!"

"Two dozen of your knights are still here in the castle, waiting for some word—anything—from you."

"But what can they do?" The prince stood, face twisted by anguish, and turned away from Bristyn as if he could seek shelter against the far wall of the room. "I tried . . ."

"You tried to get the army destroyed before the battle even started!" shouted Bristyn angrily. "You wouldn't listen to anyone's counsel, not that of the men who had been fighting these minions for a year—and not even that of your own advisor!"

"My advisor . . . Donthwal? Where is he? I've sent for him, but he didn't come. I thought—"

"He's fighting! Right now, in the streets of this city that old man is wielding a sword, standing against the minions that are trying to destroy everything he's ever dreamed of."

"Donthwal . . . with a *sword*?" For the first time the prince's eyes flickered with emotion. "But he could be killed!"

"He feels as though he *was* killed—not in battle, but in

shame. By the disgrace of you hiding in these chambers, turning your back on the city, on all Dalethica! He took the blame on himself, for all your many failures. Don't you think that's enough shame for any man?''

"No!" cried Bentram, pleading with Bristyn. "It's not . . . not his fault. It's *mine*."

"Then maybe it's about time you let him know that," the queen declared curtly, spinning on her heel and stalking from the royal apartments.

— 5 —

The defenders of Carillonn reeled backward, disheartened and terrified as the great cloud blasted the fortifications along the city's west wall. Takian tried with some success to hold his swordsmen in line, preventing an all-out surge of minions up the Roseway. Even so, the humans retreated steadily, falling back toward the castle gates against the relentless combination of the monstrous horde and its massive, lightning-spitting skyship.

"Hold that line—watch at the alley, there!" the king shouted, pointing to a crumbling gateway where sparking brutox surged. A brawny axeman stepped to the fore, slashing with his double-bitted weapon, slaying several, driving the rest of the minions back with a fanatical display of courage.

A blade lanced outward from the press and the man staggered, pierced through the heart as a half-dozen of his fellows reached his side. Cursing in hatred, they fought with vengeance and the breach was held.

"Sire!"

Randart's call somehow rose above the roar of the fight and the king whirled in his saddle, seeking some sign of the loyal sergeant. He saw the wide-bladed shortsword waving from a side alley, and guided his stallion through the crush of men, dismounting at Randart's side.

"The next street over—we've got a rout! As soon as the

lightning started, the brutox came forward . . . by Baracan, I *tried*, sire—I tried to hold the men. But they wouldn't listen, the filthy cowards . . . they ran!''

The burly sergeant's face twisted with a grief so intense that it pained Takian to watch.

"You and I both know they're not filthy cowards," the king declared, gripping the stalwart warrior's arm. "Get back there and rally them. Fall all the way back to the castle if you have to, but Randart—keep them alive! That's your task now!"

For a moment Takian wondered if the veteran campaigner would give in to despair. The anguish in his face was a palpable force, but then something hardened in his eyes.

He clapped his hand to his chest in firm salute. "As you command, Your Majesty!"

"Good—Baracan knows it's not easy," murmured the king, his praise lost in the chaos as Randart turned and raced back to his doomed position.

Another explosion rocked the ground underfoot, a heaving convulsion rippling upward, and Takian was thrown off his feet. He slammed onto his back so hard that for a moment he couldn't draw breath. A black haze edged across his vision as, straining for air, he fought to stay conscious. He saw the roof of a building across the street outlined in fire, then watched in horror as a dozen men, garments aflame, hurled themselves screaming from the upper windows.

Another bolt of lightning slashed downward from the cloud. The jagged line of fire glared brilliant yellow, like a vivid streak of sunlight in the twilit sky. The burning image remained in Takian's eyes as everything else grew black.

Then he heard the thunder, and as he finally, desperately swallowed a lungful of air, he felt the rumbling through the paving stones. At first he thought it was the resonance of the skyship's explosion, a blast that had shaken the very foundations of the Watershed.

But quickly he sensed that the cause of the vibration was

something else, a more immediate and tangible occurence. The dull resonance continued, steadily growing stronger, now shaking the cobblestones of the Roseway—and finally the king understood.

The street thundered to a cadence of pounding hooves, the clatter of heavy horses at a gallop. From somewhere Takian heard trumpets braying a brash challenge. Painfully he pulled himself to a sitting position, then staggered to his feet and took the patient Hawkrunner's reins, looking around for the source of this brazen counterattack.

"Sire!" Gandor Wade, on his chestnut gelding, clattered down the hill from the castle. "The High Prince is coming, leading the charge. Get your men clear!"

Looking up the wide avenue, Takian saw a line of palomino horses ridden by knights in golden armor, a tight formation sweeping down the street toward the battle. Massive hooves drummed against the street as the charge swept downward like an avalanche.

"Open ranks!" cried the king. "We're reinforced, men—give 'em a gap!"

Swiftly Takian's weary men scattered to each side of the street, opening a path toward the shattered, smoldering gatehouse. Minions immediately rushed forward, trying to take advantage of the opening, howling and charging up the avenue toward the castle.

But High Prince Bentram Wayn led his knights into the enemy, the speeding avalanche becoming a crushing landslide in power. The clash of weaponry, the shrieks of wounded kroaks and brutox, horses and men, rang from the white stone buildings as the battle surged like a hurricane trapped within a narrow space. Minions shrieked and dodged away, but were driven back into the killing lane by the troops gathered to each side of the road.

The small company of heavy knights, completely outnumbered, plowed through the minions like a stone ball rolling into tenpins. Kroaks flew to the side, pierced by lance and trampled by hooves, and brutox flared and sparked, driven down by deep wounds. Horses whinnied, knights cursed and shouted, and the clatter of hooves was swiftly rivaled by the ring of steel.

Bentram Wayn's riders pushed the first wave of monstrous troops aside and continued on, leaving maimed and shattered minions in their wake. The second mass of the Sleepstealer's troops tried to scatter, but they too were roughly smashed down, dozens lying in the street as the knights charged on.

Takian watched in amazement as the young heir hacked with a mighty sword, guiding his horse with his knees, urging the steed through the throng of reeling minions. Wayn's face was streaked with tears, his mouth locked in a grimace of rage as he killed one minion after another. His golden stallion fought like a true warhorse, rearing, spinning, kicking, holding his rider above the fray. The melee churned farther down the street, the momentum of the charge still unbroken.

Finally the young prince and his valiant knights turned the corner at the end of the Roseway, driving along the street beside the ruined wall. Minions streamed toward them from all sides, the enemy's uphill attack momentarily broken as all the monsters in range surged toward this new and audacious threat. Swords flailing, the Knights of Andaran pressed on.

As the last of the golden-helmed riders disappeared amid the ruins and the minions, Takian knew that he would never see them again.

— 6 —

The darkness of Agath-Trol was at last pierced by a beacon of light. The source of the illumination was fire, I knew, yet it was a warmer, brighter presence than the infernal blazes of lava and coal that I had earlier beheld.

Only vaguely did I realize that the light came from the Lord Minion himself—and this piece of knowledge was as frightening as any sensation I had ever experienced.

Nicodareus, the Eye of Dassadec, bore me in his arms, and light spilled from his body like a halo. He carried me upward, through the air, somehow driving those terrion-wings with the power to raise us both. His talons tugged at my flesh, and while the blood that trickled from my skin weakened me, it seemed at the same time to make him stronger, more hateful and vile.

Looking down from the great height, I saw Rudy across the room. Yet beyond the Iceman I saw something else, a great, seething thing in a hole in the floor. Like a slick membrane of muscle, it throbbed and pulsed, pushing black liquid through the fortress—and through Dassadec's im-mortal being.

And I knew that we had found the Heart of Darkblood.

From: *Recollections*, by Lady Raine of the Three Waters

TWENTY-TWO

Duel in the Darkness

Even the brightest light can be concealed by an
impenetrable fog.
—SCROLL OF BARACAN

— 1 —

More explosions rocked the city of white marble, but now
the *Dreadcloud*'s battery concentrated on the low wall
along the waterfront. The fringe of Carillonn along the dry
channel of the Ariak was a horizon of ruined parapet, splintered towers, and smashed, devastated buildings. Yet the
bombardment had been precise as well as awful—the three
bridges connecting the city to the west still stood, still bore
steady streams of minion troops into the wracked streets of
stone.

Takian's small company re-formed, using the respite to
pull more of the sick back from the surrounding buildings,
then readying themselves for the next, inevitable attack.

Gandor Wade fought bravely among the men, but Takian

had seen the sheen of sweat on the man's brow, knew that he was dangerously weakened by fever.

"Get back to the castle, man!" cried the king. "We'll join you there!"

"Sire—I can't go! I'll stay and fight—I must!"

Takian was about to order the captain of Shalloth back from the line, when the man went down, pierced by a minion sword.

"Bastard!" shouted the king, slashing down the kroak, then pulling Gandor's bleeding form back from the melee.

"Your Majesty . . ." Gandor's voice was weak, but his eyes flared with a martial spark. "Tell your queen . . . worthy daughter for the old duke . . . and you are a worthy king for her." With a shuddering sigh, the veteran captain gave up his last breath.

Tears stung Takian's cheeks as he gently closed the fallen man's eyes. Gripping the hilt of his sword, the King of Galtigor stood and faced the relentless foe.

Takian now had less than a hundred men left in his immediate command—and many of them were ill, forcing themselves to fight because they'd chosen to die in battle rather than on the pallet of a plague-bed. Countless warriors had been felled by the lashing tongues of lightning, or tumbling walls of rock. Still more had fallen from fever, the luckiest dragged to the rear, others reached by bloodthirsty minions before they could be pulled back.

Donthwal and the few surviving Knights of Carillonn held an adjacent roadway to the left, while a small company of Coastmen, recently arrived in the city and now led by Randart, tried to hold back the tide on the right. The High Prince and his knights had not returned, though Bentram Wayn's charge had given time for the remaining troops to retreat into the shadow of the castle.

"Sire . . . we're back to the last corner."

Takian whirled to see his faithful sergeant staggering out of an alley. Randart's face was flushed and his eyes were glazed by a rapidly advancing fever.

"Into the castle with the lot!" ordered the king. "Fal'

back over the drawbridge—we'll be there ourselves in a few minutes.''

A fresh legion of kroaks pressed up the Roseway, gaining block after block despite the lack of the skyship's destructive barrage. They rushed the buildings on each side, bashing against every door and window, clawing their way inward against the futile efforts of the always-undermanned defenders.

''Fall back—one more street!'' shouted Takian hoarsely, as kroaks churned into a nearby alley, a dozen of the brutes charging toward the street behind the defenders' line.

Hawkrunner responded like a fresh colt, dashing to block the alley mouth, allowing the king to kill a pair of the kroaks and block the advance of the rest. The stallion's hooves slashed, driving another minion back, and the weary defenders shambled up the street behind. As soon as the last of them had passed, Takian whirled his stallion and once more dashed amid his men, rallying them with his voice, his stamina, and his example.

''Your Majesty—King Takian!''

Donthwal of Andaran rode a strong gelding, handling the horse well as he reached Takian's side. The gray-haired advisor looked past the king, and his eyes, as they took in the teeming sea of kroaks and brutox, were hard.

''What of the prince?'' asked Donthwal.

Takian pointed into the mass of minions. The creatures came on steadily, crowding the street shoulder to shoulder, pressing forward with inexorable force. There was no sign of the golden helmets or proud lances of Andaran's knights, and their liege.

''His charge bought us the time to save many of the sick and wounded—he died like a great man.'' Surprisingly, the king felt an acute sadness at the passing of Bentram Wayn.

''In death, he might have atoned for some of the shame of his life,'' the advisor replied bitterly. ''But such sacrifice cannot save his city, or his world.''

''We haven't lost the city—or the world—yet, either,''

Takian retorted sharply. "How fares the fight on your quarter?"

"I came to tell you—I have four or five knights left, and they're falling back quickly. Your left is going to be exposed, but there's nothing we can do."

"Have them retreat to the castle," the king said. "We'll make a stand there."

"That's their destination. Not all men raised on Andaran choose to flee from imminent danger." Donthwal's shame thickened his voice.

"Even your princeling redeemed himself. I hope that one day you'll see that."

Donthwal shrugged, his reply lost in a renewed chorus of minion battle cries.

"Here they come!"

The shouts rose along the line as once again the black tide surged forward. The elder statesman drew his heavy cutlass and slashed at a kroak charging between two spearmen. The blade of heavy steel cleanly severed one of the minion's arms, and Takian's sword pierced its chest, finishing the job.

"Fall back—steady now!" he cried. "Into the castle, men!"

Side by side the two men fought against the enemy charge. The retreat soon brought them to the end of the castle drawbridge and there they stood while the rest of the weary company limped and crept and staggered across the wooden span.

Finally the two leaders backed across the bridge and into the shelter of the castle gatehouse, covered by a shower of arrows from the battlements and towers. The portcullis was released with a crash, and moments later the heavy drawbridge creaked upward.

Wearily the two men trudged through the crowded entryway, stepping around warriors sitting or sleeping wherever they found a patch of floor. Piles of clean rags, ready as bandages, were gathered along the walls, and several kegs of drinking water had been rolled into easily accessible locations. Takian and Donthwall stopped to dip a ladle into one of these, quenching thirsts raised over hours of battle.

Setting down the scoop, Donthwal regarded the golden king. "I'm curious about something. It's obvious that you aren't sick—that you've completely resisted the fever . . . yet you've been fighting these minions longer than any of us."

"Neither is my wife ill, though she's spent most of the last weeks in the plague wards," Takian said.

"Do you know why?"

"I'm beginning to think so. I made a guess, actually, that seems to have been proven out. Not quite a year ago, Bristyn and I found ourselves on the Watershed, at Taywick Pass. There we each had occasion to drink some Aura. Lately, I started to wonder if that was the reason for our immunity."

"Is there any way to be sure?"

"I think, yes. You see, among my Galtigor companies are many men of my brother's former legion, and several of these were at Taywick and received Aura as treatment for their wounds."

"And some of these men are in Carillonn?"

"Yes. Yesterday I identified a few veterans of the Taywick Battle, and found those that had been given Aura."

"And?"

"And all of them are healthy, though the men who have fought beside them—but never drank Aura—are almost universally sick."

"Good proof," Donthwal agreed, then shook his head with a sigh. "Now we can only hope for Aura to flow across the Watershed."

"And for Duke Beymont to come with ten thousand Corsars, while we're at it," the king said sourly. Sighing, he added, "It's our lack of Aura that made me decide not to say anything about that evidence. Without so much as a drop of the stuff in the city, I'm afraid the knowledge would only add to the general despair.''

"You're right . . . and there's no shortage of despair around here.''

Anxious to find Bristyn, Takian made his farewells and hastened through the keep, up the long, spiraling stairway to the high watchtower. He crossed the bridge to the outer wall of the castle, but the guards there reported that she hadn't been seen.

His eyes swept the city's eastern skyline, soothed by the sight of marble edifices still pristine and proud. The White-stream flowed across the island, laughing and sparkling past the foot of Castle Hill, and the lofty arches of the bridges linking the castle to the other hilltops remained standing. As Takian's gaze came to rest on the highest of the island's towers, connected to the castle by a long, spidery span of stone, he knew where Bristyn would be.

Climbing to the top of the gatehouse tower, he started across the long, lofty bridge. The street below him was empty, though an avenue a mere stone's throw away was crowded with advancing minions. Still, the king knew the enemy would take at least the rest of the night to make preparations for any attack on the high walls of the fortress.

Halfway across the high span, Takian's thoughts turned to the High King who had so loved the tower that rose into the evening sky before him. He allowed himself to walk slowly, ignoring the stain of darkness on the ground around the castle, trying to reflect on peaceful times that had once been the norm.

But the present demanded his attention, and he forced himself to study the situation below. Fortunately, for now the minions seemed content to occupy only the castle district. The deep stream separating the region of the lofty fortress from the rest of the island continued to flow, and presumably the minions wouldn't be able to dam it until they could bring some of the slow and clumsy bovars across from the mainland. The east hills and the city's port district would be safe until then.

Yet Takian knew that those regions of the city were filled mainly with the sick, so there was no real hope of respite from there. And as soon as the stream was dammed, the minions would simply spread everywhere, killing these helpless victims as slowly and deliberately as they desired.

When he neared the lofty spire of the King's Tower, Takian's pace increased unconsciously. A guard snapped to attention, letting him pass through the oaken doors into the place that had been Kelwyn Dyerston's true home.

Bristyn was in the tower's top room, now a barren and empty chamber compared to the cluttered study it had been for the High King. She went to her husband and held him, and he let her arms and her presence envelop him, as if she was a shield that could block out the nightmare of the world.

"He died in this room, you know . . . High King Dyerston," Bristyn said, blinking at the tears that formed in her eyes.

"I know . . . he lured the Lord Minion here so that Rudy could have a chance to live."

"I wonder what our Iceman is doing with that chance." The queen's words were soft and pensive, and for a moment the two rulers thought about the lanky mountaineer who had become their friend more than half a year ago. Finally, they stood on the balcony, holding each other, watching the tide of war as it lapped into the city, staining more and more of the alabaster stone with its muddy tread.

And for a time, neither of them had the strength to move.

— 2 —

"I know this bay." Rupert, the renowned bargeman, proved worthy of his reputation as he directed the flotilla of boats into the estuary of a wide, shallow stream. Danri estimated that they had moved fifty miles south from the main body of the Glimmersee.

"And I'm sure that's the wagons, under those clouds

over there.'' Neambrey sat tall in the center of the barge, and he inclined his sharp snout to point across the northern flatlands.

''Maybe another fifty miles . . .'' mused the digger aloud, knowing it would be a hard march.

Looking to the rear, Danri was again amazed at the number of boats dotting the waters of the Glimmersee. Hundreds of craft, ranging in size from small sailboats to barges and ferries as big as Rupert's *Red Swan*, had made the crossing from the south shore. They bore sylves, diggers, twissels—and one drackan—of Faerine, and Icemen, Freemen, and Lakemen from Halverica, as well as the remainder of the Galtigor company King Takian had dispatched a half year earlier. The Combined Field Army was indeed a mighty force, both in numbers and in determination. Beyond that, Danri knew they had one other significant advantage: The enemy didn't know they were here.

Within another mile they came to a broad reservoir, and Garic Hoorkin flew ahead to confirm the obvious: They had reached the minion dam.

''We'll have to beach you here,'' Captain Rupert declared apologetically. ''The rest of the way'll be on dry land—well, land anyway, though you might find a few marshes and swamps and the like.''

Winds off the mountains whipped the waves into frothing curls, and the digger was not disappointed to hear the barge captain's assessment of the situation.

''We'd better get ready to debark,'' Danri told Kerri, then looked around. ''Where's Pembroak?''

''I saw him sleeping near the captain's cabin,'' the diggermaid replied.

Danri clumped down the length of the lakeboat, ready to berate his squire, who, it seemed, had been taking altogether too many naps lately. But when he found the young digger curled on the hardwood deck without a pillow, something made him stay his hand. Beside Pembroak, placed out in the open instead of lashed with the other weapons, lay the young warrior's hammer—the tool he had so recently decided to use in favor of his long-cherished sword.

"Up . . . get up, squire," Danri said.

Pembroak blinked and stretched, running his fingers through a beard that, Danri suddenly noticed, had grown much thicker in the last few months.

"I don't suppose this was here when you fell asleep," the elder digger asked, nudging the hammer with the toe of his boot.

Pembroak looked down, then blushed in embarassment. "No. I don't know how—"

"I think you do." Danri's tone was gentle.

"Yes . . . to tell you the truth, I've been wakin' up with it for the last week. It won't be long, now."

"Well, I'll miss you, pup." Biting back a surprisingly strong emotion, Danri let Pembroak get up while he started barking orders to his warriors, getting the field army ready to debark.

"No farther by boat, brave lads, but hopefully we've made your march a little shorter," Rupert declared as his barge eased toward a sloping, grassy bank. The pot-bellied captain shook his head wistfully, clapping a hand on his gut. "If I was a mite younger, you'd see me marching with you."

As it turned out, many of the boatmen did throw in with the army, announcing their intent to join the attack against the bloodtrains. They brought an assortment of gaffs, hooks, and harpoons to augment the increasingly varied armaments of the warriors. Debarking in blustery weather, lashed by cool winds off the mountains, the Combined Field Army took shape on the marshy shore.

"Perhaps we'll get some rain," Kerri remarked, with a look toward the sky.

"*That* would be a good omen," Danri replied sincerely.

Once ashore, the band broke into two wings, planning to march on parallel routes, with a few miles between them. Danri, Roggett, and Payli took command of the left column, while Tarn Blaysmith and Awnro Lyrifell took charge of the right. Wistan Aeroel and the woodland sylves would move forward in advance of both columns, acting as scouts and skirmishers. Garic and his twissels buzzed back and forth, bearing messages and insuring that the two forces remained in close contact, while Neambrey took to the air, winging along the undersides of the glowering clouds while he determined that they were marching in the right direction. A long string of mules, each of the beasts laden with twin casks of sloshing liquid drawn directly from the Auracanal of Dermaat, plodded behind each of the army's wings.

The troops formed their large march columns on the lakeshore. Roggett walked up and down the files, asking about signs of sickness, but came back to the head of the formation wearing an expression of palpable relief.

"Everyone seems to be healthy. There's no more sign of the fever. That Aura is just what we needed," he reported.

"I had a pretty good idea it would work," declared Danri smugly, taking this as a heartening sign for their prospects as the Combined Field Army started its overland march.

The long night passed into dawn and the twin columns marched steadily, covering the vast plains at a steady, miles-devouring pace. Throughout the day, and the next night, and the next day the warriors subsisted on Aura alone, covering a distance that a fleet unit of cavalry would have been hard pressed to traverse in a similar time frame. Garic reported to Danri that the other wing had encountered some difficulties with marshy terrain, and had fallen a little bit behind the digger commander's force. Still, the second group marched hard, and the twissel said that they were coming up fast.

The third day of the march dawned gray and blustery, with the chill wind strengthening from the mountains. Roggett speculated that the breezes across the Glimmersee had given way to rain.

"Hope some of it makes it this far north," Danri muttered, looking at the expanse of parched grass and brittle brown shrubs that covered the ground to the far horizons.

"We'll have to carry our own storm to make sure it's done right," growled the Iceman.

Further reflection was interrupted as Neambrey soared into view, diving, coming to rest before the column and driving dust into Danri's face with the downdraft of his wings.

"Um, there's a problem," the drackan began hesitantly. "It seems like there's an enemy army in the way, kind of waiting for you. Oh, and they're between us and all those wagons of Darkblood."

— 3 —

Reaper settled to the ground, confident that he and his minions were on the verge of victory. The Tallon of Dassadec squatted on a broad hilltop above the crossroads before Carillonn. It pleased him to know that, a few weeks earlier, the ranks of men had stood here, harboring the foolish notion they could resist his onslaught.

The high, white wall was broken and crumbling along this entire front of the city. Black soot etched the gouges of fiery wounds, and the remnants of the once-lofty guard towers were like splintered and twisted tree trunks, ravaged by weather and worm and age.

Minions streamed by on the road, trampled the open ground up to the river bank. Thick columns choked the bridges, advancing through the wrecked gatehouses, then dispersing along wide routes that had been cleared through the streets. Other columns pressed across the riverbed, climbing toward gaps in the wall, filtering into the city by whatever path presented itself.

Now the mighty skyship lay low across the dried western channel of the Ariak. With a rumble of thunderous sturmaults, the *Dreadcloud* moved slowly, serenely, back from the smoldering city. The lightning battery in the bow was silent, in stark contrast to the flames roaring upward from so much of Carillonn.

The Lord Minion knew that the powerful ship needed more fuel, and that it would take some time to replenish the mighty lightning piles. The wagons in the bloodtrain were far back from the front, well removed from danger, waiting beside great stacks of firewood, ready to bubble the precious fuel into the sky. In a few days the skyship would be back, ready to pound the other half of the city into submission.

And until then, Reaper could enjoy a vista of ground blackened by the throng of his troops, an unstoppable horde pouring into the battered, breached city.

But a sudden note of alarm tingled within the Lord Minion's mind. He raised his massive head, listening for a hint of distant danger, and once again the tremor of warning tickled him. It was an unwelcome distraction, but a summons that he could not ignore—for the threat came from Duloth-Trol, from the fortress of the Sleepstealer himself.

Fly to me, my Talon. His master's command was urgent, demanding . . . and frightening.

Reaper sensed the compulsion in the depths of his soul and he could not disobey—in that same instant he spread his wings and threw himself into the air. With a shriek of vengeful fury, he scrambled for altitude, lifting his massive, reptilian body with the grace of an eagle.

Soon he raced through lofty skies, bearing on a straight course for Agath-Trol.

— 4 —

Wistan Aeroel reported that the enemy force had formed a line of defense along a shallow stream—an odd choice of position for the Sleepstealer's water-hating troops. Yet moments later Neambrey settled back to the ground and reported that the warriors standing against them seemed to b primarily humans—the drackan had only spotted a single minion, a brutox.

After a quick council of war, the troops in Danri's wing reached the obvious decision: They would attack with every ounce of strength they had. Some of the wagons of the bloodtrain were visible, barely a mile beyond the stream, and though the second wing was still several hours away, Danri and Roggett agreed that they couldn't risk any delay.

Soon a simple battle plan took shape: Wistan Aeroel would take his woodland sylves through the thickets and try to get around the enemy force, while the diggers and humans would make an all-out frontal assault. After scouting the enemy line from the concealment of a grove of willows, the digger ordered an immediate attack.

Roggett Becken, leading a detachment of diggers and Icemen, made a rapid sortie to clash with growling, snapping defenders along the creek. The assault team splashed through the water and chopped and hacked their way into the enemy position, and numerous darkmen streamed toward the place in a rapid counterattack.

"Charge—bring the whole line!" cried Danri, waving his hammer over his head.

With a roar the army attacked along the length of the shallow stream. Danri led the howling mass of diggers, vividly aware of Kerri charging just behind his right shoulder. He tried to veer sideways to protect her, but with annoying persistence she veered even farther, angling for a chance to attack.

Then the stream splashed under Danri's boots, and he looked up to see a leering beast of a monster that might, once, have been a human. Lupine jaws were fixed in a fangbaring snarl, and the remnants of a shirt and trousers were rags over a furry pelt that nevertheless covered the form of a muscular man. The growling, drooling warrior clutched a steel-headed spear in both hands.

The digger bashed aside the darkman's initial thrust, backswinging with the pick of the hammer to rip into his enemy's leg, crushing the skull when the howling creature fell. Around him, hundreds of diggers met the enemy in similar clashes, and quickly the waters of the shallow stream turned red.

Kerri lunged past, slashing at a darkman. The warrior of the swamp bared tooth and talon as Danri leapt to protect his diggermaid. But her sword was quick, and she killed the monster with a single stab, stumbling backward as the dead weight of the corpse fell into her.

"Good thing your sword is as quick as your tongue!" Danri told the momentarily speechless Kerri, hoisting her to her feet with a quick pull.

Neambrey flew by, landing amid a group of darkmen on the shore, rending and biting. A spear flew and the drackan howled, flapping the torn span of his right wing. He leapt into the air and tried to climb, but when he spread the membrane it tore upward and sent the wyrm cartwheeling into the stream. Splashing to the shore, Neambrey proved that even on his feet he was a force to be reckoned with, snapping and clawing, whirling about, crushing with his powerful bite and ripping with his sharp talons.

A cloud of sparks sizzled and Danri knew that the brutox was near. He charged, but then hesitated as Kerri remained behind, battling a snarling swordsman. By the time she dispatched her opponent and came after, three darkmen had lunged into the digger's path. He killed them with brutal efficiency, but the crackling minion had disappeared.

But when Danri turned around to find Kerri, she, too, was gone, swallowed in the violence around them. Frantically he charged back to the stream, looked through the surging mass of darkmen and diggers. Beyond he saw Roggett Becken, wielding his mighty ice axe, hewing a path through the enemy hordes.

Yet nowhere was there any sign of the diggermaid.

— 5 —

"Raine? Where are you?"

Rudy, heart hammering, eyes straining to see through the

shadowy chamber, clutched the Sword of Darkblood.
Lordsmiter had vanished into the murk of Nicodareus' de-
ception, and there was no more time to seek the artifact of
the gods.

A sound drew the Iceman's attention upward and finally
he saw the Woman of Three Waters, wrapped in the Lord
Minion's strapping arms, perched on a narrow ledge high
above the floor of the vast chamber. The walls of the great
chimney swept upward from there, and far above Rudy saw
the black clouds of Duloth-Trol scudding past.

"Use the power—the power we saw!" Raine called out
urgently before the Lord Minion clapped a rough paw over
her mouth.

He heard Raine's words, but the message only confused
Rudy—who was desperately afraid for her on that high
ledge. Seeking a route to climb, he observed with despair
that everywhere in this cavernous chamber the cliff was
slick and sheer. And even if he started to scale the wall, he
would be completely exposed to Nicodareus—the monster
could knock him down with a single, gliding pass.

But he had to reach her!

"His name!" Twisting free of her taloned captor, Raine
shouted the clue.

Only then did her plea register. The Iceman remembered
the black blade in his hand, raised it to point at the lofty
ledge.

"Nicodareus!" he cried.

In the blink of an eye he stood astride that shelf of rock,
a dozen paces from the Lord Minion. The Eye of Dassadec,
roaring in fury, turned to face him, casting Raine like a rag
doll toward the edge of the precipice.

Twisting in the air, reaching with instantaneous speed,
the Woman of Three Waters snatched at a flap of leathery
wing. Her fingers closed over the membrane, tugging Nicodareus backward as she slammed to the lip of the cliff.
With a catlike pounce she pulled herself away, backing into
a crack of the wall, desperately clawing for anything she
could use as a weapon.

Rudy charged, black sword extended, and the hissing Lord Minion leaped from the ledge, spreading his wings to glide toward the floor of the chamber. Nicodareus veered and darted like a bat, then spiraled around to land on his two padded feet.

Helping Raine to stand, the Iceman stood at the brink of the precipice, for the first time looking into the great pit of churning liquid in the center of the room. It was the pool that he and Raine had emerged from on their arrival here, but now Rudy saw that it was much more than a mere hole filled with Darkblood.

The slick surface, swelling and shrinking with slow pulsations, moved with the same cadence as the thrumming that had drawn them across Duloth-Trol. Black liquid, like ink, squirted and flowed and fountained in the deep pit, surrounding an obscene blob of dark flesh.

"The Heart of Darkblood," he confirmed grimly, without elation. They had found it, but without the artifact they had no way to wound the immortal flesh.

"But what's . . . look there!" Raine whispered, pointing toward a shape that moved in the dark liquid, dragging a legless torso onto the floor of the chamber with its two mighty arms. "The Guardian is still alive!"

Her hand tightened on the Iceman's arm as he watched the hulking creature, with its skin of rippling stone, drag itself from the churning pool. In its hand, amazingly, was the artifact Lordsmiter, shedding a pearly glow that brightened the entire, massive dome of the cavern.

Rudy gasped. "Lordsmiter must have been washed into the pit when I dropped it—when the fake Nicodareus melted around me!"

"Well, it's right down there now," Raine said, hope once again alive in her voice.

"Hold on to me," Rudy said, grasping her waist with his free hand. Her own arms went around him as he pointed the black-bladed Sword of Darkblood toward the floor of the cavern.

"Nicodareus!" he barked, his word a challenge and a

taunt—and then they were standing beside the Guardian, between the pit of the Heart and the raging, bristling Lord Minion. The legless creature swiveled awkwardly, pivoting on one hand while the other held the blade of the enchanted weapon. It extended the sword, hilt first, to Raine and she quickly took it.

"Come with us—attack," Rudy urged, as he and Raine started toward the Lord Minion. But now the Guardian turned away, swinging methodically across the floor of the cavern.

"What are you doing?" demanded the Iceman. Ignoring his question, the creature continued its measured advance until it came to the edge of another pool of Darkblood, a trench surrounded by a rubble of loose rock.

"We can't wait for it," Raine said, and Rudy knew she was right.

The Eye of Dassadec stood tall, awaiting their attack. The Iceman rushed first and Nicodareus bashed him away. With a downward thrust of his wings, the Lord Minion leaped high into the air—but not quickly enough to avoid Raine. She slashed upward and the tip of Lordsmiter carved a deep gash in the monster's foot.

Howling, Nicodareus landed and flew at the Woman of Three Waters. She stabbed, slicing the side of his chest, but then he bore her to the ground, slashing toward her face, pinning her weapon hand to the floor. Rudy charged and thrust and the Lord Minion snatched the Sword of Darkblood away as if he were taking a toy from a child, sending it clattering across the room. The monster blocked the pit of Darkblood as he rose over Raine's battered body, glaring triumphantly at the agonized Man of Three Waters. The Lord Minion's feet pinned both of the woman's arms as he beat his chest with his fists.

"I will allow you to watch her die," chortled the Eye of Dassadec, his voice burbling like a vat of boiling blood.

Something moved across the chamber, but Rudy had eyes only for his beloved, bruised and still at the feet of the roaring monster. He moved sideways, but Nicodareus pivoted with casual arrogance, ready for an attack.

The movement across the room grew more distinct. With a flicker of his attention, Rudy could see a large shape dragging itself across the floor, behind Nicodareus—and then the Iceman forced himself *not* to look. He had recognized the legless Guardian, but now it was astride something . . . something huge, a thing that crawled steadily across the floor.

"Is this your ultimate reward?" asked the Man of Three Waters scornfully, gesturing to the dark, lofty chamber. "To lie here in wait for your master's enemies?"

Nicodareus threw back his head and laughed, a thunderous, deafening sound that assaulted Rudy's ears and shook the air around him. The unarmed Iceman took a step forward, feinting an advance, insuring that the Lord Minion remained fixated upon his mortal enemy. Raine struggled on the floor, the artifact Lordsmiter out of reach to her side.

The source of movement behind Nicodareus was clearer now. Rudy held his attention on the ghastly face of the Eye of Dassadec, but he was aware of the stony Guardian, trunk planted upon the back of a large, four-legged creature, arms outstretched, reaching toward the Lord Minion.

The supporting being was a Deep Guardian, the Iceman saw now—though that hapless creature was covered with scars, and its gnarled legs moved only slowly. But it advanced steadily, too, a step closer, then another. Rudy tried not to stare at the mangled face of the battered creature, at the cruel wounds marring its head and flanks.

But the crushing mandibles of its powerful jaws and the sharp horn spiraling from its snout were intact. The High Guardian reached out and seized the flexing wings of the Lord Minion from behind. Nicodareus shrieked in disbelief as the two powerful arms pulled him hard.

The Deep Guardian's horn emerged from Nicodareus's chest in a shower of black gore. Eyes bulging, the Lord Minion roared a dying scream, the sound gurgling away, leaving his mouth gaping and clamping silently. Then the

Guardian's mighty jaws closed around the Eye of Dassadec's torso, rending and crushing.

Rudy closed in, snatching up Lordsmiter as Raine scrambled to her feet. He slashed at the Eye of Dassadec, driving the keen blade into the monster's torso and limbs, repeating the blows over and over as the Deep Guardian ripped the monster to pieces.

TWENTY-THREE

World of Three Waters

A mortal artisan can spend decades, even
centuries on a great endeavor, and the caprice
of an angry god can obliterate the masterpiece
in the blink of an eye.
—THE SYLVAN BARD

— 1 —

"Rudy, stop!"

The Iceman felt Raine's hand on his shoulder, heard her
words through the haze of his fury.

Lurching backward, he looked strangely at the blade in
his hand. Lordsmiter was spattered with black gore, enough
to almost obscure the artifact's pearly blade. Nicodareus
was dead—the Iceman had *seen* him die, knew that this
gory flesh on the floor was all that remained of the Lord
Minion.

Yet still he wanted to assail him, to hurt him more.

"The Guardians tore him apart, the two of them together," Raine was saying. "Our old friend seemed to
bring the Deep Guardian to life . . . somehow . . . they came
from that trench."

He looked, saw the joined creatures crawling away, approaching the far wall of the vast chamber. The damaged High Guardian rode squarely atop its counterpart. The wounded flesh, the stump that had carried the creature for hundreds of miles, was pressed to a gap in the other's carapace.

Unhesitatingly Rudy went after them, watching as the horn on that scaly snout smashed against the cavern wall, powerful jaws starting to scoop away the broken rock. After a few blows, enough of a tunnel had been excavated that the forequarters of the Deep Guardian were already out of sight.

"Their injuries broke each of them . . . but now they're a single being," observed Raine, moved.

"And they're going back to the Watershed," the Iceman replied, intuitively understanding the long trek ahead of the pair. "Farewell, friend."

You must perform your task . . . Then the Watershed shall have no more need of us.

"But . . ." Rudy was startled by the declaration, made as the High Guardian ducked low, vanishing into the quickly growing tunnel.

"He's right. Now it's time to do what we came to do," Raine said, nodding toward the pit in the center of the vast chamber.

Grimly, clutching the hilt of the artifact in both hands, Rudy stepped forward, slowly approaching the Heart of Darkblood. He could picture it perfectly now, the massive mound of flesh throbbing and flexing beneath the gently churning surface. Clearly he imagined the wide connecting passages leading into the stone walls of the pit—it was through one of these that Rudy and Raine had been pulled into this chamber. Darkblood swirled in constant motion, sucked downward from the surface, forced into those tubes and pulsed away.

The slick surface roiled and throbbed, squeezing the great mass of inky liquid. The Iceman visualized that fluid surging through the passages, the "veins," of this inanimate fortress. That circulation gave the Sleepstealer his vitality—just as surely as a man's flowing blood gave him life. Looking upward, Rudy regarded that lofty patch of sky, and wondered if the vast chimney might even provide a way for the god of Duloth-Trol to breathe.

"Rudy . . ." He heard Raine's whispered word from behind and halted. "Whatever happens . . . I love you," she said simply.

For a moment he weakened, wanting to turn and go to her. "I'm glad—If you didn't love me, I never would have made it this far," he replied, starting toward the pit once again.

A sound like a whirlwind roared through the cavern, blocking what little light spilled from above. Rudy saw a great creature spiral into the huge shaft, wings spread like the sails of a galyon. The beast turned a crocodilian face downward and he saw the glowing fires of its eyes.

"Reaper!"

Raine's voice was like the snapping of a dry stick. The Man of Three Waters knew she was right, that they faced the last, the most awful of Dassadec's Lord Minions. The monstrosity swept downward like onrushing doom, plunging to the cavern floor, coiling protectively around the pit of the Heart to glare wickedly at the two intruders.

A rumble of sound emerged from the mighty body. It might have been laughter, or merely deep, resonant respiration. Rudy stared in disbelief, wanting to cry out against the injustice of fate, against the cruel fortune that had hurled one last, mighty obstacle into their path.

"We've got to try!" Raine declared, sidling away from the Iceman. "Be ready!"

Rudy moved to the left, but Reaper slashed out, casually batting him across the room. Tumbling through a bruising roll over the rocks, the Iceman clung to the sword of the gods, frantically seeking some hope, however futile. Perhaps the Guardians would come back . . . perhaps . . .

In his heart he knew there could be no more hope. The truth burned in bitter pain, but was inescapable: The Lord

Minion was too great, the Man and Woman of Three Waters too weary and small, to overcome this last obstacle. Lordsmiter hungered for the Heart of Darkblood as if the sword were a sentient being—even more, a creature that sought the blood, the vitality, of the Sleepstealer. Yet the Lord Minion lay coiled, as large as a castle wall, between the man and his objective.

Kill them, my Talon—slay the intruders in my name!

The command of Dassadec was a thunderous message in the chamber, not a thought or a sound so much as a sensation understood on the most primal level. Rudy raised the sword, knowing he was doomed, ready to die fighting.

But then Reaper rose with majestic dignity, stretching his wings with arrogant disdain before he slowly stalked away. The Man and Woman of Three Waters watched in amazement as the mighty black serpent crossed to the wall of the great chamber, coiling casually on the floor—and leaving open the path to the Sleepstealer's heart.

— 2 —

"There—look out for da rock!"

Darret's worried face peered down from the rigging and he gestured wildly, but Anjell's full concentration was centered upon the great wheel of the galyon's helm. She steered around a massive pillar of stone that jutted from the shallows off the starboard bow, easing the big galyon to port while she studied the obstacle. Black waves cracked at the base of the spire, which rose from the sea like the twisted, slimy trunk of some terribly diseased tree. It was strange to realize that this was the first piece of ground she had seen close up in many weeks.

"How deep?" called Anjell loudly.

Haylor, in the bow, pulled on his sounding line. "Way deep!" came the shouted reply.

"Okay, now back to starboard!" came the cry from above.

Anjell again cranked on the wheel and the vessel slowly drifted into a vast anchorage. More of the rocky spires rose from the right side, arrayed almost like fence posts in a curving, natural breakwater. The waters behind the barrier were still and calm, though the ship remained a good distance from shore.

"This seems like some kind of harbor. Maybe the minions made it—and that mountain *has* to be Agath-Trol!" Anjell was convinced now, and no longer afraid. Though even the base of the massif was far away, she felt certain that Rudy was inside, and since the galyon had sailed this close, there just *had* to be a way to make him know that they were here.

Haylor released the linchpin and allowed the anchor chain to rattle through the slots, while Darret did the work of three sailors, hoisting on the lines to furl the mainsail. Only when the canvas was lashed tightly to the boom did he slide down the lines and join the others on the deck.

"What we do now?" the boy wondered. "Dat mountain's still pretty far away."

"Well, I don't think we should go over there. I mean, that would be silly!" Anjell declared. "No, we just have to wait until Rudy knows we're here."

"Well, if you know where he is—can't you tell him we're over here?" demanded Darret. "You know, use some magic? Like when you blew dat wind!"

"No," the girl replied sadly. "Whatever magic I have, well, it doesn't work that way. I don't know how I could send Rudy a message."

"Ah, but then, maybe you do!" Haylor said brightly.

"I can't!" But Anjell objected without conviction, suddenly remembering Haylor's earlier faith in her. She scowled as he repeated the assertion.

"You *can*," insisted the little sylve.

Anjell glared at him sternly. "How do you know so much, anyway?" she demanded—and then remembered something else. "You know why the grownups fell asleep and we didn't, don't you? Well, you just better tell us!"

"That sleepiness, well that was a surprise, I assure you. As for the other . . . it was only legend, really . . . ancient stories. But I had to see for sure."

"What stories?" Darret's voice was a low growl as he stood protectively beside Anjell.

"About humans drinking Aura, and becoming sorcerers—or sorceresses, I should say. It is said that, a long, long time ago—more than a thousand years—there were human magic users. They drank Aura, and became enchanted."

"*Any* humans who drink Aura?"

"Well, no. Just children. The legends say that an adult will be unaffected by the water of Faerine, save for the healing effects that we all know about. But children—now, that's a different story! And the younger you begin, the more dramatic the possible effects."

"You mean—I *am* a sorceress? And Darret's a sorcerer?"

"You have become the first human sorceress in many centuries," Haylor concurred. "Darret is older, so it is very hard to say with him. But we know that he has not succumbed to the soporific effects of the air, so that means something. Still and so, it is you who have been blessed with great power."

"You mean, like blowing the wind into the sails," Anjell said, thinking that it sounded funny to be called a sorceress, even if that's what you knew you were.

"And more. Why, I'll bet pretty soon you'll be able to do things you can't even imagine."

"How do you know so much about all this?" Anjell asked again. "I know sylves don't get to be Auramasters and tutors until they're grown up."

"Yeah! How old *are* you?" Darret pressed.

Anjell nodded, tapping her foot impatiently. "Don't tell us that you're just a sylvan kid."

"No, not 'kid.' Actually, I have lived for some time. Many have come to know me as Wysteerin Hallowayn." The silver eyes sparkled as Haylor gave them a gleeful grin.

"The Sylvan Bard? The one we're always hearing about?" demanded the girl in disbelief.

"The same!"

"But how—"

"Oh, I *never* let anyone know what I look like. Otherwise, they'd act all funny around me—you know, if they thought I was going to write a song or something."

"But how old are you?"

"As old as the Watershed, and as young as you see!"

"Dat's no kinda answer!" Darret objected.

"But why did you come here, then?" Anjell wondered, her head whirling.

"Well, you see, your uncle is the best hope of all the Watershed. And your uncle's best hope is, of course, you. So I thought I would come and help you."

"And how can you do that?"

"Well, I remember some things about the Olde Magick . . . it wasn't like Auramagic, you know, not the way the sylves practice it now."

"Olde Magick isn't Auramagic? Well, what *is* it, then?"

"The Olde Magick has real power, as you saw in the wind that moved us along the coast. And it is capable of violence, as well, dark and dangerous spells . . ."

The Sylvan Bard looked toward the black mountain, then back to the human girl.

"And those are the spells, I fear, that you may need to master."

— 3 —

Storm clouds glowered over the battlefield, which had been churned into a sea of mud by Faerines, darkmen, and humans. The little stream was red with blood, the banks trampled, and lined, increasingly, with the dead of all kinds. The fight had already lasted hours, but Danri was not aware of his own weariness, so frightened was he by Kerri's absence.

The tide of battle had swirled violently, and he had been seeking her everywhere. But the digger had seen so sign of his maid, and with each passing minute, his fear grew more acute. He so dreaded the thought of finding her among the corpses that he was unwilling to look down, telling himself that she was—yes, she *had* to be—still alive.

Neambrey swept past, biting and clawing a darkman. With a flip of his head, the drackan tossed the mangled creature into the ranks of its fellows—then pounced on another hapless mutant, bearing the beast to ground with rib-crushing talons. Beyond, Roggett and Payli fell back with the Icemen from a stubbornly-held section of river bank. The big warrior limped, clutching his ice axe in a bleeding hand, while the diminutive woman faced the pursuing darkmen. She wielded her digger blade with deadly skill, and the brutes showed a ready willingness to let the humans get away.

"There you are, you digger!"

Kerri's voice made his heart soar, and Danri felt her hand in his. His throat tightened with emotion as he bashed one, then another darkman, to the ground.

"Get back from here, to safety in the rear!" he begged. "Please—do that for me!"

"I won't!" cried the diggermaid, jabbing her shortsword into the gut of a menacing bandit. The monster fell, flailing at her feet until she kicked it away. "Look at Payli—what an inspiration!"

At that moment the woman of Neshara was rallying hundreds of Icemen, warriors who had been rebuffed in their attempt to break the enemy line. With their tiny commander charging in the lead, waving her sword of digger steel, the Halvericans raised a lusty cry and pounded toward the darkmen on the bank of the stream.

Howling madly, Roggett leapt halfway across the waterway, lurching through the mud to spring up the far bank with ice axe flailing. Two darkmen went down in the first instant, and others fell back. Seconds later, the vengeful men of Neshara had elbowed through the gap, and other darkmen turned from the bank to contain the breach.

But Danri saw his chance, quickly gathering a hundred or more of his own warriors into a tight pack behind him. They pushed ahead steadily, a solid wedge of Faerines led by Danri, Kerri, and Neambrey, and grimly forced a gap into the darkmen's line. Each counterattacking mutant was faced by a sturdy digger protected by his own shield and the overlapping ranks of his neighbors.

Sparks flared nearby and Danri caught a whiff of Darkblood, then saw the brutox hulking above the mass of the darkmen. The big creature lunged, seizing a digger from the wedge and twisting the hapless warrior with spine-snapping force. Kerri charged forward, raising her sword, but the minion whirled with shocking quickness, taloned paw lashing out—and Danri's heart all but stopped beating.

And then Neambrey was there. The drackan's jaws snapped onto the beast's massive wrist, crushing bone and gristly flesh. The brutox howled, breaking away from the scaly wyrm, lunging toward Danri.

Darting forward, the digger raised his hammer, eyes locked on the brutox—but a snarling darkman leapt into his path. Danri brought the weapon down across its fanged face, and when the mutant went down he crushed its skull with one final, plunging blow.

But the brutox had once again been swallowed by the battle, and the digger commander dared not leave this tight formation to seek it. Instead he bashed right and left, venting his frustration on the darkmen in reach of his hammer. One deliberate step after another he led the wedge in a slow, relentless advance, feeling the darkmen start to yield, to slowly fall back from the bank of the stream.

Cool winds swept across the field, and Danri sensed the hint of rain in the moist fullness of the air. Remembering the clouds blowing north from the Glimmersee, he was lifted by a momentary hope. But then he realized that these darkmen not only fought beside water, but some of them had charged *into* the stream during the fight. Clearly they did not have the aversion to the pure liquid that was the hallmark of any true minion.

Abruptly the skies opened up, rain showering down in gentle sheets as the clouds continued their slow migration from the lake onto the plains, drifting northward. Still the darkmen fought, holding the press of the attacking field army to slow progress. Danri shouted and cajoled, wielding his hammer with crushing effectiveness, striving to break through the thinning line of darkmen.

There was a great shout from the right, and the Faerines and humans sensed victory as the enemy troops wavered. Some of the darkmen turned, howling, and ran into the swamp—and still the sounds of battle swelled, weapons clashing with renewed vigor as the line of defenders steadily gave way.

"The second wing of the Combined Army is here!" reported Garic Hoorkin, suddenly buzzing behind Danri's ear. "They're attacking over there!"

"About time!" groused the digger, though he was elated by the news. More and more of the darkmen broke and ran, vanishing into the rain.

"And Wistan Aereol's sylves are all the way to those big wagons!" the twissel declared. "You just have to finish off this battle and you'll be there, too!"

The reinforcements rapidly folded back the line of darkmen, and the surging diggers rushed through remnants of their scattering foe. Finally the corrupted, craven humans scattered through the tangled wetland, seeking only escape—and for the most part the attackers let them go.

Danri jogged ahead, seeking the brutox, but again he failed to find the minion. He speculated that the monster had possibly ceased sparking in an effort to hide among the mass of its defeated troops. Knowing the minion would be discovered soon, Danri clutched his hammer and vowed to be ready.

Letting the survivors flee, the diggers and humans raced to the bloodtrain. Dozens of massive wagons were parked in long rows, while huge piles of dry timbers had been stacked nearby. The tall iron tanks, sides streaked with rust and gummy Darkblood, loomed far over the tallest men, and even the stone wheels of the great wagons were taller than Danri.

Beyond the bloodtrain, a huge herd of bovars had been tethered. Presumably they'd had some caretakers, but those minions had apparently fled with the arrival of the Combined Field Army.

The sylves had already begun the careful work of uncapping the numerous vats. Each tank had a spigot near the bottom which could be released to drain the liquid slowly, and a large iron plug in the upper side. The sylves had discovered that when this cap was removed, the spigots drained more quickly, so Wistan Aeroel's archers were busily occupied in scrambling over the vats and pulling or knocking off the iron lids.

All across the plain the great wagons were being opened, men and Faerines jumping back to avoid the foul stuff that flowed out. Stains darkened the ground in expanding swaths, hissing and foaming as the rain splashed into it.

"The water seems to be diluting it," Danri observed hopefully, as the ground was quickly covered with a gooey and smelly, but apparently nonlethal, mixture.

"It's okay as long as you don't drink it," reported Wistan, who was overseeing the destruction of the bloodwagons. "A few sylves got slightly burned from splashes, but Aura repaired those wounds quickly."

"Any sign of the brutox?" asked the digger, who had still not seen the minion since the collapse of the darkmen line.

"No—we've passed the word to be on the lookout for it, though."

Danri stalked through the camp, still seeking the minion that had commanded this dark legion. Humans and Faerines were everywhere, and he didn't see how the monster could go undetected for long.

"Pull those caps—stand clear there!" he shouted, pausing to watch as several humans wrestled with the great, iron plug in the side of one of the vats. Just as the Darkblood began to trickle out the men scattered, and the cap came off with a surging of inky stain.

The rain still streamed, not a downpour but a steady shower. The water from the sky mixed with the black elixir draining onto the ground, and slowly the Darkblood of Reaper's army fizzled, bubbled, and disappeared.

— 4 —

Direfang crawled partway from beneath the wagon. His broken wrist throbbed until he lapped up a trickle of Darkblood from one of the ruptured vats. Gradually the agony faded, though the limb remained stiff and unwieldy—and it jabbed him painfully when he dove to the ground and crawled behind a large stone wheel to avoid a party of humans coming toward him.

In his good hand the brutox clutched a massive sword he had taken from a wounded darkman. His mind seethed with hatred and fear as, everywhere he looked, there were humans or Faerines stalking among these precious wagons.

Beside a tall Iceman he saw a human woman who reminded him of his captive, the sacrifice who had escaped. That vexing prisoner had been the start of his trouble, Direfang remembered. How he hated humans—and especially the females. He glared at the woman before him, who, though she was very small, stood with an air of confidence that Direfang found utterly infuriating.

And that fury could no longer be contained. With a roar, the brutox rushed from beneath the wagon, tusked jaws spread, talons reaching, anxious for the kill. Direfang's bellow would freeze his prey in terror, then his jaws would taste the hot blood—

But the Iceman beside the woman whirled so quickly, decidedly *not* paralyzed by terror. And he had one of those accursed crossbows!

The steel-headed bolt punctured the brutox's chest and

he went down, thrashing, clutching at the deadly shaft that
had torn into his heart. Direfang's eyes grew dim, and
sparks flickered across his vision as he struggled in vain to
remove the cruel barb.

He saw the face of a vengeful digger. Then he saw the
head of the digger's hammer, expanding rapidly in his vision.

Then he saw nothing at all.

— 5 —

"Now!" Raine said. "Use Lordsmiter!"

The Talon of Dassadec, leathery lip curled in a mocking
smile, watched the Iceman in apparent amusement. Rudy's
eyes flicked from the Lord Minion to the woman to the
pulsing presence in the center of the chamber. But the Iceman wasted no further time in pondering Reaper's bizarre
decision—instead, he charged across the chamber, sword
raised, aiming for the pit where the pulsing Heart was waiting.

His clean dive cut the surface of Darkblood and his momentum carried him far through the smooth liquid. With
shuddering force he stabbed Lordsmiter into the slick, black
surface of the heart. The artifact of the gods hissed through
the corrupt flesh as the Iceman still plunged forward, immersed in the pulsing, seething muscle, the force of his dive
pushing him through the wound he had himself created.

The Iceman hacked to the right and chopped to the left,
slicing the keen, enchanted steel through the immortal
heart. He fought with an insane frenzy, stabbing at any flap
of the shredded muscle that waved within reach of his
blade. He found smaller and smaller pieces, yet still slashed
wildly, cutting into even these remnants.

Finally he splashed to the edge of the pool, covered in
sticky blood and gore, gasping from exertion—and hatred.
He still clutched Lordsmiter, and felt the sword pulsing
with tangible energy.

Around him the cavern trembled, audible tremors rocking the air, shivering the bedrock, as the death throes of
Dassadec began, a wail rising though the air. Rudy looked
up to see that the Talon of Dassadec had risen high, back
arched like an aggressive—and impossibly huge—alley cat.
The leering smile had vanished, replaced by a savage snarl
that bared fangs the size of longswords along the length of
those massive jaws.

"*Now* I will kill you!" cried Reaper, trumpeting in exultation, leaping at the Iceman. At the same time, the
ground heaved underfoot, a deep, fundamental wrack taking
hold of Agath-Trol. Stones broke free from the wall and
the seething gore in the pit boiled upward, billowing high
into acrid black smoke.

Raine leapt toward Rudy, lashing into the churning pool
of black liquid to seize the Iceman's arm. The force of her
dive pulled him back from the Lord Minion's first, slashing
bite, the monster's jaws snapping shut just beyond the tip
of the gleaming sword.

The eruption came from beneath the Heart of Darkblood,
emerging as a flood of viscous liquid spuming upward. A
shriek echoed through the chamber, and the Iceman realized
that the cry came from the walls, from the very bedrock of
the fortress. Pressure rose as the essence of Dassadec
washed through the cold stone of his fortress, kindling explosive, violent release.

The Iceman felt himself hurled wildly into the air. Raine
clung to him like an acrobat, seizing his left wrist with both
of her hands as the eruption gained in force. Together they
rode the surge of Darkblood up through the shaft of the
mountainous chimney, faster and faster as the thunderous
convulsion swelled. Rocks fell from the cliffs and ceilings,
and the whole mountain trembled as the force of the blast
lifted them still higher, ever faster.

The explosion rumbled upward, a spuming cloud bearing
the Man and Woman of Three Waters. They rode the eruption, swimming for their lives through steam and Darkblood, feeling the mountaintop shatter around them. There

was nothing solid beneath the pair, but still the pressure forced them upward.

And then the mountain was *below* them, and black clouds all around. The blast dissipated into churning vapors and gusting winds, leaving the man and woman sailing, floating, then tumbling back toward the ground.

The smoky vapors of the explosion coalesced into cool plumes, and these swirled like pennants from the cracked and splintered summit of Agath-Trol. The Man and Woman of Three Waters fell onto one of these vaporous streams, finding themselves supported by the spongy surface.

Then they were floating, borne through the sky on a cloud of Darkblood. Rudy had a vivid and surprising thought of Anjell before he turned his attention back to their tenuous support. He knelt on the dark, porous surface, straining for Auramagic—and hoping that his power would have some effect on this tarcloud.

With an exercise of will he broke the spuming tail free from the mountain, guiding it away, for some reason choosing to float southward. The shred of skyship was hard to control, not nearly as responsive as an Auracloud of Faerine, but still it moved—and answered, if sluggishly— to the commands of his mind.

"I think I can fly it!" he exclaimed. "I'll try to bring us down a bit, out of the overcast."

"Good—and look! Agath-Trol is still suffering!" Raine replied, pointing to the shattered mountaintop.

But Rudy wasn't listening.

"Can you feel that?" he asked.

"What?" She turned, looked at him, then shook her head.

"It's Anjell—I swear it is! She's calling . . . from over there." He pointed, now seeing a vast coastline as they dropped below the overcast, an extent of black sea expanding to the glowering horizon.

"I don't believe it," he gasped, drawing Raine's attention to the sight. "It's a ship . . . it's got to be the *Black Condor*!" He pointed to the tiny speck of the vessel on the placid surface of a massive lagoon. Even from this vast height the raised fore and stern decks of the vessel clearly marked it as a galyon.

"But how . . . you're right!" Raine's disbelief became a shout of joy. "It's here!"

Rudy sagged back into the cloud, willing to accept without questions the arrival of such miraculous aid. It was enough just to drift, to feel them floating in the general direction of the ship.

"What's . . . oh—no! More trouble." The Woman of Three Waters spoke urgently, and the Iceman turned to look behind them.

He saw that the black mountain had not been destroyed by the convulsion, though a great portion of the summit had apparently been blown away. The sky was a mass of black smoke, churning destruction . . . and something more.

And then the vicious form of Reaper flew into view, mouth gaping hungrily, massive wings bearing the Talon of Dassadec outward from the smoldering wreck of Agath-Trol—and after the tarcloud and its two escaping intruders.

— 6 —

Takian awakened suddenly, aware of the coolness of the air, sensing Bristyn's warmth against his side. The king and queen had slept where they had been sitting, against the wall on the parapet of the King's Tower, loftiest vantage in the city.

Gingerly Takian turned his stiff neck, careful not to wake his bride—but she nuzzled into his beard and wrapped her arms more tightly about him. He decided to stay for a moment, to soak up her warmth, holding her with a tenderness that nearly broke his heart.

It was over, he knew . . . the war was lost, and humankind ended. Then how could it seem like enough, for now, to just have a quiet moment with his queen?

Dawn wrapped the city in a murky embrace. Gray clouds

covered the sky, with a tinge of blackness marking the minion destruction to the west. Cool breezes mocked the royal couple with a hint of moisture from the south.

Footsteps clattered up the tower steps, and Tray Oldar, accompanied by Donthwal, burst through the door. The servant's wrinkled face was wreathed in a broad grin, and the silver-haired diplomat's eyes were moist with emotion.

"Sire! The men stricken with fever started getting better last night! Drinking the water from the brook, from the Whitestream, is what's doing it!" Tray's ruddy skin was flushed as he reported the news. "Once we learned that, Lord Donthwal here set men to taking the stuff all over the city, getting it to every sickhouse—and I ran up all the stairs to tell you!"

"Aye, Your Majesty," the advisor of Andaran agreed, his stern facade softening with emotion. "The fever has broken, everywhere."

"Perhaps you got your wish," Takian said, rising slowly, stunned and elated by the news. "Could it be that Aura has come to flow over the Watershed?"

A clamor arose from across the Whitestream, atop the city's eastern heights. Over that far hilltop a file of spear tips came into view, glittering in the sunrise. Shortly thereafter the line of their silver-armored bearers could be seen.

"Are they marching already? Those who were sick last night?" asked the king incredulously.

"No!" Donthwal replied, shaking his head in confusion. "They were gathering into units, certainly—but no one gave orders to begin a counterattack."

"And those are *clean* helmets, fresh tunics and armor!" Bristyn had risen, and now she stood at the parapet, looking to the undamaged quarters of the city.

The shouts reached them from the streets, from the balconies of manors and the shacks of slums.

"It's the Corsars. Duke Beymont has come!"

"It's Beymont and the men of Corsari!"

Now the fresh troops, the first columns led by their dashing young nobleman himself, were clearly visible. They came from the waterfront and swept over the hilltops. In a concerted charge down a dozen streets and avenues they surged across the Whitestream with loud cheers, driving toward the castle. Thousands of Corsars were already in view, pushing the outnumbered minions back along each of the main avenues. Lifting his gaze Takian could see that the river beyond the island was crowded with the masts of a great fleet.

"These are just the beginning," the king declared in awe, as the Corsars left kroak and brutox corpses scattered through the streets around the castle.

"And wouldn't you know it?" Bristyn said in wonder, reaching a hand over the parapet, palm upturned to the sky. "I believe it's starting to rain."

— 7 —

The tarcloud was already sinking, drifting lower under the force of the winds lashing away from the coast. The galyon had begun to take form, specifics of masts and rigging coming into view, but now the Iceman halted in agony. The ship was so close, but he knew that he didn't dare continue.

Behind them, the mountain crumbled but Reaper came winging steadily on, flying without visible urgency, yet still closing quickly toward the shred of dark cloud.

"I can't take us down to the ship!" Rudy groaned. "We'll just bring Reaper after them—dooming the galyon as well as ourselves!"

He allowed the black skyship to drift as Raine nodded, understanding. Finally the Man of Three Waters stood, Lordsmiter in hand, ready to face the Talon of Dassadec.

"Uncle Rudy—come on!"

The Iceman staggered, startled by the sound of the voice—as if it originated at his elbow. He whirled around, reassuring himself that Anjell wasn't here, on the cloud with them.

"It's okay—you can come down to the ship. It's the safest thing!" urged the girl, in that startling disembodied voice. "We can help you—but you've got to hurry!"

The stubborn sense of correctness, the strong insistent tone, clearly marked the voice as his niece's—it was unquestionably Anjell speaking.

In that instant he decided, turning his concentration to bringing the cloud down toward the sea. The Iceman strained for speed, but the tenuous skyship just drifted along—though it did descend, and go in the direction he wanted.

Yet Reaper, with jaws gaping, closed in steadily. Now the Lord Minion dove, jaws gaping wide enough to swallow the man and woman in a single bite. Rudy knelt, trying to push his little skyship lower, closer to the galyon.

But it was clear they wouldn't make it. Reaper, grinning lethally, was too close, coming on too fast. Raine took his hand and, together, they faced the onslaught of death.

The lightning bolt that crackled from the galyon's rear trebuchet exploded with flaring brightness, hissing into the sky and flying past the cloud like a blazing spear. Stunned by the following echo of thunder, Rudy spun, saw Anjell on the wheel deck. She waved, then pivoted the heavy weapon to correct her aim.

But with a scream of rage Reaper had curled away, leaving black scales floating downward in his wake. The smell of burned flesh lingered as, winging strongly back toward shore, the Lord Minion vanished into the swirling smoke.

"How . . . how did . . . ?" Raine shook her head, dazed—and not just by the lightning bolt. "Apparently he's happy enough just to get back to his mountain," she added looking toward the ruin of Agath-Trol.

The tarcloud slowly descended, drifting closer to the galyon. Rudy steered as best he could, drifting along about masttop height.

"It's in some kind of anchorage, behind those spires of rock," Raine noted as they neared the ship.

"Bold sailing to take her there—but Kestrel was ever

the audacious captain,'' Rudy declared. ''And look—
there's Darret.''

The boy was aloft in the rigging, and he tossed a line as
the skyship drifted closer. Soon the Man and Woman of
Three Waters were aboard the galyon, where a delighted
Anjell was explaining far too many things at a time.

''Why don't we raise de anchor?'' Darret suggested.
''There'll be lots of time for stories on the trip back home.''

— 8 —

Reaper flew back to the crumbling, abandoned mountain,
striving for altitude, ignoring the bombardment of smoke
and tumbling rock that still showered through the air. He
spiraled lazily, inspecting Agath-Trol, not displeased by
what he saw.

Though the ruined palace teemed with minions, it was
empty in the way that mattered most to Reaper. Agath-
Trol's immortal liege was departed, dragged off to the
realm of the gods by the destruction of his heart of flesh.
Dassadec, the Lord Minion's only master, was gone . . . and
there was none to compete with him for the rulership of all
the dark realm.

Reaper finally swept into the great, arching entryway, the
hall from which legions of minions had marched forth over
many thousands of years. He glided above the smooth black
avenue, abandoned now, where tens of thousands of kroaks
and brutox had once shouted the praises of their master . . .

Their *former* master.

Slowly, regally, the mighty Talon—and he was his own
Talon, now—coiled upon the lofty throne. Agath-Trol had
a new master . . .

And at last he had come home.

EPILOGUE

Don't knock on the door if you're afraid of who
might be at home.
—DIGGERSPEAK PROVERB

We heard the story first from Anjell, then, later, from Dara
and Kestrel as well. The appearance of the ship off that
darkened shore was a miracle so far beyond Rudy's and
my expectations that, for a while, my Iceman and I needed
time just to believe, to accept, the fact of our own survival.

It seemed right and proper that it was Anjell who brought
us out of there—Anjell, whose reputation as a sorceress
would grow steadily through the years, whose life and legacy would leave its effect on all three realms of the Watershed. She had brought the ship here, had driven the Lord
Minion off with her lightning magic, and then blew a wind
to carry us back home.

Darret was not so affected by the tasting of Aura, for
even at his adolescent age he was too old to undergo the
transformation to sorcerer. Instead, he and his captain
would make a name and fortune for themselves, sailing

where no other seafarers dared to go. In the years after the war, as the scattered minions slowly made their way back to Duloth-Trol, it was Kestrel and Darret who first reopened the sailing routes to Westhead. Together—and in later years Darret under his own flag—they would contribute more than any other sailors to the annals of ocean-going adventure.

I often wondered if Kestrel's wanderlust was the sign of a broken heart, for it was on our return to Spendorial that Dara Appenfell gently declined to plight her troth to him. As the galyon sailed up to the docks of the sylvan city, Dara's eyes rose to the mountains, and we all knew that she was picturing the face and hearing the music of a dashing bard.

Rudy and I decided to return to Halverica overland, with Dara and Anjell. We traveled slowly through newly peaceful Faerine. The Suderwild remained a dark and dangerous place, but many of the minions had started scattering, slowly, back to the south. Finally we started for home via the newly opened route of Wilderhof Pass (or Kerri's Pass, as many of us would call it).

As after the Sleepstealer War of ten centuries earlier, many diggers elected to stay in Dalethica during the subsequent period of peace, lending their talents to a multitude of rebuilding tasks in Carillonn, Shalloth, and farther realms as well. By the time of our arrival on the Watershed, the pass had already begun to see steady traffic as curious diggers, and even some humans, made trips back and forth.

We rested for a long season at the Inn of Two Waters, the place with the spendid bar of white marble. Indeed, at the time of our arrival Danri was just installing the slab of alabaster stone. It was from him that we learned Pembroak had vanished on the last day of the war, to commence his Digging Madness.

Awnro Lyrifell was waiting there too, and upon his proposal Dara accepted, and our band of travelers became a wedding party, moving on toward Neshara. The stain of Darkblood still marred parts of Halverica, notably Dermaat,

but Rudy's town had already been restored to much of its
former beauty. The arrival there of Bristyn and Takian,
fresh from the rebuilding of Shalloth, completed our circle
in the mountains.

Rudy and I chose to live in Neshara, in the Appenfell
chalet where my husband was the new patriarch. Through
the years we left here often, and sometimes for long periods, but always we returned to the mountains and the chalets and the flowers, to the peace and serenity of this
peak-shadowed vale. It was here that my Iceman died, and
here he is buried. And I shall rest here as well . . . at a time
not many years in the future.

Today, as the sun sinks over the ridge of the Watershed,
and the Glimmercrown fades to purple and violet in the
creeping dusk, I sit on the porch of that elegant chalet and
remember the man who had tried to climb the mountain,
who had met his first death—and his second birth—at the
base of its precipitous wall.

And even now, when the wind sifts down from Aura-
shrouded Faerimont, I can sense my Iceman's spirit in the
heights. He comes to me, borne by dreams, and together
we walk the high crests of the Watershed, and ride clouds
of magic through the limitless skies beyond.

From: *Recollections*, by Lady Raine of the Three Waters